# RELICS OF DAWN

## A STORY CARVED IN TIME

## A.W. DAVIDSON

*For our Future*

# DECONSTRUCTION

## WILDLIFE REFUGE #7 – CYCLE 2276

Kaia held her breath and pressed her ear to the bunk's exterior wall. There was no trace of thunderous footsteps outside, only the sound of rain pummeling the observation facility as it had for hours. *The mommy phara's eggs need her,* Kaia thought. She listened one more time. Nothing. She sighed, pulled a hood over her head, and looked back to the video on her viewpad.

A reporter raised his eyebrows and tapped the news desk. "The climate is changing, yes, but does the Council really know best? We'll return to our non-stop coverage of the Tragedy in Tremva after the break." The video cut away to an ad for an in-home nature projector, featuring over one hundred landscapes from the "breathtaking past."

Kaia rolled her eyes the same way her daddy did whenever it came on and she could almost hear his voice saying, "That's just what we need! A greedy corporation profiting from pictures of nature before other greedy corporations ruined it."

She set the viewpad down on the mattress and pulled her purple blankie off the top bunk, then over her head to hide from the storm.

Her suit's protective coating crinkled as she raised her knees to make a little tent and rested the viewpad against her legs.

"Play the Tremva deconstruction again," she told the pulsing red dot at the center of the screen.

A dark city skyline filled the display. The camera panned across the towering buildings of downtown Tremva to the trash-laden harbor, where crowded refugee ships sat low in the water, steaming toward the open ocean. The broadcast zoomed in on a long pier, where Kaia knew the deconstruction was about to begin. At the end of the pier sat an iridescent orb twenty cubits wide, with protestors gathered around to hurl insults at it, as if that would stop the Council from signaling the orb to start. The crowd parted for a lanky man in a red full body habsew suit making his way to the front. This was Captain Set, the one who dared to defy the Council's evacuation order. A chill ran down Kaia's spine as he stepped out into the open space between the protestors and the shimmering sphere. She wondered if he knew what was about to happen as he examined his reflection on its smooth surface.

He turned to face the protestors and scanned their faces before looking to the city beyond.

Kaia noticed his chest rise and fall and wondered what he was thinking as he looked out at the crumbling four-story seawall enclosing the city. The camera zoomed in on his face, visible through his helmet's visor. *He looks sad.* She had seen a photo of the same seawall from before she was born and thought the mural of a beach at sunset looked pretty. But now algae stains marred the picture's vibrant hues. Did Captain Set remember how pretty it used to be? Or maybe he remembered when the sea level was lower, and the beach was real? It was hard for Kaia to imagine a real beach without pictures like the one on the wall, or nature projectors like the one her father despised.

The man pointed to the city. "We will not abandon Tremva. Deconstruction is not the only option! Soon, the entire world will see that"—he pumped his fist in the air and shouted— "WE MUST..."

The protestors chanted in response, "STOP THE COUNCIL!"

Captain Set joined in and everyone repeated, "STOP THE COUNCIL! STOP THE COUNCIL!"

At that moment, a piercing siren blasted through the viewpad's speakers.

Kaia cringed when Captain Set's knees buckled. He and everyone in the crowd raised their hands to cover their helmet microphones the way she remembered doing to stop the same type of siren. Although, this time, the sound was warning them of something much worse than the hailstorm that buried her schoolyard under two cubits of ice.

"They can't do this to us!" Captain Set yelled and rushed toward the tranquil orb. Kaia knew nanomechs stayed in suspension only until the Council sent the signal. She knew it was not smart when Captain Set drew his elbow back, curled his gloved hand into a fist, and punched.

Ripples raced across the sphere's surface, like the waves behind the departing refugee ships. The siren dropped several bone-shaking octaves as it faded away.

The protestors roared when Captain Set pulled his hand out and raised it in triumph. He turned and looked at the crowd, but they fell silent, eyes widening.

A man pointed at him and yelled, "The air! Protect him from the air!"

Captain Set lowered his hand as pieces of his glove flaked off and blew away in the wind. He dropped to the pier and writhed in agony. Kaia winced at the memory of the time a fern thorn poked a pinhole in her habsew and let in the same hot, acidic air that burned her skin. The camera zoomed in on Captain Set's face as it scrunched up in pain.

"MAKE THEM STOP!" he yelled, but the nanomechs pulled his protective suit apart molecule-by-molecule, just as Kaia had seen them do to the miniature model city in class. A few people helped Captain Set to his feet and rushed towards a small boat. They lowered him into its berth and sped away as the pier disintegrated behind them.

The camera zoomed out to a wide view of the city. Kaia's breath lodged in her throat. The Council's deconstruction plan, unleashed, was terrifying. The nanomech sphere melted into a thousand glistening rivers, flowing across the waterfront toward downtown Tremva. Within seconds, the seawall turned to a pile of gray dust, and the harbor-front transit tube sank into the shoreline. Everything Jacana-made was broken down to its most basic elements and returned to the bare soil below. The silver tendrils advanced through the city streets and scaled the city's empty skytowers.

Except—Kaia gripped the viewpad hard, knowing what was about to come—they were not quite empty.

Near the top of one of the apartment buildings, at least 150 floors up, a bulky white habsew suit stood out against the dingy gray of a balcony. The video closed in on the man. His arms held a small furry animal that was flicking its tail and shuddering. *A pet affi.* He stood, stroking its tiny body with one hand and leaned over the balcony rail. Streams of nanomechs climbed past him to the top of the building. He stepped back and seemed to look straight at the camera. He held the animal close as the balcony melted away beneath his feet. Kaia's heart sank with him as he plummeted into the massive cloud of dust, still cradling the pet affi.

Distant thunder rumbled beyond the facility wall, startling her from the image on the screen. The patter of rain rose above its usual din.

"Pause," she said. She squeezed her damp eyes shut and let go of the viewpad. It slid down her legs, coming to rest against her stomach.

Kaia first witnessed the Tremva deconstruction on her viewscreen with her parents two days ago. They explained why deconstruction was necessary. She understood that most cities could not survive sea level rise, the droughts, the hypercanes, or the multitude of similar tragedies a warming planet had in store for her civilization. Her young mind still struggled to comprehend it all. It was inconceivable that deconstructions like this would happen over and over in every single city except one: Puna, her home. She missed it even though she also loved being at the wildlife refuge. She knew it would never be the way it was when her family left for the assignment, because the Council was sending so many refugees to Puna, the last place not wrecked by climate change.

Kaia pulled the blanket away and shut off the viewpad. Her gaze settled on a photo taped to the bottom of the top bunk. Her father's eyes were wide in mock terror while she sat on his lap, laughing. A phara eye the size of a dinner plate and a gigantic mouth of jagged teeth loomed through the thick glass behind them. Her heart swelled thinking of that day again. It was the day her parents accepted the assignment to the phara wildlife refuge. Best of all, the Council said they could take Kaia with them. They went straight to Puna's zoo to celebrate. At the phara enclosure, Kaia impressed everyone as she rattled off facts about the ferocious giants to other kids, and adults, in an impromptu lecture on how there was only one phara nesting ground left on the planet of Nu and how important it was to save them. She grinned from ear-to-ear when a zookeeper thanked her for educating the visitors, because the zoo received more donations than ever before.

*My family,* she thought, smiling at the picture. Her thoughts wandered back to the man left behind in the skytower, and she frowned. After the accident, the newsfeed reporter found out who the man was and shared a photo of him with his family standing under dappled rays of light shining through an artificial tree canopy. Kaia recognized the background as the old-growth forest exhibit at Puna's Natural History Museum. The man and woman wore wide smiles, hands resting on the shoulders of their two cute kids. The girl was a toddler, and the boy looked about Kaia's age with his awkward grin. Maybe she could figure out which school he was going to after the Council resettled his family. The viewpad should have that information, she knew, and turned it back on when a familiar thud rattled the bed frame. She set the viewpad down and pressed her ear to the exterior wall to listen again. There—another thud, distant but unmistakable.

"The mommy phara is coming," she whispered and leapt up, dragging her blankie on the floor as she ran toward the observation room.

The door slid open, and Kaia smiled at the sight of her parents standing in front of the observation window. Dark acid rain streaked down the glass, but she knew they were still monitoring the nesting ground by the way they hunched over the consoles and their fingers danced over the glyphpads. They were the smartest grown-ups she knew, and she hoped to do important work like them when she grew up.

Her father looked up to the window. "Anything on the sensors, Rhea?"

"What do you think, Ory?" her mother snapped back.

"Right, sorry," he said.

She straightened up and rubbed her temples. "No, no, I'm sorry." She turned toward him. "It's not your fault. It's the Council's. Only two wild pharas left on the planet, and we can't track them. Did you hear anything back on that work request for the tracking sensor tower?"

He shook his head. "The Council still won't authorize a work crew to come out with all these storms."

"Wildlife is not their priority these days," she lamented.

"I'm sure it's the next phase of the Dawn Project."

She nodded in agreement. "It's getting all the money."

"And all the attention." He rested his hands on the edge of the console and gazed outside.

"What do you think it's all about?" she asked, arms crossed.

"I don't know, but I'm afraid forcing all those people from their homes is going to cause even bigger problems, no matter how promising the Council's plan might be."

"You know they couldn't stay, Ory."

"I know, but the 'Tragedy in Tremva,' as the newsfeeds are calling it, will only make things worse. I can't get over that an innocent person died while the world was watching."

"Not the best start to the project."

"Captain Set would be dead, too, if the protestors hadn't gotten him to the boat in time." He shook his head. "It will be much easier for him to win hearts and minds now."

"Seeing all this resistance and division over the Council's actions reminds me of the early days of the third great war."

"You're right, it feels like that. And you're also right that the

Council had to do it," her father said, glancing over to the center viewscreen.

Her mother followed his eyes and took a deep breath without saying a word.

Kaia knew the pattern of circles on the screen represented phara nests. She also knew there were no longer forty-two of them left. All the circles were red, with one glowing green exception.

Her mother grimaced. "Rapid change never ends well—for us or for the animals."

"Even the last one is worth saving," her father reminded.

She exhaled. "Is it?"

"Hey," he reached over and rubbed her shoulder, "It is worth it, Rhea. We're doing our part while thousands of other scientists are doing theirs. Our lives are going to make an impact, I'm sure of it."

A clap of thunder caused Kaia to take a step backward. She peered around the edge of the doorframe. Another flash of lightning followed, revealing the wetlands outside the window.

Her mother waved a hand toward the bunk room door. "I'm just afraid of what the future holds for—"

"For what, Mommy?" Kaia said, taking a cautious step forward.

Another thud shook the facility. Light fixtures swayed, causing shadows to dance around the room. Kaia ran to her mother's side.

She bent over and patted Kaia on the head. "Hey, it's okay."

"I'm not afraid," Kaia insisted. "I'm excited to see the mommy phara!" She stood on her tiptoes to look out the dark window. "What were you and Daddy talking about?"

Her mother looked up at him. In that moment, Kaia thought her eyes seemed sad, like Captain Set's had been in the video.

She kneeled down to Kaia. "Well, my little Chirps, the world is changing, and sometimes change is scary because it means things will be different."

Kaia pointed to herself. "I'm not afraid of things being different," she proclaimed. "Other kids are, though. I had to teach them that just because wild pharas are big and scary doesn't mean we shouldn't save them. They take care of their babies just like our mommies and daddies take care of us!"

Her father chuckled. "And people always listen to you, Kaia. Now, what do you say you do some, uh, field observations of the phara for your class back in Puna?"

Kaia jumped up and down. She loved studying the pharas and couldn't wait to be a real biologist. "Do you think I can work at the zoo when I grow up?"

Her mother bent down and patted her head again. "You can do anything you want, Kaia. You're in control. Never forget that."

Ory walked across the room and pulled a large case from its compartment in the wall, then scooted it across the floor toward the console. "Here, hop on this so you can see outside."

"Careful, honey, that's the emergency medical kit," her mother said, shooting her father what Kaia called her "I mean it" look as he helped her onto the case.

Kaia stood up tall and peered outside, trying to identify the dark shapes made blurrier by the rain on the glass. "Daddy, can we turn the lights on?"

"Sure, Chirps," he replied and swiped down from the top of the glyphpad.

The facility's exterior lights hummed to life. In the clinical white light, Kaia saw the remains of the phara nests on the wetland outside. The facility sat on a small hill where the forest thinned out to yellowing tufts of grass. A wide, rushing stream wound through the marsh on its way to the sea a few hundred cubits away. She struggled to imagine a bunch of scientists like her parents studying all the living nests, until she started counting all the broken eggshells floating in the deepening mud puddles. There used to be many more wild pharas in this coastal forest, but now there were almost none left.

Kaia looked to the edge of the woods. "I still don't see the phara."

Her mother glanced outside. "Don't worry, I'm sure she's still on her way here. She stops by to check the nest like clockwork."

Her father added, "Maybe she's walking through soft mud, so we can't feel her coming."

Kaia reached up and touched the window. "Daddy, how much longer is it going to rain?"

"Let's find out." He drew a circle on the glyphpad and swept a line halfway around it. A radar map appeared on his viewscreen.

The vast, swirling arms of a hypercane storm covered the narrow sea that divided the continent. He swiped to the right, and a red line appeared on the image. "It won't last much longer, but it will make landfall soon."

Kaia caught the concerned look he flashed to her mother before smiling again. She decided the storm's tentacles looked scary because they were so close.

Her mother knocked on the wall. "We'll be safe in the facility."

Another thud. Kaia shrieked in delight, "The mommy phara must be close!"

The ground shook again, and this time, a huge leg passed by the window.

Kaia jumped up and down. "There she is!" she squealed, clapping as the other leg strode past. The mother's tail whipped back and forth for balance as she slid down the small hill to the stream.

Water flowed around the mother phara's ankles as she waded across the water and into shadow past the outside lights' range.

Kaia's voice quivered. "What was that red stuff on her legs?"

"It looks she must have gotten hurt," Rhea said.

"By what?"

"I'm not sure, but it must have been big." She turned to Ory. "Please switch to the spotlight."

He moved his finger up the glyphpad and the light outside focused onto the mother phara as she reached her nest.

Kaia cupped her hands and brought her face closer to the window to marvel at the giant. She saw them many times at the zoo, and even more since they'd come to the wildlife refuge. Still, each sighting felt as exciting as the first time she met the amazing animal. They were so strong and tall!

Rhea nodded to the data feeds on the viewscreen above her console. "The mother is in range. Her heart is racing, and her core temperature is too low." She looked up as the phara collapsed to the ground with a loud thud.

Kaia yelled. "We have to help her!"

Rhea looked to Ory, then to the airlock.

He shook his head. "It's too dangerous."

She turned back to the window. "I have to, Ory. She's the last female."

Ory rubbed his hand down his face and exhaled. "Keep your distance, though. Okay?"

Rhea chewed her lip.

"Hey, I'm serious," he said.

Rhea nodded, already lifting Kaia off the medical supplies. She kneeled and reached for the case's clasp to open it. Kaia did not know what any of the vials inside were for, but their pretty colors always fascinated her.

Rhea snapped the case shut again. "Everything is here." She stood and walked toward the airlock at the rear of the facility.

Kaia held up a helmet. "Here you go, Mommy."

"Thank you, honey," Rhea said, bending over and kissing Kaia's forehead. "I'll make her feel better, I promise."

Ory turned his chair around. "Kaia, why don't you grab yourself another case to stand on and let your mother get going? I'll even let you press the airlock button…"

Kaia hugged Rhea's leg and bounded toward the red button on the wall.

Rhea lowered the helmet over her head and checked the seal around her neck. She stepped over the threshold inside the small, brightly lit chamber and turned to wave. "Keep an eye on Daddy," she said and winked. "Now press!"

Kaia mashed the red button, and the airlock door slid open. She turned to her father and grinned. "I'm the head biologist of this facility now."

He chuckled. "Rhea, be careful out there."

"Always," her mother said as the airlock door slid shut.

Ory stood close to Kaia and pulled Rhea's camera feed up on his viewscreen. The stairs looked slippery from the rain as she stabilized herself by leaning against the saucer-shaped shuttle docked to the facility. As she trudged across the ground, mud built up on her boots until she arrived at the stream, which Ory thought looked higher now than it had when the phara crossed. Rhea's face was visible on a small overlay in the corner of the camera feed. He gulped as her eyes narrowed and her mouth tightened as she tried to keep her balance while wading across the knee-deep stream with the bulky medical case in tow. By the time she reached the other side, sweat beaded on her brow. Her exterior camera showed flattened clumps of grass dotting the landscape. The spotlight flickered, and they heard a thud as Rhea tapped the side of her helmet to turn on her headlamp. She looked down to step around the mother phara's muddy footprints.

"Kaia, I bet thirty of your footprints would fit inside this one I'm looking at right now."

Kaia laughed. "And you think my feet are big!"

Ory chuckled, too, then asked, "Rhea, how is it out there?"

"Hot. I can almost feel the sticky air through this suit," Rhea said. She looked up, and the camera showed the dark figure of the mother phara lying on the ground ahead. "I'm almost there," she said, in a lower voice this time.

Ory crossed his arms, then uncrossed them, trying to relax as Rhea approached the nest.

"I can't see Mommy's light outside," Kaia told him.

"She is getting close though, see?" he said, pointing to the viewscreen.

Kaia leaned away from the window, transfixed.


Rhea crept up to the phara. The mother lay still, her body curled in a wide arc around the outside of the nest like a protective mountain range. Her short arms twitched in the mud between breaths. Rhea lowered herself to her knees and set the medical case down. She opened it, pulled out the handheld scanner, and aimed it at the mother.

"The cuts on her leg go to the bone," she noted, continuing to scan up the immense body, "and she has three fractured ribs. Her core temperature is still falling." She lowered the scanner to the ground. "Too low..." she trailed off.

"Is it too—" Ory asked but did not finish.

"I-I believe so. Her injuries are severe," Rhea replied.

She heard him sigh.

Rhea continued observing the way the mother phara's stomach rose and fell, each breath growing shallower than the last. She shut the case, picked it up, and took a few cautious steps closer until the mother raised her head and snarled. Rhea froze. The mother sniffed the air again, then laid her head back down in the mud. Rhea exhaled, not realizing she'd been holding her breath.

The mother wheezed. Each time she blinked, her eyes stayed shut a little longer.

"It's okay, momma," Rhea whispered.

The case felt extra heavy in her hand, because Rhea knew she could ease the pain of the mother's last moments. She turned around toward the facility and shielded her eyes from the spotlight. *Kaia should not have to see this, too,* she thought. She raised her hand to the side of her helmet, flicked off her camera, and flashed her headlamps.

The spotlight from the facility dimmed. Ory had understood. Another of the many reasons she loved him. They'd been on the same wavelength since their first date on the plateau overlooking downtown Puna.

She heard Kaia's protest. "Wait! What are you doing Mommy? I can't see anything!"

"Kaia, I need privacy to help her, okay?"

Rhea eased the case down in the mud again, opened its clasps, and removed a blue vial. She drew back the feathers on the mother's neck and pressed the injector to the brown scaly skin below.

She looked into the fading orange eyes of the magnificent creature. *I'm sorry for everything we've done to you.*

Rhea exhaled as she pulled the trigger. The blue liquid disappeared into the mother's veins. The phara's last breath rattled, then faded to a hiss. Rhea reached up with a tender touch and slid the mother's eyes shut. She tossed the empty injector into the case and draped her arms over the mother's snout, allowing herself to cry for a moment while the unforgiving sky rained down on them.

Ory tried to divert Kaia's attention to lightning on the horizon, but she demanded to know what was happening. "Mommy, is she okay?"

"Hey, shhh, Kaia," he said. He thought he heard a sniffle through the microphone.

"It's okay. She's sleeping now, honey," Rhea said. "Ory, you can raise the lights."

He swiped up on the illuminated triangle. The spotlight brightened outside.

"Are there babies in the nest?" Kaia asked.

On the console viewscreen, Rhea's camera feed reappeared. The mother's body cast a shadow over a depression on the ground.

"There are two eggs," Rhea said, stepping down into the depression.

Kaia jumped and clapped. "Two!"

Ory mustered a shallow smile. "Are they both—" He paused and looked over at his daughter, who was squinting through the big window. "Are they both healthy?"

Kaia looked up at him. "We can help them while their mommy sleeps!"

On the screen, Rhea's hand reached out and rested on the first egg. With a jerk, her hand skipped to the second one. This time, it lingered in a caress. She whispered into her helmet, "Ory, Kaia, you're looking at the last baby phara on all of Nu."

Kaia shrieked, "Watch out, Mommy!"

Ory's heart raced when he looked out the window.

The mother phara rose on her hind legs.

Rhea's camera feed swung from the eggs to the looming silhouette of the phara above her: equal parts majestic and terrifying.

Ory panicked as the image on the viewscreen turned chaotic: boots slipping in the mud, dark sky, dead trees, and falling rain flashed on camera as Rhea scrambled backward, trying to get out of the nest and back away from the mother. The phara's long mouth rose to the sky as she let out a heart-rending roar to the storm above. The mother took a single step forward; her eyes blazed in the headlamp's light. Another low, guttural roar started but turned into a cough that spattered blood onto the Rhea's helmet. The mother's eyes rolled back into her skull. She collapsed, sending muddy water in every direction.

Rhea screamed.

"Mommy!" Kaia yelled.

"Are you okay?!" Ory said, the lump that formed in his throat threatening to choke him.

Static cracked, and Rhea spoke through clenched teeth. "Momma's head landed on my leg."

Ory and Kaia looked to each other, both letting out shaky breaths.

Ory sprang into action. "Is it broken?" he asked as he rushed toward the airlock.

"I-I don't think so," she said. "But I'm stuck."

"I'm coming." He put on his helmet and snapped the seal shut around his neck.

Ory internalized Kaia's fear and let it focus him as her eyes darted between the window and the feed from her mother's helmet.

"Kaia," he said. She turned around. "I need to go help your mother."

She nodded, hopped down from the crate, and headed toward Ory. "I want to go with you."

Ory bent down and looked into her eyes. He placed his gloved hands on her shoulders and squeezed once. "Do you remember the stream, Kaia?"

Kaia nodded again.

"Well, it's getting deeper with all this rain. I'd have to carry you, and I might lose my balance. It's too dangerous, okay?"

Kaia looked at the floor. "Okay..."

"Good." He patted her shoulders. "We will be back soon, Chirps.

Besides, we need you to stay here and let us know if the Council sends a storm warning."

She nodded again, pecked his helmet in the general location of his cheek, and raced back to hop on top of the supply crate.

As Ory made his way down the outside stairs, he flipped on his helmet camera. "Kaia, you should be able to see my feed now."

"I can see it, and Mommy's, too," Kaia confirmed.

"Good girl."

Ory headed to the nest, trying to balance speed with caution. He made his way through the grass, which was more of a mud slick now with the accumulating rain, and down to the stream. As he waded in, the once knee-deep water surged up to his thighs, threatening to knock him off his feet.

"Daddy be careful," Kaia begged.

"I'm fine, Chirps," he said, panting, trying to reassure himself as much as Kaia. He trudged through the water with careful, deliberate steps until he reached the other side.

The inside of his helmet fogged up, but he stumbled on toward Rhea.

"Rhea!" he yelled. "I'm almost there."

"Be careful," she warned as he approached.

The facility's spotlight faded.

"Kaia," he said, trying to keep his tone even, "please don't lean on the glyphpad."

"Oh, sorry," she said. The spotlight returned.

He fell to his knees next to Rhea and pulled the scanner from the medical case still wedged in the mud. He swiped the scanner up and down her body. "You twisted your ankle." He paused where the mother phara's jaw pinned Rhea's leg to the ground. "But nothing looks broken."

"Mommy, you're okay!" said Kaia.

"Yes, I'll be fine, Kaia. I just need to get unstuck." Rhea used her arms to prop herself up. "Ory, see if you can lift momma's head enough for me to get out."

Ory put the medical scanner in the pocket of his habsew. He

crouched down and slid his fingers under the mother's jaw. "One, two..." He lifted until his thighs burned, but he only managed to raise the phara's head a fraction of a cubit.

"It's no use," Rhea groaned.

He looked toward a dead tree nearby. "I'm going to find a branch so I can get some leverage." He stood up and began walking away but stopped when he noticed one egg rocking back and forth.

"Wait, I think it's hatching, Rhea."

"Now?"

"Now," he said, pointing to the egg.

It wobbled from side to side until a crack appeared on its top.

"It's coming!" Kaia's squeal was loud through the helmet.

"Go help, Ory," Rhea said. "We need to get it to the facility's incubation chamber."

He looked at her leg.

"I'll be fine. Go," she demanded. She reached down and pressed a red button on her suit's forearm controls. "I'm recording our camera feeds and transmitting them back to Council headquarters in Puna. This may be the last time anyone sees a hatching in the wild."

"Maybe it will inspire them to spend some money on preservation again," Ory said while scooting over to the nest. He cupped his hands and was scooping up the egg when the top popped off. "Kaia, look!"

She squealed with joy. "It's a baby phara!"

A fuzzy white arm popped out. Ory reached up to help pull the eggshell away. Its tiny head pushed another piece off with a small growl. It clawed at the sky as rain pattered its face.

"It's so cute!" Kaia shrieked.

The baby phara chittered, then froze. Ory felt it in his boots. The ground was shaking again. He looked down to the nest and saw ripples radiating in the puddle at the bottom.

He stood up to scan the edge of the forest. The clouds were darker, but there was nothing to explain the rumbling.

"What is it?" Rhea asked.

"I'm not sure," he said. He bent down to hand the baby phara to her and pointed back to the tree. "I'm going to get up higher to check."

Rhea cooed at the baby and lifted its tail. "I see you're a healthy girl, aren't you?" she said.

Ory reached the tree and scrambled up the empty branches. Clinging to the central trunk, he peered into the distance. There was nothing but curtains of rain in between the flashes of lightning. Then he heard it: another roar. *The father.* Not close yet, but he knew they would not have much time.

He clambered down as fast as he could and jogged back to Rhea.

Fear filled Rhea's eyes when she asked, "Was that a roar, Ory?"

"I'm not sure," he lied, "but we need to get back now." Ory pushed the branch under the mother's head and rested his body weight on the other end. The jaw budged enough for Rhea to pull her leg free before the stick broke, and the mother's head dropped back into the mud. Ory wrapped his arm around Rhea. "Can you stand?"

She tried and groaned, "Not by myself."

"Here," he said, wrapping his arm around her and lifting her up, "I've got you."

She winced in pain but used her left leg to support herself.

The baby phara, now cradled in Rhea's arms, chirped at the excitement as they made their way toward the stream.

Another roar. Closer this time.

Rhea turned to Ory. "I'm pretty sure that was the father."

"Hang on," he said, pulling her along as much as he was supporting her steps.

This time, there was no mistaking the deep, distant cry.

"What was that?" said Kaia. "What's going on?"

"It's okay, Kaia. It must be the daddy phara," said Rhea.

The father began roaring again, but something cut it short. A low, rolling thunder reverberated under their feet.

Ory paused to listen. "That's not a phara…"

"Whatever it is, let's keep moving," Rhea said, wincing at the pain. "It sounds like it's coming this way."

Ory pulled her forward and said, "You're right, we need to go."

"Mommy, Daddy, what's happening? Can you feel that? Everything is shaking inside."

He looked to the facility and saw the lights swinging from the ceiling. "Don't worry, Kaia, we're almost there." Thunder clapped.

"H-hurry!" Kaia cried; her voice thick.

Ory and Rhea slid to a stop at the stream. Except it wasn't a stream anymore—raging white-capped rapids flowed over the banks on both sides.

Ory panted inside his helmet. He looked at Rhea, then to the water. He tapped off the transmission mic so Kaia could not listen.

"The water is too deep, Rhea. And the current looks too strong."

Rhea nodded. "It would wash us away in no time."

Ory looked over the facility in frustration. They were so close, yet it may as well have been all the way to Puna.

That's when it occurred to him. "I'll radio for help."

Rhea glanced down at the baby phara sheltered in her arms, then up at Ory, her expression desperate. "What can they do, Ory? They'll never make it here in time."

He pointed to the docked shuttle. "We may not need them to get here if headquarters can fly that to us."

He tapped the side of his helmet to get long distance comms. "Come in, Puna. This is Ory Badra at Wildlife Refuge No. 7, requesting emergency assistance."

A flat voice crackled through the helmet, "Puna Control Center, go ahead, Ory."

"We're stuck outside in a storm with an impassable stream between us and the facility. We need someone to fly our shuttle over to us."

There was another voice in the background.

"Uh, one moment," the man said.

His voice sounded muffled as he spoke to, or more like argued with, someone; female, older, and angry.

Her smoky voice grew louder when she picked up the comm herself. "Ory, we're looking at the radar, and we've got bad news. The storm made landfall near you, and it doesn't look good. Is Kaia safe?"

"She is in the facility," he confirmed.

"Good. You need to get her into the shuttle."

"Okay, we'll do that now." Ory switched back to local comms and looked at Rhea as he spoke. "Kaia, I'm talking to headquarters, okay? We can't get across the stream, and the storm's getting worse. We need you to get to the shuttle—"

Kaia's frantic voice burst through the comm, "Daddy, behind you! The trees are disappearing!"

Ory turned, and terror gripped him.

Distant treetops shook, then sank into a wall of water.

"A storm surge," he said, unable to process the severity of what he was seeing.

Rhea yelled, "Kaia, get to the shuttle!"

"But I won't be able to help you," she protested.

Her father raised his voice. "Do it now."

"But I—"

"Kaia," Rhea said over the comm. "You need to listen. Get in the shuttle, now. Puna is going to fly it over to pick us up, so go."

Kaia stepped away from the observation window and disappeared into the facility. The swish of a door sliding open and shut followed her footsteps.

"Okay, I'm inside."

"Good, get strapped in, and I'll talk to you again soon, okay?" Ory pressed the comm button on his helmet again. "Puna, a storm surge is coming. Kaia's in the shuttle. You need to come and get us fast."

The woman on the other end clicked her tongue. He could almost see her shaking her head when she replied, "It's unfortunate, you know, this Tremva situation. It has forced us to make some tough calls."

"What situation? What do you mean?" Rhea demanded.

The woman continued, "We're dealing with mass protests aboard the refugee vessels. Captain Set's shenanigans have riled everyone up. People are angry, distrustful of our plan, of the whole Dawn Project itself!"

Rhea fumed. "Have you considered that it's not only Captain Set? You forced people from their homes. A man died in Tremva! Do you expect them to thank you?"

"We don't expect them to thank us, not yet," the woman cleared her throat, "but the Council's work is critical to the future of all Jacana, and we need to turn this tide. We need to give the people something else. An event or, say, tragedy to rally around."

Ory listened in horror as a thousand sickening cracks filled the air, closer now. He noticed the shuttle's lights turning on and the landing gear retracting.

"Look, we can talk about this later. Just get the shuttle over here."

"Well, that's the thing..." the woman said, her voice trailing off.

Ory's heart sank as the shuttle rose. It moved in the opposite direction, away from the storm surge.

Away from the facility.

Away from the stream.

Away from *them*.

"No!" Rhea shouted.

The woman on the comm sighed. "As I said, it was a tough decision, but your sacrifice will help us continue the Council's plan. And do not worry about young Kaia. The Council will watch over her. We've noticed she's quite precocious, that sweet girl. We'll make sure she continues your work. She will be more than yet another child refugee. Kaia will be a figure all Jacana can get behind."

Ory yelled at the top of his lungs, "You won't get away with this!"

"I suggest you use what time you have left to say goodbye to your daughter. And consider your words carefully. This is all she will have left of you. Oh, and I would be remiss to not thank you for your noble sacrifice. I will personally ensure that it is not in vain."

The transmission clicked off.


Kaia didn't understand what was happening. The shuttle was moving, but not toward her parents.

"Kaia, can you hear us?" Ory's voice boomed through the console. The glyphpad lit up with commands, as if entered by a ghost.

"I can hear you, Daddy!" she replied. "Wh-what's happening? Where are you? I don't see you. I-I think something is wrong with the shuttle." She set aside her blankie and reached for the controls.

They flashed red, locked. Not that she knew how to fly a shuttle, anyway.

"Kaia," Rhea said through tears, "listen, we don't have long, okay? We need you to remember that our people, our species, are the reason the world is dying. We are the reason for these hypercanes, the reason the animals are all going extinct. But you have a gift, Kaia. You have a way of making people understand. You can make them care, just like that day at the zoo. They listen to you, Kaia."

Her mother's words lodged in her subconscious. "Where are you? Why won't this thing stop?" Kaia slammed down on the emergency button, but the shuttle kept moving. She could no more stop the shuttle than she could stop the storm surge. She remembered a video glyph and scribbled out a rough box with a triangle on the front on the glyphpad. The interior helmet cameras from Rhea and Ory appeared on the shuttle's viewscreen.

"Mommy! Daddy!" she cried. "I can see you now. Can you see me?"

"Yes, Chirps, we see you." Her father had tears in his eyes.

Rhea said, "You're in the pilot seat now, Kaia."

Kaia realized that the shuttle wasn't turning around.

It wasn't going back for her parents.

Tears began streaming down her face. She picked up her blankie and squeezed it against her chest. "Mommy, Daddy, I n-need you."

"You'll be okay, Kaia. You're strong and brave," Ory said.

Rhea cleared her throat. "We are so proud of you, Kaia. So proud of everything you've done and for all the things you will come to do." She coddled the baby phara and Ory wrapped his arms around her.

Behind them, the storm surge burst between the trees at the edge of the wetland. "Run!" Kaia yelled.

The dying forest transformed into a barrage of deadly missiles as it raced toward her parents unimpeded. Ory and Rhea pulled themselves close and clung to the baby phara.

Rhea did her best to soothe their daughter. "We will always love you, Kaia."

Ory turned to the approaching torrent, then back to Kaia in the shuttle. He looked into his daughter's eyes on the video feed.

"Remember what your mother said, Kaia. People listen to you. You can help them understand what we've done. You can—" he choked back tears. "Kaia, you can save the world from us."

Her parents' video feeds went dark.

Kaia jumped up and pounded on the console. "Nooo!" she yelled at the blank screen. "Nooooo!" she yelled again as the crushing wave washed away her entire life.

She looked up at the dark acid rain streaking across the cockpit window and thought of the recording from Tremva, of the boy and girl whose father died in the deconstruction. Her life felt deconstructed now, too. She slumped into the pilot's chair and pulled her hood down tight. Her mother and father's last words played on repeat while an unseen hand transported her into an uncertain future.

*"We will always love you, Kaia."*

Her feelings swirled—fear—sadness—anger.

*"Kaia, you can save the world from us."*

She forced her eyes open and stared into the darkness ahead while a new, grown-up feeling transcended all others.

Determination.

*Mom, Dad, I will.*

# ERUPTION

## ACT ONE

# ERUPTION

## A NEW MASS EXTINCTION

# A.W. DAVIDSON

# CHAPTER 1
# CLIMB

## UXMAL RUINS - 2034 CE

Alan put his hands on the white pyramid's next step and pulled himself up with a groan. *How fortunate,* he thought, that the drill site was so close to the ancient city of Uxmal. He knew his team of students could sustain their energy at the rig all night, core sample after core sample, on nothing but the possibility of discovery. He decided to leave them to it while he checked out the ruins.

"Why in the world did the Maya build such tall steps?" he huffed.

Geological fieldwork like this reminded him decades had passed since he was the newly minted Alan Pearce, PhD. He was no longer the young hotshot geologist who scaled Mount Kamen in Siberia for a single rock sample to research the cause of the Great Dying—the largest mass extinction on Earth due to a climate change 250 million years ago. He still remembered the speech:

"And that is how the lava eruptions, also known as flood basalts, can release enough carbon dioxide to kill almost every living thing when they happen too fast. Earth lost ninety percent of its species in this Siberian Traps eruption, including this little critter, the trilobite," he had explained to the crowd in front of a picture of the enlarged two-eyed bug fossil.

From there, his unique approach to studying climate change by focusing on Earth's geology had earned him tenure at the University of Chicago and a coveted seat on the Geology Committee of the United Nations Climate Council. Now the only thing he scaled was a mountain of paperwork for a single field outing. He shook his head just thinking about all the international travel requests he had to file to get his graduate students here for the project. He looked up at the next step on the pyramid. His legs ached in protest.

*Okay, time for a break*, he thought.

He took a moment, inhaling the warm, humid air. A bead of sweat trickled down his brow and he wiped it away with a red handkerchief from his shirt. At least he didn't need to manage a flashlight, too: the white limestone stairs glistened in the light of a full moon. His breathing returned to normal. *Almost there*. He reached out, put his hands on the next step, and pulled himself up.

"Eighty-nine," he exhaled, "ninety." He took a deep breath. "I made it!" he shouted from the top of the white pyramid. He looked up at the temple standing guard over the peak. Its flat roof rose twenty feet into the air, and the white limestone facade stretched thirty feet in both directions. He hobbled toward the front of the temple and ran his hands across the wall. The Maya carved a deep crosshatched crystal pattern into the stone on both sides of the door. He stepped back and noticed the temple resembled a woven basket. *The pattern must have some cultural significance*. He took a mental note to ask his wife Louise what it meant. He knew the rocks; she knew the people.

They got married during undergraduate studies, much to the chagrin of both sets of parents. His dad, the classic image of behind-the-times, was livid when Louise, a dual-major in anthropology and linguistics, went on to graduate with a bachelor's degree and then continued to become the first Dr. Pearce in the household, beating his son to an accepted PhD dissertation by two whole days. Alan, the other Dr. Pearce, could not have cared less and beamed with pride when his wife completed her final thesis defense. But he had her on one point, his father liked to remind him: the UN called Alan first. Louise was close behind, though, and now served as the head anthropologist on the Climate Council's Relocation Committee. He felt lucky that she was spending her sabbatical with him on a research trip to Mexico.

"Professors get musty without some fresh air," he loved to joke.

"And fresh ideas," she always added with a smirk.

Now that his thighs had stopped burning, he felt the straps of his backpack digging into his shoulders. He pulled the bag off and removed a thermos from the front pocket. He smiled as his finger ran over a large dent in the stainless-steel base. Back in 2019, the Relocation Committee sent Louise to study the remote Easter Island inhabitants to predict how their culture might integrate with the mainland if they needed to evacuate due to the increasingly severe cyclones. Alan accompanied her, and although he'd intended on taking a break while she worked, he could not help himself from inspecting the stonework of the mysterious Moai head carvings. He was entranced by their maroon capstone hats when he took a step backwards, right off the ceremonial platform.

His thermos was not the only thing that ended up with bumps and bruises.

Alan held the thermos at his waist and twisted the lid, but it did not budge. He stopped to shake his right hand. "Stupid arthritis," he muttered. "I hate getting old." He stretched his fingers and tried again. This time, the lid squeaked open, followed by coffee splashing out onto his beard. He wiped his chin on his shoulder and flipped the lid over to pour. The heat passed through the cup, still too hot for him to drink, but also too hot for this weather. "Stupid humans," he said. "Thanks for this July heat in January!" He pursed his lips across the top of the coffee and blew. Hearing a groan, he whirled around.

It sounded like it came from inside the temple.

Alan took a few steps and stood in front of the door and raised the cup to blow on his coffee again when there was another sound—this time more like a whimper. Goosebumps rose on his arms as he turned his right ear toward the temple.

He walked back to his bag and pulled out a flashlight. "You better not be trying to give your old professor a heart attack," he called out, hoping that perhaps one of his students was inside trying to scare him. When he returned to the temple door, the dark chamber within seemed to swallow the light until it fell upon a wide stone face staring at him from the back wall. He gulped and raised the flashlight higher. Carved feathers sat atop its head like a crown. The almond-shaped eyes angled down. He followed their gaze with his flashlight. A stone altar, large enough for a body, dominated the center of the chamber. He walked through the door and squatted next to the platform. He shone the flashlight along its side. A chill went up his spine despite the muggy air. Blackish streaks ran down the stone's rough surface. He closed his eyes, trying not to imagine them as fresh blood pouring over the sides as the Maya sacrificed humans on this spot.

Standing back up, he put the flashlight in his pocket and tried to shake the grisly thought from his mind. He peered out the doorway and saw the kite-shaped constellation of Orion.

It reminded him of the complicated relationship his species had always had with the stars—believing the dots of light were gods for so long. Louise always pointed out that ancient deities had such power over the minds of humans that often religious monuments were the last remaining traces of entire ancient civilizations. To modern eyes, the monuments appeared beyond their engineering capabilities. But Alan knew not to underestimate the will of thousands of people. From this pyramid in the Uxmal ruins outside Chicxulub, Mexico, to its mound cousins north of St. Louis, Missouri, to the pyramids across the ocean in Egypt, countless souls poured themselves into the impossible constructions. The altar's red streaks flashed in his mind again, but this time, his shoulders relaxed. Modern humans were more likely to build grand monuments to honor influential leaders and civic pursuits rather than centers of worship for gruesome rituals.

He looked down at this coffee, blew over it one last time, and was about to take a sip when he heard the shuffling of feet outside the chamber. His heart pounded in his chest, certain someone else was on top of the pyramid. At that moment, a dark figure stepped into the doorway, framed by the glow of moonlight.

Alan threw his coffee at it. The shadowy figure let out a yelp. He fumbled the flashlight out of his pocket, held it with both hands, and found the switch. The shaky beam illuminated a woman raising her hand to shield her eyes.

"Alan! What are you doing?" Louise yelled, trying to wipe the coffee off her shirt. "Get that light out of my face!"

Alan let out a jagged breath. "Louise! I'm so sorry. You scared me half to death!"

He lowered the flashlight and the hair on his arms laid back down.


Louise took a moment and rested her hands on her hips while catching her breath. She then lifted the mosquito net from her face.

"I thought you'd hear me since I was cursing my bad knees all the way up. It's such a long climb," she said. She wiped the sweat from her brow with her forearm.

"My mind wandered while I admired Orion," he said, pointing to the constellation. Looking back to the altar, he shivered. "The echo made your climb sound like the ghost of a long-dead shaman. Let's get out of here."

"Gladly."

Louise stepped out into the moonlight and blew a tuft of red hair from her face. Her milky skin—lined with age but still beautiful to Alan—radiated in the light.

"What were you thinking about?" she asked.

He smiled. "Oh, I was just wondering who else would have followed me into the Mexican jungle on a wildly speculative scientific expedition."

Louise rolled her eyes. "Alan, you're great and all, but don't kid yourself. This is a great use of my sabbatical from academia because many believe the Mayan civilization collapsed due to local climate change. It is hard to imagine a better place to launch my own research for the Relocation Committee."

She reached up to his face and pushed the damp gray hair off his forehead. He felt his skin warm like a seam of black coal soaking up the midday sun. She could still make him feel flushed even after thirty years together.

She poked his chest. "What kind of anthropologist would I be if I gave up the chance to examine these ruins up close?"

He grinned, pointing to the coffee stain on her green shirt. "An anthropologist not at risk of being scalded by a hot beverage."

She laughed. "Hazards of the job, I guess. How can you drink that in this heat, anyway?"

He toasted her with his thermos cap. "I need the caffeine if I'm to make it through the last night of drilling."

"Smart," she said, now eyeing his coffee.

"Permit expires tomorrow at noon, sharp. I am told you do not want to push it with the Mexican Archaeological Police."

"Do the Archaeological Police actually exist?" she asked.

He shrugged. "I have heard stories, and I don't want to find out for myself. My funding will evaporate if I don't find a crater under these ruins, and I'll have to come up with another plan to save the world."

"Alan, you're right about this. I just know it. And as much as I'd like for the UN's volcano plan to work and reverse the terrible damage we've done to this poor planet, I'd feel much better knowing there are other options, too." She paused and looked back to the temple. "And this has been an enlightening trip for me. I have never studied Mayan culture up close and personal. I believe we have underestimated the ancient population supported by this region's ecology."

"Well," he started, "what I want to know is why such short people built such tall steps!"

Louise laughed. "That is a good question. They are more suited to Scandinavians than the Maya."

With the temple at their backs, the pair looked out over the last relics of the civilization at Uxmal. The white pyramid was twice as tall as the surrounding forest, affording a full view of the spacious stone plaza. Placid moonlight bathed the ruins in a milky white glow. The imposing two-story Governor's Palace flanked its right border, while the steep, pitched roofs of the House of Pigeons rose above the forest to the left. At the opposite end of the plaza, the squat House of Turtles stood guard by the ancient gates.

The view was a rare treat because most people were no longer allowed on the pyramid. Decades of acid rain had softened and dissolved the limestone, leaving it too fragile to handle the footsteps of a thousand tourists a day.

Alan reached for Louise's hand and sighed. He closed his eyes and listened to the jungle. The whir of cicadas served as the backdrop for a chorus of tree frogs. The occasional whoop of a distant howler monkey reminded him he and his team were not the only primates awake tonight.

He opened his eyes and looked east, past the stone plaza, and saw harsh artificial light shining up into the trees. A narrow scaffold rose from the center of the light, poking through the tree canopy. Alan imagined his fifteen graduate students gathered around the small drill rig, watching with anticipation as it pulled up sample after sample.

Louise saw the gleam in his eye. "You are proud of them, aren't you?"

He grinned. "Very much. They want to sort out how to repair the climate even more than I do."

"The worst climate problems are still to come and will be theirs to solve," Louise said with a sigh.

"Very true. And they were all raised with more appreciation for the earth's ecology than I ever learned in school—makes them better geologists than I'll ever be." He pointed to the drill site. "That rig was their suggestion, you know. When I was in school, we had to clear trees to make way for the equipment and then put holes at least a foot wide all over the place. The kids found this new-fangled thing that doesn't need much space to operate and can drill a shaft hundreds of feet deep and only two inches wide."

"No wonder you're pleased. I understand it leaves no lasting environmental impact. We've already stressed the rainforest enough," Louise said.

A terrible grinding ricocheted around the plaza and into the temple's inner echo chamber, which turned it into a spine-tingling dull roar. Alan and Louise covered their ears until the scraping stopped.

A howler monkey yelped in response, then fell silent. An eerie calm settled over the ancient city. Even the cicadas and tree frogs grew quiet, disturbed by the unnatural metallic screech. Alan pictured the students all bending down to study the latest core sample from deep below their feet, and now wished he was down there, too.

A young woman's shout rose from the forest. "We've got it!"

# CHAPTER 2
# PYRAMID OF THE PROPHET

## UXMAL RUINS – 2034 CE

Looking down from the pyramid, Alan and Louise saw a light winding through the trees toward them. A young woman jogged into the plaza, her flashlight casting eerie, jagged shadows across the ruins.

Alan put his hands on his thighs and leaned forward. "Is that you, Daxia?" he yelled.

She paused at the bottom of the staircase. "Yes, Dr. Pearce! I have something you need to see!"

"Well, come on up!"

"The view is spectacular," Louise added.

As Daxia scaled the pyramid, Alan chuckled to himself. She ascended at least twice as fast as he or Louise could.

Louise rested her hands on her hips. "Well, she's in a hurry. She must love the work as much as you do."

He nodded. "She does. No other teaching assistant has come close. I am going to miss her when she decides on a PhD program."

"Has she decided what she's going to study?" Louise asked.

"Not yet. That's the rub with getting dual degrees. She's still going back and forth between getting her doctorate in environmental geology or paleontology."

Louise patted his back. "Well, either would be useful to the Council if she wants to stay involved in climate change research. And, if you ask me, a dual-degree holder myself, two are better than one." She winked.

"Ouch!" Daxia yelled from below.

Louise shouted, "Careful!" as Daxia took the steps two at a time. "I can't believe she can do that, let alone after midnight in this heat."

"Oh, to be young again," Alan said.

Daxia scrambled up the last step, breathless. She looked to him wide-eyed. "Dr. Pearce, how did you survive the trip up here?" she asked, wiping sweat from her brow.

"Hey now, same way you did, thank you very much."

Louise grinned. "Except it took him about twenty times longer."

His eyebrows flattened. "Excuse me, but did you get up here any faster?" he said, looking at Louise.

"Maybe I did, maybe I didn't."

His flashlight caught something in Daxia's hand, something big and gleaming. His pulse quickened. *Could this be it?*

Daxia brushed a curtain of her sopping black hair behind her ear and nodded toward the temple's chamber.

"Go sit, dear," Louise said.

Daxia ambled to the altar after her sprint to the top. She lifted herself up on the edge of the stone slab and collected her breath.

Alan raised a hand to discourage her from sitting there, but guessed she was oblivious to the altar's true purpose and decided it might be best not to mention it.

"So, what did you find?" he asked, no longer able to contain his excitement.

Taking a final deep breath, Daxia held her hand open and shined the flashlight on a rock. Alan reached for it and a piece broke off, falling to the ground and fracturing into a million tiny crystals.

"That has to be shocked quartz!" Alan exclaimed. He could not believe his luck. If they had failed tonight, it could be years before he got funding to try again.

Daxia nodded. "You were right, Dr. Pearce. We reached the Cretaceous-Paleogene boundary layer, and sure enough, there's your shocked quartz!"

He raised his fists and shouted, then embraced Louise in a bear hug. "Finally!"

Louise laughed as Alan twirled her around. He set her down, and she grabbed his cheeks for a kiss.

Daxia turned away. "Geez, get a room, you two."

He looked at the chunk of rock in his hand. "How wide was the layer?"

Daxia grinned. "Based on the sample we pulled up, the K-Pg layer is wider here than anywhere on Earth we've found so far. All the evidence points to this being a second rim of a single crater structure, because, as your model shows, the dust layer would be thicker the closer we are to the impact."

Louise's smile turned serious. "But I thought we already found the rim fifty miles from here?" she asked.

"That is the inner rim and this, we think, is an outer rim," he explained. "There are two."

"Very rare for an impact crater," Daxia said.

Alan rubbed his chin. "You're right. I can think of only one other like it on the planet," he remembered. "It is much smaller, though."

Louise turned to Alan. "How big is this one by comparison?"

"I'll show you," Alan said, waving toward the door with his palm up.

They stepped out of the temple and stood facing the sky. He waved his arms over the moonlit landscape. "See the horizon?"

Louise nodded.

"Now imagine the crater stretching about eighty miles past that."

She turned to him. "Unimaginable."

"Very imaginable, for me. There is no doubt we are standing on the outer rim of a crater almost one hundred miles wide."

Louise's eyebrows shot up. "One hundred miles wide? The impact's consequences would have been—" her voice faded.

"Technically, 93 miles wide according to the model, but yes... the impact was devastating," Daxia said.

"Cataclysmic," Alan offered. He looked down at the glimmering rock in his hand. "Did you plug this new data into the simulation?"

"Yes, according to Harris and Bowell's models," she began, and pulled her phone from her pocket to scan the notes, "the simulation determined the asteroid was at least six miles wide."

"Six miles?" Louise asked. "That is hard to believe. A single stone, six miles wide? How did that not destroy the world?"

"It did," Daxia said. "It killed almost everything."

Alan chuckled. "As far as we know, anyway. I wish we knew more about the event. That settles it, Daxia! You must get your doctorate in paleontology, so we can get a better handle on the specifics of this impact."

Daxia laughed. "You know I've been considering it, Dr. Pearce, but as we both know, it's easier to get research funding for environmental geology than paleontology these days."

Alan closed his eyes and rubbed the back of his neck. "Unfortunately, I do know, Daxia. I would even say paleontology is downright unpopular. The politicians don't understand how animals who died tens of millions of years ago can tell us about the ones dying today."

Louise smiled weakly and squeezed Alan's shoulder. "Well, they funded you this round. I'm sure they'll continue."

"I hope you're right," he said.

Louise sighed. "People can be very short-sighted at times."

He sighed in return. "Overconfident may be a better description. But regardless of what the Geology Committee thinks, it may take a bunch of small meteorite impacts to save the planet if their man-made eruption isn't successful. Looking at this large crater will give us the data we need to complete the impact model for my plan."

Louise put her hand on his shoulder. "You're right. The data is important no matter what they say."

"These findings should convince the Council's Geology Committee to fund at least one more round of research. Every bit will help."

Daxia stood next to him. "Don't be modest, Dr. Pearce." She took the stone from his hand, its crystals glistening under the moonlight. "This little rock is the scientific discovery of the century."

"We still have so much work to do to convince everyone that micro-impacts are a viable option," he said, looking out over the ancient city.

Moonlight bounced off the waxy, green leaves of the jungle below the pyramid. The forest was alive with the nightly chorus of creatures.

"Look at that," Louise exclaimed, pointing to the sky. A tiny dark circle passed in front of the full moon. "I wonder how many people are mining up there as we speak?"

"Three hundred, I think," Daxia stated as the asteroid transited across the moon and back into darkness.

Alan raised his eyebrows. "And if it works, that's just the beginning. I'm glad Asteroid Resources Inc. is well-funded, because those space rocks may be our best chance for survival."

Daxia sat down at the edge of one of the pyramid steps and looked back up at the brightest star rising on the horizon. "Maybe I should focus on astrobiology instead. No use in studying this planet's present or past life if it will all end up in the trash."

"Let's hope not," Louise said, sitting down next to her.

Daxia laughed under her breath. "Tonight reminds me of the last time I looked up at the sky, like, really looked. I was eight years old, camping with my dad while he studied Egyptian nightjar bird nests in the bushes." She pointed to a bright star hanging above the horizon. "I asked him what star that was, and he told me it wasn't a star at all, but a planet called Venus." She put her hands down behind her and leaned back. "A whole other planet floating out there. My little brain couldn't imagine it."

Alan sat down next to her and pointed to the constellation of Orion.

"I remember lying in the cool grass as a boy, imagining what life must be like on the ten planets circling the stars of Orion. I even remember the three stars in the belt—Mintaka, Alnilam, and Alnitak," he said with pride.

"Ten planets? You know there are over forty, right?" Daxia said.

"It was only twenty-one last I knew! But there were only ten when I was a boy. I stopped paying attention as I got older and my interest in geology grew."

Daxia smiled. "When I got older, I wished aliens from one of those planets would visit and help us save our world, but my father always said there was a good chance they'd be fleeing theirs because they used up its resources."

"The fact that aliens haven't visited us yet might mean they destroyed themselves like we are about to do. Maybe they couldn't stop their climate change, either."

Daxia frowned. "We need research like this because I'm pretty sure aliens aren't coming to show us how it's done."

Louise put her hands between her knees and shrugged. "That is not a new idea, you know—that the wisdom to save our home may come from the heavens." She looked at the three stars in Orion's belt. "Did either of you know that some fringe Egyptologists believe the ancient Egyptians aligned the three great pyramids of Giza to those three stars?"

"Like, the Egyptians worshiped the stars?" Daxia asked.

"Perhaps," Louise said. "Some go even further and suggest aliens from those stars visited Egypt and gave them a vast store of knowledge. Conspiracy theorists say it's all documented in an encyclopedia called the *Book of Power*."

Alan chuckled, "Lunatics."

Louise entertained the notion for a moment longer. "I agree with you, but it is puzzling that pyramids often occur in sets or multiples of three in ancient cities. All ancient societies in the northern hemisphere seemed to focus on the same three stars."

Daxia nodded to a gap in the distant treetops. "Well, if they're going to come help us, they'd better hurry. This jungle will be farmland in a few years."

Louise inhaled and nodded. "The UN has tried to curb deforestation, but there are just too many mouths to feed."

Alan nodded. "Earth is suffering on a scale we have never seen and soon its people will be, too. All those ethicists concerned about re-engineering our climate are going to find themselves on the losing side of the argument when everything goes south."

Louise looked down at her feet. She raised her head to Alan and Daxia. "Do either of you know the name of the pyramid we're sitting on?"

Alan and Daxia exchanged a glance, shrugged, and shook their heads.

Louise crossed her legs and turned toward them.

Alan's eyes lit up. "Oh, wait! Yes, I do. I read the plaque at the bottom." He puffed his chest. "This is the Pyramid of the Magician. Take that, Dr. I-have-a-second-degree-in-linguistics!"

Louise rolled her eyes. "That is a poor translation for the tourists who come to gawk at it. This pyramid's true name is *Pirámide del Adivino*. A more direct translation is Pyramid of the Prophet."

Alan raised one eyebrow and looked to Daxia.

Louise smiled. "I know you two do not believe in fate."

"Only you liberal arts people talk about fate," he joked.

She tilted her head. "But you cannot deny the coincidence that this discovery of yours may predict the future."

Alan turned the shocked quartz over in his hand. He never believed in fate. It felt too much like religion. He looked back at the sacrificial altar, trying not to imagine a shaman thrusting a human heart to the heavens while crazed crowds chanted from the plaza below.

*That's where religion leads*, he thought. He shuddered again, then forced his mind back to the crater and all the extra work needed to fill in the gaps in his impact model. "If I'm right, it might be our only chance. I hope the UN Climate Council listens to us."

# CHAPTER 3
# LITTLE AFFI

**BY KAIA BADRA**

I was once was a child,
but now I have grown.
Little Affi, you taught me
the destructive seeds
my people have sown.

As the sun sank
into an industrial haze,
I knew we had reached
the end of our days.

Your fur was so soft,
when you curled up in my hand.
How could I know,
you would inherit the land?

You were meek underfoot,

and easy to ignore,
as you hurried and scurried,
across the forest floor.

You were scouting for food,
when you crested the hill,
and saw our great city,
unusually still.

The ground shook in a quake,
and you sniffed at the air,
sensing danger was close,
but it was already there.

Heat poured from below,
spreading out in a fan,
engulfing our city,
as your future began.

It was too hot for you,
so you fled to your nest,
and curled up safely,
as the chaos progressed.

We left your world in ruins.
and fled to the stars.
Little affi, you taught me
the planet was now yours,
not ours.

You came into your own,
growing up, too,
so now, Little affi,
it is time for Me to teach You.

# CHAPTER 4
# EXODUS

## MONTU CITYSHIP - CYCLE 2296

Dramatic, hopeful music echoed around the hollow heart of the *Montu* cityship's central plaza. Kaia stood with her back turned toward the stage as tens of thousands of colonists filed in to watch the Exodus ceremony. She remembered seeing the first *Montu* schematics right after her parents died. *Twenty cycles ago,* Kaia thought. Had it really been that long?

Kaia clasped her hands in front of her and gazed up at a long, bright light beam illuminating this cavernous space. Like sol, its warm glow cast shadows that danced between buildings carved out of the asteroid's interior as they gently rotated around its central axis. Centrifugal force held everyone's feet to the ground, which was the only artificial gravity scientists devised in the cycles leading up to the Dawn Project. Her species made amazing progress but reflecting on it brought a familiar pang of guilt and regret that if previous generations of Jacana had done more, a fleet of cityships would not be necessary. Now, every Jacana soul was a refugee fleeing a dying world. They would live here, spinning on a spaceship traveling at a fraction of the speed of light, oblivious to the astronomical wonders they would pass on their way to a new home on the planet Duat.

She heard footsteps to her right and turned to see Enki walking toward her, eyes zoned in to the viewpad in his hands. His silver habsew suit, the one all project geologists wore, reflected the lights of the circular city. He kept up his pace and almost bumped into her.

"Hello Enki. Looking for your seat?" she said, pointing to an empty chair in the front row.

Enki stopped and looked up from his viewpad. A confused look spread across his face.

She reached over her shoulder and pulled her hood back on, then adjusted it so the translator speakers covered her ears.

Enki did the same with his own suit's hood. "Sorry, I forget the babel hood sometimes."

"It's okay."

He looked to the empty chair. "Thank you, though I do not like the front row," he lamented. "At least I do not need to give a speech," he said, eyebrows raised.

Kaia puffed her cheeks and said, "I hope this is my last one."

"The project will be over soon, and you will be free."

*Free.* The word stuck in her mind. It was hard to say if she knew what that felt like because she dedicated her whole life to the Dawn Project. Without the project, what would she do? She pushed the thought aside and glanced at Enki's glyphpad. "What are you doing on there?"

He turned it around and held it up to her.

She saw a graph with several lines racing to the upper right while others stopped moving at all. "What am I looking at?"

Enki huffed, "As a project leader, you should know a thermoviewer readout when you see one!"

Kaia smiled. She was used to his reactions after months of working with him on the final phases of the project. His odd ways could appear self-absorbed and his obsessive interests prevented him from seeing the connections she could. But, that's how people with the tism were. His mind was an unmatched powerhouse and she was proud to have him on the project. In fact, her society depended on people like Enki. People who would forgo meals, hygiene, relationships—anything to doggedly pursue their interests. Those obsessions lead to breakthroughs in science that led the Council to devise this grand plan to save their world. As they threatened nature, could it have created more tism in the Jacana young? Her mind began diving into the question, planning to search the journals, but now was not the time. She snapped it back to the present.

"I know this is a thermoviewer readout," she said. "I meant why are some of the readings disappearing?"

"Oh, yes, I am trying to find the answer. The nanomechs should be near the planet's mantle in a two to three hours so I expected the temperature to rise, but not failing thermoviewer sensors."

Kaia felt her heart quicken. Phase one of the Dawn Project would begin soon.

Enki tapped the viewpad. "Wait, they are back."

"The readings?"

He nodded. "I will need to investigate when we get back to the *Meridian*." He glanced over to the stairs leading down to the shuttle docking bays. "When is Captain Apep picking us up?"

"As soon as the ceremony is over, I hope," she said, noticing Councilor Horus approaching them.

"Good," Enki said, and resumed tapping around on the viewpad.

The Councilor's deep black robe and babel hood gave Kaia the impression he was walking in the shadows as he drew near.

He stopped next to Enki. "How is everything looking, my friend?"

Enki's eyes darted up from his glyphpad then narrowed. "It would be going better if you had listened to my advice and reinforced the bore hole so the nanomechs could work without the risk of it collapsing."

Councilor Horus chuckled, "Still stuck on that, are we boy?"

Kaia fumed inside. Councilor Horus did as he pleased, only Head Councilor Hegira could force him to listen.

Enki kept a straight face, and said, "Even without a collapse, pieces of the wall could break off and destroy the drilling nanomechs. Or worse, prematurely detonate the puncture explosives."

"Don't you worry," Councilor Horus said, patting him on the back. "I designed them to be so resilient that a little heat and falling rocks won't take out enough of them to make a difference."

The wheels were turning in Enki's head, that much Kaia could tell by the way he just stared at Councilor Horus, fingers still moving over the glyphpad with a will of their own.

Councilor Horus raised a chastising finger, but Enki flashed a patronizing smile and turned his back. He then waltzed over to his seat, leaving Kaia alone with the Councilor.

"Who does he think he is?" Councilor Horus said, pointing at the empty space next to her, dumbfounded.

She tried to break the spell with a smile. "Why don't we sit down?"

Councilor Horus seethed for another second, then a jovial veneer spread across his face. "Of course, Kaia. Are you ready for your big moment?"

Her eyes swept over the crowd again, now mostly seated and murmuring amongst themselves.

"I am as ready as any of us can be for what we are about to start."

"Good," Councilor Horus said and bowed. "Now, let's go sit with the others," he said, gesturing to the front row.

Kaia wondered where Head Councilor Hegira was, then saw her clutching Councilor Itzamna's arm as he guided her down an aisle to the front row. She rushed over and bowed to Councilor Itzamna, "I'll take her from here, thank you."

Councilor Hegira looked up at her and smiled. "Thank you, dear."

After losing her parents, Kaia could have been just another orphan, but Councilor Hegira convinced her she could play an important role in helping the Council with their plan to save Nu from total devastation. Over the cycles, Hegira became the closest person Kaia had to a mother.

Kaia felt Councilor Hegira's strong grip on her arm and not an ounce of weight leaning into her. *Another tactic?* Kaia wondered if this frailty could be a technique in Hegira's impressive cache of political savvy. Nobody could match her array of methods used to inspire, or persuade, others into acting on her wishes. Kaia loved her for it. The

Dawn Project would be nothing without Councilor Hegira. And, the natural world would be suffering, forever.

The societal division her parents thought the Council could never overcome was settled shortly after their death, and perhaps in some small part because of it. They became martyrs, and Kaia became the child whose story weaved through every dinner conversation around the world. Her whole society seemed to agree all at once that it was time for Captain Set and Head Councilor Hegira to negotiate a tenuous peace so the Dawn Project could begin. Both sides ended up agreeing it was time to leave the planet, and that Captain Set would command a cityship, this cityship, the *Montu*.

The lights dimmed as Kaia and Head Councilor Hegira took their seats. The massive viewscreen above the stage brightened. Loud, dramatic music accompanied a video of each new destination planet. The camera flew above a barren, ruddy landscape and zoomed in on a waterfall the same color as the canyon walls around it. Kaia tried to remember, was she 15 or 17 cycles old when the Council scientists found this world and named it Midgard? There were so many planets, *so many uninhabitable ones*, she also recalled. They seemed to announce new planet discoveries around her birthday, one cycle older, a handful of new planets found, and often only one that could serve as a new home for her species. The Council used the opportunity to celebrate her life, reflect on her tragedy, and remind all Jacana of their important work.

As the camera swooped over another planet's desolate landscape, Kaia wondered what her parents would think of the Dawn Project. They would agree with the goals, of course, but would they also agree with the methods? When she was a child, her people sat at the brink of extinction on a dying planet, and the path through it was anything but clear.

But she was no longer the teary-eyed little girl building support for the Council by reliving her trauma on home viewscreens.

And her society no longer acted like apathetic school children squabbling over a toy while they ignored a deadly ice storm rolling in.

Everyone paid attention now.

The Council bestowed the title of "Head Biologist" Kaia when she finished her studies at eighteen cycles old. The next nine cycles she had a singular focus, along with the rest of Jacana society: The Dawn Project, her civilization's grand plan to save the world, from them.

The video ended and a spotlight shone on the center of the stage. Kaia heard a rustling to her left and saw Councilor Brahma standing up and ambling toward the stage.

Councilor Hegira leaned over to Kaia and whispered, "He made an odd choice of headwear."

Kaia nodded in agreement. "But you tried to tell him."

"That I did," Councilor Hegira said and crossed her arms.

Councilor Brahma's headwear looked like a stick decorated with a stack of shrinking plates. A conical headpiece was typical of most Council members, but she thought his looked more like the skeleton of one. The side flaps had large dots that almost looked like eyes, giving the unsettling impression that he had three faces. Overall, it failed to convey the power he intended, she thought.

Thanks to all the rehearsals, Kaia knew the speech's lines better than he did. Still, a rush of hope passed through her each time she heard the Council's plan to ensure the future of life on Nu.

Councilor Brahma clasped his hands. "Our departure... Our Exodus, is an opportunity to create a new world, a better world, for everyone." He stopped, his gleaming eyes staring into the crowd.

Kaia winced, wondering who had coached him on the dramatic pause, then realized it might be his own idea. He was always the one prodding her to speak with more passion, more tears, as she retold her tragedy for the newsfeeds. *More people will pity you, which will make them believe in our cause,* his words echoed in her mind.

Councilor Brahma pressed a glyphpad on his forearm, and a three-dimensional landscape materialized in front of him. Skeletal trees dotted the rolling landscape that spread out under a polluted orange sky.

"After Exodus, the two ultimate acts of our grand project will set a plan in motion to repair our climate over millennia." He stepped back and spread his arms wide while the scene enlarged for all to see.

A blue sky crested the horizon and pushed away the haze. The brown clouds faded to pure white, and it started raining. Crystal clear rain, not the acidic brown drizzle that generations of Jacana knew. The space between branches filled in as leaves appeared. Vibrant green grass spread over the dry soil. The scene revealed a world unrecognizable to any living Jacana. Councilor Brahma clasped his hands in front of him once more. "This is the future of Nu."

*As best we can tell from the simulations,* Kaia thought but never said out loud.

Councilor Brahma crossed his arms over his chest and bowed, then stepped through the lush landscape and took his seat.

Councilor Shiva took the stage with a youthful energy and confidence. A downward facing triangle dominated the front of his suit. A scarf resembling the scaly skin of a uraeus covered his neck. As he pressed his forearm glyphpad, Tremva's skyline appeared in front of him. He looked down, and the city crumbled to the ground in a cloud of dust.

"Deconstruction has helped nature reclaim our majestic cities." He held up a finger. "Except one, the jewel of our civilization." A new skyline, much larger than Tremva's, appeared in front of him. "Puna."

Kaia heard Councilor Hegira take a deep, prideful breath.

Skytower after skytower filled the screen. Kaia imagined each one full of the minutiae of daily life. The lives and lifestyles that now threatened the planet that gave birth to them.

"If we are to create a new world," he said, "we must first erase the remains of the past. While our society has moved beyond divisive faiths, I cannot help but say that the location of our last city appears fateful."

Puna's skyline shrank to reveal the layers of Nu's crust below it. "Two acts of destruction will renew our planet. The first begins beneath our feet. An immense geothermal force powered our city, and now we must tap into it to save our planet." A red column rose through the layers beneath Puna until it erupted onto the surface, dwarfing the skytowers.

"The second act will come from above. There are one hundred small asteroids waiting to impact over thousands of cycles."

A small field of dots formed in the blackness above Puna and began orbiting the planet at different speeds. One fell to the surface, creating a cloud of dust that encircled the planet.

"The impact dust will work in balance with the eruption to continue a cooling trend until our home achieves a stable climate once again."

Kaia had grown numb to the geological details after hearing them so many times; that was Enki's area, not hers. This time she paid close attention, though, because the plan was only hours away from becoming a reality.

The councilor's face turned grim. "Our home will be no place for a civilization during its recovery, so we must leave it behind to heal, and then perhaps," his chest rose, "future generations of our people can return."

The image zoomed in on the blackness of space. A double-ringed ship filled the viewscreen. "After our cityships are underway to the destination planets, eleven brave Jacana, including our beloved Kaia Badra, will stay behind on the *Meridian* to complete the final steps of the Dawn Project."

Kaia winced at hearing 'beloved' precede her name. She knew many felt that way about her, but she never felt special, even now.

Councilor Shiva looked to her and smiled warmly before continuing. "This team of scientists will monitor the initial eruption before leaving to wait for five hundred cycles to pass on Nu," he explained. "Our scientists determined that this is the ideal time for phase two. Thanks to near-light-speed travel powered by the *Meridian's* lightdrive, only a few hours will have passed for them. Upon their return, they will place each of the hundred asteroids into orbit, ensuring an impact on Nu every thousand cycles. Once that is complete, the team will join the *Montu* colonists on Duat within weeks of the cityship's arrival. We wish them success and a safe journey to their home." Councilor Shiva crossed his arms and bowed.

Councilor Vishnu was up next, Kaia knew, and watched him rise gracefully from his seat and sweep onto the stage with a flourish. She smiled to herself. She'd always found herself distracted by the long shoulder pads he wore—they stretched so far away from his body that he looked as though he had four arms instead of two. He paused and took a deep breath to let the well-practiced stern expression settle onto his face.

"It is critical that we protect and preserve the ecosystem of each of the new worlds we colonize," the councilor explained. "We must follow the legal commandments developed by our best and brightest Jacana socio-environmental scientists."

The image flashed, and the rules appeared as he read each glyph out loud:

1. Maintain a population under 500,000,000 in perpetual balance with nature.
2. Guide reproduction wisely—improving fitness and diversity.
3. Unite with a living, new language.
4. Rule passion—faith—tradition—and all things, with tempered reason.
5. Protect people and nations with fair laws and just courts.
6. Let all nations rule internally, resolving external disputes in a world court.
7. Avoid petty laws and useless officials.
8. Balance personal rights with social duties.
9. Prize truth—beauty—love—seeking harmony with the infinite.
10. Be not a cancer on this world—leave room for nature.

"We inscribed these rules on the surface of each cityship and posted them in every common area onboard. In addition, each cityship possesses five stone slabs with these rules engraved in each of the eight Jacana languages. Your ship's assigned Council members will place them in prominent locations on the surface of each world. I urge you to follow these rules. Our society must not ruin another planet. Let these be guidestones to an age of reason."

The glyphs faded away, leaving Councilor Vishnu alone in the spotlight. Kaia smiled, *just where he likes to be*. She remembered a time, many cycles ago, that she didn't want to go in front of the cameras anymore and he agreed with her. Now that she was older, she recognized it was probably because it would mean more time on camera for himself.

The councilor relaxed his shoulders and held his chin up. His eyes softened. "We must never forget the final rule. Leave room for nature," he repeated. He clasped his hands and bowed, then took his seat.

Kaia stared at the empty spotlight. Her heart began to race and her palms felt clammy. *This is it, the last one,* she knew. It all came crashing down on her at once. Twenty cycles of her life built to this very moment. She convinced her people to save their home by reliving her tragedy over and over. But now, an uncertain future lay ahead. After this speech, everything would change. The Dawn Project would begin, her future would begin. *What will I do... after Dawn?*

Kaia felt something on her knee and looked down to see Councilor Hegira's hand resting on it.

"Kaia," the councilor said, "it's your turn my dear."

"Of course," she said, snapping herself back to the present. Endless rehearsals prepared her for the moment, for the words, but not for the feelings. She stood and tentatively made her way to the spotlight. She was used to pushing through panic, because each time new data on the climate poured in, it revealed their predictions were wrong, again. The world would be uninhabitable even sooner than scientists thought. Kaia's society existed on the brink. The flames of extinction licked at the edges of their civilization.

Her bright green suit shimmered in the light. The crowd fell silent. She squinted, unable to see any of them. She closed her eyes and saw her parents, beaming with pride. *We did it,* she said to them. *Everyone understands now. We're saving the world from us.* She opened her eyes. The surface of ancient Nu projected behind her, lush and green.

"This is what our home looked like two thousand cycles ago. No great cities, no pollution. Nu is pure, unsullied by Jacana industry. But it was not to remain this way." Kaia swirled her finger on her forearm glyphpad to speed up time. "This is what happened when we discovered kohl."

An unnatural haze developed through the green. "Our cities grew faster than ever. Our population exploded. We spread out over the surface, decimating ecosystems in our wake."

Gray spots formed where polluted rivers met the sea, then spread across the entire ocean. "We poisoned the atmosphere with the by-products of kohl. The blue sky disappeared, and the oceans began to die."

She felt the shame emanating from the crowd. "These were the early cycles of mass extinction. Then the superstorms came, for us." A dying Nu was replaced with the final scenes from her parents' helmet cameras. "The superstorms came for... me." She told the story of her tragedy, one last time.

There was not a dry eye in the audience as her younger self screamed at the torrent of water rushing toward her parents. The video faded to black, and Kaia stepped into the spotlight.

"Many people gave up their livelihoods to work toward the goal we are achieving today. Some people lost more; some lost their lives fighting to preserve Nu. Now, we will become a divided people. Each group alone, out of reach, on alien worlds. Those who wish to return will reunite on a healed Nu. I will leave you with the words of one such person, my father, Ory Badra: 'We did this. We can save the world from us,' and today, we are doing just that."

She bowed to the audience, and a wave of bows swept back in return.

"Best wishes to you all on your journey to the stars."

# CHAPTER 5
# LATE FOR CLASS

## UNIVERSITY OF CHICAGO - 2034 CE

Alan tightened his seatbelt and looked out the taxi window as 59th Street sped past. He noted green buds dotting the branches of the trees in Hyde Park. *Spring comes earlier every year*, he thought, and flicked on the radio.

"Thank you for listening to 91.5 WBEZ Chicago," said a woman with a smooth radio voice. "Today is the first day of March, and it looks like it's coming in like a lion."

"Doesn't it always nowadays?" he asked out loud.

The woman continued, "Severe storms will move in over the next two hours, and the National Weather Service has already issued a Tornado Watch."

"Wonderful," he said, shaking his head.

Alan caught glimpses of the sky between two-story brick houses. Dark clouds loomed in the distance.

A man's voice chimed in, "As you may recall, last year saw a record 204 tornadoes in Illinois. NOAA's investments in early warning systems are paying off, though. There were no fatalities last week when eleven tornadoes caused chaos over much of the Peoria metropolitan area."

"You forgot to mention tornado outbreaks are not supposed to happen in February," he admonished and switched off the radio.

The car lurched, heaving him against the seat belt.

"You've got to be kidding me! Again?" he demanded to know from the car.

A computerized, genderless voice replied, "I have experienced an error. One moment, please."

He sighed. "Gee, I had no idea."

The city's driverless electric taxi program was off to a rough start. The system crashed—often. Remote operators spent more time in control of the taxis than the taxis spent controlling themselves. The vehicles were a step up in other ways, though. Natural light streamed into their glossy white interiors through an all-glass roof. Riders enjoyed an unobstructed view over the steering-wheelless dashboard. A large central touchpad replaced the glyphic knobs and dials; simple swipes and gestures over its illuminated symbols controlled the radio and temperature.

Alan drew a square on the taxi's touchpad to access his calendar, but it buzzed, not recognizing the symbol.

"I apologize for the inconvenience, sir," came the response from the car's speakers.

He scoffed and turned away, seeing his reflection in the side window. He reached up to smooth out his grey hair. *All this fancy technology is doing is turning me into an angry old man.*

The car jerked forward and began moving again. He knew technology like this reduced the need for everyone to have their own hulking piece of steel that spent more time sitting in a garage than on the road. Or worse, those ride share drivers who spent all their time driving around looking for fares and creating more pollution than if they just stayed at home, but these driverless taxis never seemed to work.

Alan pulled a stack of papers out of his bag and read the top sheet. A bulleted list of chicken scratches outlined today's lecture. It would be a good one. Today would be the day he told his students what the team had discovered in Mexico, an exclusive preview before the Climate Council approved his paper for publication.

The car slowed, announcing, "Your destination is eight hundred feet ahead, on the left." It rolled to a stop, and Alan stuffed the paperback into his bag. He reached for the door and pulled the handle, but found it was locked.

"I'm already ten minutes late to a forty-five-minute class!" he told the faceless voice, exasperated.

"I am sorry," the voice said, all trace of human sympathy scrubbed by an algorithm. "We're having trouble with the automatic fare system today. Please touch your payment method to the illuminated reader," it instructed.

Alan looked at the pulsing blue circle on the touchpad. He double tapped his watch to access his credit cards. He moved his wrist to the circle but stopped short. Enough was enough. His taxes subsidized this program, and that should be payment enough. He lowered his arm into his lap and looked at the dashboard, longing to see a steering wheel. There was a single red button. He glowered at the light of a security camera mounted above the touchpad, hoping the remote operator was watching, and raised his fist.

"Whoa!" a woman shouted, jumping back in her office chair. The man in the cubicle behind her turned around.

"Is everything okay?" he asked.

She rubbed her eyes. "Yeah, just another Luddite passenger making me wish I had stayed at John Deere's remote operation center instead of taking this job. Nothing beats steering a tractor through a field at sunset." She shrugged. "That system wasn't perfect either, though. As the farmers would always say, remote driver systems are put together with duct tape and bailing wire."

Her colleague laughed. "They may be right."

She exhaled and puffed her cheeks. "Here we go."

She leaned forward and watched the man in the car.

The man still held his clenched fist to the camera. She was sure he would flip her the bird because most everyone did when there was a problem, and with the current state of the system, that was a lot of birds. He raised his other hand and pretended to crank his finger up, but to her surprise, his middle finger stayed put while his index finger extended. Then, staring into the camera, he lowered it to the red button and held it down.

The operator knew what came next: the car's lights flashed; the horn honked three times. A calm, automated voice announced, "For your safety, please check your surroundings before exiting the car."

The passenger turned to the now-unlocked doors and pressed down on the handle.

"We have another runner," she sighed, shaking her head. "That's the third one this afternoon." As the man opened the door, he turned back to the camera and winked.

"It's okay," her coworker said, pointing to his own screen, where a young man in another car screamed at the camera. "This guy's manual payment didn't work, either. The whole system must be down."

"Typical." She shrugged then stood up to stretch and turned off her monitor. "I know we're supposed to be saving the planet and all with this project, but let the dang sea level rise if it means I don't have to deal with this worthless tech anymore."

# CHAPTER 6
# THE MERIDIAN

## MONTU CITYSHIP - CYCLE 2296

Kaia and Enki waited next to the *Montu's* airlock. Her whole body felt more relaxed now that the ceremony was over. She could get back to what she loved most, her work, and the live specimens in her lab on the *Meridian*. Enki was still zoned into his viewpad and she wondered if he even watched the Exodus ceremony.

His uncanny ability to tune everything else out reminded her of the first time she met this odd new colleague in his lab after a Council meeting. He was hunched over a magnifying lamp, examining a dusty black rock, never pausing his work while she introduced herself.

"Oh, I know who you are," he stated.

Kaia fumbled, "Oh—"

He turned around, this time interrupting her. "So, am I supposed to feel pity for you? The little girl who lost her parents at the tender age of seven." He turned back to the stone. "All Jacana have suffered through tragedies, Kaia Badra." He laid the black rock down, picked up a smooth green one, and held it under the light. "Your tragedy was merely..." he paused to choose his next word, "public."

She sat down next to him. "You wanted to say propaganda, didn't you?"

He looked up at her, wide-eyed. "That is not—"

"It's okay, I know your type. You aren't the only Captain Set supporter in the project, you know."

He shook his head. "I do not involve myself in such political distractions."

"I did not ask for your pity, and everything I said, everything I did for the Council, was because I believed it was the right thing to do," she said. "I was only a child. I've worked hard to stand on my own accomplishments." She looked down. "But it's impossible. No matter how hard I try, everyone sees me as the little girl whose parents died."

He tilted his chin up in thought. "I do not know of your scientific work. I shall examine your file in more detail."

Kaia stood and said, "Please do. I'm sure you will find it more interesting than whatever you think you learned about me from newscasters."

He nodded and turned back to his work.

She had smiled as she stepped out of the geology lab, happy to have met someone who would judge her for her achievements, not her childhood losses. That first awkward exchange was one of her favorite memories of their friendship because the whole thing was classic Enki.

The airlock behind them buzzed and the light above the door turned green. Through the window, Kaia saw three figures removing their helmets and pulling babel hoods over their heads.

Kaia tapped Enki's shoulder. "Captain Apep is here to pick us up."

He looked up and nodded, then stuffed the viewpad in his pocket.

They both turned to face the door as it slid open.

An unfamiliar flutter in her stomach replaced her eagerness to leave the *Montu* when a man inside stepped forward.

He bowed to her. "Hello, I'm Captain Apep," he said in a too-cool, confident voice.

She bowed to the captain in return. "We've met, briefly," she said. "I'm Kaia."

He smirked. "Yes, indeed you are," he said, bowing again.

Kaia felt herself blush. The neon orange lines contrasted against the suit's deep blue color, angled in a way that accentuated the captain's wide shoulders. The parallel gray lines running over his hood highlighted flecks of silver in his eyes. *Why do captains always have the best-looking suits?* She first met him during an early mission briefing but never got beyond small talk before the press whisked him away for an interview. She remembered a strange sensation that day, which, after further analysis, she chalked up to a mild attraction. Her work consumed every waking moment and all these cycles later she still knew little more than that he was a tugship captain before the Exodus.

Captain Apep clicked his tongue and she snapped back to the present. "I decided to come pick you and Enki up myself so I could also drop these two off," he said, stepping aside to reveal the other two people with him. One was a woman, a bit younger than him, and a much older woman, hunched over but with the same bright eyes as Apep.

"This is my sister, Helena," he explained, "And my mother, Leda."

Kaia bowed, "Very nice to meet you." She elbowed Enki, and he matched her bow, with a slight sigh of impatience.

Helena took Leda's hand and guided her out of the airlock. "We're traveling to Duat onboard the *Montu* because—"

Leda shushed her. "Helena and Apep think I'm some old warbler and the medical facilities on the *Montu* are better than the *Meridian's* but really it is because the *Meridian* is a tin can compared to"—she waved her arm over the view of the ship's open plaza— "this wondrous creation my Apep helped make! And an 'old warbler' like me needs her space!" she quipped with a healthy dose of side-eye to her son.

Apep chuckled. "Yes, mother, there is much more space on this ship for you to flit around in."

Captain Apep swiped up on his forearm glyphpad and the coordinates for their quarters appeared on Helena's glyphpad. "Follow those directions, and let me know if you need anything before we all leave." He bent over and hugged his mother, then stood and hugged Helena. "I'll see you both on Duat. Be safe."

Helena hugged him again. "You too, Apep," she said and turned to hold Leda's arm. "Now, mother, let's get you to your quarters so you can get some rest."

Kaia bowed. "It is a pleasure to meet you both."

Helena nodded, "You as well, Kaia. You have been an inspiration."

Leda raised her eyebrows. "Kaia, do you see what these two put me through? You're a woman of the Council, surely you can do something!" she pretended to hiss, but a slight smile gave her away.

Kaia bowed again, "Of course, I'll talk to Head Councilor Hegira about your treatment right away."

"That old bat won't do a thing," Leda said, then coughed. The shine in her eyes dulled. "It was nice to meet you." She coughed again as Helena walked her down the corridor.

*Old bat?* Kaia recalled a comment from Councilor Hegira that there was more to Apep's story, but it was his to tell. Now she wondered how Leda was involved.

Captain Apep put his hands on his hips and whispered. "My mother is not a fan of the Head Councilor, as you can see."

Kaia whispered a neutral response. "Well, there are others who feel that way, too."

Captain Apep clicked his tongue. "She has her reasons, let's leave it at that."

His mother rounded the corner, but first paused and smiled a warm smile toward Kaia and glanced at Apep, then back to Kaia, and winked before she went out of sight.

Captain Apep cleared his throat. "Where is the Head Councilor, anyway?"

Kaia filed the curiosity about his mother away for the future. "She and Councilor Horus will be taking a separate shuttle."

Captain Apep nodded once. "Just as well," he said then waved Kaia and Enki into the airlock.

Captain Apep nodded toward the airlock. "Shall we?"

Enki strode past them into the airlock, then pivoted around on one foot. "Aren't you two coming?"

Kaia tried to steal another look at Captain Apep, and found he was already stealing one of her. They both looked away and stepped forward into the narrow doorway, bumping into one another.

He hung back. "Sorry, after you," he said bashfully.

Kaia grinned as she stepped through.

Apep followed and pressed a button on the wall. The airlock door slid shut. "Enki, can you get the other side now?" he asked, pointing to a button on the opposite wall.

Enki turned around and pressed it. A whoosh of air hissed as the other airlock door opened into a small cargo bay where another crew member sat on the last seat, almost tucked behind a bulkhead.

Captain Apep walked through first. "Kaia, Enki, welcome to my shuttle. It's just a short ride to the *Meridian* so take a seat anywhere you like." He turned and strode toward the cockpit at the front.

Enki looked around the shuttle's cargo bay and announced, "I will identify an optimal place to sit now." He walked toward the empty seats next to the other crew member. The man wore a pristine blue suit. A handheld viewpad in his lap illuminated his sharp nose and thin mouth. The man did not look up to introduce himself when Enki sat down next to him.

Enki leaned over to get a closer look at the image on the viewpad. It was a line drawing that looked to be an engineering schematic of an engine.

"Is that a lightdrive?" he asked, feeling a tingling of anticipation.

The man nodded.

Enki pointed to what appeared to be closable fins behind it. "What are those?"

The crew member looked up, and their eyes locked. Enki felt a flash of recognition, not of familiarity but of a deep intellectual resonance.

The man bit his lip before speaking. "A new design to control photon output. I am trying to devise a way to control individual output levels so the engine can run longer by varying the energy from any given photocell." He used his finger to circle the processing unit at the front of the engine. "From there, I will create an algorithm to adjust the vents, so I don't have to do it myself."

Enki leaned in to inspect the diagram. "What will that allow us to do?"

The man raised his eyebrows. "The more efficient the engine, the closer to the speed of light we can go before it overheats, and the—"

"More time dilation we can achieve," Enki said, astonished.

"Yes, that is correct. We will be able to travel closer to the speed of light and dilate more external time."

"But why would you want to do that?"

"Well, let's say someone wants to come back and check on Nu. With this change, they could." He tapped the viewpad. "And these engine modifications will make their timing more accurate."

"I understand," Enki said with an unconscious smile—he was capable of the same obsessive focus for as long as he could remember. "However, it is disconcerting that the margin of error in these calculations remains so large. I assumed Ra would have figured this out by now, given our cityships will soon be hurtling through interplanetary space."

The man glanced up with a smile. "Those big lightdrives are crude compared to the one I designed for the *Meridian*. They can't go as close to the speed of light. If they did, we could have just dilated time enough for Nu to heal and come right back. There would be no need for new colony planets. I'm talking ninety-nine point nine, nine, nine, nine... You get the point, more nines than you can count as a fraction of the speed of light. The engine can take us to the edge of when time itself would stop for anyone on the ship as millions of cycles race by outside. At that speed, you can miscalculate and be off thousands of cycles, or more. It is important to design the algorithm to get the timing right."

"W-wait," Enki stuttered. "Are you...?"

The man bowed. "First Officer Ra, inventor of the lightdrive, at your service."

Enki bowed even lower. "The pleasure is mine."

They both smiled then huddled closer to the viewpad screen, ready to apply their shared enthusiasm toward solving time dilation ratios and cell outputs required to the ten-billionth decimal point of precision.


Kaia and Captain Apep watched the exchange in stunned silence. She leaned closer to him, "I haven't seen Enki this excited since, well, ever."

The captain replied, "Yes, it looks like First Officer Ra has found a friend."

"Ra? Ra Meridian? He's the ship's first officer?" Kaia said in disbelief.

The captain nodded. "Yes, that's the one. His father padded Councilor Horus's pockets enough that the Council agreed to name the *Meridian* after their family. The deal included Ra being the captain, too, but he wasn't interested in that. Ra only cared that the Council agree to continue funding his lightdrive work, and they did."

"Does that make it awkward to work with him?"

Captain Apep crossed his arms and shook his head. "Not at all. His father may have been a game-the-system type, but Ra is smart and too modest for his own good. I doubted him at first, too, but I've learned to value him as my second-in-command. His knowledge of the physics powering our ships is second to none."

"Good." Kaia looked back to them. She smiled. "Enki could use some friends who aren't rocks."

"Couldn't we all? There are only eleven of us left on the *Meridian*, you know."

"And now we all have something in common," she offered. "We will be the last Jacana left in our star system."

"Only for a few days, if all goes according to plan," he reminded her, then uncrossed his arms and nodded to the cockpit. "Would you like to join me up front? The view is better up there."

"Sure." Kaia felt her smile widen just a little more as she took a seat in the copilot's chair next to Captain Apep. He lingered larger-than-life in her mind—older, maybe wiser, too. But now that she saw him up close, she remembered that he must be about the same age as her. He had a youthful appearance without a trace of gray. *He belongs on a poster for overachievers.* Square jaw, sharp nose, posture erect, eyes focused straight ahead. Here was the third most powerful member of the project after Councilor Hegira and Councilor Horus, yet his tranquil demeanor put her at ease.

Captain Apep turned and nodded. "Are you ready to leave the *Montu?*"

She buckled the belt over her lap and nodded. "More than ready."

He swiped his hand over the glyphpad and a clang reverberated around the shuttle as it undocked. The gentle curve of Nu's horizon appeared on the bottom of the viewscreen as the shuttle turned. Sol peeked over the edge of the planet, turning the reddish-brown atmosphere a brilliant golden yellow.

Kaia sighed. "You're right. It is beautiful."

Captain Apep angled the nose of the shuttle down toward the surface for a better look at their home planet. "It gets me every time. I know it wouldn't be that color without all the pollution, but it's still pretty."

Below the thin atmospheric glow, Puna's urban plan emerged from the landscape. Semi-circular lakes separated each concentric ring of streets. A ribbon of beige land divided the round city from its agricultural zones. To the east, a massive plateau rose over the cityscape. A grid of thousands of black marks dotted the flat-topped landform.

Kaia leaned forward to examine them closer.

"Those are the populator rocket launchpads," he said and swiped down on the control glyphpad.

The shuttle angled upward and shuddered as the blackness of space filled the viewscreen. Her hands clenched the seat's armrests. It hit her, then, that this might be her last glimpse of home before the final phases of the Dawn Project.

Captain Apep continued moving his hands over the glyphpad, and the shuttle veered back for a better view of the *Montu* cityship. The massive, cratered asteroid was no longer a dead stone floating through space, it was the temporary home for five hundred thousand Jacana souls on their way to a new home. Pipelines weaved over the jagged surface between towering antennas and machinery vents as the asteroid rotated on its axis to create artificial gravity for the new occupants. Clear ecopolymer bubbles covered some excavated depressions and offered a glimpse of the interior. Bright green fields stretched out below a few domes designed to harness the light from sol and other stars on the journey.

Kaia pointed to the cluster of antennas near the largest dome. "Did you get to see the *Montu* while it was being constructed?"

Captain Apep clicked his tongue. "Yes, I saw all of them. My crew handled five of the fourteen asteroids that became cityships. We brought them here for the nanomechs to hollow out."

Captain Apep removed his fingers from the glyphpad as autopilot took over their short flight to the *Meridian*. He leaned back and rubbed his neck.

Kaia thought he looked tense. She scooted back into her chair and turned to him. "Is everything okay?"

"I'm trusting all that is left of my family to Captain Set on that ship. I hope he keeps his word."

Kaia cocked her head. "Why would he go back on it?"

Captain Apep shrugged. "I find it hard to trust people who didn't even agree with the evacuation plan in the first place."

She cleared her throat and watched him as she continued, "I believe we should all trust Captain Set's sincerity when he made amends with the Council and calmed the Resistance. We have to put our differences aside and focus on the future, not the past."

Captain Apep looked out the front. "I'm doing my best to stay focused on the mission, which is the most important thing."

Kaia held her hands in her lap and interlocked her fingers, then nodded in understanding. "Yes, it is." She untangled her hands, even though it still did not sit well with her. "And besides, you won't be separated from your mother and sister for long."

He smiled and said, "I do look forward to our reunion on Duat." Then, he maneuvered the shuttle away from the *Montu*.

Kaia's eyes widened as all fourteen cityships came into view, each pair pointed toward different extrasolar planets like a flock of birds ready to scatter. Jacana scientists spent over one hundred cycles searching for new homes for their society, but the stellar cartography probes only discovered seven habitable exoplanets. They hoped to find more habitable worlds like Nu, but they did not. It made their world, and their mission, even more important. Ten billion people once called this planet home. Now, fourteen cityships housed seven million battered souls, the remnants of their civilization's clash with nature, and each other.

Captain Apep looked to the chronometer next to the glyphpad and said, "Anytime now, captains."

"Anytime for what?" Kaia asked.

His eyes lit up, "Look! There they go!"

She looked outside to see an iridescent sheen of violet lights moving along the dark pipelines of each asteroid's exterior, like the surface of a feather in the sunlight. The starry sky behind each cityship wavered as the lightdrives spun up.

The space in front of each ship condensed into sharp rings of light, and the space behind them stretched to blackness. And just like that, they disappeared, accelerating toward new worlds, riding a photon wave that would carry them to their new homes. The great flock divided.

Kaia's eyes were wet with tears, and when the *Montu* vanished, she looked over to Captain Apep to see his were damp as well.

She reassured him, "They'll be okay."

He sat up straight, and Kaia heard a hint of a sniffle as he breathed in.

Captain Apep rested his hands on his lap. "I'm glad I didn't have to watch this alone."

With the cityships gone, she noticed the field of shimmering lights beyond the orbit of their moon, Iah. *Phase two*, she recognized. She didn't like to admit it, but the next part of the Council's plan scared her more than the eruption. Kaia felt Captain Apep's eyes on her.

"Asteroid guts," he said.

She raised one eyebrow. "Asteroid guts?"

"Yeah, all one hundred iridium cubes came from the nanomechs mining out interior living spaces on the cityships," he said then looked out the window. His jaw tightened. "Smarter people than me figured out we also needed to fling asteroid guts at Nu to save it."

"I know the plan," she reminded him and looked back outside. "But I'd never thought of them as asteroid guts." She chuckled, realizing Captain Apep's joke helped her shake away a little bit of her apprehension about phase two. Kaia knew Enki's meticulous planning would maximize each impact's cooling effect without also killing every living thing for thousands of cubits. "The timing will be everything."

He nodded. "That it will. We'll be setting their orbits when we return to Nu after our little light speed jaunt." He looked at her. "And then let's hope Ra's calculations are on target."

They both watched the asteroids, one hundred in all, reflect the varying colors of yellow sunlight, the gray surface of Nu, and the pure white of the moon as they spun, waiting to fulfill their purpose.

Kaia started to break the silence then realized she was rising out of the chair. Captain Apep laughed then reached out and took her hand, guiding her back down into the seat.

He glanced at the chair's clasps. "You'd better tighten your seatbelt. We're slowing down, and the gravitational effects of our acceleration will dissipate."

She gawked at the captain's hand on hers and tried to say something, but her mouth had turned dry. All she could manage was a weak, "Okay."

Captain Apep smiled. He looked into her eyes and squeezed her hand before letting go.

Kaia's mouth curled into a blushing smile. "It's been a long time since I felt... weightless."

·  ·  ·

Kaia felt her body push against the seat belt as the shuttle slowed. Through the window, the *Meridian* came into view. Shadows danced over the ship's cylindrical body as two habitat rings spun around it, seeming to be moving in slow motion. She watched two crew members talking as they strolled along on the curved floor of one ring on their way toward the ladder that led to the main corridor running the length of the ship. At the end of the corridor sat a smaller ring, the bridge ring. The ship looked delicate, almost fragile, compared to the massive bulk of the cityships. She felt a tinge of renewed unease, even though she'd spent the past few weeks settling into her onboard lab, preparing her team for each of their missions. But now the realization set in; the *Meridian* was no cityship, and there would be no retreating into several hundred cubits of rock in case of danger. A thin layer of metal was all that separated her from the merciless vacuum of space. Worse still, there would be no one left to rescue them if something went wrong.

Beside her, Captain Apep tightened his lap belt and pushed back into the seat. "Hold on," he instructed. "I am initiating the docking sequence."

He put both hands on the control glyphpad. The engine's roar faded as he worked the controls by swiping over glyphs. Small thrusters flared in intermittent bursts to align with the *Meridian*'s docking ports. Kaia heard a metallic clanging and clenched her jaw. She peeked back into the shuttle. Enki was sitting straight up with his eyes closed, holding onto his seat. She closed her eyes, too, and took deep breaths to relax.

The screeching stopped.

"Docking completed," Captain Apep announced.

She opened her eyes, let out her breath, and released her grip on the seat.

"It's okay, Kaia," Captain Apep said, nodding to the finger-shaped depressions in the foam armrests. "It gets a little easier every time."

There was a brief buzz, and a green light illuminated above the cargo bay door.

Captain Apep unbuckled himself and floated out of the chair, finding the zero gravity handholds with ease. "Kaia, I'll meet you on the bridge when you figure out which way is up."

"Wait, I'll come with you," she offered as she let go of the chair. Her head bumped into the ceiling.

The captain chuckled before he was able to stop himself.

Wrapping her arms around the chair, Kaia said, "On second thought, I'll be right here."

"Suit yourself," he said, and floated through the doorway.

Enki drifted up to her, pointing to the last man heading toward the door. "Did you know that person is Ra Meridian?"

She nodded. "Captain Apep told me. It's nice to know we have the lightdrive inventor with us for the final mission."

"He knows far more than how a lightdrive works. Ra also grasps the physics of space and time on an instinctual level. It is remarkable."

Kaia smiled. "Sounds like you with your rocks."

"They are not rocks, they are the products of temperature and pressure on elements over eons," he said, "but, yes, I suppose so. On that note, I need to go to my laboratory and enter the updated sensor readings into the eruption simulation."

"I'll join you after I stop by my lab," she said.

He quirked a brow and nodded toward her seat. "Do you need assistance?"

When she realized she was still holding onto the seat for dear life, she straightened up, cleared her throat, and said, "No, thank you."

"Very well." Enki turned and pulled himself through the hatch.

Kaia puffed her cheeks, then let go and floated upward until her hands found a railing to pull herself toward the docking port and into the main corridor. The ladder down to the labs lay a hundred cubits to her right. She took a deep breath of recycled air tinged with the ever-present hint of sterilizer and pulled herself toward the ring access tube.

# CHAPTER 7
# A REMINDER

## BIOLOGY LAB - AD CYCLE 0

Kaia pulled herself along the corridor on her way to the biology lab. She wanted to go straight to the geology lab with Enki to check on the eruption first, but no one else onboard the *Meridian* was qualified to take care of the animals. She stood in front of the biology lab door and read the plaque with satisfaction: *Ouranos and Rhea Badra Biology Lab*. In a moment of courage, she stood up to Councilor Horus and refused to let him auction off the name of her lab to the highest bidder and instead named it after her parents. Memories of her team's work on the project hit her like a whirlwind. The long final hours they'd spent gathering and indexing critical samples. It was hard work, and they gave up their personal lives to get it done.

She envisioned her team busy at work, holographic projections of each of the seven destination planets floating above the lab tables. Her chest swelled with pride as she thought about the thousands of packets of freeze-dried seeds packed in storehouses on the cityships. Plants, vegetables, medicinal herbs—everything they would need to start over. Little vessels unto themselves that would feed generations of Jacana colonists.

She wrapped her hand around the door handle and twisted. It did not budge. When she leaned forward and pushed with her body, nothing. She groaned in frustration and leaned on the door again, this time putting all her weight into it. It shot open, and she tumbled to the floor. Jumping to her feet, she looked down the hall to make sure no one had seen. *Whew.*

She slid the door open to unleash a cacophony of screeches from the cages along the back wall.

"Sorry!" she yelled. "I know it's past feeding time! Hush now and let me change clothes."

She stepped into the lab. Silence replaced the usual frenetic activity and a single planetary holograph hung in the air above the nearest lab table. On it, a deep blue ocean surrounded a circular arrangement of skinny continents—Duat. A pale blue dot orbiting a middle-aged star. Their probe's limited readings indicated many plant species from Nu could survive there. It was the most home-like world of all the seven deemed habitable.

Below the projection, glyphs spelled out a farewell message: *Have a safe trip and enjoy your new home!* They signed it, *Always Your Team.* Kaia had been so busy preparing for her final trip to the *Montu* that she forgot to say goodbye to them. She smiled to think they remembered her, though. A fond memory of celebrating Freya's birthday surfaced. She would never forget the look on her face when a furry little affi jumped out of the gift-wrapped box. And the look on Loki's face after Freya had put the affi down his shirt made her laugh out loud. She hoped they would stay out of trouble on the *Asgard* as it journeyed to the third colony planet, Midgard. The Exodus ceremony highlighted the majestic waterfall in the planet's grand canyon but hid the fact that it was a single landmass adrift on the vast ocean world. Space would be at a premium if their colony succeeded. Perhaps another Jacana skytower city would bloom on the planet.

A squeal from the back wall brought her back to the present moment. She looked down at her glittering green suit. *Time to change.* She opened her locker door and pulled out her dull green crew habsew. Its pantlegs unfolded down to the floor. The locker door creaked as she moved it out of the way to change into the new suit. Deep red bangs fell over her forehead as she pulled her old hood off. She brushed them aside and pulled on the clean hood with a built-in babel.

Kaia reached over to the glyphpad on the forearm of her fresh suit and drew a symbol. The fabric tightened, and the wrinkles vanished as the hydrothermal circulator warmed her skin. She rolled her shoulders back and stretched her neck, then leaned in to the mirror hanging next to the locker. Deep blue eyes stared back at her, and she felt a lump in her throat—her eyes looked just like those of her father.

She tried to fight the urge to care about her image, but always being on camera as a young girl made it near impossible. There was always someone on hand to get her ready for whatever clip the crew needed to shoot that day. Applying her makeup then fixing it between tearful takes, choosing just the right shade of blue clothing to invoke the optimal level of trust and empathy.

Kaia could still hear Councilor Hegira's soft voice reassuring her from the director's chair. "I know it is hard, dear, but you must tell your story. Remember your daddy said you can save the world, and you are, Kaia. You are."

Kaia raised her hand to wipe a tear from her eye. She would give it all up to have her parents back.

It was the right thing, not because the Council said so, but because Nu needed saving, she reminded herself. She exhaled, searching for the sense of relief she expected to come now that the Council didn't need to broadcast her personal tragedy for support. Unfortunately, relief was nowhere to be found.

Instead, all she could conjure up was the unknown of stepping onto the open field on Duat where they would set up the first colony. The Dawn Project always provided her with a sense of purpose and a path to walk down. But now, her future felt like that faraway, alien plain: a wide, formless canvas. She looked around the dark lab and imagined landing on the surface of Duat, trying to feel anything except the sense of loss that still consumed her thoughts as she took a few steps toward the specimen cages.

She walked past shelves of sample jars. A menagerie of tiny

creatures and plants sat embalmed in colored fluids — all incompatible with any destination planet but important for preserving Nu's history.

There was another squeal.

"Coming, coming, but you have to quit making that awful noise."

She crinkled her nose—the cages needed cleaning, too. She squatted and looked inside the temporary home of her favorite, the nathus. It shared seventy percent of its DNA with Kaia. She admired its big, bright eyes, its grasping hands, and powerful lower legs. Even its shrill vocalization was reminiscent of a Jacana child's shout. It scampered to a dark corner at the back of its cage and curled up in a nest.

She scooted over to the next cage, which held an affi. It looked nothing like her. Four stubby legs supported its fur-covered body that could fit in her hand. Two front teeth, perfect for sawing through saplings, stuck out of its mouth. It looked up at her and ambled to the cage door, squeaking louder and faster. She laughed, turning to the feed bin behind her, and pulled out a small handful of seeds.

"I guess I found the hungry one," she said. "Okay, little girl, here you go."

She put her hand next to the cage, and the affi reached over, plucking the seeds from her palm and stuffing them in its cheeks. It scuttled away and stashed the load in the fresh hole in the foam. Then, it hurried back and resumed squeaking.

Kaia shook her head. "Hey, no more for you right now. You didn't even eat what I just gave you." She put her finger through the bars to pet the affi, but it nipped at her. "Ouch! You're lucky I have my gloves on," she scolded.

The affi made a barking squeak, which Kaia interpreted as having more than a hint of attitude.

She wondered about the future of all these animals on Nu after the Dawn Project. The affi did not tolerate heat well but could burrow into the ground to escape it during the hottest parts of the day. But, nathuses also had their limits. Unyielding global warming already made it an endangered species, just like the Jacana would have been without habsew suits.

Passing the remaining cages, Kaia examined each creature and hoped with all her heart that on a future Nu, their species would flourish once again. "Okay, everyone, time for me to go check on our plan to save the planet for your brothers and sisters." The affi seemed to chitter goodbye.

Kaia headed for the door when she heard a knock. This time, she pulled the door up before trying to slide and it opened right up. An advanced degree in biology and a leadership position with the Council must be what it takes to discover the trick.

In the corridor, a hunched figure in a gold suit looked up. Kaia smiled, seeing the warmth in Councilor Hegira's green eyes. The old woman returned the smile and stepped into the lab. A circular disk sat askew on top of her hood. She often joked that her unusual headpiece was just to distract people from the wrinkles around her eyes.

Kaia crossed her arms over her chest and bowed. "I'm happy to see you, Councilor. Can I help you?"

Councilor Hegira put her hand on Kaia's shoulder to steady herself. "I came to check on you. This is all so exciting. Do you feel it, too?"

*Exciting?* It was hard to describe, but her feeling wasn't excitement. She settled on saying, "I'm doing fine, Councilor."

The councilor gave Kaia a pat and plodded over to the nearest lab table. She pulled herself up onto a stool with a groan.

"And how many times have I said that when we are alone, you can stop with the '*Councilor*' business? Call me Hegira."

"Yes, Hegira."

The councilor smiled. "Now, Kaia, I think I know how you feel right now. When I was your age, I remember feeling empty and rudderless each time a mission was drawing to an end."

Kaia felt her shoulders sink. "You're right. That's what this feeling is."

Councilor Hegira patted the stool top next to her. "Come, dear."

Kaia looked at the floor, shuffled over, and took a seat. Another deep breath, then she leaned back on the lab table, fingers fidgeting in her lap.

Councilor Hegira rubbed Kaia's back. "I want to show you

something." She withdrew her hand and faced the table's viewscreen. Councilor Hegira drew a series of symbols and tapped the glyphpad.

Kaia spun to face the table and rested her chin on her elbows.

Councilor Hegira smirked at Kaia. "This will cheer you up."

The viewscreen flashed to life. The video showed waves of grass moving with the wind. A river wound past a tree and stretched to the horizon, appearing to touch the sky.

There was movement along the river's edge. Kaia leaned on the table to get a closer look.

A pair of long necked mimis stood tall, munching on the tree's leaves rustling in the light wind. Two young ones squeaked with joy as they chased each other along the riverbank.

"The world looks so alive," Kaia said.

One young mimi put its two front legs in the water and bent down for a drink. The water seemed to rise to meet its head. A splash of white appeared. The long, tooth-filled mouth of a sobek broke the surface and clamped down, narrowly missing the young mimi's leg. An adult mimi rushed over and stomped the ground, sending ripples into the water. The sobek hissed, then sank under the surface where it would wait for its next shot at a meal.

Councilor Hegira's eyes lingered on the screen. "My mother recorded this video on her trip through the first wildlife refuge. Her generation was the last to see the planet so, as you say, alive."

Kaia sat up straight. A wave of energy washed over her.

The councilor continued, "And that world will live again thanks to your work."

"I hope so. I only wish I could be here to see it."

They watched the young mimi go back to chasing its sibling through the tall grass. Kaia noticed a wisp of gray under the councilor's hood.

The councilor looked down. "Kaia, may I ask you a serious question?"

"Of course."

"The first time I met you, you said you wanted to study biology so you could run the zoo someday. Do you regret giving up that dream to join the project?"

Kaia had asked herself that question a few cycles earlier when she worked alongside Artemis Agrotera, Puna's last zookeeper, on a plan to transfer the animals to cityships.

She smiled. "I wanted the next generation to understand what we lost and why we need it back. So, I think the project ended up being a bigger and better platform to inspire kids than the zoo."

Councilor Hegira nodded. "And you did inspire them, Kaia. Enrollment in biology classes increased after you began your speaking tour in schools. You touched an entire generation. Countless lives, both Jacana and wild animal, will be saved on other planets thanks to you."

Kaia leaned back against the table. "Thank you, putting it that way makes me feel better, but I've got to say, I envy the next generation's biologists."

"Envy?"

Kaia nodded and made a circle with her hands. "They will have whole new worlds to study—new ecosystems, new animals, new natural cycles."

"Sure, you won't be leading discoveries across multiple worlds, but I think you'll have plenty to do on Duat. Your curiosity won't let you sit back while others go out into the field and study whatever creatures exist." Councilor Hegira reached over and patted Kaia's knee. "But I know what you mean. My studies of our civilization's history were important and prepared us to leave. Now, new scholars will be the ones using history to make history. My greatest contributions are behind me…" she lamented.

"You sound unsettled, too," Kaia said.

Councilor Hegira considered it for a moment. "I am, but it warms my heart more than anything else. I am old. Now I can rest. You still have many more productive cycles left, so don't feel discouraged. These feelings will pass. There is always a new challenge ahead."

With a flourish, Hegira placed a hand back on the edge of the table. "Let me tell you about the early days of the project. When you were only a child."

Kaia nodded in silence.

"The Dawn Project, of which I was the only director at the time, was a joke. The laughingstock of the Council—and of our entire society. No one cared about our plan because no one cared about conservation until species after species went extinct faster than the simulations predicted."

Wetness filled the corners of Kaia's eyes. Any mention of extinction reminded her of the day she witnessed the last phara die, and worse.

Councilor Hegira didn't notice, or pretended not to. "There were so few animals left alive that our wildlife refuges were almost empty. We convinced them to push some funding our way, though most of it still went to other Council affairs. I shudder to think how much money we wasted building flood walls for coastal cities like Tremva. The ocean was rising, and no wall was tall enough in the end. That impractical work continued for more cycles, and then everything changed. The tragedy of your parents' deaths changed everything."

Kaia could not fight it anymore. She leaned into Councilor Hegira as she fought back tears.

The councilor caressed Kaia's head. "Your parents started you on this journey, and it will all be over soon."

"But I feel so lost..."

"Their deaths woke people up and lit a fire in you that will never go out. You will find another way to express it."

"So, what do I do next?" Kaia asked, dabbing away light tears.

"Oh, dear, don't worry about that right now. Enjoy what you have accomplished. Take some time to realize that you *have* accomplished something important, the most important mission the Jacana have ever had. You had a stronger purpose and have achieved more in your few cycles than most of us can dream of achieving in a lifetime."

Kaia closed her eyes. She inhaled through her nose and exhaled through her mouth until her breathing returned to normal.

The councilor patted her knee. "I'm glad we had this talk, Kaia. Now, I need to get out of here. This lab is depressing. What is it with scientists and this dim lighting?"

Kaia looked around the lab with fresh eyes and decided it *was* too dark. All the workstation lights were on their lowest setting, just as her team had preferred. "The projections are easier to see without the bright lights on."

"Always the consummate scientist," Hegira said as she stood and straightened her back. "You know you can come to me anytime you need something, my dear."

"Thank you," Kaia said. She used her new trick to swiftly open the door for Councilor Hegira, and they walked into the corridor together.

"Where are you off to?" Councilor Hegira asked.

"I am heading to see Enki in the geology lab."

Hegira smirked. "Enki? Still spending all your free time with him?"

Kaia's laughter echoed in the empty hall. "Oh, no, not like that, Councilor!"

Councilor Hegira nodded once and smiled. "He's a fine young man, but," she gave Kaia a knowing glance, "if I were a pretty young one like you, I'd have my eye on that Captain Apep."

Kaia's mouth fell open. This was a new side of Councilor Hegira, and she liked it.

# CHAPTER 8
# KOHL

## GEOLOGY LAB - AD CYCLE 0

Enki leaned forward with his elbows on the geology lab's center table, his eyes focused on a numeric grid hovering in the air, which was growing denser by the second. He picked up a silver stone from the table and was fidgeting with it while looking at the projection.

Kaia stood in the doorway, observing his movements the same keen way she had with animals in their natural habitat on Nu. His silver, form-fitting suit matched the silver of the table. The color no longer served to reflect heat, but instead seemed to be camouflage, allowing him to hide from the rest of the crew while in his lab. Her gaze wandered past Enki, past the hologram he was studying, to the topographic maps and fact sheets lining the walls in neat rows. Aside from the same basic layout, their labs were completely different. Where her shelves were a jumble of samples and half-full beakers, Enki's was all rock samples, labeled and arranged in tidy rows.

She imagined his mind was the same way; everything he knew stayed hovering on the surface, accessible at a quick glance. It was the only way to explain what some called his genius and others called his ignorance to most normal Jacana social behaviors.

Enki's brow furrowed, his face a picture of intense concentration as he mulled over the numbers.

"I cannot make sense of these estimates," he said aloud.

"Why not?" Kaia asked.

He jumped up and whirled around to face her, dropping the stone in the process.

They both winced as it hit the floor with a metallic clang that reverberated around the lab.

Enki puffed his cheeks and exhaled then turned back to the matrix. "I did not hear you come in," he said.

"Sorry, I didn't mean to startle you." Kaia picked up the stone and handed it to him. Dozens more rock samples were spread out in a row on the table. *He's been staring at those for hours,* she thought.

Enki set it down between two other stones. In a single motion, he turned back to Kaia. "I wanted you to see this," he said, pointing to the matrix.

"Is this the data from the eruption on Nu?"

"Yes, it is still processing. It needs more time, but I can already see that some readings are off-target by several orders of magnitude."

A progress bar under the matrix read, "22% Complete."

"Have you spoken to Councilor Hegira or Captain Apep about it?" she asked.

"No, I do not wish to share conjecture based on an incomplete simulation."

She nodded. "Good choice."

He looked up at her. "Speaking of Captain Apep, did he share any notable information on the trip over?"

Kaia smiled to herself. Time seemed to speed up to a blur when she spent it with Captain Apep and she tried to remember. "No, just normal stuff, I guess. You've heard of *small talk,* right?" She bumped her shoulder into his.

"Small *talk* is best left to small *minds,*" he quipped.

Kaia noticed he raised a hand to brush the spot where Kaia's shoulder had just touched him. As if he could brush off the contact like a speck of dust on his pristine habsew. Kaia was powerless to suppress the laugh that bubbled up. "How is the calculation coming?"

He looked at the progress bar on the projection.

"It is twenty-four percent complete," he said.

Kaia sighed. She wanted to know the results but did not want to sit in silence while the system finished. "You know," she pointed to the rocks on his table, "you've never told me what got you interested in geology."

"I believe I indicated that in my Dawn Project personnel file. Did you read it?"

"No..." This was going to be another conversation she'd have to pull out of thin air. "I'm trying to talk about something other than the project. We're friends, Enki, because we've worked together so long but you've told me very little about your past."

"That is because you could read it in the file, making this conversation a waste of time."

"Enki..."

"Fine, you are inquiring as to why I wanted to be a geologist when so many of our generation instead wanted to become biologists due to your parents?"

Kaia frowned. She shifted her weight to one leg and leaned against the table. "I suppose geology didn't get the same surge of interest that biology did when my parents died. But I'd like to know more about why you got into it."

"I grew up in Leneum, before the resettlement," he began.

"Yes, you've told me that," she shrugged, "but I don't know much beyond that."

"I do not suppose a Puna *elite* like you would," he said, waving his hand through the air.

There was a hint of truth in what he said, but he had sounded judgmental, angry even. *Is he upset with me?*

He ran his finger over the rocks and stopped on a black one. "Leneum was a primary source of the problems on Nu because it was a mining city." He picked up the stone and held it in the air. It was semi-reflective despite its rough surface, more like a dark, crystalline fluid than a rock. "As I am sure you know, this is kohl. It took many people to pull this resource from the ground in the quantities necessary to satisfy our civilization's limitless thirst for energy. Miners and their families made up the majority of Leneum's population. Once they mined the kohl, transporters carried it to power plants where they burned it to create energy for all of you *big city* people to have lights at night."

She rolled her eyes at him, now that she understood he was teasing her in his odd way.

He tossed her the chunk of kohl and looked down at the black dust that now coated his gloves. "Not the cleanest mineral," he said and brushed the dust onto the legs of his habsew. "Fossil fuels fascinate me. Sometimes they are a solid rock, other times a liquid, and sometimes even a gas. Each form has a high energy density when compared to similar natural products."

Kaia nodded, noticing black dust now coated her gloves, too. "And burning it turned out to be the largest unplanned environmental experiment of all time. And it was not an accident. In retrospect, it was companies motivated by greed that led to our irresponsible actions," she said, setting the kohl back on the table. A tiny piece flaked off, creating a shiny, mirror-like sliver.

Enki rested his hands on the table and leaned down to look at the flake. "The energy contained within it was too great for our civilization to ignore. We wouldn't be here on this ship—or in this situation— without it. Ironic, when you think about it." He straightened up and let his shoulders relax.

Kaia spotted the rare loosening up and asked, "Why didn't you want to be a miner like every other kid from Leneum?"

"My parents were not like the other miners. They paid little attention to my interests and cared more about drinking tekhit and carousing with their friends. No value was placed on education, either, unless it was the kind that kept you alive thousands of cubits below ground in the mines. My life improved when one of my teachers noticed my intense interest extended beyond what Leneum's schools could offer. I spent most weekends at her house where she and her husband fed my curiosity with more geological facts than I would ever learn in class."

Kaia pulled a stool from under the table and sat down. "What did your parents think of that?"

He shrugged. "They did not care. They tried to get me to play with their friends' children, but I was not interested. Everyone called me 'shy.' I am not shy, we had nothing in common, and I preferred it that way. I was interested in things they thought were boring. Most of them only wanted to play miner and argue about who got to be the supervisor." He crossed his arms and puffed out his chest in mock authority.

She laughed at this rare display of humor.

He placed his hands back on the table, a serious expression settling on his face.

"I owe my teacher and her husband a lot," he continued. "My favorite part was learning about volcanoes and rocks—even kohl, of course. I could not escape my roots."

Kaia smiled. "You were lucky to have them."

"I was. They once took me on a cruise ship to the Frovinia Islands."

Kaia wrinkled her brow. "Where?"

He scoffed. "You have not heard of Frovinia?"

"Sorry," she said, taken aback. "No."

"It is a volcanic chain in the middle of the ocean," he said. Kaia noticed that his animated speech seemed to have absorbed some energy from the kohl. "One had been active for over one hundred cycles and was still erupting when I visited. We took an air tour over the summit and looked down right into the crater. I could feel the heat of the boiling magma through the airship's hull."

"Sounds exciting. Most kids never had that kind of opportunity, even me," she said.

Enki nodded. "It is a shame." He looked up at the simulation.

"It sure is." The percentage complete crept up to twenty-six percent, she noted.

"If more kids had seen that volcano the way I did, biology wouldn't have been the only popular area of study for my generation. I can't help but think if we had more geologists, Councilor Horus might have considered my eruption ideas. Or at least spent some time to investigate. As it was, he seemed bent on rushing through the planning process." Enki looked up at the progress bar. "Which is why I am worried that something is wrong. We should have taken more iterative measurements."

"In my experience, Councilor Horus and careful study don't mix," Kaia lamented. "I remember, an interviewer asked him why the Council was starting its research from scratch instead of building on what was already in the scientific journals. I believe he responded, and I quote, 'Old academic research is better left to the dusty halls of scientific history.'"

If Enki was right, and something was wrong with the eruption, what would that even mean for the project? For Nu? *Let's hope he's wrong.* But even then, she knew better.

Enki gave a hesitant nod toward the progress bar. "Thirty-one percent. It should not take this long."

"It isn't going to go any faster with us staring at it," Kaia said. "I think I'm going to go to the bridge and get my station set up for our departure." She pushed herself away from the table and stood up. "See you there?"

Enki said nothing, his eyes still on the progress bar. She had a bad feeling about this, because this was a new level of strange obsession, even for him. She glanced at the progress bar and tried to ignore the growing sense of dread in her stomach.

*Thirty-seven percent... until he learns what?*

# CHAPTER 9
# ANTHROPOCENE 201

## UNIVERSITY OF CHICAGO – 2034 CE

Alan, now doing his best to act professorial since he was Dr. Pearce, walked into the classroom twenty minutes late. He was shocked to find the students still seated. When he was an undergraduate, everyone abided by the ten-minute rule, so he was expecting his Anthropocene 201 class to give up and leave. *The rule must not apply anymore.* He wondered what other changes to the unspoken rules of student life had slipped by over the years.

Daxia waved him in. "I was about to dismiss the class."

He made his way to the front of the room and sat his papers on the table. "I'm so sorry, taxi trouble…"

"Hey, hey, no rants today," she said and smiled.

"Deal. Thanks for keeping them here, Dax."

"Don't thank me—it was the cliffhanger you left them with last week. They must genuinely want to know what we found in Mexico."

He rubbed his hands together. "Then let's get started."

Daxia gave a quick nod and took her seat.

He stepped over to the lectern. A small blue circle appeared on its touchpad. He held his watch to it, and the touchpad flashed his name and displayed his files. He tapped on the first presentation. The students quieted as the projector's fan kicked on and a screen descended from the ceiling behind him.

"It's a miracle," he said. The students all laughed—any other day, he would have treated them to another episode of *Dr. Pearce versus The Projector*.

He stepped around the table and sat on its front edge.

"Last week, we reviewed how mountain ranges can affect the regional climate." He pressed his watch, and a picture of snowcapped peaks rising above a desert appeared behind him. "As a refresher, who can tell me what is happening in this photo?"

A young man raised his hand.

Dr. Pearce pointed at him. "Yes… Um…" Then he looked to Daxia.

"Jason," she mouthed.

He raised his eyebrows. "Jason, yes, what is happening in this photo?"

"Is it the Atacama Desert?" Jason asked.

Dr. Pearce nodded.

Jason cleared his throat. "The Atacama exists because it is in the rain shadow of the Andes and the Chilean Coastal Range. The clouds let go of their moisture as they ascend to get over the mountains, leaving no rain for the other side. Air and ocean currents also play a role, but the mountains are the main reason."

Dr. Pearce gave him a thumbs-up. "Jason is right. Most geologists— myself included—believe the Atacama has existed in some form since the mountains formed between twenty and forty million years ago. Officially, though, it is three million years old, and even that makes it the oldest desert in the world." He reached down and swiped his watch. Photos of the Atacama's sandy, reddish dirt scrolled by on the screen. He saw his students starting to look down at their phones.

"Today, I promised we would cover how what Daxia and I learned in Mexico will guide the United Nations Climate Council to reverse climate change."

The students looked up again.

A line chart appeared on the projection, with a gentle downward slope for the first half, then three sharp descents on the second half. Near the right edge, the line was near-vertical as it raced toward the bottom of the chart.

"This graph shows the number of species that have existed during the last twenty-five thousand years," he explained.

He pointed to the first downward step, labeled 9,500 BC. "Here, you can see the number plummeted as Earth came out of the last ice age. We used to think these creatures died out because they couldn't handle the temperature change. These were gigantic animals, some of which still exist today in much smaller versions. Imagine beavers as big as bears and wingless birds twice as tall as us. Others might look familiar, but covered in fur, like the great woolly mammoth. They evolved this way to survive the extreme cold."

Dr. Pearce turned back to the class. "However, we now understand they did not die of natural causes. They died because humans spread across the globe and ate them." He pressed his watch, and people dressed in furs began throwing spears into a huge woolly rhinoceros appeared below the graph.

The class's eyes widened. He pointed to the far right of the graph where the line seemed to fall off a cliff.

"This spot is about 1930 CE, only one hundred years ago. Wild species began to disappear faster than ever. As you know, we're not doing a lot of hunting these days, so it must be something else."

He turned back to the class, somber. "In fact, Earth has not seen dying at this pace since the end of the Cretaceous, when the dinosaurs went extinct. Some scientists say that point, in 1930, is when a sixth mass extinction began. Others say it was thousands of years earlier when we started clearing land for agriculture. Either way, there is no doubt we're now living in a time where we're changing the climate faster than evolution can keep up, so it makes sense to name this geologic epoch after us. Welcome to the Anthropocene."

A student raised her hand. "Dr. Pearce, there is still no consensus that human activity is causing—"

"Let's put the cause aside for this lecture because, even though it is wrong, it does not matter for what I'm about to tell you. Nothing will change the fact that the climate is changing. Just like nothing will change the fact that we're going to run out of fossil fuels and will need to find alternative energy sources whether oil companies like it or not. But right now, entire ecosystems are dying because of fossil fuels; never mind the contributions of microplastics and other pollutants doing their part. There is no arguing with the numbers." He sighed, "It sounds defeatist, but history shows it will be impossible to gather enough political will to prevent a far-future catastrophe. Humans are not good at thinking beyond their own lifespan. So, it is hard to blame anyone and is pointless to argue over it. We need to accept that our behaviors are not going to change."

He tapped his watch, and a black-and-white photo of a dune surrounding a farmhouse and windmill filled the screen.

"Dorothea Lange took this photo in Texas in 1938, at the height of what we now call the Dust Bowl. It was the first time the United States experienced environmental mismanagement combined with natural cycles of drought. Despite the warning signs, poor farming techniques disturbed thousand-year-old topsoil, degrading the rich organic layer in less than twenty growing seasons. The result was land desertification, leading to a decade of dust storms. The storms were so bad, and so frequent, that people could not even go outside. Five hundred thousand of them lost their homes and left behind land that had been in their families for generations."

He swiped on his wrist. The iconic image of a concerned mother and her two children in a refugee tent appeared behind him.

"The local economies took two decades to recover from the catastrophe. And remember, it was not a *natural* disaster. It was our fault."

He saw a few students squirm in their seats, satisfied he was reaching them.

"But the Dust Bowl was a regional disaster," he continued. "Let's see what will happen if today's climate change continues on a global scale."

He brought up the graph of species decline again and pointed to

1930. "Starting from the Anthropocene and going forward." A menagerie of animals replaced the graph.

"First, many of our largest animals will continue to decline until they are extinct." On the screen, modern elephants, rhinoceroses, and giraffes all faded away.

"Next, desertification will lead to fewer bushy plants, which will leave less for herbivores to eat." Deer, elk, buffalo, and more disappeared.

"Since carnivores eat herbivores, there will be fewer of them, too." Lions, wolves, and bears all vanished. Animals continued to fade one by one until the screen was white.

Dr. Pearce crossed his arms. "Total extinction." He stood and paced back and forth in front of the table.

"It is not only the animals who will suffer, though. Hurricanes will grow so large they will reach a new classification called 'hypercane.' And don't forget floods, severe thunderstorms, droughts, and dust storms that will force the human population into fewer and fewer habitable regions. Some areas will become more inhospitable than Mars, if you can imagine that. It's not a stretch to say humans will need a space suit to walk down the street. Or that we will need population control measures unthinkable in today's society."

The Chicago skyline faded onto the screen. Futuristic half-mile-high skyscrapers soared above the familiar John Hancock building and Sears Tower.

"Cities will grow so dense that we will need to engineer ever-taller structures to accommodate all the climate refugees. Earth will be so unrecognizable that we may as well give it a new name."

One student yawned and closed his eyes. Dr. Pearce clapped his hands, and the student snapped to attention.

"I know this is probably your last class before break but stay with me. I'm just getting to the best part."

Dr. Pearce swiped his watch again, and a top-down wireframe of Earth spun between two olive branches. Superimposed on the graphic was *United Nations Climate Council*.

"As you know, the United Nations created a Climate Council to address the challenges of our changing world. Many of their initiatives focus on renewable energy and sustainability, but I am skeptical that any of them will succeed. That requires cultural change and political cooperation like the world has never seen, and humans just don't like each other enough to work together. Resistance is already growing in response to strict regulations and carbon taxes."

He waved his hands toward the class. "And if we cannot change behavior, what else can we do?"

The term *Geoengineering* appeared below the Climate Council logo.

"Nothing short of re-engineering the planet," Dr. Pearce said. The earth at the center of the seal morphed into a satellite view and zoomed into a tiny island in the Pacific Ocean.

One student raised her hand and said, "Dr. Pearce, haven't they tried that with the genetically modified algal blooms and only created more problems?"

"Yes, they have, but what I am talking about is using geology, not biology."

He pointed to the dot of land in the middle of the ocean on the screen.

"This is Réunion Island. An interesting spot in the Indian Ocean, just east of Madagascar. Earth's crust is thin at this spot because of a magma chamber just two miles below the seafloor. This tiny island may be the key to reversing climate change, or at least buying us more time to change our society."

A red-headed student raised his hand. "Didn't the other Dr. Pearce, your wife, study the population there?"

Dr. Pearce laughed. "She did." He gestured to Daxia. "Daxia and I both went with her to study the hotspot. That trip led me to study geoengineering in the first place."

He pressed his watch again. Nothing happened.

The screen turned blue. *NO INPUT* blinked where his image had been. This time when he pressed his watch, harder, it just beeped in protest. He rubbed his forehead.

"Good times never last. Remember that, class."

He marched over to the wall and pressed another button. The

projector shut off, and the screen rose, revealing a whiteboard. He began drawing a wavy blue line near the bottom of the board. Above it, he drew a green arc with a dimple at its peak just above the blue line.

"Let's try this again." He pointed to the green shape. "Pretend this is Réunion Island."

He put down the green marker and picked up a black one. The drawing looked like a sprawling tree until he picked up a red marker and added streaks and flames to the island's base. It was a mushroom cloud. Satisfied with his sketch, he turned back to the class.

"The crust is so thin here that we could drill into the volcano and detonate a nuclear bomb. The result would be a type of eruption powerful enough to pause climate change... a fire fountain," Dr. Pearce said, pointing to the mushroom cloud.

Several students looked at him like he was crazy. One even started packing her bag to leave.

Dr. Pearce ignored her and looked back at the whiteboard.

"The reason this plan might work is thanks to something you cannot see." He drew three more arcs high above the crude island and labeled each band: troposphere, stratosphere, and space. Above the stratosphere, he drew several black squiggles radiating off the explosion.

"This man-made volcanic eruption would deliver millions of cubic feet of sulfates to the atmosphere. Sulfur compounds are exceptionally efficient sunlight reflectors. The latest studies predict reflecting 1.8% of sunlight back into space would stop climate change in its tracks. Imagine re-engineering the climate in a matter of weeks by popping the cork on this island."

He turned back to the class and saw the gears turning through their intense gazes.

"The world would be a whole degree cooler in less than a year. Now, it isn't without risk. Models predict significant damage to the ozone layer."

He drew an *X* through a slice of the atmosphere. "If that happens, we may still have to wear protective suits outdoors to prevent exposure to carcinogenic levels of solar radiation. There are no guarantees when tinkering with Earth's natural cycles, as we've already been doing for hundreds of years."

He picked up an eraser and rubbed it over the explosion until only the island in the sea and atmospheric layers remained.

"The only force we know that can cool the planet for a tremendous amount of time is a dust-filled atmosphere."

Above the layers of atmosphere, Dr. Pearce drew a black circle.

"This is Gigantia. It is the first asteroid we are mining for its heavy metals, like iridium." He redrew it in the stratosphere, this time adding a fiery red tail.

He made a fist and slammed it into his opposite palm. "Impact."

The red-headed student raised his hand again. "We reviewed the asteroid impact extinction theory last week in Paleo 101." He looked to Daxia and pointed. "She was there, too."

Dr. Pearce nodded. "Daxia, your department is doing a good job scaring these kids! Why don't you do the honors and tell them what we found in Mexico?"

Daxia stood up to join Dr. Pearce at the front and began, "What you learned last week is already outdated; you can thank old textbooks for that. We now know the Chicxulub crater on the Yucatán Peninsula in Mexico is twice as large as once thought."

The class looked even more rapt than before.

Dr. Pearce fluttered his fingers through the air above his head. "It stirred up so much dust and caused so much destruction that it affected the climate for millions of years. We know this because the impact left a layer of iridium-laden ash spread over the entire planet, known as the Cretaceous-Paleogene boundary, or K-Pg boundary for short. Our drilling discovered that it is thickest around the Gulf of Mexico and thins out the farther you get from the peninsula. Our discovery about the Chicxulub crater's true size was key to creating an accurate model for the climate change we see in the fossil record after this ancient impact.

The red-headed student looked worried.

Daxia raised her finger. "However, we still cannot account for the amount of iridium in the K-Pg boundary, even when factoring in the size of this impact."

Dr. Pearce drew a crosshatch matrix on the whiteboard. "The only way our model predicts the right amount of dust is if there are more impact craters out there. At least five more, maybe ten more, depending on asteroid size."

Daxia sat on the table and pointed to the asteroid turned meteor. "The good news is that we are at least two or three hundred years away from having to take this desperate step. No one, none of us, knows how far humanity will advance by the late 2200s. If you look that far into the past from today, there were no computers, cars, or modern medicine. Civilization progresses at an ever-increasing rate."

Dr. Pearce drew several more circles between the black marks of space. "And we don't need multi-mile wide asteroids. My hypothesis is that small impacts could work better than a few large ones, targeted to less populated areas, of course. But if that doesn't work…" He trailed off for a moment. "Let's just say I wish I felt hopeful that we can address climate change without more drastic measures." He drew a huge black circle above the Earth. "The good news is we have found over 2,400 planets beyond our own. If we sent probes, I suspect we'd find less than one percent of those are habitable for humans. What I am suggesting is nothing less than evacuating the entire planet. It may take a catastrophe to save it. Let's all hope technology progresses enough by the time we need to leave."

The entire class seemed to be holding their breath. "So, what are you studying next?" asked a student in the front row.

Dr. Pearce set the marker down and rubbed his hands together. "I plan to use the rest of our funding from the Geology Committee to develop and refine our impact plan. We need to figure out where all that iridium in the K-Pg layer came from, and our recent work at the Chicxulub crater will keep us busy for the next ten years, or at least until I retire. I'm trying to convince Ms. Daxia Ling here to stay onboard to help until we have finished the model."

Daxia smiled. "You need to get more funding first."

The students laughed, and Daxia returned to her seat.

"I'd like you all to remember just one thing from this lecture before you go on spring break." He removed a rock from his bag. Its tiny, embedded crystals glinted like diamonds in the light. "This is a tektite, composed of sixty-six-million-year-old shocked quartz from the Chicxulub crater."

He turned the stone in his hand.

"Unless you believe aliens will swoop down with some tips to save us from ourselves, you'd better prepare for dramatic action to reverse the damage. Without it, Earth will not be habitable for your great, great grandchildren."

The students seemed to blink in unison, and he heard several gasps.

He sat on the table again. "But that is far in the future. For now, have a good spring break! Enjoy those beautiful seaside resorts before the beaches disappear!"

A few students laughed, and others rolled their eyes as they packed their bags.

Daxia stood and smiled at them as they filed out of the classroom. "And enjoy a break from Dr. Mood Killer!"

She waved the last ones out and sidled over to Dr. Pearce, who was still sitting on the table.

"The classic pre-break buzzkill from Dr. Pearce."

He smirked. "The future is grim if they do nothing; it may be in their hands. Maybe that will wake them up from their apathy long enough to realize this is not an exaggeration."

"Yeah, but right before spring break?"

He shrugged. "Climate change is real and it will be up to them to do something about it."

Daxia pulled out her phone. "That reminds me: I thought you would like this quote I read in an old article about the K-Pg impact event." She scrolled down. "A science writer named Matthew R. Francis wrote, 'We are not the dinosaurs. We are the asteroid.'"

He considered that for a moment. "I like it," he decided and held up the shocked quartz. Its tiny broken crystals left a fine white powder on his hands. "We are the asteroid," he said, wiping the dust off on his pants, "here to finish off a dying world."

# CHAPTER 10
# INTRODUCTIONS

## MERIDIAN BRIDGE - CYCLE 0

Kaia poked her head through the entryway to the bridge. The breathtaking sight made her pause in wonder. Six consoles formed a vertical wheel around the main viewscreen. To her left was a row of workstations where three crew members in pressed blue suits monitored the glowing gauges and graphs on their screens. The floor's gentle spin created just enough gravity to keep the crew's feet on the decking, although several still used the foot straps on the floor to steady themselves.

She noted what was on their viewscreens as each one rotated past. "Lightdrive propulsion, ship's systems, crew health," she whispered to herself.

Next, a long wooden table came into view—the Council's section. She imagined the hushed meetings that must have taken place there as Councilor Hegira put the final eruption steps in motion. Enki's unmanned geology workstation rotated into view. Nu's surface temperature, and seismic activity lit up the screen above. Next to it, the biology station's viewscreen was empty, conserving energy while it waited for her to take her position. The mission station and helm came into view, where First Officer Ra and Captain Apep interpreted the data summary streaming in from each workstation. Their intense focus assured her that nothing would go unnoticed. She felt a rush of confidence in the Council's greatest, and last, project. The whole picture spread out before her in a way she'd never experienced while sifting through samples in the biology lab.

The entire planet of Nu hung in the center of the bridge, giving the impression that this was a control panel for the world. In a way, it was.

She wrapped her hand around the ladder and climbed down to the small seating area behind the helm. The handrails helped her stay grounded as she stumbled off the viewing platform toward the biology station. Kaia's feet found the loops on the floor as she steadied herself and drew her login symbol on the glyphpad. The transparent screen came to life. The biological sensor readings from the surface floated in the air above her console with the large main viewscreen behind it. She felt her body begin to lean.

Captain Apep's unmistakable laugh came from the mission console on her left. "I can tell it's been a while since you've been on the bridge. The motion here is a bit… different."

Kaia turned around without letting go of the workstation.

"I wish we could have found some way to create real gravity before this whole project was necessary," she said, flexing her arm to keep herself upright against the spin.

"Me too," he admitted. "But we had other things to figure out, like how to save the planet," he flipped his hand up. "Or, more importantly, whether Eve or Jezebel wore the golden habsew better," he joked.

Her mouth tightened as she remembered how many Jacana went along with the mindless celebrity gossip instead of taking the time for critical thinking about the global situation. "People have different ways of facing reality," she offered.

"Sure, like denying it," he said with a sarcastic smile.

With a start, she felt her stomach burn and a wet feeling rising in her throat. Her hand flew to her mouth—she was about to be sick. Captain Apep offered his arm, and she took it.

"Here, look at me. Don't look around." He placed his other hand on her shoulder. "There you go. Now, slide your boots out of those straps."

She took a deep breath and slid each foot out of its loop.

He looked into her eyes. "That's much better, isn't it?"

"I'm still feeling... strange," she said as she swayed to one side.

"Whoa there, be careful. Let's go for a walk."

She looked to her right; the floor curved away and above them. "A walk might help," she agreed.

His gaze circled the bridge and settled on her. "How about we refresh your memory of the bridge? And, you can get to know this skeleton crew a little better. I'm sure they'd like to meet our resident hero," he said with a playful, deep bow.

She held her hand to her chest. "I'm not the hero here. They are. They're the ones seeing this plan through."

Captain Apep tilted his head back. His eyes softened, then he said, "You're one of the good ones, Kaia."

"I'm glad you think so," she said, unsure why she said it.

The next stop was the Council's section. It was an open space on the otherwise cramped bridge. A long, narrow table dominated the space. Its rich wood top sat in stark contrast to the glass and metal that made up the rest of the surfaces. A holoprojector displayed a single fern leaf rotating in the air above the table.

Captain Apep ran his hand along the table's beveled edge as they walked past. "The Council wanted this to be in another section of the ship, but I insisted it be on the bridge. I like to solve problems by bringing people together in the moment, not separating them from the action."

Kaia furrowed her brows in consideration. Working together without everyone at a viewscreen for quick access to data felt old-fashioned to her, maybe even inefficient.

He must have sensed her hesitation and added, "We might not be in this mess if the Council had tried to bring people together where the worst effects of climate change were felt, instead of looking at videos from the comfort of a well-insulated skytower in Puna."

She glanced down at the table to avoid the captain's eyes then back at him again. "They listened to you about the table. Maybe they will listen to you about other things," she offered.

He nodded to the spinning leaf. "Well, I think that's because this is my ship, but this is still the Council's show. I don't expect Councilor Hegira to change amid our most important mission."

Kaia looked up across the main viewscreen toward the helm; anywhere but at the captain. She tapped the table and finally met his gaze. "Let's keep moving."

The captain picked up his pace and caught up with her just as she arrived at a workstation she'd seen upon entering. "This is where we monitor the crew's vital signs and the habsew systems," he explained.

Two suited figures hunched over the glyphpad. The closest one looked up. His beady eyes studied her, then he bowed as a wide smile spread over his face. "Kaia! How exciting that you're here to see history being made! I'm Professor Thoth." He rocked on the balls of his feet then kicked the other man's foot. "Kaia and the captain are here."

The man turned around.

"*Hrmph*," he said. "Nice to meet you, Kaia. My apologies for Professor Thoth here." He kicked the young man's foot in return. "Thoth might have been our brightest intern before he finished his degree, but if you ask me, he needs to cool his lightdrive and focus on making sure the computers stay operational instead of being awed by our more famous crew members." He said with a slight bow. "No offense."

She recognized the crooked nose and smooth gold hood covering the top of his bald head. "None taken. You must be Dr. Khnum," she said.

"That's right." He turned back to the console. "Now if you'll excuse me," he pointed to a grid of eleven line graphs on the viewscreen, "I'm trying to make sure everyone's habsews keep up with their bodies during all this stress." He looked to Professor Thoth, then Kaia and Captain Apep. "We aren't all spring chickens, you know."

"I am all too aware of that these days," Kaia said, reaching down to massage her right elbow, a painful reminder of her graceless exit from the shuttle earlier.

Captain Apep stepped forward. "Sorry, Dr. Khnum, we'll leave you to it." He turned to Professor Thoth, who was still staring at Kaia. "Thoth, are you finished with the archival duplication?"

"Uh," he gulped and straightened his back. "Not yet, sir."

"Best get to it then, yeah?" Captain Apep said and started heading toward the next station.

"Yes, sir," Professor Thoth said, sliding his feet back into the stabilizers in front of the systems console.

The captain turned around backward as he passed an imposing woman. "Kaia, have you met Pakhet?"

There was no hiding the woman's muscular physique, yet Kaia saw the soft-featured face of a gentle giant. "Nice to meet you, Pakhet."

The woman's shoulders were at eye level, but something about her demeanor made it feel as though she were looking up at Kaia as she spoke. She brushed away a yellow tuft poking out from under her babel hood. "You as well." She bowed. "You are my hero, you know—seeing you on the newscasts so many times, wise beyond your years, talking about how important all this work would be," she said, waving her arm around the bridge.

"Thank you," Kaia said. She raised her eyebrows. "I hope I don't disappoint you, since I am not larger-than-life in the flesh."

Pakhet laughed with ease. "I have to look down to see most of those I look up to."

Captain Apep smiled at the exchange. "Engineering runs in Pakhet's blood. She would have been heiress to the great Milas Manufacturing fortune had the Council not taken over the company."

Pakhet grimaced. "The Council taking control wasn't all bad. We didn't have the money to reinforce the factories in New Sifan so they would have been destroyed without the government's intervention."

Kaia rubbed her sore elbow again. "My grandparents on my mother's side owned Fortuna Asteroid Mining before the Council assumed control."

"Well," Captain Apep shrugged, "I guess we wouldn't have the cityships or," he knocked on a support beam, "the *Meridian*, without your families' expertise."

Kaia left it at that and smiled. "I'm glad you're here, Pakhet."

"As am I," Pakhet said with a bow.

The Captain and Kaia bowed in return and walked toward the helm.

She looked to him. "Pakhet seems excellent for the job."

"Why, thank you. I've never met anyone as humble as she is, given her family's wealth." He turned to her. "Speaking of being humble reminds me of you."

Kaia blushed and kept moving.

Captain Apep continued, "There are only eleven of us on the ship now," he fell into step beside her, "and everyone has given up a big part of themselves for the greater good. Choosing to stay behind was a big decision."

"I am in good company," she replied.

"Indeed you are," he said with a proud smile.


They completed their loop around the bridge and stopped next to First Officer Ra at the helm.

Captain Apep inhaled a deep, prideful breath and said, "Well, that's everyone. Except Nef and Mirik."

Ra nudged Kaia. "Whatever those two are up to, it probably is not good."

He and the Captain burst into laughter. "Thick as thieves, as the saying goes," the captain said with a grin. "You'll meet them soon enough, I'm sure."

"They sound like fun," Kaia said.

Captain Apep grinned even wider. "That's one word for them," he said and faced the helm.

Kaia pointed at a furry lump below the viewscreen. "Is that a—?"

He leaned against the glyphpad. "A stuffed affi? It sure is, meet Rex. I've had him since I was seven cycles old."

Kaia covered her mouth to hide the giggle. "Sorry."

First Officer Ra rolled his eyes. "Don't get me started on that thing." He sauntered over to the ship console to the left of the helm. "Mirik gave that to the captain after—"

Apep raised his hand. "I'll explain it to her later."

First Officer Ra nodded. "Sorry, sir, I thought she already knew."

"It's fine," Apep said and turned to the viewscreen. He waved for Kaia to step up to the helm with him.

She tried to keep her eyes away from the stuffed animal out of fear she'd laugh again, though she took a mental note to make sure he told her what it was all about.

There was a loud clang from behind, and they all spun around. Councilor Horus was at the entrance to the bridge, holding himself upright by wrapping his elbow around a rung on the ladder.

Captain Apep rushed over. "Here, let me help you, Councilor."

Horus brushed him away and stood free. "I'm fine. Don't you have a ship to run?"

Captain Apep bowed. "Yes, Councilor."

"Then get to it," the councilor said, making his way to the mission console between the helm and Kaia's station.

Captain Apep strutted off to the helm after a quick glance at Councilor Horus's feet to make sure they had found the floor loops. He then reached down and drew a rectangle on the helm's glyphpad and swiped up. A video from the surface of Nu filled the bridge's main viewscreen, grabbing everyone's attention.

Captain Apep looked at the orange-gray planet. Vast storms swirled over the dead, overheated oceans. "A wonder to think we lived there."

"Not only did we live there," Kaia replied, moisture filling her eyes. "We evolved there. We were born there."

Captain Apep leaned forward. "There's something I've always wondered," he said. "Kaia, in your professional opinion, do you think the few animals left below will appreciate our saving the world for them?"

She shook her head. "Not the way we want them to."

"I suppose not, but it is a comforting thought."

"I take comfort in knowing, or rather hoping, the Jacana will no longer destroy their worlds. How could they, after seeing what we've done to Nu?"

Captain Apep clicked his tongue. "Each cityship's council will make sure it does not happen again."

Kaia nodded. "I worry about that, too. Some were more promising than others, but none were as lush as we'd hoped to find."

Councilor Horus scoffed. "I see you're still trying to tell it like it is, Kaia. That isn't a good idea since it doesn't inspire confidence in the Council's plans."

She fought the urge to raise her voice. "Truth is always the best route."

Horus let out a belly laugh. "Someday you'll learn, child. And you know, we didn't interpret the data on our own planet very well, either."

"You think we could have done better? Why didn't you—"

"Of course we could have," Councilor Horus interjected. "We knew we were messing the place up when I was fresh out of my incubator."

Captain Apep frowned. "A shame we needed incubators in the first place."

"Councilor Horus has a point," Kaia conceded. "Scientists have been telling everyone we needed to curb kohl emissions or else the world would die. Teachers taught it in school, but we never changed our lifestyle until we had to, and by then, we were out of time."

"Speaking of time..." Captain Apep looked toward the chronometer on the outer edge of the main viewscreen. Cycle 2296, Day 33. He held down the comm and raised his wrist to his babel. "Attention, crew, I am resetting the date." The clock's numbers blinked to zero, and AD appeared before the word Cycle. Jacana time was starting over on the *Meridian*.

Captain Apep looked around the bridge. "The Exodus is complete. We will now track the date in relation to the Dawn Project's initiation. It is After Dawn, or AD, Cycle 0. We plan to return in AD 500 to begin phase two after Enki confirms the eruption is working. Then, we will depart for Duat, where a new future awaits us all."

He lowered his voice and leaned against the console. "Kaia, what are the chances a cityship will discover there is already intelligent life on their new home?"

Kaia shook her head. "We found no evidence of civilizations, but I admit we have limited data."

"If we do come across one, let's hope it has figured out how to balance civilization with the planet's ecosystem."

She took a deep breath. "Yes, *hope* may be all we can do if that happens."

"Kaia!" a voice yelled from above. "Captain!" it said again.

She and Captain Apep spun around and looked up to see Enki scrambling down the ladder.

Kaia rushed over to him, "What is it?"

He ran past her and went straight to his console.

She jogged up behind him, "Enki, what's wrong?"

He stopped his furious glyphpad gestures and turned to her, his forehead creased with wrinkles.

"It is happening again."

Captain Apep leaned forward. "What is?"

"The *sensors*," he urged. "Sensors are going offline and not coming back. I cannot be sure what is happening below." He huffed and pointed to the graphs. "Maybe if I tried checking the..." he gestured on the glyphpad and the screen flashed red. He pounded the console.

Kaia put her hand on his shoulder. "Enki, it's okay, just take a breath."

"But we need to know if the eruption is going to work before we leave!" Enki insisted.

Kaia paused and inhaled; he was right. "What did the simulation show?"

"I would show you, but I am unable to fit the necessary data on this diminutive screen."

Captain Apep strode up next to them. Kaia saw him make nervous eye contact with the other crew members before he said, "Enki, let's go take a look at it, together, at the Council table. It has a holoprojector." He bowed and nodded to the long, curved table a short distance around the bridge.

Enki was darting towards it before Captain Apep finished his sentence.

Captain Apep turned to Kaia and shook his head. "Odd bird, that one."

She crossed her arms. "But he's the smartest person I know by a thousand cubits."

"I can tell," Captain Apep replied.

She nodded over to Enki, "I better go see what he's found."

The captain glanced around the bridge again and shook his head when Professor Thoth began walking toward the table. Kaia noticed his subtle authority. *Stay there,* his eyes said, and the professor looked back down at the console. "I'll keep the crew away for now, but let me know what Enki found."

# CHAPTER 11
# SIMULATION

## MERIDIAN BRIDGE - CYCLE 0

A number matrix floated in the air above the table until Enki placed his finger on the glyphpad and swiped to the left. Kaia watched a spinning blue square fade in, rotating faster and faster as the simulation loaded. It stopped and exploded into a million points of light.

They watched in awe as Puna's skyline hung above the table. Buildings stained by acid rain disappeared into the smog. It would be easy to forget they were on the bridge and not back on the plateau taking in the pre-eruption cityscape.

Enki held his hand suspended just above the glyphpad and said out loud what Kaia had already been thinking. "What if it shows that we will fail?"

Kaia placed her hand on his shoulder and cast her eyes toward the simulation. "It will work," she reassured him.

If only she could reassure herself.

Enki took a deep breath and tapped the glyphpad to start the simulation.

They watched the nanomech orb pierce the crust as the tiny machines drilled and deconstructed layers of rock, descending toward the magma chamber deep below the city. The skyline sat silent until a blinding flash filled the projection. When the light subsided, a dark form rose above downtown's center. Kaia felt her pulse race the same way it did each time she saw a simulation of the eruption.

The head of a mushroom cloud reached the top of the projection's upper boundary and disappeared.

The glyphs "Insufficient Data" flashed over the simulation.

Kaia blinked, hard. "What happened?"

His fingers were zooming over the glyphpad already. He looked up at the frozen simulation, then at her, his face blank. "It needs data from the sensors to continue the simulation." He glanced back at a small screen above the glyphpad. "And they are all offline, now. The last reading showed pressure far above its design threshold."

Kaia could feel Captain Apep's eyes on them, and she motioned for him to come over.

She read the glyphs again. *Insufficient Data.*

Captain Apep positioned himself between the projection and the rest of the crew trying to get a glimpse from their stations around the bridge. He spoke in a hushed voice, "What is it?"

Enki began to say, "The thermal sensors are—" when Kaia heard another man yelling.

"The thermal sensors are fine!" She recognized the voice as Councilor Horus right away, and an angry one at that.

Captain Apep reluctantly said, "Well, everyone will know now."

Enki ignored the exchange, still troubleshooting the simulation. He restarted it and swirled his finger to fast-forward. The skytowers began swaying and shaking then stopped.

*Insufficient Data.*


Councilor Horus burst around the corner, "What are you three doing?"

Councilor Hegira was behind him now, unable to keep up.

She sat down at the end of the table and took one look at the paused simulation. "Enki, what does 'Insufficient Data' mean?"

He stood up straight and said, "The simulation requires live input fro—"

"It means what it says!" Councilor Horus interrupted.

Councilor Hegira glared at him. "Horus..."

He shirked away.

Enki continued. "The simulation requires live input from thermal sensors in the bore shaft in order to predict the outcome of the eruption with a high degree of accuracy."

She nodded once. "Why aren't we receiving the data?"

Enki looked to Councilor Horus, who was glaring at him. "I believe it is because the drill shaft is collapsing. I recommended we create a latticework to suppo—"

Councilor Horus flew toward the table. "The shaft is fine! It does not need any reinforcements. It is probably the sensors you designed. That was shoddy work, and you know it!"

Enki pulled his shoulders back. "The sensors are performing above the design limits."

"That's a lie. There's no way—" Horus began.

Councilor Hegira slammed her hand down on the console. "Horus, enough." She rotated the stool to face Enki straight-on. "How do we get the simulation the data it needs?"

"I need to go to the surface and take direct thermoviewer measurements."

Kaia stepped forward, "Enki, are you sure that is safe?"

He looked up for a moment, then back. "There is an observation platform on the plateau overlooking Puna. It should be safe to observe from that distance."

Councilor Hegira rubbed her thighs. "It's settled. Let's not waste time. Enki, you have my authorization to go to the surface and take your measurements. I want us to be certain the eruption will work."

Councilor Horus scoffed. "It will work. Besides, Phase 2's asteroids can clean up any mess an imprecise eruption might make."

She glared at him. "We need to be certain, Horus."

"Of course," he said with a bow.

Enki was still standing, stiff as a board. "There is one problem."

"What is it?" Captain Apep asked.

"I can't fly a shuttle."

Kaia stepped forward. "I'll fly him in the biology shuttle."

"Kaia, is that wise? Autopilot should suffice." Captain Apep asked.

She strode over to Enki. "We'll use autopilot in space, but when we get to the surface, where there is *gravity*, I'll be fine. I flew biologists all over Nu collecting samples to prepare for the Exodus."

Captain Apep looked to Councilor Hegira for confirmation.

The Councilor bowed from her seat. "You may go."

Kaia bowed in return. "Thank you," she said and began heading off the bridge with Enki in tow.

Councilor Horus scoffed. "This is ridiculous." He shook his head and mumbled, "Completely absurd."


Captain Apep watched Kaia and Enki climb up the ladder and disappear into the corridor. It all happened so fast, and he knew so little of the eruption's science. He did not know how to respond, or how to feel.

He took a tentative step towards the table. "I do not want to alarm the crew. I need to make another round and ensure everyone is busy with preparations to leave Nu."

Councilor Hegira bowed. "Very well."

He stepped away from the table and rounded the corner behind a beam. Councilor Horus was muttering something to Councilor Hegira. The captain turned around and listened just out of view.

"Hegira, you can't be serious."

"I am," she said firmly.

"But the plan, it has to work!" Horus insisted.

"And if it doesn't, we have…" her voice trailed for a moment. "The other one."

Apep heard Councilor Horus sigh and say, "The earlier Council was right to reject it. It's unthinkable."

"What is unthinkable," Hegira began, "is losing our dear Kaia."

"You're growing soft in your old age, Hegira," he said.

The chair creaked when she stood. "That may be, but we need her. And you know it."

Captain Apep tiptoed away.

His mind raced.

*It is time Kaia learned the truth.*

# CHAPTER 12
# OVERLOOK

## PUNA PLATEAU - CYCLE 0

Kaia kept an eye on the altimeter as she placed both hands on the shuttle's glyphpad. *Coming in a tad hot,* she noted and adjusted her right hand down one hundredth of a cubit. Most people used autopilot, but every time she tried her mind flashed back to the shuttle flying away while a storm surge approached her parents.

When she turned 16, she spent an entire cycle learning how to operate a shuttle in all kinds of situations. It was unusual for a biologist to pursue a pilot certification, but no one questioned her. Almost twenty cycles after her first interview, she could still hear the newscaster's voice: *What ran through your mind when the autopilot malfunctioned?*

Her tearful, timid seven-cycle-old self had replied, *"I wished I knew how to fly the shuttle so I could save Mommy and Daddy."*

And now, after hours of rigorous training, she did.

A cloud of dust rose from the ground as the landing jets slowed its descent onto the plateau. Scratches and dents marred the fern leaf insignia etched into the shuttle's green exterior. It looked as tired and broken as the withered bushes on the ground.

"Touchdown," she said.

Enki unbuckled his seatbelt. "I'm going to get started right away."

"Good idea," she said.

Enki got up and pulled a suitcase-sized container from the cargo bay. He used his foot to kick the button that lowered the cargo ramp.

Kaia noticed some dust blow in from the plateau. "How long do you need?"

He looked down at his viewpad. "The eruption should start in less than 30 minutes, so, less than that."

"Be safe, Enki."

"As always," he replied as he ducked through the cargo bay door and shuffled down the ramp.

The grinding of the nanomechs at work in the bore shaft outside made her skin crawl. She crossed her arms and stretched her neck—it was going to be a long half hour. She decided to review the temperature data while she waited. A line rose, indicating that it was rising as the eruption neared. *I'll just worry myself to death if I look at that,* she decided.

Kaia swiveled the pilot's chair away from the viewscreen and toward the shuttle's front window. The view was not what it used to be, she thought. Pollution coated the once grand skytowers of downtown Puna. Still, many former residents had visited this overlook before they left, unable to resist one last glimpse at the final city of their fleeing civilization.

Her breathing slowed as memories washed over her. Puna would always be her home. She felt her eyes watering up at the realization that there would be no more sunsets behind the skyline. No more people rushing to their jobs on the wide avenues in Plutus, the financial district. No more holiday decorations illuminating the narrow streets of Clio, the historical district. No more lazy strolls through Puna's zoo.

*The zoo.*

She sighed and looked down at the worn photo taped to her console. Her father looked so happy, Kaia in his lap and him pretending to be scared of the phara behind the glass at the Puna City Zoo. Even though the colors had faded over time, she could still see hints of the hidden smile at the edges of his blue eyes.

She slumped and pressed a button on the right side of the window. The horizon twisted left as the shuttle turned. Dead bushes scraped against the metal hull and made her wince. The cockpit gave an impression of safety and isolation from the world, but the sound outside reminded her of the deception. Earlier generations thought they were separate from the natural world. Their rapid technological advancement cultivated an illusion of supremacy over nature. Her ancestors ignored the signs, the scratches outside their own window. Her generation knew better, though. They suffered tortuous pain in searing heat; the superstorms leveling entire cities. It took the death of billions to convince older generations that they could not control nature.

*Nature always wins in the end.*

The shuttle's rotation slowed to a stop. Kaia rested her elbows on the controls below the window and drew a deep breath at the amazing sight. Exodus rocket launchpads stretched into the distance, where two days ago the last colonists shot into space in the Dawn Project's final evacuation. Her mind wandered to the cityships. How far away would they be by now? She began drawing a symbol on the glyphpad to find out when the ground trembled below her shuttle, through the landing gear, into the cockpit, and into her bones.

Kaia spun back around to the window and leaned forward to look outside.

An explosion knocked her back into the chair.

Her vision blurred.

It felt like someone was squeezing her skull.

The shuttle creaked and tilted to one side; its landing pads lifted off the ground and slammed back down. An eerie silence followed, making her wonder if a booster had misfired, but lighted glyphs indicated everything was normal. She looked up to the window and saw a shock wave roar through the air.

*Enki is still outside!*

Kaia jumped out of the chair and ran to the airlock. In seconds, she reached for the helmet and twisted it on, ensuring the babel speakers fit over her ears. The gloves crinkled as she pulled them over her wrists and twisted the seal. No time for a safety check.

She pounded the exit button. A burst of hot air rushed in, and she darted out. Fear gripped her tight when she looked up toward sol to get her bearings. A dark mushroom cloud rose high above downtown Puna.

"Enki!" she screamed.

# CHAPTER 13
# ERUPTION

## PUNA PLATEAU - CYCLE 0

Dead grass crunched underfoot as Kaia raced toward the edge of the plateau. The mushroom cloud over Puna reached high into the clouds and spread out above the city.

Kaia looked down and touched the orange comm button on her wrist.

"This is Kaia to the *Meridian*. Come in, *Meridian*."

She heard nothing but the hiss of digital voice compression artifacts.

"*Meridian*, anyone, please respond."

A brief buzz, then a silvery male voice replied, "This is Captain Apep. Go ahead, Kaia."

"Captain, Enki is not responding. Has he contacted you?"

"One moment, please."

She heard the captain's muffled footsteps and him speaking to First Officer Ra in a hushed tone. "Anything?"

There was a pause.

"Nothing, sir," Ra said.

"Kaia, there is too much interference."

The captain's voice grew concerned. "Kaia, it isn't safe. There is too much interference. If something happened, we wouldn't be able to—"

"I'm not leaving him," she insisted.

She heard the captain sigh over the comms. "Understood. We will monitor your signal. Be quick, you don't have much time," he ordered.

"Yes, Captain."

A wall of dust rolled in and obscured her view of the plateau. A chemical scent filled her nose. She hoped it was just the habsew's air filter working overtime, because a broken seal would cut the search short. Her eyes scrutinized the seals around her wrists while she waited for a puncture warning from her suit. She patted down the front and sides; no holes or tears, no warnings in her visor. The ground trembled. Kaia looked toward the edge of the plateau again. The air was clear down below.

"Captain, I felt another groundshake," she said.

"Yes," someone replied, but something garbled the signal. "The nanomechs reached—" a man said between coughs. "The nanomechs reached the mantle. The nuclear shock wave took almost twelve minutes to reach the surface," the voice recovered and continued in a flat, matter-of-fact voice. "Our eruption is about to begin."

She gasped with relief. "Enki! Are you okay?"

"I am. The energy release exceeded my calculations."

"Where are you?" she demanded to know.

"I am still on the observation platform."

"I'm on my way," she yelled and began running.


Kaia's helmet fogged up as she approached the cliff to look for the platform. A warning flashed in the visor. Her suit's internal temperature was climbing. Its pump struggled to circulate enough coolant to keep her safe, so she slowed to a jog.

She reached the edge of the plateau and looked to her right. The observation platform jutted out over the precipice. Enki hunched over the thermoviewer's screen, while its delicate sensors swayed overhead.

She couldn't believe the hulking machine popped out of the two suitcases from the shuttle.

When she reached the platform, she put her foot on the first step and felt the metal treads through her boots. She looked down and froze in terror. The ground lay hundreds of cubits below her feet through gaps in the floor planks. Her mind screamed. *Don't take another step.* She reached out to hold on to the railing and made her way to Enki's side.

"I'm glad you're okay," she said.

"As am I," he replied, oblivious to the terrifying scenarios that had played out in her mind when she thought he was in trouble.

"Are you almost finished?" she asked.

He looked down at the screen and blinked. "Thermal sensors are still, but my manual data gathering is successful."

"Will you have enough to complete the simulation?"

"Yes," he said with an affirming tone.

Kaia looked toward downtown. "Well, make it quick." A flock of bahis squawked as they flew away from the skytowers. "We need to get out of here before it starts."

"I will," he said and leaned closer to the thermoviewer to scrutinize the gauges. His adjustments came to a halt.

"What is it?" she asked.

Enki reached up, turned a dial, and waited for the reading to update, but none came. "I still cannot determine why the sensors failed at an alarming rate. There is collapse, as I warned about, but something else is happening."

He drew a few vertical glyphs and waited for the on-screen result. It occurred to her that the fact that he preferred to observe the scene with scientific instruments instead of his own eyes made him the perfect geologist for the Dawn Project. Remote monitoring was all they could do once they left the surface.

Enki stood up, brushing dust from his shoulders. "I have eliminated other explanations. It can only be that Councilor Horus's estimates of the magma chamber are inaccurate. I anticipate the eruption will be much stronger than he expected."

"Is that a problem?"

"Unknown," he said. "I recommended we use fewer nanomechs to drill and more to reinforce the shaft while taking iterative measurements."

"Councilor Horus was eager to prove his little inventions would work without modification from others."

"My simulation should have included the fact that the more autonomous nanomechs involved, the harder the drilling is to control."

"How bad is it, Enki? Is there anything you can do now?"

"No. Like I said earlier, I could have taken more precise measurements at regular intervals to be sure, but Councilor Horus told Councilor Hegira they were unnecessary. I fear he is no longer making decisions as a prudent scientist."

Kaia nodded. "It was all downhill when he started caring more about his image rather than if what he was saying was true."

"Mmm, yes." Enki agreed. "I never understood why he did not outright reject Captain Set's proposal to stay on Nu. I am certain Councilor Hegira's threat to revoke his seat on the Council was what changed his mind."

She shrugged. "I think he was afraid of leaving home along with everyone else. Now, I'm glad he stayed the course with the Council and didn't join Set's Resistance in their fight to stay on Nu. I still don't believe Captain Set cared about staying on Nu, though. I think he saw an angle to gain power by pandering to people's fear of leaving."

Enki considered what she said for a moment. "But, staying was illogical and dangerous. It was not an option, no matter how people felt. The Council, Councilor Hegira herself, tried to tell them."

His head tilted to the right. Kaia knew feelings confused him. She smiled, knowing he had the best intentions, despite discounting the emotional implications of logical decisions.

"Yes, Enki, you're right. But remember that sometimes people find it easier to decide based on their feelings, especially in the face of inconvenient truths. I know it is hard to understand."

He blinked several times. "I am sorry, but your lack of friends led me to assume you do not possess a superior interpersonal understanding, either."

"Ouch," she said and laughed, "but a good one."

He smiled, pleased with himself.

A warning message flashed on the thermoviewer.

"What's that?" she asked.

Enki gripped the edges of the display with both hands. "I-I am not sure yet. These readings seem off, indicating more lava pressure than I expected."

The platform trembled under their feet.

"What is going on?" Kaia asked.

Enki raised a finger to his mouth, his eyes sparkled with excitement. He pointed toward the skyline. "The eruption is beginning."

It was disconcerting to see the great city so still. No constellation of apartment lights dotted the skytowers. No airships floated above them; no holoboards projected above the commercial center high-rises. Only dark buildings, dark streets, and an eerie quiet.

Then the ground shook again. The buildings began to sway.

Kaia and Enki knew what to expect. They'd watched the simulation hundreds of times, but academic discussions and scientific diagrams were inadequate preparation for reality. The sight still took their breath away. Layers of accumulated pollution sloughed away from the facades, creating a roiling dust cloud. Kaia's body stiffened as the ground vibrations continued. She could almost feel the anticipation rolling off Enki. The coming destruction was a testament to their determination to save their home from themselves. Kaia felt her heart torn—first soaring into the clouds at this amazing achievement, then sinking to the depths of her stomach when she remembered why they were doing it. The Dawn Project, her life's work—and the work of countless scientists before her—culminated in this purposeful act of erasure to destroy the last epicenter of Jacana civilization.

The time was upon them.

There was a loud explosive burst, then a seething fire fountain shot into the sky, eclipsing the two hundred-story skytowers around it. Entire city blocks burst into flames. The glow was too bright for their helmets' visors, and Kaia and Enki raised their hands to shield their eyes while they adjusted to the light. Searing rivers of magma snaked through the streets, oozing between the buildings, consuming them in fire as it flowed past. Smoke from countless fires rose high above the city.

"And so—" he started.

"It begins," she finished.

The platform rattled as the groundshake rolled on. They saw lava burst from the ground and spread out in a fan, engulfing the city as their future began.

A loud metallic screech ricocheted through the air, and the tallest skytower in the Aristotle research district began to sway. The tower served as a beacon for researchers across Nu to improve the state of their world. New technologies, like the translating babel speakers, allowed for connections between people like never before. Now, the imposing building leaned hard to the right and stopped. Sheets of glass shattered and fell like snow as the tower's superstructure failed—much like the trappings of her society when the planet could no longer sustain the weight of civilization. The Great Tower of Babel seemed to collapse in slow motion. Tumbling concrete slabs splashed into the lava, sending waves of magma radiating through the streets. Clouds seethed and sizzled above the scene. Lightning struck the building-top antennas, its thunder mixing with the crashes of the crumbling city.

Kaia backed away from the railing and sat in the platform's built-in chair as Enki bent closer to the thermoviewer. The lava fountain surged taller in the distance.

Enki stood and held onto the railing. He gestured toward the flame-engulfed skyline. "Do you believe the Council knew this would be necessary when they relocated everyone to Puna?"

Kaia considered the possibility as she watched another tower fall in a cloud of dust and flame. She took a deep breath. "Yes. They didn't tell everyone why at the time, but I'm sure they knew. We built a great city, each building certified as environmentally friendly, but it was too late. We were not meant to live packed tighter than affis in their burrow, but it was the only way we could."

"Interesting you mention affis," he said.

She gave him a quizzical look.

He tapped the railing. "I have read that they sometimes come together in large groups then run straight off a cliff en masse. Do you think we are doing that now? All of us leaving at once into the unknown?"

She laughed and shook her head. "That's a myth, Enki. Affi's, like most of their furry kind, migrate and sometimes—"

The ridge shook. Enki fell, catching himself on the thermoviewer's antenna. He glanced down at the screen, "Wait—Kaia, a new plume is coming up right under us. It…" His voice wavered.

"What, Enki?" She leapt to her feet.

He double-checked the screen and looked up at her, wide-eyed. "This is not a plume drilled by the nanomechs."

The platform creaked and tilted away from the edge of the cliff. Cases of equipment slid into him, almost knocking him off.

"We've got to go!" Kaia yelled.

The platform shook again, tilting farther. She saw the valley floor cracking open. A new lava fountain rose from the fissure to meet them.

The thermoviewer rattled loose from the platform and fell toward the magma. Flames consumed the antenna and its internal circuit boards, leaving nothing but the thick metal case to drop into the boiling pool below.

Kaia grabbed the ladder and pulled herself up the metal planks and onto the flat ground above. Certain Enki was right behind her, she took a moment to catch her breath when a loud wrenching caused her to swing around. She watched in horror as the platform's supports gave way. It slammed against the rock wall with only a single tube of metal holding firm as the floor swung below the ridge, taking Enki with it. Kaia fell onto her stomach and reached over the edge. Enki grabbed her hand, and she pulled him up just as the last support pipe failed, sending the platform plummeting.

They both lay on their backs, out of breath, coughing and covered in ash. Enki slid up the tinted layer of his viewport.

"What is that?" he asked, pointing into the distance.

Kaia saw it, too. She could just make out the sleek silhouette of a black shuttle from the *Meridian* touching down a few hundred cubits away. A bright white light shone toward them as the cargo bay door opened and a ramp descended.

A thunderous boom shot through the air, and the ground fell several cubits. They jumped to their feet and sprinted for the shuttle as fast as their habsews would allow.

She yelled to Enki, "I've never seen this on any simulation!"

Another lava plume erupted as a slab of rock fell from the cliff.

Enki gasped between words, "Nor have I. We will need to monitor it from orbit. There is nothing else we can do." Boiling splats of lava were falling all around them. "We need to hurry!"

Just as they reached the shuttle, the ground heaved, tossing them both into the cargo bay. They landed hard on their stomachs and gasped for air. The ship ascended as fast as the ground fell out from under it.

The first thing Kaia saw from her graceless sprawl on the floor was an imposing pair of dark blue boots.

"I was wondering if you two planned to become part of the fossil record," she heard Captain Apep say. "Are you okay?"

The metal floor grating dug into her hands as she lifted her shoulder. She looked over to see Enki lying on his stomach, his hands still shielding the back of his head from the lava bombs.

"Yes, I think so." She nudged his arm. "Enki, we're safe now."

He looked up from the floor toward the front of the cargo bay to avoid the captain's gaze. His eyes settled on two grimy crew members along the wall who were pointing and whispering at the two disheveled newcomers.

Kaia puffed her cheeks and exhaled. She pulled her legs under her body and stood all the way up. Enki sat upright and brushed the volcanic ash off his suit. The fine gray dust settled into a circle around him.

Kaia looked down at her own habsew and pulled it tighter around her waist, aware that it was billowing out thanks to a damaged air pump.

Two other crew members, a woman and a man in dirty habsews, smiled and waved at Kaia and Enki.

Captain Apep bowed to each one, "Kaia, Enki, meet Nef and Mirk."

Enki stood in front of the woman, cleared his throat, then pointed to himself. "I am Enki, a geologist." He motioned toward Kaia. "This is—"

The woman's face flashed with recognition and settled into a warm smile. "Everyone knows Dr. Kaia Badra." She reached up and smoothed back fuchsia-colored bangs from her forehead. "Welcome aboard, both of you."

The lanky man next to her said, "Nice to meet you, Enki. I'm Mirik." He pointed to the squat woman next to him. "And the rude one here is Nef, short for Nefertiti. But, let me tell you, weird name or not, she'll either kick your butt or fix your ship all day long, depending on how you treat her." He rolled his head forward to the captain. "We used to be good enough to fly with Captain Apep, but now," he wiped caked grime off his glove, "we just do his dirty work."

Enki cocked his head.

Mirik slapped his knee and burst out laughing. "Get it? Dirty work!"

Captain Apep chastised them. "I'm standing right here."

Mirik's eyes widened, then he shrugged playfully.


Kaia was not in a joking mood. She turned to Captain Apep and said, "We need to get Enki back to his simulation, fast."

"Done," Captain Apep said and jumped up to the cockpit. "You're welcome up front again. The view of the eruption is going to be spectacular."

Kaia straightened her hood. "Thank you."

He motioned to the empty copilot's chair. "Have a seat."

Mirik tapped Nef's shoulder and whispered, "Looks like the captain's gone and replaced us."

Nef punched Mirik's shoulder and looked to Enki. "Sorry about him. It's nice to meet you both," she turned toward Kaia and bowed, "in person."

"Likewise," Kaia said with an uncertain smile and made her way toward the cockpit.

She heard Mirik giggle then whisper, "It's about time he spent time with someone other than his job."

She took a seat and buckled herself in. "A spectacular view is not the word I would use, Captain."

"That bad, huh?"

She took a deep breath. "Just get us to the ship." She pressed the comm button on the console. "Councilor Hegira, we're on our way back to the *Meridian*. Meet us at the Council table. The eruption is failing, fast."

# CHAPTER 14
# PUBLICATION

## UNIVERSITY OF CHICAGO – 2034 CE

Dr. Pearce entered his office with Daxia close behind him. Weak sunlight filtered through the pollution-hazed windows to light up the jumbled stacks of papers rising from the floor, like replicas of Chicago's skyscrapers. When he approached his desk, the computer screen brightened, showing 1,776 unread emails.

Daxia snickered and pointed at it. "You're a little behind on your email, Dr. Pearce."

"If you think that is bad, you should see this!" He pointed to a stack of papers that started on the floor and rose almost as high as his shoulder. "That's the snail mail!"

Daxia wrinkled her nose. "Speaking of snails, it smells like some died in here."

"Sorry," Dr. Pearce pointed to a brown container on his desk, "It's probably last week's Philly cheesesteak."

Daxia waved the smell away in disgust.

Dr. Pearce pulled the latest additions off the top of his mail stack and thumbed through them. He paused, took a manila envelope from the bunch, and held it high, turning to Daxia with a grin. "This is it!"

"You got something important in the mail?" She leaned over to get a closer look, "The paper mail?"

He cocked his head toward the computer. "Sure, they know I don't read any of that."

She gave him a look he could not decipher but knew wasn't good, then she read the return address. "United Nations Climate Council, Geology Committee. Open it!"

He scooted a stack of mail over and sat on the edge of his desk while he fumbled with the clasp, then pulled out a letter. He slammed the manila envelope down, blowing loose papers into the air. He felt his face flush. "The Geology Committee will not allow me to submit our paper on the Chicxulub crater to any journals!" he yelled. "I'm going to give them a piece of my mind right now!" He fell into the chair behind his desk and began pounding away on the keyboard.

Daxia picked up the letter and scanned it then reached over the desk and held her hand over his. "Take a deep breath, Dr. Pearce. I'm sure there has been a mistake."

He stopped and clenched his fists above the keyboard.

Daxia let go and took a seat in the worn leather chair on the other side of his desk. "Why would the committee suppress such an important discovery?"

Dr. Pearce leaned back in his chair and raised his arms behind him. "They must have talked to my department head! Dr. Lucas has made it clear he thinks I'm a crackpot. Wasting money on an impossible and," he made air quotes, "*crazy* plan. But it isn't crazy! You've seen the same thing in our data as I have, yet he won't even look at it."

Daxia leaned forward in the chair. "There is more work to do at Chicxulub, though. We have not considered the asteroid's mineral composition, or the rock strata at the impact site, yet."

He pointed to a contour line map of the Chicxulub crater on his wall. "You're telling me! The dust is key. If a lava eruption at Réunion Island won't work, then some future generation will be up the creek without a paddle. It's not like they can work their way out of trouble by blowing up even more volcanoes. I mean…"

There was a knock at the door.

Dr. Pearce lost his train of thought and huffed, "Come in."

The door creaked open, and Louise stepped through. The tension in his shoulders released at the sight of her. No matter how stressed he felt, she could always calm him down.

"Oh good," Louise said. "I'm glad you're here. I wanted to hear about yesterday's lecture," she said, sitting down in the second chair. Her polite smile transformed into a crinkled-nose grimace. She glanced around. "What on Earth is that smell?"

Dr. Pearce picked up the envelope. "That is the putrid smell of the Climate Council's foul Geology Committee."

"Aren't you *on* that committee, Alan?"

He huffed again in response.

Daxia gestured toward the cardboard container on his desk. "Would you like some of last week's Philly cheesesteak?"

Louise rolled her eyes, then looked back at Dr. Pearce. "Well, how was the lecture?"

He sighed, mumbling, "It was fine."

Louise turned to Daxia again, who raised her eyebrows and tilted her head toward the letter lying on top of the manila envelope. Louise leaned forward and skimmed the words, but Dr. Pearce snatched it up and chucked it into the trash. "The Geology Committee decided not to approve our Chicxulub research for publication."

Louise's voice softened. "Alan, I knew you would be—"

He lurched backward in surprise. "You knew about this?"

She frowned.

He raised his eyebrows. "I'll take that as a *yes?*"

"They called and told me this morning."

Dr. Pearce pursed his lips and rubbed his pant legs. He wished the committee would give him bad news without leaning on Louise to deliver it, but he felt an inner cringe when he remembered the last time the committee chair had given him bad news in person.

He cleared his throat. "Well, as you know, our simulations show that the meteorite that created the Chicxulub crater is not large enough to account for the amount of iridium dust in the K-Pg boundary layer. We still can't explain it, not by a long shot."

"Can't a computer simulate that?" Louise asked.

Dr. Pearce laughed. "Not a chance."

Daxia cleared her throat. "It could be simulated," she said, then explained, "The problem is that we need baseline data from the real world to build a model that we can then use for a simulation."

Dr. Pearce rifled through the papers on his desk and pulled out a photo of a core sample. He pointed to a gray layer on the otherwise brown slice. "That line that marks the end of the dinosaurs sixty-six million years ago. Our goal was to determine the timing and size of known impacts that deposited the K-Pg layer. That helped us devise a formula to estimate the amount of dust stirred up by an impact. Our civilization may need to do the same thing to cool this rock down someday. I hope future generations of humans evolve a bigger brain than the Geology Committee members have inside their skulls. I mean, where do they think this data is going to come from?"

Louise placed her hand on the edge of his desk. "Alan, not everyone on the committee agreed with the decision. Your lecture yesterday created quite the controversy."

He cocked his head. "My lecture?"

She nodded and pulled her smartphone from her purse to thumb through the news.

He looked to Daxia, expecting her to know.

Daxia shrugged. "Nobody told me anything."

"Ah, here it is," Louise said and showed them her phone.

"PROFESSOR SAYS MASS EXTINCTION THE ONLY WAY TO SAVE EARTH FROM HUMANS" read the article's headline.

"That is not what I said!" Dr. Pearce yelled at the phone screen. "They're sensationalizing so more people click it and they get more eyeballs on their advertisements."

Louise put the phone back in her purse, ignoring the accurate comment about the business model of modern so-called news. "The committee felt they would lose the public's trust if they discovered we were even investigating such an option."

"That's ridiculous! No one in their right mind—me included—would ever consider slamming a six-mile-wide asteroid like the

Chicxulub into the planet if there was a single human soul still on it. I am only trying to study past impacts to build a model in case their eruption plan fails. If they release too much volcanic gas, too much sunlight will be reflected. The Earth will turn into a popsicle! Astronomers have found so many frozen wastelands around other stars. That's basic planetary science, and the committee is choosing to —" He had to stop to catch his breath.

Louise leaned back in her chair. "Alan, it's only human nature that the committee does not want to acknowledge that their plan may fail."

"Well, one possibility of the model I am investigating is multiple small impacts in uninhabited areas, happening over thousands of years. This would continuously stir up dust that blocks sunlight and cools us down. It doesn't need to be one big one!" He sighed, dejected. "How are we going to finish the model now?"

Louise's voice hardened. "Alan, need I remind you that Dr. Lucas, your own department head, is on the Geology Committee?"

He grumbled.

She clasped her hands and leaned forward. "Of course, word got back to them. They did not appreciate you sharing what should have been confidential information during your class lecture."

"They are my findings, and I can share them when I please!" he protested.

Louise tilted her chin up. "There's more I haven't told you yet."

He leaned back in his chair and put his hands behind his head, waiting to hear it.

Louise looked at the food container then up at him. "Not now. I'll tell you over lunch. Now throw that disgusting mess away."

He stood from his desk and picked up the container. His finger poked through the grease-soaked bottom. He went right past his trash can and toward the door.

Louise pinched her nose and asked, "Alan, where are you going with that?"

"Dr. Lucas's office is a couple of doors down, and I hear he likes Philly cheesesteak."

Louise glared at him.

Dr. Pearce smirked. "What? He likes biology too," he held up the package, "and I expect there is plenty of organic material in here to study by now!"

# CHAPTER 15
# FAILURE

## MERIDIAN BRIDGE – CYCLE 0

Kaia felt woozy as she pulled herself along the gravity-free corridor toward the bridge. Enki was already near the doorway.

"Enki, don't wait for me, load the data and start the simulation as soon as you get there," she said.

"I will," he replied and disappeared down the ladder.

She raised her hand and examined the fine black soot covering her glove. She rubbed her fingers together and it sloughed off, floating through the air. A lump rose in her throat and she grabbed onto the railing again. The docking bay door shut behind her and Captain Apep came floating out.

"Kaia, we better get you to gravity," he said.

She nodded, doing her best not to throw up.

He took her arm and pulled her toward the ladder.

"Down you go," he said.

The gravity grew stronger with each step down. Her stomach settled as her feet touched the floor. She backed away from the ladder and leaned against the wall. Apep hopped down and turned to face her.

"You and Enki are leaving a trail," he said.

Kaia raised an eyebrow.

Captain Apep pointed to the wall. "Look behind you."

She spun around and saw a shadowy outline of her suit against the wall.

"I'm sorry," she said and felt her face flush.

"Don't worry about it at all," he reassured her. "We can clean it up later." His eyes followed dark marks on the floor leading to the Council table. "Shall we?"

Kaia nodded. "I hope we got enough data."

"Who needs data? You two saw what happened, firsthand."

She hesitated. "And what we saw was not according to plan."

"I'll gather the crew at the helm to brief them on what happened while you two get a look at the simulation."

"Understood," she said and stepped down into the bridge.

Kaia made her way to the conference table. She hung back to watch Enki as his hands flew over the glyphpad entering the data into a new simulation.

He looked at the simulation clock, then at a dial, and shook his head. "There. That is the one. It has the same magnitude and timing as the groundshake that caused the viewing platform we were standing on to collapse."

Kaia leaned back from what was about to happen.

Countless small lava fountains burst from the ground all over the city. Buildings in every district crumbled, falling into widening canyons as the ground sank with the release of pressure.

Enki shook his head. "It is all happening too fast. More fractures, more fountains, more lava in far too little time."

"Why should it matter how fast it happens?" Kaia asked, dreading the answer based on the worried look on Enki's face.

He paced around the table, analyzing the projection from every angle. "I told Councilor Horus we needed to be careful in our calculations. This is a delicate process, and the model is imperfect. We studied natural lava eruptions to create the estimates." He pointed to the shaft as it continued to collapse. "But boring through the crust and using a nuclear charge is not a natural event."

"Natural or not, why does extra lava matter?" she asked.

"The lava itself is not the trigger for climate change. The volcanic off-gassing is, and it is critical. Now, the timing and amount are incorrect."

Fountains continued to appear all over the simulated city. Enki touched the glyphpad to pause the simulation and pointed to the brown clouds coalescing above the lava. "The eruption needed to happen over thousands of cycles to minimize the volume of volcanic sulphate gases released at once."

She crossed her arms, growing impatient. "Where will this leave us, Enki?"

"You will not find the results satisfactory." he swiped back on the glyphpad. The projection flickered.

She gasped.

A white, desolate world replaced the vibrant planet. No forests, no oceans, no land.

"What happened?" she asked.

He pinched his fingers on the glyphpad and zoomed in to Puna.

Kaia leaned in for a closer look. Dark, slender shapes poked through the ice. "Skytower ruins? How is that possible?"

Enki examined the dark shapes. "The ecosystem, the rain, temperature changes, it all should have eroded Puna as the climate cooled."

"But your simulation doesn't show a healthy ecosystem," she pointed out.

He accessed the biodiversity graph from the glyphpad. The line representing the number of species on Nu dropped to zero.

Kaia felt her hopes turn to dust, like a chunk of burning kohl. "Because there is no ecosystem at all."

Enki leaned on the table. "If the simulation is accurate, the eruption will release thousands of cycles of volcanic sulphates in less than six months because the drill shaft failed too soon. Snow will fall in even the warmest places, causing more light to reflect back into space. The asteroids will stir up snow rather than dust. Even if there was dust, there would not be rain to clear the sulphates from the air."

"Our probes to other planets showed life can survive in ice, though," she offered.

Enki shook his head and peered across the white globe that was Nu. "Not on this snowball. The level of sulphates will also destroy the ultraviolet light blocking quality of the atmosphere that protects life from the sun's rays. Anything that may have survived the eruption will die due to radiation poisoning."

Darkness filled her mind. Those creatures in Councilor Hegira's video... no, all creatures, would go extinct. Forever. "Are you certain the eruptions will continue to multiply?"

He shot her a look that told her he thought she should know the answer already, then drew a symbol on the glyphpad. A view from the *Meridian*'s exterior cameras replaced the ice planet image.

Kaia counted over twenty lava fountains gushing from a long fissure stretching across downtown Puna. A skyline of fire dwarfed the tallest buildings, splitting the city in two. There was no sound, but their minds filled in the metallic screeching of buildings collapsing into one another amid the thunderous roar of the eruption.

Kaia fell back into a chair and shook her head. She wanted to cry. No, she wanted to scream.

Enki cleared his throat and said, "It is expanding faster than my updated simulation—"

More fountains erupted as the rift extended into the fields beyond the city. "What have we done, Enki? What have we done?"

"We have failed, Kaia." His face sank. "No, worse than failed. We turned runaway warming into runaway cooling. The climate change this brings will not stop until long after everything on the surface is extinct."

Kaia studied a temperature graph next to the simulation. "What's this?" she asked, noticing a near-vertical, downward slope on the line.

Enki nodded once. "That is the tipping point where the ice feedback cycle grows out of control. We need to act before then to prevent a catastrophic freeze awash with fatal radiation."

Kaia stood and hit the table. "Enki, we can't let this happen." She suddenly felt the eyes of the whole crew upon her, and she didn't care. "We have to do something!"

Captain Apep rushed over. "Have to do something about what?" he asked. Pakhet, Professor Thoth, and Dr. Khnum took tentative steps up to the table beside him.

Enki did not hesitate. "If this simulation is correct, and I believe that it is, the eruption will fail."

"And the asteroids will have no effect," Kaia added.

Dr. Khnum was the first crew member to speak up. "Fail? What do you mean fail? As in, we have to start over?"

Enki shook his head. "Starting is not the problem. Stopping is." He swiped on the glyphpad to switch back to the simulation. A white orb replaced the chart.

Professor Thoth approached the projection. "Is that a nanomech orb?"

Kaia sighed. "No, that is Nu, one hundred thousand cycles in the future."

The professor frowned. "That sure isn't what I'm used to seeing from this simulation." He looked to Enki. "Well?"

Enki launched into a second explanation. "The eruption is too strong, too soon. It is creating a high concentration of volcanic sulphates that will lead to runaway cooling. A deep freeze like that will cause the ozone layer's destruction. Asteroid impacts will do nothing. They may even make it worse."

Captain Apep put his hands on the table and leaned forward, examining the glaciers carving their way across Nu's surface.

Kaia slouched. "Everything will die, faster than it would have had we done nothing at all."

Captain Apep tapped both hands on the table. He made his way to the railing overlooking the big viewscreen at the center of the bridge. He tapped a command on his glyphpad and the surface of Nu appeared. A storm was forming over the sea east of Puna. The last great city was always a bright spot on their home, but now it was not the glow of life. It was the burning of destruction.

He turned away from the viewscreen and met each crew member's eyes. Saving Enki's for last. "Enki, how did this happen?"

Enki shook his head and clicked his tongue. "I told Councilor Horus that we needed more testing to validate the number of nanomechs required, and to test the structural integrity of the bore shaft. He always said we did not have time, that I had all the data I needed. I should have forced the issue, presented the numbers in a way that he would have known it, too."

Kaia raised her hands to her face and rubbed her eyes. She rested her elbows on the table and lowered her head between them. "We have failed." She held her eyes closed. "*I* have failed."

Captain Apep went to Kaia and placed his hand on her back. "That's not true, Kaia. This is not your fault."

She felt the pressure of years of effort being threatened, and blurted out, "You wouldn't understand! I dedicated my life to those poor animals below. You've only spent the last few cycles on this project, and only as a fly boy hauling rocks around in space."

Pakhet gasped. Dr. Khnum and Professor Thoth looked down at their feet.

Captain Apep's face chilled.

Kaia saw the expression spread across his face and shirked away at her own words. "I'm sorry. I didn't mean that. I just... I don't know what to do next."

Captain Apep took a seat next to her. "Kaia, you don't have to know; we'll work on this together. We have the best and the brightest on this ship for a reason." He smiled at Ra, Nef, and Mirik now making their way to the Council table. "Nobody came this far to give up now."

She looked up and took a deep breath to collect her thoughts. "Enki, can you add ecosystem and species data to your simulation? I want to know what species have the best chance of survival. Maybe we can figure out a way to prevent a total extinction."

Enki furrowed his brow in thought then said, "Yes, I believe that is possible."

"Good. So, what do we do? Try to start another eruption?"

Captain Apep cleared his throat. "I like where you're going, but I recommend we slow down just a bit. Enki, how sure are you sure about the total extinction?"

Enki, unphased by the grim projection, said, "99.3 percent chance, or greater."

"That's pretty high," said the captain. "But that does leave some room for the simulation to be wrong."

"That is a .7 percent possibility," Enki confirmed.

Captain Apep saw the orange glow on Nef's face when she leaned over the main viewscreen where Puna was burning. "Next question: how long until the eruption ends? That seems to be the next logical milestone we can use to verify that your simulation is correct."

Enki swirled his finger on the glyphpad, back through time on the simulation until all the ice melted, past the impacts, right to the point where the eruption's glow faded. He glanced down at the datestamp. "One hundred and six cycles, but we should be able to verify the trend in less than a week."

"One hundred and six? That's a flash compared to the five hundred cycles we expected," Captain Apep noted.

Kaia nodded. "We will need to come back before that."

The captain knocked once on the table. "I suggest we start by telling Councilor Hegira and Councilor Horus."

Kaia scowled. "Council Horus's caution-to-the-wind approach to science is part of the reason we're in this situation in the first place. Nothing got priority unless it also served to pad his bank account."

"My bank account?!" Councilor Horus's voice echoed around the bridge. They all looked over to the ladder and saw him lowering himself off the last rung. His robes were a wrinkled mess as he huffed toward the projection. Councilor Hegira was a few steps ahead of him, nearing the table already.

Enki glared at Councilor Horus. "As Kaia said, we have failed." He proceeded to explain the results of the simulation in detail, ending with his hypothesis of what went wrong and why. "The shaft collapse doomed the eruption." He looked at Councilor Horus. "We should have been more cautious. We also should have taken more measurements, as they would have shown we needed to reinforce the drill shaft."

Councilor Horus glared right back, not missing the accusation in Enki's words. "Yes, thank you for that retrospective genius, Enki." He glowered at Kaia. "And what do you propose we do?"

"Why are you asking me?" She pointed to Enki. "He is the one who could have prevented this in the first place if you'd listened." Enki balled his hands into fists at his side.

Councilor Horus narrowed his eyes. "Because you, Kaia, are the one people listen to around here," he said, waving his arms over the crew. "Whether I like it or not."

Kaia started to say something when Councilor Hegira raised her hand.

"All of you, please." She faced Enki. "So, what do we do to fix this?"

"My calculations show the cooling will reach a tipping point, that much is certain. After that, there will be nothing we can do."

Hope tinged Councilor Hegira's voice, "So, are you saying there is a chance of success if we act soon?"

"Yes, but that assumes we find another solution. The asteroids will not be enough to turn this around, even if we impact them all at once."

Hegira nodded. "What do you propose?"

"I do not know yet," said Enki. "I need time to study the data, time to plan. Perhaps we could recalibrate the impacts or create more asteroids."

Councilor Horus's laugh was dripping with sarcasm. "And where would you propose we get more asteroids? The *Meridian* isn't a tugship, you know."

The crew remained silent. Kaia could feel the tension in the room.

Councilor Hegira spoke. "Well... there was another plan. An earlier Council rejected it." She raised her eyebrows at Councilor Horus. "Perhaps it is time to tell them, Horus."

He shook his head and whispered, "Absolutely not..."

Councilor Hegira rested her elbows on the table and leaned forward. She looked straight at Enki, then Kaia. "There may be another option for phase two."

Councilor Horus jumped to his feet, causing his chair to tip over behind him and hit the floor with a crash. Fuming, he turned to Councilor Hegira. "You cannot be serious."

Everyone at the table was murmuring. Kaia assumed they were asking themselves the same thing she was: *What does she mean?*

Councilor Hegira stood. "Everyone, back to your stations. We will reconvene tomorrow." She addressed Kaia and Enki. "I will see the two of you in the geology lab." She turned to Captain Apep. "Actually, you too, Captain. The three of us have much to discuss."

# CHAPTER 16
# COMBINATION

## GEOLOGY LAB - AD CYCLE 0

Kaia noticed the way Captain Apep held out his arm to help Councilor Hegira down the step into Enki's lab then guided her to the table at the center. He must have grown up with grandparents around, she thought and filed the observation away in a place that would soon be overflowing with thoughts of Captain Apep.

Enki stepped up beside her, and she whispered to him, "What do you think Councilor Hegira has up her sleeve?"

"I cannot be sure," Enki said. "But I am certain you heard the rumors of another plan, too."

"I did, but no one seemed to know the details. 'Unacceptable' was the word I always heard used to describe it."

Councilor Hegira reached for the table to steady herself as she sat on the stool in front of the glyphpad. Hegira would not explain herself to any of them, because she revealed so little of herself after all these cycles, even to Kaia.

Councilor Hegira began drawing symbols that none of them recognized. The glyphpad beeped in acknowledgment, and Hegira looked to the doorway where Kaia and Enki still stood.

"Come over here and join me and the captain."

Captain Apep stepped aside and gestured for them to stand next to him. Kaia and Enki took their places at the lab table. The light field hovering over the surface morphed into columns and rows of numbers. The matrix extended beyond the borders of the projection.

Enki leaned forward, clicking his tongue as he analyzed the image. "This appears to be a simulation dataset, but a very old one. It is from a time before we could visualize this amount of information in real time."

Captain Apep asked, "What is it simulating?"

Enki snapped his fingers. "I have seen something like this before. It was in geology class at school, many cycles ago," he put one hand on his hip as he leaned against the table. "There are several empty data cells. It looks unfinished."

Councilor Hegira nodded. "Enki is right."

Enki swirled his finger on the glyphpad, and the numbers scrolled faster. They all watched as his eyes scanned the symbols filling the air. It seemed endless, but then the matrix started thinning out. Enki remained focused on the numbers that remained, his face contorted with intense concentration.

The scrolling stopped, and Enki squeezed his eyes shut. He rubbed circles into his temples.

Kaia tapped him on the shoulder. "Enki, what is this simulating?"

He backed away from the table and sighed. "This is a model of the asteroid impact that happened on Nu tens of millions of cycles ago."

Kaia turned to Councilor Hegira. "What do you expect us to do with this old dataset?"

The councilor looked up at the data. "I expect you to complete it, of course. At one time, there were those on the Council who thought our best course of action was to mimic this, shall we say, *large* impact event. But they were in the minority, and they put all our resources toward the eruption plan paired with smaller impacts. Perhaps something in here can save us from failure."

Kaia felt her mind spin. "But that asteroid was enormous. What would we do with an asteroid the size of a city?"

Councilor Hegira took a deep breath. "Kaia, my dear, what did you learn about this ancient asteroid impact?"

Kaia wracked her brain. "That it caused massive destruction—" she paused in thought, then it hit her, "that led to an explosion of life."

"Yes." The councilor nodded.

"But," Kaia's voice hardened, "only after it killed seventy percent of organisms on Nu."

"Is that not better than what is going to happen now, Kaia?" Councilor Hegira offered. "And what else happened in that explosion of life?"

Kaia sank onto the stool. "Us. We evolved in the period of climatic stability created by the destruction." She saw Captain Apep's face turn a bright shade of pink.

He raised his voice. "Councilor, have you gone mad? We could not get an eruption right. What makes you think we should even think of attempting destruction on that scale? And where would we find the time to get asteroids that size?"

Kaia saw his question hit then bounce off Councilor Hegira and realized the councilor was several steps ahead of them.

Hegira pulled up the exterior camera feed and zoomed it in. "Here are your big asteroids," she proclaimed.

Kaia saw the field of one hundred shimmering stones. "Of course."

Captain Apep put both hands on the table to examine the stones up close. "Of course, what?"

Kaia made a scooping motion with her hands. "The nanomechs created those from the cityships." She turned to him. "Asteroid guts, remember?" His puzzled expression indicated he wasn't following. She saw the gears turning in Enki's head, though. *He gets it.* "Enki, would it work?"

"Yes, it is conceivable."

"What are we talking about here, Kaia?" Captain Apep asked.

"We could use the nanomechs to create a single large asteroid from some of these smaller ones. We could recreate the natural impact event from seventy million cycles ago." She turned and swiped on the glyphpad to make the simulation matrix reappear. "Enki? Can we fill in these gaps?"

"This model is almost two hundred cycles old, and technology has made huge strides since then. We know an impact of that size happened, and we know that it changed the climate. But the data is inconclusive at best. Geologists stopped studying it to focus on the eruption as the primary initiative. I would need to review the climate models from that period. Oh, and we would need to review the biodiversity estimates, as well as the—"

Kaia put her hand on his shoulder and squeezed. "Short answer, Enki?"

He paused then said, "Yes, we can fill in the missing data."

She turned back to Captain Apep. "See? We know more about geology now, more about biology. We could mine the data from our archives and complete this simulation."

Councilor Hegira nodded. "There is no *could* Kaia. We *must*."

"Yes, we *must*." Kaia stared at the projection, trying to imagine how one could boil the intricacies of Jacana evolution down to numbers on a spreadsheet.

"You realize that if we do this, the wildlife you have spent your life studying will die, Kaia," said Captain Apep. "Worse, we will be the ones who finish it off."

Kaia sighed and started to speak, but Enki held up his finger. "Wait, you need to see this again."

Kaia crossed her arms as he went to the glyphpad.

Enki drew a few symbols, and the Nu they recognized appeared above the table. He pressed down. Lava poured onto the surface again, and ice caps began to form.

She watched in horror as the ice spread from the poles all the way down to the equator, consuming everything.

The white orb that was once a planet hung in the air above the table. Enki explained, "If we do not try again, nothing will survive."

Kaia trudged past the shelves upon shelves of rock samples in Enki's lab. Their cold lifelessness gave her a chilling preview of a Nu devoid of life. She slumped onto a stool and uncrossed her arms. "If we can't figure out another plan, rocks like these will be all that remains."

"But if we try the bigger asteroid plan, how do we know any species will survive?" Captain Apep asked.

Enki swiped the simulation away, and the matrix returned. "That is why we must fill in these empty cells—to know for sure. We also need to add data for the current level of volcanic sulphates from our failed eruption."

Captain Apep knelt in front of Kaia. He placed a hand on her knee. "What do you think?"

She turned the situation over in her mind and tried to shove away the gnawing dread away. Another explosion of diversity might happen if they stabilized the climate. It happened before and it could happen again if they succeeded. She shrugged. "Unless Enki has another solution, then… we don't have a choice."

Councilor Hegira rose to her feet. "Kaia, I want you to lead this new effort. You have always been the face of our plans to save the planet."

Kaia jumped up, straightening her back. "Yes, Councilor."

"The crew trusts you," Councilor Hegira added. She looked at the matrix one last time. "Assuming Enki's simulations return positive results, the scope of this plan will be frightening, especially in light of the failure of the eruption. You, no—*we*, must depend on that trust if we are to convince them."

"I understand," Kaia said and looked at the floor.

"Good." Councilor Hegira shuffled toward the door. She stopped and put her hand on Kaia's shoulders. "My child, this is your opportunity."

"Opportunity?" Kaia frowned. "Creating a mass extinction of the world is not the kind of opportunity I was hoping for next."

Hegira took her hand off Kaia's shoulder and began to walk away. "It is up to you to redefine that legacy. Are you here to save a few species, or to save life itself?"

Kaia took a deep breath.

Hegira resumed her departure. "Enki, make haste on your analysis.

We need to know if this can work, and soon," she said, waving goodbye.

The door slammed shut, leaving the three of them staring at each other in silence.

Kaia faced the projection, then looked to Enki. "What do we need to do first?"

Enki reached over to a shelf and pulled off a shining silver stone. He tossed it back and forth between his hands a few times then handed it to Captain Apep.

"What is this?" the captain asked.

"Iridium. It is what composes the small phase two asteroids," Enki said between swipes on the glyphpad. "Very heavy, as you can see. We'll need a way to move a lot of it once the nanomechs combine them."

"Like a tugship?"

"Yes."

Captain Apep smiled wide. "You asked just the right person."

"I know," Enki said. "I read everyone's profile, as they asked us to do, and I know you were an asteroid tugship captain prior to this assignment."

Captain Apep chuckled, now tossing the stone between his own hands. "Of course you did. I'll see what I can find in the abandoned mining depots out there, Enki.

He strutted over to another table and rubbed his hands together before setting to work. Kaia could tell he loved a good challenge. The old asteroid mining companies guarded their survey data, lest the competition discover the richest deposits without paying for the expensive multi-cycle exploratory work.

She turned to Enki. "What biological data do you need to complete the old model?"

"I need numbers from previous mass extinctions. Not just animals, but also plants. I need biodiversity estimates, species that are likely to survive, and anything else you can pull from the last few hundred cycles of research."

"On it." Kaia went to a smaller table in the lab. She drew a symbol on the glyphpad, and projections of animals large and small filled the air in front of her. The habitat and tolerances of known species were well-studied areas. Generations of scientists explored the question of which animals would survive the climatic destruction wrought by Jacana industry.

Enki turned back to the table at the center. "I am going to pick up where the old model left off with our updated knowledge of Nu's geology."

Captain Apep rubbed his face. "If this works, I'm not looking forward to telling the crew what it means for our mission."

Kaia leaned toward him. "You don't think they'll be able to put aside personal concerns to save our home?"

"They will, but they won't like it. Maybe we can keep some of the details to a smaller, need-to-know group."

"There are too few of us to keep secrets from one another." She turned to the simulation and squared her shoulders. "I have been the face of this project since I was a child. I should be the one to tell the crew."

# CHAPTER 17
# OPPORTUNITY

## CAFÉ LOGAN – 2034 CE

Alan held open the door to Café Logan for Louise and Daxia. They thanked him as they stepped inside.

A cheery young man behind the counter adjusted his hat and greeted them. "Welcome, what can I get you today?"

Alan stepped up to the counter and winked at Louise before turning back to the cashier. "I'll have a Philly cheesesteak."

Louise was next. "I'll have a southwest turkey wrap," she turned to Daxia, "and what would you like, dear?"

Daxia shook her head. "Oh no, you don't need to get my lunch."

Louise smiled. "Please, it's the least I can do to apologize for this oaf." She nudged Alan. "You've put up with him longer than any of his other teaching assistants."

Daxia laughed. "Well, okay, I'll take the wrap too. But no need to apologize. I've worked with him long enough to understand when he's putting on a show."

Alan turned around, a fake stern expression on his face. "Hey, you two, I'm right here."

They all shared a hearty laugh.

Alan pointed to an empty table in the corner by the window. "I'm going to go snag us the best seat in the house."

"Thanks, Alan." Louise said and held her phone to the payment pad.

Daxia watched Alan walk toward the table, steadying himself every few steps by grabbing chair backs. "He reminds me of my father."

"You haven't given us an update on him in a while. How is he doing?" asked Louise.

Daxia looked down. "Not well, I'm afraid. I should have told Alan weeks ago but can't bring myself to do it."

"Tell him what, dear?" Louise asked with a frown.

She sighed. "I—I got a call from his longtime friend, Jian. My father is not doing well but is afraid to tell me."

Louise frowned. "I'm sorry to hear that."

Daxia looked up. "Jian thinks I should come back to China to look after him. He even found me an opportunity to be the excavation director on the Yixian Formation."

Louise's face lit up. "The Yixian? That sounds like a dream job, Daxia! Most paleontologists would give up everything for a chance like that."

Daxia mustered a smile. "I know, but I hate to leave Dr. Pearce and his research. His work feels more important than studying all the bird fossils buried in the Yixian."

"Don't say that. All scientific research is important, even if it isn't obvious in the moment," Louise said.

"Perhaps, but I doubt ancient birds are going to help us save the world."

Louise smiled. "Some of the biggest discoveries have come from the most unexpected places."

The cashier cleared his throat. "Your card, ma'am."

"Oh, thank you!" Louise said and stuffed the card back into her purse. She turned back to Daxia. "For the record, I think you should go."

Daxia smiled in return but said nothing.

Louise put her arm around Daxia as they walked to the table.

.  .  .

Alan patted the table. "There you are. I was beginning to think you'd both abandoned me like the council."

Louise rubbed his head as she sat down next to him in the booth. "Hush, you."

Daxia slid into the seat opposite them.

Alan smoothed his white tuft of hair and crossed his arms. "So, Louise, you said you had more to say about the news from the Climate Council?"

"Yes, great news," she beamed. "The UN invited me to be the chairperson for the Relocation Committee Conference in Matheran, India!"

Alan exclaimed, "That's wonderful! It is about time they recognized your brilliance!" He uncrossed his arms and gave her a hug.

She held up a finger. "But wait, that is not all."

He leaned back in the booth. "Oh?"

She smirked. "I played hard to get."

Daxia laughed along with Alan.

"Hard to get, eh? How so?"

"Well," she leaned forward on the table, "I told them I happen to know the world's pre-eminent geologist."

Alan smiled.

"And I reminded them what is near India."

"Nepal? The Himalayas?" he offered.

"Try again."

Alan rubbed his chin.

"I'll give you a hint," said Louise. "What is near the central east coast, *geologically*?"

Daxia raised her eyebrows. She held her hands together then, mimicking a rumbling sound, moved them up and spread them apart in the shape of an oval.

Alan felt a jolt of energy when he recognized the cloud shape Daxia was making with her hands. "The Deccan Traps! The second largest lava flood basalt eruption ever discovered! Well, after the ones exoplanetary geologists have found on Mars."

Louise nodded. "They want you to go with me to India and study them, since an eruption is still the Council's primary solar radiation reduction strategy for reversing climate change. They would like to know precisely when it occurred and its duration."

He sighed. "A trip to India would be fun, but..."

Louise put a finger to his mouth. "Shh. I knew what you'd say to that. I'm not done."

He closed his mouth.

"I negotiated something with the Relocation Committee, too."

He tilted his head to the side. "Relocation?"

"Well, do you know who is paying to relocate people affected by the rise in sea levels?"

He nodded. "Oil companies, with their taxes, and through the nose, I've heard."

"And one such company is conducting oil drilling exploration off the coast of Mumbai."

"You don't mean..."

"I do. They want to stay in the committee's good graces, so they offered to fly you and Daxia out to their largest ship, the *Finality*."

His eyes lit up. "Don't tell me you asked them to let us visit the..." he lost his words out of excitement.

"I did," she said with a grin.

He leaned over and gave her a big kiss with his bear hug. Alan held her tight for an extra moment then leaned back, "My Louise. You always drove a hard bargain."

Daxia raised her hand. "I am not following. What is off the coast of Mumbai?"

Louise turned to her. "Ages ago, France discovered a strange landform on the seafloor during marine surveys."

"Are we talking about the Shiva structure?" Daxia asked Alan. "In the Arabian Sea?"

He nodded. "We know there is a depression of some sort, but no one is sure what created it."

"How will another sonar survey help your research, though?" Daxia asked.

"It won't, but the *Finality* can do far more than sonar, it's a drillship."

Daxia sat up. "That means—"

Alan raised his hands, still unable to believe his luck. Or rather, unable to believe his wife's negotiating skills. "It means we can pull up cores and look for shocked quartz deep below the seabed!"

Daxia clapped. "We can determine if it is an impact site, and if so, measure the amount of iridium in the strata and the width of the K-Pg boundary layer in samples of seafloor strata."

He nodded. "That may be the missing piece of the puzzle. We can finish the impact model!"

Louise grasped Alan's hand. "Remember, you need to help them finish the eruption model by studying the Deccan Traps as well, or this whole deal is off."

He looked up. "Yes, of course. We'll need two teams. Louise, can you lead the one to the Traps?"

Louise glanced at Daxia with concern. "Will you keep an eye on him? He gets seasick, you know."

"Yes, I will do my best," Daxia said and laughed.

Louise turned back to Alan. "Then yes, you let me know what you're looking for and give me your best team so I can handle the Deccan Traps. But you'll owe me."

Alan wrapped his arms around her again. "Thank you! Thank you!"

A server walked toward the table, balancing three plates on her arms.

"Food is here," Alan said.

The server first set the wraps down in front of Louise and Daxia. "Be careful, this plate is hot," she said as she sat the Philly cheesesteak in front of Alan.

Alan sized up the sandwich and felt full without touching it. "I can't eat this. My mind is racing with all the planning we need to do."

He noticed that Daxia's smile had faded, and she was not touching her sandwich either. "What's wrong?" he asked.

Louise put her hand on his shoulder. "Alan, I believe Daxia has some news for you."

Daxia looked up at Louise, then at Alan.

"Go on, dear," Louise urged.

Daxia hesitated. "M-my father's condition has worsened. He needs me back in China."

Alan felt a nudge from Louise. He put on his best concerned smile for Daxia. "I'm sorry to hear that, I hope he is going to be okay."

She nodded. "He just needs someone to look after him. But I hate that I have to leave—"

"Don't you worry about me, I'll be fine. In fact, I'll make some calls, see if I can find you a good teaching spot," he offered.

Louise spoke up. "Daxia has already found something." She smiled at Daxia. "Go on, tell him."

"A family friend has found me an opportunity to manage the excavations on the Yixian Formation."

Alan could not contain his excitement. "That's amazing, Daxia!"

The pained expression had not left her face. "And... I will need to leave before the summer is over."

He waved his hand and thought about what Louise would say. "Oh, that is no big deal. I will have my hands full with the findings from the Shiva structure, anyway." He slouched as the realization set in. "Will you at least be able to come with us to India?"

"When is the trip?" Daxia asked.

Louise pulled out her phone. "The conference is two months away, and the *Finality* will be at the Shiva structure in six weeks for a one-week trip."

Alan started to worry. "Six weeks? That doesn't leave much time to get ready!"

"That's why you need to start your medical evaluation soon and give them a few exact coordinates so they can plan well ahead of time."

"I will," Alan said, turning back to Daxia. "So, are you up for one last adventure?"

A smile widened across her face. "Yes, I'll go. My new position starts in September, and I have an aunt who has agreed to look after my father until then."

"Wonderful! It's settled." Alan clasped his hands. "It will be just like Mexico. The Council won't be able to ignore us after this! We're going to solve the most, dare I say, impactful mystery on the planet!"

# CHAPTER 18
# FOUR STRIKES

## MERIDIAN BRIDGE - CYCLE 0

Kaia cooled her hands on the mug of chilled karkade tea Captain Apep handed her as the crew gathered once more. The all day and night data crunching reminded her of her final project at school some ten cycles earlier, which felt like a lifetime ago. Now, she was once again at the Council table ready to share important news with the crew. At the opposite end sat Councilors Hegira and Horus. Captain Apep stood against the wall, watching First Officer Ra make his way over from the helm. Along the table to her left sat Dr. Khnum and Pakhet.

While Kaia swiped through her notes, waiting for the remaining crew to gather, Dr. Khnum whispered to Pakhet, "Do you know anything about this other plan?"

Pakhet shook her head and whispered back, "Nothing for certain, though I was checking the engine readouts when I heard Captain Apep ask First Officer Ra how hard we could push the lightdrive before it would give out."

"You don't think they're planning to use the ship to..." Dr. Khnum's voice faded as his mouth fell open.

"No, they would never," Pakhet said, leaning away. Her gaze flitted toward Kaia. "Well, maybe."

Kaia felt the apprehension radiating from Pakhet. *You'll know soon,* she thought.

Professor Thoth walked by to take his seat, but first tapped Kaia on the shoulder. "Mirik said you're going to ask for volunteers to stay behind with more nanomechs to terraform Nu. I have no one to meet up with on Duat and would love the opportunity."

Kaia set the viewpad down. "Thank you, but that won't be necessary, Professor."

"Well, just so you know, I am up for any plan." He bowed.

Councilor Hegira stood, and everyone hushed. Professor Thoth took his seat, and everyone directed their attention to the councilor.

"Thank you all for coming again. We have continued to monitor the eruption below and—" she looked down at the table for a moment, "we can confirm Enki's simulation is accurate. The eruption will fail."

The crew seemed to lower their heads in unison.

"There is an alternative, though." Councilor Hegira gestured to Kaia. "Have you completed your analysis?"

Kaia thought about the data they'd gathered and what she was about to tell the group. Captain Apep gave her a reassuring nod.

She pulled her shoulders back and clenched her jaw. She picked up the viewpad and held it over her stomach. Councilor Hegira's trust gave her more confidence than she knew existed within her. "Yes, Councilor. Enki, Captain Apep, and I stayed up all night working on the simulation. It's based on very old data, but we have filled in the gaps to the best of our ability."

The crew sat in silence, exchanging nervous glances.

Kaia drew a circle on the glyphpad and pressed the center. Above the table, the rotating fern leaf flashed off, replaced by an image of Nu. Angry black clouds poured over the planet as the eruption raged amid the remains of Puna.

"First," she began, "I believe everyone needs to understand a bit of Nu's history."

She made eye contact with a few crew members.

"Once life began on Nu, it has never stopped evolving. It is part of the planet's story, from the first organic molecules to the first single-celled organisms, to the complex animals, and ultimately to us, the Jacana. The strand of life has remained unbroken for billions of cycles. All life is connected, dependent on one another, originating from one another."

She looked down for a moment and took a deep breath. Anxiety mixed with the same wonder she always felt when thinking about the mysteries of their home world.

"That unbroken chain of life, though, is not without some close calls." A line graph appeared on the projection, marred by a handful of deep valleys. "This line represents the number of species on Nu for the last 350 million cycles." She pointed to the first dip. "Each valley represents a massive die-off, often because of climate change driven by geological forces. Mountain range uplifts or volcanic eruptions that would make our eruption look like the old decorative fountain in Xi Shi Plaza."

Professor Thoth raised his hand.

"Yes, Professor?" Kaia asked.

He pointed to the final decline. "That last extinction was caused by—"

She cut him off. "Us," she stated. "We caused it, yes. It took us too long to admit it to ourselves, but we did. Our dependence on kohl changed the chemistry of the atmosphere and led to runaway global warming. That, as you know, is what the Council designed the Dawn Project to repair, starting with the phase one eruption, followed by the phase two small asteroid impacts. As Councilor Hegira said, the plan as it exists will fail... but there may be one other option for us to save Nu."

Councilor Horus tapped his fingers on the table. Kaia wished she could move along faster, but still felt the *why* was just as important as the *how*.

She pointed to the mass extinction on the graph prior to the Jacana-made one. "Something happened about seventy million cycles ago, before any Jacana or any recognizable ancestor had evolved. Nothing on

Nu caused this mass extinction, though." A swipe on her viewpad revealed an elevation map showing a deep depression on the surface. "It was a massive asteroid impact."

Dr. Khnum shrieked and turned to Pakhet. "You were right! They're going to ram the *Meridian* into the surface to create another eruption!"

"I didn't say that!" Pakhet shouted. "Kaia, all I told him was that I heard Captain Apep and First Officer Ra discussing the lightdrive."

Kaia shot a pointed look at Captain Apep. He shirked away a bit and mouthed, "*Sorry.*" She returned her attention to Pakhet and put on a comforting look. "We will do nothing of the sort, Pakhet."

Councilor Hegira spoke up. "Kaia, let's jump to the part where you're proposing what we do." She glared at Dr. Khnum. "Or some of us might die of suspense."

Dr. Khnum huffed and threw his shoulders back. "Yes, get on with it."

Kaia looked down the table. "Councilor Hegira shared a two-hundred-cycle-old impact model for this very crater. It was part of early studies of the mass extinction. However, whoever started the model never finished it."

She tapped the viewpad and switched to a seafloor view of the crater, then zoomed in so everyone could get a better look. "The asteroid that excavated this crater is the same one that led to a mass extinction. After that, the climate stabilized again, a period that led to the evolution of our species and to the rise of our civilization."

Several crew members leaned in to look at the crater.

Nef was the first to speak up. "Pardon my simple question, but why won't the smaller asteroids we already have work?"

"That's a good question." Kaia turned to Enki. "Can you explain the completed model to the crew?"

As Enki made his way to the end of the table next to Kaia, Councilor Horus scoffed. "Whoever came up with it must have been a crackpot. The Council rejected these dangerous plans long before any of us were alive. They saw what a waste of resources it was before they finished the model."

Kaia shot Horus a stern look then stepped away so Enki could respond. The councilor's behavior during this crisis might not have surprised her, but that didn't make it any less annoying. His leadership skills were atrocious.

"You are correct, Councilor Horus," Enki said. "As Kaia explained, the Council chose not to complete the old model." He held the viewpad up and tapped the glyphpad. The projection changed to an incomplete three-dimensional matrix. He shuffled his feet, then looked up at the crew.

"But the scientist who devised it was not a crackpot, they were brilliant." He glared at Councilor Horus then turned back to the crew. "We made some significant updates to the model by filling in gaps in the data."

Councilor Horus leaned forward with more than a hint of interest now. "And...?"

Enki lowered the viewpad. "It works."

Enki pointed to an empty section of the matrix. "This missing data represents the current biome of life." He tapped his glyphpad, and numbers began to appear in the empty slots where he pointed. "Thanks to Kaia and generations of biologists before her, we now understand the ecosphere's role in planetary renewal." The empty section filled in.

He pointed to another sparse part of the projection. He tapped his glyphpad again and more numbers appeared. "This section represents the geologic processes set in motion by an impact." He glanced around at the crew. "The simulation now incorporates plate tectonics, volcanic eruptions, earthquakes, erosion, and the rise and fall of entire mountain ranges combined with the previous model used for the Puna eruption."

He tapped his glyphpad again, and the data filled the rest of the empty sections. He pointed to a few of them. "This section is climate on a global scale." He pointed to another newly completed section. "This section is the ocean temperature, chemistry, and tides."

One section remained empty. "This section represents us, our entire society and its impact on the climate."

Enki drew a symbol on his glyphpad, and the empty spot

representing the Jacana impact filled in with data. "The model is now complete."

He tapped the viewpad and a view of the Jacana-made asteroid field appeared above the table.

"The answer is simple. These asteroids are too small now. Even if we sent all one hundred down at once, it is not possible for them to throw up enough dust to affect the long-term climate. We need something bigger."

Councilor Horus waved his hand in the air. "They abandoned it for a reason, you know. The conditions that existed seventy million years ago were nothing compared to what we have today. Not to mention the damage from our failed eruption. What makes you think one large impact would fix all this?"

Enki shook his head. "You're right, one impact would not be enough to fix the damage from our failure." He paused and set the viewpad down on the table. "We need four."

"*Four* impacts?!" Councilor Horus slammed his fists on the table and shouted. "You're *crazy*! You've completely lost it."

Enki nodded and tapped on the viewpad screen. Four crystal-shaped asteroids appeared, hovering above the table, each larger than the next. "Based on our simulations, this shape seems to work best, and I have identified impact locations. The largest asteroid needs to be 21,120 cubits in diameter."

Professor Thoth shouted, "That's the size of Puna!"

"It is, but it is also the best way to stir up enough dust to undo our damage. Not only will that dust shroud Nu and lower its surface temperature, but it will remove the sulphates from the atmosphere over time to create long-term stability once the dust settles."

Councilor Horus rolled his eyes. "And where are we going to get asteroids that big?"

Enki tapped the viewpad again, and the projection returned to the asteroid field. He nodded to Councilor Horus. "They are already here, though it will require some work."

Kaia noticed the councilor's body language change from frustration to... was it interest? "Councilor Horus, can you configure your nanomechs to recombine one hundred asteroids into four large ones?" she asked.

He let out a belly laugh. "Of course they can, but you can't be serious! This is your great idea? Our only hope?" He swiveled his chair to face Councilor Hegira. "They put this plan aside the first time around, because it's ludicrous! We're going to leave a bigger mass extinction in the fossil record than anything Nu has seen before! Are we going to destroy the world to *possibly* save it?"

Kaia offered her thoughts. "The chain of life has existed for billions of cycles. We must not stand back and do nothing while the legacy of life on Nu ends because of our mistakes."

Councilor Horus opened his mouth, then closed it.

Councilor Hegira glared at him. "We must do this, *Councilor*. Unless you have another plan you haven't told us about?"

Kaia saw him collapse into himself, and the timbre of his voice softened.

"Of course," he said with a bow toward Councilor Hegira. "The nanomechs are at your service, Kaia. If I may ask, though," he turned to Enki, "how long will the recovery take?"

"I am still finishing my simulation, but... the current range is between sixty and seventy million years, similar to the original large impact that caused the prior mass extinction."

"And how will we know it worked? We'll be on Duat, long dead by then, I should hope."

Kaia sighed. "You're right, Councilor, we can't know for sure if it worked. We'll only have one shot."

"We have one checkpoint, though," said Enki. "Based on our simulations, the ideal time to start the new phase two would be 107 cycles from now versus the 500 cycles we planned. That is when the current process will stabilize to some extent, yet is still before it reaches the tipping point." Enki looked to First Officer Ra. "Is your algorithm complete?"

First Officer Ra sat up straight, seeming a little flustered about giving a presentation without notice. "Yes," he looked around the table. "Captain Apep found tugships at an abandoned mining depot in the asteroid belt. We will travel there using the lightdrive, and I have made modifications to our travel speed that would allow 107 cycles to pass on Nu in just a few hours for us. We will also change our trip to Duat to ensure that our arrival remains as close to the *Montu's* as possible. I still need to work out those details."

Nef and Mirik exchanged a glance, then Mirik spoke up. "I'm sorry, but I want to know what I'm signing up for here. How can you be sure we'll still show up on Duat at the right time, Ra? There is a big difference between 500 cycles and 107 cycles."

"Ah," First Officer Ra acknowledged. "My lightdrive modifications have allowed for greater precision in approaching the speed of light. If we were to travel *at* the speed of light, time would effectively stop for anyone on the ship while it continues on outside. But if we control how *close* to the speed of light we travel, we can control the time dilation with a high degree of accuracy, so we can arrive at the asteroid field, let the nanomechs do their work, and start the new impact plan at the right time. We'll then adjust the trip to Duat so we still arrive at the same time."

Enki jumped in to add, "And at 107 cycles in the future, we'll be able to confirm whether the eruption stabilized as predicted. If it did, we can assume the overall simulation is correct, and initiate the four impacts as planned. If it did not, well, we still have time to reassess."

Nef jabbed Mirik's arm. "What they're saying is we have to go fast to go slow, just not as slow as we had planned."

Mirik crossed his arms with a smug grin. "By all means, carry on, then."

Kaia noticed him bump Nef's elbow in agreement.

Councilor Hegira stood, and everyone quieted down. "Thank you, First Officer Ra, for your studious work on the lightdrive to make our alternative solution possible. And thank you, Enki, for completing this old simulation model. Last, thank you, Kaia, for bringing everyone together and sharing it with us." She looked around the table. "Raise your hand if you're in favor of pursuing this plan."

Kaia tensed up, unsure how the members of the crew were going to respond. A few exchanged glances, but no one moved. She took a deep breath and smiled.

"I've spent my entire life trying to save many of the species that will die with these impacts. Species like the phara that my parents..." she felt familiar tears welling up in her eyes. "Species that my parents gave their lives trying to save." The projection faded away to a flat video.

An image of a baby phara hung in the air, cradled in a pair of suited arms. The video panned up, and a raging torrent of water and broken trees raced toward the camera. The image switched to an unmistakable face. Tears poured down his cheeks, then came a voice. "Kaia, you can save the world from us." There was a crushing sound, and the projection went black.

Many crew members looked away, unable to witness the video's conclusion.

Kaia pressed her glyphpad, and snowball Nu appeared. White, desolate, dead. "My parents gave their lives, and I have dedicated my own to trying to save our home. All of our sacrifices, all of your sacrifices, all the sacrifices of our entire civilization will be in vain —*everything* will die if we do nothing."

She saw a collective grief sweep across the crew's faces followed by a montage of feelings as each one processed her words: understanding, fear, grief, and resignation. But no one said a word, not even Councilor Horus.

After a moment of silence, Councilor Hegira stood and clasped her hands in front of her robes. "This is a dangerous plan. One unlike anything we've ever attempted. Bigger even than our original plan... and let's face it, the scope was already complex. But we must remind ourselves that we are endeavoring to save the world—nothing less. The world that we destroyed."

Kaia looked over the crew as whispered discussion swept the room. She felt hopeful. They were at least considering the plan.

Then, almost in unison, every hand went up around the table. Councilor Hegira smiled. "Good, very good." She sat back down. "Kaia, what do we do next?"

Kaia felt a sudden burst of pride. This was the start of something new. "First, Captain Apep, we need to get the tugships from the asteroid belt. And we need to do it at light speed."

"*Near* light speed," First Officer Ra corrected.

"Yes, thank you. We want to slow down time for us, not stop it," she acknowledged.

Captain Apep rested his elbows on the table as he spoke. "So, we need to get started now, right, Enki?"

Enki nodded. "Yes, we have a limited window of time. After the eruption ends, the cooling will reach a tipping point where even the large asteroids will not work. We need to be sure that does not happen."

Councilor Hegira rested her hands on the table and nodded once. "Very well, let's get underway to the asteroid belt to retrieve the tugships at once."

Councilor Horus looked over to Councilor Hegira. "I hope you know what you're doing."

Hegira waved him off and stood to make tearful eye contact with each of them: Enki, Ra, and Captain Apep. "You've done remarkable work." Her gaze settled on Kaia. "All of you."


Captain Apep took his place at the helm. "Time to get moving." He rubbed his hands together and turned to First Officer Ra, who was sliding his feet into the floor straps. "Is the lightdrive ready?"

Ra held one finger down on the glyphpad and drew a circle next to it with his other hand. The viewscreen above his console blinked on, displaying an image of the photon vents opening and closing. He swiped up to see the data behind the recommended lightdrive settings. Row after row of numbers appeared on the viewscreen until a progress bar replaced the data.

Captain Apep noticed Enki heading toward them. "Here comes the odd one…" he warned Ra.

Ra looked up and grinned. "Oh, he helped me complete the algorithm."

"Carry on, then," Captain Apep said with a surprised smile.

Enki stopped next to Ra. "What are you calculating?" he asked, leaning in to examine the view screen.

Ra shook his head. "The precise output required from each photocell."

"Very good." Enki hesitated for a moment, then returned the smile with an awkward amble toward the geology station.

Captain Apep chuckled and noticed the progress bar on Ra's viewscreen had finished and a new dataset appeared. They were almost ready to put Ra's engineering to the test. The next few hours could mean life-or-death, not only for Nu, but for the entire crew. So many things could go wrong. He took a shaky breath to try and prevent the thought from overwhelming him.

"New settings confirmed, Captain," Ra said, interrupting his worried thoughts.

"Thank you." Apep took a moment to look around the bridge, nodding to each crew member, many of whom were stiff with apprehension. He locked eyes with Pakhet at the engineering console to his left, cleared his throat, and asked, "Are you ready?"

She clasped her hands behind her back and nodded once. "Engineering is Go, Captain."

He nodded and looked to the next console.

"Other than some elevated heart rates, the crew is Go," Dr. Khnum said.

"Excellent. Professor Thoth, systems look good?"

"Yes, sir. Systems are Go."

Apep turned to the geology station on his far right. Enki was drawing complex symbols on the glyphpad and changing the data on his viewscreen faster than Apep had ever seen.

"Geology, are you Go?" Apep asked.

Enki remained engrossed in his work.

Kaia raised her voice but kept it calm. "Enki, are you ready?"

"Wha—? Of course," he said with a slight roll of the eyes as he trained them back on the work.

She turned to Captain Apep, nodding with a slight smile playing across her face. "Geology is Go."

Captain Apep nodded and returned the smile. He waited for Kaia to leave for the biology console next to him and slide her feet into the straps then asked, "And is Biology Go?"

Kaia nodded. "Biology is Go," she said.

Captain Apep took a deep breath and turned to the *Meridian's* controls. "We are Go. Awaiting your orders, Kaia."

He heard her gasp and turned to her again. He chuckled to himself, realizing he'd been doing that a lot and found it quite pleasant, in fact.

Kaia's wide eyes were on him, her head thrown back. "My orders?" Her voice was a higher pitch than normal.

He bowed his head. "This is your mission, Kaia. You should be the one to give the order."

She turned to see Councilor Hegira leaning forward out of the shadows.

The councilor waved her hand toward Kaia with a flourish. "Kaia, the order is yours to give."

Kaia turned back to the Apep. He could see a range of emotions crossing her face in rapid succession as she considered the councilor's words. He assumed she was as overwhelmed by this moment as he was, perhaps even more. There would be no going back, no guarantee that the lightdrive wouldn't malfunction and burn them all to pieces, or if Ra's calculations were off, take them to a time that was too late for Nu, and too late for them to join their families on Duat. He could almost see her shoulders bow with the true weight of the decision before her.

She looked around the bridge, meeting the stoic gaze of each crew member.

"Kaia?" Captain Apep said.

She pulled her shoulders back. "Captain, take us to the asteroid belt."

"Yes, Kaia," he said, his respect for her growing even stronger than it had been before. He knew it was a big jump from simulated images projected in the air above the Council's table to the reality of the actual event. If one thing was certain in his mind, it was that Kaia Badra was the strongest person he knew.

Captain Apep turned back to his console, drew two glowing circles on his glyphpad, and pressed the center of each one. The ship turned away from the asteroids. Distant stars dotted the blackness of space, filling the viewscreen. A rumbling bellowed from deep within the ship. The photocells spun, creating trillions of photons per second. The noise settled into a low hum as the energy output rose. The star constellations outside warped, their faint light condensing into an intense illuminated ring at the center of the viewscreen.

"Feels a little shaky—is the ship holding up?" Apep yelled over to Pakhet.

Pakhet peered at her glyphpad to examine the details. "Everything looks good!"

Bright white bursts appeared in the ring of starlight as the ship rode a wave of light faster than they had ever gone before. As far as Apep knew, faster than *anyone* had ever traveled before.

He held onto the console. Kaia was shielding her eyes but seemed okay. He pointed to the luminous circle of light on the main viewscreen. "What do you think, Kaia?"

"I think," she began, "this will take some getting used to."

They both glanced over to the chronometer.

Kaia asked, "What do you think the scientist who came up with the impact model would say if they could see us now? Two hundred cycles later?"

Apep gave a simple shrug as entire cycles flew by in the blink of an eye.

*AD Cycle 3*
*AD Cycle 11*
*AD Cycle 18*
*AD Cycle 29*

# IMPACT

## ACT TWO

# IMPACT

## ASTEROIDS THROUGH TIME

# A.W. DAVIDSON

# CHAPTER 1
# LANDING

## MUMBAI - 2034 CE

The morning light shone through gaps in the plane's window shades. It had been a very smooth flight, with none of the turbulence Alan was expecting due to the perturbed jet stream. The fast-moving current of high-altitude winds hadn't been stable since the late 2010s. He looked around at his team in the dim cabin. They were all asleep, their heads tilted to the sides, some with mouths agape. How could they fall asleep with such exciting research ahead? He rubbed his neck and yawned— no way he was going to fall asleep. Too many thoughts filled his mind.

The chilly plane cabin reminded him of riding the school bus on cold winter mornings before the sun came up. His thoughts drifted from the bus to the school playground, where other kids chanted his nickname.

"Alpee! Alpee!" they yelled, as he scrambled up a tree higher than anyone else was brave enough to climb.

Anyone who knew him from elementary school still called him Alpee. Alan often used this as his "fun fact" during icebreakers at conferences. When people asked how he got that nickname, he explained it was a shortened combination of his first and last names.

But that was only half of the truth; the half he told people now that he was an esteemed academic professional with fifty years of experience.

The full truth was he peed his pants on the first day of kindergarten. One too-clever bully put together Alan's first name and last initial along with wet pants, and "Alpee" was born. All the kids taunted him before the teacher realized what was happening. They jeered as he ran out of the classroom, down the hallway, and out the door.

"Alan, is that you?" his mother asked from the kitchen as he crashed through the screen door. "What happened?" She looked down at his pants. "Oh, honey, it's okay."

He sobbed. "All the other kids are meanies," he said, with tears streaming down his face.

His mother gave him a tight hug. "Don't worry about the other kids. You are smarter than them."

He wiped his eyes and rubbed the tears on his sleeves. "But they don't like me, Mommy. I want them to like me."

She pursed her lips. "It doesn't matter if mean people don't like you, Alan. Don't let them get to you."

He sniffled and nodded.

By the time Alan was twelve years old, everyone still called him Alpee. But no one remembered why. What they did know was that he was always up for an adventure. He was the first one to pick up an injured bird on the playground. The one who was not afraid of the dark at sleepovers. The one who would always get the baseball when it went into the creepy neighbor's yard. Alpee did not seem scared of anything, or anyone. And he was smart, smarter than all of them, and now they knew it. He was the one who always asked questions the teachers could not answer.

"Why did the crocodiles survive but the dinosaurs didn't?" he asked a flummoxed fifth grade science teacher.

Alan could still hear their voices, "Alpee! Alpee! Alpee!" as he wriggled into a dark drainage pipe to save a cat. He felt the culvert shake then tilt down. He opened his eyes and found himself on an airplane.

The graduate students were still asleep, and he was glad no one saw him doze off. He put his hand on his neck and stretched, feeling his spine pop. To make things worse, his neck was sore. He rubbed it again as the plane began its descent into Mumbai.

Louise mumbled something, still asleep in the next seat, her head hanging toward her lap. He turned to her and felt pride sweep over him. It was an incredible honor to be invited to the Relocation Committee's first ever summit.

Neither of them had been to India before, but all their colleagues warned him to avoid the street food unless he wanted to get sick with Bombay Belly and spend his whole trip in the bathroom. He chuckled to himself, doubting anything could top the bout of Montezuma's Revenge he picked up while studying the Chicxulub crater in Mexico.

*Another adventure with you,* he thought as he admired the way a single tuft of hair fell over her cheekbone.

The plane hit a spot of turbulence and Louise stirred awake. She rubbed her eyes and blinked.

"Why are you staring at me, Alan?"

"Oh, I, um, wasn't," she could tell he was fibbing by the way his eyes darted back-and-forth. "I just wanted to raise the window shade to see out but didn't want to wake you up."

She looked around the plane. "Are we landing soon?"

"I think so," Alan said, pointing to the digital map display on the seat in front of him. "But you can never trust these things."

"You mean you can't," she joked. Louise yawned and stretched her arms. "Okay, let's see what's out there." She pulled the window shade up. "Look, honey!"

In the distance, several super-tall skyscrapers poked through cloud cover. Despite the sun glinting off their shiny facades, they looked rather utilitarian, like steel beams rising straight into the sky, with row upon row of dark-tinted windows.

"What are those?" Alan asked.

"*Those* are the first mile-high buildings," she said. "The first of their kind, purpose-built to house refugees."

"They look so much bigger in real life."

She nodded. "They won't be the last, so we should get used to seeing them. It's the cheapest, easiest way to house the people pouring into Pune from the flooding coasts."

The plane descended farther beneath the clouds.

Alan shook his head in awe. "I didn't realize Pune was so big, either."

Louise looked over the sprawling grid of streets and towers encircled by farms. "Out of the entire world, this region is one of the least affected by climate change. The temperature is still reasonable, and the monsoon rains are reliable. So, the crops can still achieve high yields."

"It's no wonder everyone wants to come here." He sat back in his chair. "This is the future, isn't it?"

"Yes," she said. "Rising seas and superstorms will force more people to abandon their homes. The Climate Council would like to get ahead of the rush by forcing people to move earlier, but I think there would be a lot of resistance."

Cranes jutted from the steel scaffolding of more towers under construction. Louise saw tiny yellow dots swarming the structures and realized they were workers' hardhats. They looked like little bees busy at work. A few of the buildings were not clad in eco-glass yet, so she could see into the orderly layout of compact housing units zipping past her window.

Louise looked away and leaned back in her seat.

"What is it?" Alan asked.

She thought of the families about to move into the spartan apartments. "Sometimes, I worry this isn't a good idea. History shows us that when you mix so many people of different cultures in a small space, it can be great, or it can be a powder keg of civil unrest."

Alan patted her hand. "That's why we need people like you working on this problem, too. Climate change is as much about people as it is about weather patterns over time."

She smiled. "Don't underestimate your field's contributions, Alan."

He shrugged. "I don't know a single climatologist or geologist who has figured out a way to factor human culture into our climate models and simulations."

"You have a point there," she said and turned back to the window as Puna's towers faded into the distance.

Alan leaned over and looked out, too. "Ah, that must be Matheran," he said, pointing to a small village on a plateau above the clouds. "And look over there! It's the Deccan Traps!"

Louise saw jagged, forested hills surrounding a small village. "The hills?"

He nodded. "They formed in a natural volcanic eruption then eroded over millennia. We still have so much to learn about them. Even though I disagree with the Climate Council about the eruption, I'm glad they're interested in learning more about it."

"What is that line going up the plateau?" Louise asked, pointing to a thin mark running up the mountain to Matheran.

"That's the railway you'll take to the top." He pretended to pull a whistle. "Choo-choo."

She laughed and looked at the village. "Hard to believe that place is going to be swarming with anthropologists for the conference in a few days."

The hills around Matheran faded into the distance, and the Arabian Sea came into view. Louise smiled to see the look of anticipation light up her husband's face. It wasn't the water but the land below the sea that was the real source of his excitement.

"Just think," he said. "A huge, mysterious landform laying a few miles offshore could hold the clues to saving our future."

The research team took inventory of their gear—all fourteen boxes and ten bags of it. They divided everything into two piles. The drilling equipment was for the Deccan Traps, while the X-ray fluorescence spectrometer was for the boat. The plan was for Alan and Daxia to board a helicopter and land on the drillship, *Finality*, which was already out at sea. Louise, on the other hand, would lead the land drilling team headed for Matheran. She hoped they could finish their work before the Relocation Committee conference began.

A child's cry pierced her thoughts. She turned and saw a river of people disembarking from another airplane onto the tarmac. They weaved around a woman in a hijab, weighed down with multiple duffel bags. The poor woman was also trying to comfort a crying child. A young man ran over to help with the bags as the woman lifted the child into her arms and disappeared into the mass of humanity.

Louise adjusted her wide-brimmed straw hat and walked over to an official-looking man in a bright yellow vest. She tapped his shoulder. "Who are those people?" she asked.

He looked up from his clipboard. "Them?" He pointed to the weary travelers.

She nodded.

"That is the first bunch of refugees from the Maldives. Their home island, Kondey, is going to be underwater soon and there is nowhere left to go on the other islands. Which, if you believe the Climate Council's simulations, aren't going to be above the waves much longer, either."

Louise sighed. This scene was all too common in the world of sea level rise. "Where are they going to live?"

The supervisor looked down at his clipboard and traced his finger across a row on the paper. "Pune, skyscraper fourteen. So new it doesn't have a name yet!" he said, with incongruous enthusiasm.

She mustered a smile, knowing this man had nothing to do with the refugees, but still frightened by how their plight seemed like nothing more than a checklist to him. "Thank you," she said and walked back to the students.

Louise found Daxia and asked, "Which of the teams is coming with me?"

Daxia pointed to the group on the left. "You're going with the graduate students. The *Finality* has its own drill crew."

Several students were busy opening plastic containers to check the metal piping for damage.

"Good, it looks like they know what they're doing."

"They're some of the best."

Louise nodded her approval. "How long will it take you and Alan to get the first sample after you land on the ship?"

Daxia held her hands up to shield her eyes from the sun. "Should only be a couple of days, as long as the weather holds." She reached into her pocket and handed Louise a piece of paper. "Here's where you're going in case GPS doesn't work. Dr. Pearce insisted I print it out."

Louise opened the folded map. It showed the train route with a circle drawn around the Mumbai railway station and another around Matheran.

Daxia pointed to the first station. "You can board the train here at the airport."

"Thank you, and don't worry about me. I was always a better navigator than Alan." She folded the map and slid it into her back pocket. "Seriously though, Daxia, please keep a close eye on him. He doesn't have what you'd call sea legs."

Daxia gave her a reassuring smile and a thumbs-up. "Yes, ma'am." Louise looked at her half of the team. They seemed to have everything in order, so she wound between the crates over to Alan and poked his shoulder.

"Okay, time to go our separate ways, honey."

He glanced up from the latch of a crate he'd been fumbling with. His hands raised into the air and words came rapid fire out of his mouth. "This is going to be great! Safe travels, and I'll call you from the satellite phone as soon as I have results."

She had never seen him so excited. Alpee, the young boy from the stories he'd shared with her through the years was on full display. She loved this man with all her heart.

He wrapped his arms around her and gave her a quick kiss. "I can't wait to prove those Climate Council buffoons wrong. Little asteroids are the only way to go!"

"I'm sure they are," she said, with a last squeeze.

Louise joined her own team and was heading to the train when she heard him say, "Ah-ha!" The latch must have finally clicked shut.

# CHAPTER 2
# LITTLE ONES

Councilor Horus sat in the dark in his quarters, leaned back in his chair, and crossed his arms over his stomach. He liked the way the lightdrive made the *Meridian*'s hull hum as it traveled to the asteroid belt. *Maybe we were always meant to be an interstellar people,* he thought as the star trails whizzed by outside the oversized porthole. He looked up to a medal on the wall, awarded to him for his superior achievement in leading the effort to create a societal structure that would keep the Jacana alive. The Council equipped the cityships with enough supplies to support generations of Jacana on their new worlds. But survival would also require strict rules for every aspect of life. No one would have children, change jobs, or eat more than their allotted rations without the approval of each ship's council.

Was he annoyed when Councilor Vishnu pulled rank and read the ten commandments on stage at the Exodus ceremony? Yes—yes, he was. Those were *his* rules. It had also been his idea to carve them into solid rock and set them up on every new planet.

Councilor Horus's favorite rule was the one about languages. He thought of the third rule again:

*Unite with a living, new language.*

Those irritating babels—he hated the hoods, or having the smaller ones shoved in his ears all the time. *A single language, what a dream that will be!* He was pleased with himself. Everything, thanks to him, was orchestrated flawlessly in the final cycles leading up to the Exodus. His desire to guide society toward maximum performance in preparation for their long voyages was the reason he entered politics—or, as he called it, "the game."

The Jacana's slow progress as a species had long frustrated him because he knew social engineering and strong guidance would help them advance faster. However, the only way to promote these ideas was in politics—a profession that disgusted him—until he realized it was the fastest way to manipulate beliefs in the unfortunate absence of dogmatic spirituality. Now, he knew the age-old secret weapon wielded by every politician. People are not moved by facts, but by feelings. And so, he scared them to death.

To ensure his victory for a seat on the Council, he filled his campaign with images of dead creatures, burning forests, and flooded cities. He never hesitated to use them when his opponents supported less radical measures to save their world. The ruined climate turned out to be a perfect villain for his political crusade and rise to power. Was he capitalizing on fear? Sure. But he knew his ideas to address society's problems were better than everyone else's.

He looked up at the numerous small frames on his wall, each containing a photo of him shaking hands with a different donor. He knew the rich stood to lose the most, so he courted the wealthy. They gave him money, so much money that he raised more for the Dawn Project than Hegira herself. And more importantly, the wealthy gave him media exposure to spread his ideas in exchange for luxury accommodations aboard the Exodus fleet. Who else would have natural wood furniture and pristine granite countertops in their private bathrooms? Only Councilor Horus's donors, of course. As he told

Councilor Hegira in his justification to her: "All cabins will have what a Jacana family needs; some will simply be a little better appointed."

He imagined each cityship humming along. They would reach their destination planets, and the society he facilitated would spread throughout the galaxy. There was just one problem—the Jacana *always* left destruction in their wake.

His primary concern was never for Nu. He could not care any less about the environment beyond its use as a political motivator. Without better guidance, he knew damaged ecosystems would be an imperfection on the otherwise-flawless Jacana image. So, he had to pretend to care, and it helped that his nanomechs were now part of the backup plan. There was a hint of pride when Kaia said his invention could be instrumental in fixing the last blemish on the Jacana's history that could be attributed to him.

Councilor Horus leaned forward to the glyphpad sitting on his desk just below the porthole. He swiped and activated the holoprojector.

Four translucent crystals floated before him. He reviewed the plans for the final shapes and sizes of the four rocks his tiny machines were to create. A sharp, back end met angled sides leading to an even sharper leading edge. Drag would be minimal, and dust would erupt in every direction. Councilor Horus considered his tiny machines.

"Are you ready, little ones?" He rubbed his hands together. "I just need to make a few modifications. I promise it won't hurt." He studied the four crystalline forms. "Hmm, atomic graspers should do the trick."

He drew a symbol on the glyphpad, and a nanomech orb replaced the crystals in the projection. The sphere appeared opaque. He rubbed his hands together and then pulled at his fingers, cracking each knuckle to loosen up. It had been a long time since Councilor Horus's hands were busy with actual work.

As he zoomed in, the microscopic latticework of interconnected machines became visible. The three-dimensional structure was a precise arrangement of nanomech chains angled at forty-five degrees. Councilor Horus always thought of Nu itself as a disorderly orb. Every life-form, including the Jacana, was connected to the others in a disorganized mesh of irrational behaviors and inefficient interactions.

He felt more attached to the little machines—with their rigid structure and clear roles—than to his own species.

He continued zooming in until a single nanomech filled the display. It spun in the air; its specifications listed next to it.

"We need to modify your protuberances," he told the projection, "for maximum grip strength." The enlarged nanomech looked like an insect—four jointed legs draping below its polygonal body and four jointed arms sprouting upward.

"No need for these drilling and splitting appendages," he said as he pulled the attachments from each arm. "We'll need the graspers, of course, and a heating element."

He swiped through a menu of nanomech components, looking for the smallest graspers he could find. He chose one that resembled a set of tiny insect pinchers, made from the same iridium as the asteroids.

"Ah yes, this one is perfect." He dragged two of them to the nanomech's arms. "Now, something to melt the iridium, so it fuses at the atomic level."

He swiped through more components and found a friction pad that oscillated over ten thousand times per second.

"That should generate enough heat." He dragged it onto the projection. "Perfect."

Something else caught his eye. A wide, flat circular disk with a fuzzy texture.

"Yes! A polisher to buff out any seams created when combining crystals." He dragged the component onto the nanomech and leaned back, satisfied. "For what is destruction without a little style?"

His thoughts wandered to Jacana history. A utopian society emerged when they finally dropped the doltish mythology that divided them for the science that united them. Never mind that they wrecked the planet on their way there and slapped the names of the old gods on cityships, and each other. *Imagine if society had come together even earlier.*

The nanomech now resembled a piercing, prickly insect at the back and a friendly, fuzzy creature at the front. "You may not be pretty, my little chimera, but you are perfect."

He smiled, then pinched his fingers on the glyphpad. The projection zoomed out to show the whole orb. He leaned back in his chair and crossed his arms. "We wouldn't be in this mess if it was this easy to manipulate the Jacana."

*That's it!*

The spark of an idea.

The tingle of anticipation.

He knew the feelings well.

Kaia said something about new creatures evolving after the impacts. *I can break the cycle of destruction*, he thought. "Evolution just needs a little guidance."

He looked back at the photos and analyzed each Jacana in them. The shape of their bodies, so flexible, so adaptable to many environments. He studied the handshakes. Those hands, with their fingers, *they could do anything*, he thought.

"That's it!"

He drew a stick figure on the glyphpad. An androgynous Jacana body appeared in the air. Two legs and two arms stemmed from a core that supported the prize, the head that held the powerful brain. He zoomed all the way into a twisted strand of the figure's DNA. Another symbol, and a new nanomech appeared on the right.

"Ahh," he gasped. The nanomech seemed to reach over to the DNA while the projection flashed red and buzzed.

"You're too big," he said, pointing at the nanomech. "But there are other ways."

He remodeled the nanomech, placing several sword-shaped appendages on its body.

"That should do it."

The nanomech reached over to the DNA again and slashed off a piece.

"Excellent."

He swiped again, and the nanomech disappeared, replaced by a blinking cursor.

"Now, we need to tell you what to do."

He inspected the Jacana figure. "Bipedal, that is a feature to keep. Two hands, and keep the opposable thumbs." He continued to scrutinize the figure and fine tune the nanomech as the cursor accepted his instructions.

The Jacana figure disappeared. A wireframe sphere appeared to the left of the nanomech. With a swipe, the nanomech moved into it, then shrank and filled it with millions of copies.

The sphere of secret nanomechs spun in the air in front of him. It was a perfect shape, composed of millions of perfect individuals. Each one with a purpose, unlike so many Jacana. His heart swelled with pride. "You'll do better than us, right, my little ones?"

# CHAPTER 3
# MINING DEPOT

## MERIDIAN - AD CYCLE 48

Captain Apep was heading back to the bridge as they neared the asteroid belt. Ahead of him in the central corridor, Councilor Horus pulled himself toward the front of the ship. The councilor's robe flowed in waves behind him, reminding Apep of the sea. He glided up next to him and asked, "Are you all finished with the nanomech changes?"

Councilor Horus stopped and made vicious eye contact. "Do you think I'd be heading to the bridge already if I wasn't?"

"Sorry, of course not."

The councilor huffed and pulled himself along the railing, then turned his head. "Shouldn't you already be on the bridge, Captain? I thought you knew how dangerous the asteroid belt can be, but perhaps I was incorrect in that assumption."

"I do, and I am sure First Officer Ra has it under control," he said without a hint of concession.

Councilor Horus snorted and kept moving. The captain caught his glare one more time as the councilor turned to climb down the ladder onto the bridge.

Captain Apep muttered to himself now that Horus was out of earshot. "Was it something I said?"

"I hope you know you don't need to worry about him," a voice said from behind.

He spun around to see Kaia coming toward him and his heart picked up its pace. "I try to stay on everyone's good side, but I'm not there yet with Horus."

"Let me know if you figure it out," she said as she floated up next to him.

The ship pitched forward, forcing them to hold on to the railing with both hands. There was a clang from the bundle of pipes running the length of the corridor. "That's just Ra adjusting course to rendezvous with the mining depot."

She let go of the railing with one hand but held firm with the other. He thought he saw a hint of fear in her eyes.

"We should get up there," she said.

"We should. You first?"

She obliged and pulled ahead of him, then spun around, planted her feet on the ladder, and climbed down. *She's got the hang of it now,* he thought.

Captain Apep waited until she was all the way down then started down himself. As soon as his feet hit the floor, First Officer Ra announced, "Sorry for the swerve back there. The depot isn't where the old orbital plan said it should be, but we're on the right track now. Pakhet thinks an asteroid may have pulled it a little farther out. The Council stopped tracking everything after the Exodus."

"No damage, though?" Captain Apep asked.

"None," Ra replied.

"Good," he said, watching Kaia make her way to the biology console. He scanned the rest of the bridge and noted that everyone was present and focused on their viewscreens. The two councilors, as usual, were busy whispering to one another.

Captain Apep stepped up to the helm and took control, guiding the *Meridian* into the belt with both hands on the glyphpad. He looked over at the empty mission console on his right. "Kaia?" he said loud enough for her to hear him.

She looked up from the biology console.

"You're in charge here," he said. "Why don't you step over to the mission console?" She took a tentative step back, then looked at Enki, who nodded to the mission console and mouthed something that looked like *Go*.

She looked back to the helm, said, "Of course, Captain," and swiped the graph on her viewscreen away.

He couldn't help but notice how the shadows danced over the contours of her fitted green habsew. In answer to his heart, which had started its own little dance of sorts, he scolded himself. *She's still a colleague, you idiot.* And yet, the mission would be over soon, so he allowed his thoughts to linger on her two seconds longer.

*You shouldn't go there until you tell her the truth.*

Kaia gave a quick smile, then slid her feet into the floor loops at the mission console. She peered up at the main viewscreen and did a double take.

"The asteroid belt not what you imagined?" he asked.

She lowered her chin. "Well, it is not at all how the Council portrayed it," she said.

On the radar, he saw two large asteroids in the blackness, separated by thousands of cubits. "Yeah, it's rare to see more than three at a time. I've never seen a cluster like movies showed."

Councilor Hegira overheard the comment and leaned forward in her chair. "Well, we had to do something to get you kids more interested in space."

"Oh," Captain Apep chuckled. "I remember the advertisements on the holoboards. They made space jobs look like a blast! It got my attention."

On the viewscreen, a solitary stone spun end-over-end.

Councilor Horus chimed in, "I do seem to recall that we took some artistic liberties."

Captain Apep smirked. "That's for sure. I don't recall seeing anything about the *glamorous* quarters of a mining depot. All my hormone-addled adolescent brain remembers is racing around space in a shuttle as it weaved between a dense field of asteroids several times bigger than the *Meridian*." He nodded to the single asteroid outside. "Reality is a bit *different*."

Kaia narrowed her eyes. "It almost makes me feel sorry for anyone who chose to work here."

"It's not so bad—almost feels like home to me."

"Home is nothing like this," Kaia said.

He noticed her shoulders tensing up as the ship passed within a shuttle's width of the stone. Moving his right hand to the left caused the *Meridian* to steer farther away from the asteroid. He turned back to Kaia and saw her relax.

"Captain!" First Officer Ra shouted.

A screeching alarm echoed around the bridge. Captain Apep turned back to the viewscreen just in time to see the web of scaffolding from an old mining rig coming right at them. He swiped right on the glyphpad, steering hard to starboard. Blue jets erupted all along the *Meridian*'s cylindrical body to avoid a collision, but another abandoned rig was dead ahead.

"Ra!" he shouted. "Why aren't these showing up on radar?"

"They're just webs of steel, no central mass for the sensors to detect," Ra explained.

Two consoles away, Pakhet watched the thruster output. "You're going to need more power to clear it!" she shouted.

"Give me all you can," the captain shouted in return. The rigs loomed ahead. "We still aren't turning fast enough!"

"Sorry, Captain, that is all I have!"

He saw the fear return to Kaia's face as she braced herself against the console. He looked around the bridge at the other crew members. There was Dr. Khnum, Professor Thoth... No, no way a doctor or a professor could help. Nef and Mirik stood on either side of the councilors. "You two, any ideas?"

Mirik was holding onto the railing for dear life. "You know I'm not an idea guy, Captain!"

Nef pointed to Enki. "Looks like he's working on something!"

"Enki!" Captain Apep shouted.

Enki looked up from the console. "The nanomechs! They could deconstruct it." He pointed to the mining rig growing larger on the bridge's central viewscreen.

Captain Apep spun around to the Council platform. "Councilor Horus, do we have nanomechs to spare?"

Captain Apep could hear him thinking in the silence, then Horus said, "Yes, I saved a few."

Councilor Horus drew a symbol on the glyphpad in front of him and swiped up with both hands. A small orb shot forward and dissipated into a cloud. The scaffolding seemed to vanish, deconstructed in seconds.

The entire crew exhaled at once.

Councilor Horus raised his voice. "You're all very welcome."

The captain bowed. "Thank you, Councilor Horus." He turned to the rest of the crew. "Right?"

They all bowed as well, although some lower than others. He noticed Enki barely leaned forward at all.

"Okay, everyone," Captain Apep said, adjusting his babel hood and taking a deep breath. "Abandoned drilling equipment is everywhere in the belt. Stay sharp."

"Not for much longer," said First Officer Ra. "We are near the depot, Captain." Two radar echoes appeared on the viewscreen just outside the border of the mining zone. "We will pass the one on the right first, an asteroid, then the depot is next," he said, studying each spot on the screen.

Captain Apep steered the ship past the asteroid and noticed geometric scars across its surface.

"What are those lines?" Kaia asked.

"Strip mines. That must have been one of the first ones we mined, before we figured out how to tunnel into them to get at the minerals we were after."

The asteroid moved off the screen, replaced by a small cube at the center that grew larger with every second.

"I assume that's it, Ra?" Captain Apep asked.

First Officer Ra looked down at the radar. "Yes, that's the correct mining depot."

The captain turned around. "Nef, Mirik, go prepare my shuttle."

"Yes, sir," Nef said and bounded toward the ladder with Mirik in tow.

Captain Apep stepped over to the mission console. "May I?" he asked Kaia and gestured to the console.

"Of course." She stepped to the side.

He reached down to the glyphpad and copied the main viewscreen's image, then stepped back. "Kaia, can you please zoom in and search the structure for tugships?"

"Yes, but point me in the right direction."

"Ah, yes, one second." He spread his fingers on the glyphpad and zoomed in on the cube. An enormous wireframe shape projected out from the screen. Twelve long beams outlined each side, while two motionless habitat rings dominated the center.

"The tugships should be right about," he circled the main support beam holding the two habitat rings with his finger, "here."

She stepped back up to the console. "I'll see what I can find."

"Thank you." He headed back to the helm, but Kaia stopped him with another question.

"How long ago did we abandon this place?" she asked.

Captain Apep stepped up next to her, brushing her arm. He drew three horizontal lines on the glyphpad. The depot's log appeared on the viewscreen. "The last crew member disembarked two cycles before we started the eruptions."

"And the tugships will still work?"

When she didn't move her arm away, he allowed himself to absorb the feeling of her closeness. "Yes, they should be fine."

"Good," she said, leaning into him even more, a smile playing at the corners of her mouth.

"Would you like to join us?" he asked. "We could use an extra hand —if you don't have any more pets to feed." He smirked again.

Kaia shrugged. "Sure, I'll join you."

. . .

As soon as the captain's shuttle docked with the depot, Kaia unbuckled her belt and floated away from her seat. She pulled herself toward the docking port, past Mirik, Nef, and First Officer Ra. Captain Apep glided into the cargo bay from the shuttle's cockpit.

She caught Captain Apep watching her and felt warmth creep up her neck. Her shift from Doctor Kaia Badra, an accomplished biologist, and a leader on the Dawn Project, to Kaia, a giddy teenager, was never so pronounced as when the captain was around.

"Looks like you're getting better at that," he said.

"Well, maybe you were a better pilot this time," she quipped.

He chuckled. "That must be it."

"Sorry to interrupt, bosses." Mirik pointed to red lights around the door. "No pressure over there. Looks like we need to seal up our habsews."

Captain Apep motioned for Kaia and the pilots to follow. They unbuckled their belts and tightened their suit clasps.

Kaia reached down and twisted the seals on her wrists. She noticed that Captain Apep missed one on the back of his neck and floated over to help him.

"You can hold on to my arm if you're feeling queasy," he said.

She laughed out loud. "Turn around."

He raised an eyebrow then turned.

Kaia tugged on the clasp. "It's a good thing I'm here to make sure you don't get sucked through an open hole in your suit," she said, grinning. She felt the warmth of his skin as she rubbed the seam to check the seal.

Behind them, Mirik snickered until Ra cleared his throat. When Captain Apep turned back, his face was bright red. Ra gave Kaia a subtle thumbs-up.

"Hang on to something," Captain Apep said. "It's going to get windy in here."

She wrapped her arms around the cargo bay's tie-downs as Captain Apep turned the handle on the door. A rush of air pulled her toward it. The port hissed until the pressure equalized.

"You three first, spread out to the right. Kaia and I will head left," Captain Apep instructed the pilots.

Ra let go first, then Mirik and Nef pulled themselves through the docking port and headed down the depot's corridor.

Captain Apep put his arm in front of him and bowed. "You're next."

She peeked into the depot and hesitated. "How far do you think we'll have to go before we find working tugships?"

"They're close. Your scan showed several docked in both directions," he said and pulled himself through the doorway.

She paused and whispered, "See you soon," to the shuttle. Its bright lights and comfortable chairs called for her to stay. The memory of jumping into the cargo bay to save herself from the eruption filled her mind and made her heart race. *Calm down, it will be fine,* she told herself.

The light on Kaia's helmet flickered on when she entered the depot's dark corridor. Inactive screens and glyphpads covered the round walls. There was no power, even for the emergency lights. She was expecting cobwebs, maybe traces of water stains and cracks in the superstructure. But the whole place felt as though the Council decommissioned it yesterday.

Plants and animals would have invaded an abandoned structure on Nu by now. But here, the familiar, natural reclamation of Jacana-made structures was nonexistent. These abandoned depots might be the only trace of the Jacana in their sol system if their plan succeeded.

She looked around for a railing and saw Captain Apep already halfway to the next docking port. She grabbed a pipe along the wall and pulled herself along to catch up to him.

Kaia tapped his foot once she got close. "Did you ever come to this depot during your time as a tugship pilot?" she asked.

He continued toward the darkness. "Yeah, even spent a whole cycle here moving rocks around before they made me captain." He stopped in front of an open docking port and attempted to bow, which looked kind of awkward without gravity. "After you."

Kaia stifled a giggle and pulled herself through the opening and into the tugship. She floated toward the console and noticed a scrap of paper taped to it. Her headlamp illuminated the front of a ripped postcard featuring a bright red X covered a fern leaf—the symbol of resistance to the Council. The graphic represented freedom and the desire to make Jacana society great again. Those who loved the symbol valued industry over environment, free enterprise over regulation—all the things that led to their dire situation in the first place. In the end, it stood for a societal schism that came close to killing them all and taking Nu with it, until Captain Set and Councilor Hegira negotiated a treatise.

Captain Apep saw her staring at the symbol. "Is everything okay?" he said.

"Yes. Yes, I'm fine," she said.

He pointed to the console as he settled into the pilot's chair. "I guess this pilot was a member of the Resistance."

"Looks that way," she said, an edge to her voice. Kaia knew it wasn't personal, yet had always felt that anyone who opposed the Council was dismissing her story. Dismissing the death of her parents. She brought her hand up to wipe her eyes but met the helmet visor instead.

Captain Apep turned away then shook his head. "Just remember, it didn't stop Captain Set from accepting a cityship from the Council in the end."

Kaia shrugged her feelings away as best she could and maneuvered herself into the copilot's chair. She looked at the postcard again. "I spent my childhood trying to convince people that the Council's plan was necessary."

"And you convinced many," Captain Apep offered.

"What's worse is that later, I learned that some Council members profited from the same industries that were killing our planet," she said.

"Some Council members were—or, well, still are—swayed by wealth like most other Jacana."

She narrowed her eyes. "Yes, Councilor Horus has no qualms about taking kohl money."

Captain Apep nodded but said no more. He pointed to his comm, signaling that someone on the *Meridian* could be monitoring their conversation.

"Can you turn on the tugship's power?" he asked.

Kaia nodded and reached up to the console to flip the primary power toggle. A small viewscreen glowed to life in front of his seat. The cockpit lit up, button-by-button, and the control lever vibrated.

They sat in silence as the system finished its automatic calibration.

She reached up to remove the Resistance's anti-Council postcard. "Sometimes it feels like I spent my whole life studying the biology of Nu—a field of study that will be meaningless when this plan is over." She flashed her eyes to Captain Apep. "Maybe I shouldn't be so hard on the Resistance. They probably felt something similar, knowing their jobs may mean nothing after everyone left Nu," she said, grasping for a connection to the ones who fought so hard against everything she believed in.

All Jacana lives mattered, including the ones who disagreed with the Council. There was no reason to dwell on the hate that divided their society in its final days.

He put his hand on her shoulder. "I don't know about the Resistance, but the part about you, Kaia, is not true. Even if your work loses meaning, you will never become meaningless," he said.

She ripped up the postcard and threw the pieces behind her. They both smiled as they floated away. *It's in the past,* Kaia told herself.

Captain Apep pretended to tap the side of his helmet and mouthed, *"local."*

Kaia nodded and drew a symbol on her glyphpad. *Local Comm Only* appeared on her visor.

He did the same. "There, now we can have a private conversation."

She tingled with anticipation. "Something you want to ask me?"

He glanced down at his forearm to ensure she activated privacy mode for him, too. "Yes, there is something we need to discuss." He puffed his cheeks and took a deep breath. "Do you trust Councilor Hegira?"

She leaned away from him, smile wavering. "Of course." Her

stomach dropped. This was not where she thought the conversation was going. "Do you not trust her?" she asked.

He chewed his lip then looked down. "Yeah, I mean, only a bit, about some things... I don't know."

"What do you mean?" She saw him sigh and knew he had to get something off his mind.

He took a deep breath and continued, "Sometimes she leads your ideas, even tells you how to feel. It's just, well, it makes it seem like maybe she's controlling you."

"She has a lot more experience than me—than any of us for that matter. She's trying to save the world. That's no small feat. I can forgive her for being a little..."

"Pushy," he offered.

"Pushy?" Kaia crinkled her nose.

He raised both palms. "Sorry. It's just that she never asks for ideas from anyone else. It seems like she knows what's going to happen before the rest of us do. It's a little suspicious, don't you think?"

"Are you trying to say you don't agree with the impact plan, Captain?"

He shook his head. "No, nothing like that. I know it is the only way to go." He sighed.

Kaia grimaced. "Thank you for the vote of confidence, Captain."

"You're doing an amazing job, Kaia," he said in an attempt to redeem himself and change the topic. "I mean it."

She cleared her throat and glanced back at the control panel. "Is the tugship's system still loading?"

Captain Apep took the hint. He glanced at the viewscreen.

"It looks locked up," he said.

She pointed to the battery indicator. A thin red line ran across the bottom. "Not enough power."

"I should have known," he sighed. He drew a new symbol on his forearm glyphpad to open the comm channel again. He held up his hand and spoke into his wrist. "Ra, Mirik, Nef, any luck?"

"No, sir," Mirik replied. "They must have used every last drop of juice before shutting 'em down."

Captain Apep turned around and smacked the wall of the tugship.

Kaia watched him think, head tilted to the side, eyes focused on something she could not see. She wracked her brain too, then it hit. "What about the constructors?"

Captain Apep looked up then raised a finger in the air. "That could work! Did you see them on the scan?"

"Yes, they are attached to the habitat rings."

"Ah yes, the builders used their rockets to initiate the spin so the crew quarters would have centrifugal gravity. They use liquid fuel, you know?"

She shook her head.

He continued, "There wasn't enough electron power available until after the constructors finished the generators, so they ran refined liquid kohl."

"It is hard to imagine we brought fuel from Nu all the way out here."

"You know, I never really thought about it, but you're right."

She floated up from the pilot seat and pulled herself toward the docking port. "Let's go get them."

Kaia was already on her way to the junction tube leading to the rings when she looked back to see Captain Apep paused at the port door, speaking into his comm. "Ra, head for the rings then spread out. We're going to try the constructors."

Kaia marveled at the scale of it all as she pulled herself along the hallway with Captain Apep at her side. "These habitat rings are so much bigger than the *Meridian*'s. I mean, the floor almost looks flat."

Captain Apep nodded and pulled himself forward. "Yeah, I wish the *Meridian* had one large ring like this instead of being divided into the two small rings and the bridge," he said.

"It's too bad we can't make these things spin again," Kaia said. "I would really like to stand on a level surface for a bit."

Captain Apep breezed past her, above what used to be the floor. "The constructor's hatch should be right up here."

She paused in front of a half-open door. A placard read *Captain Hephaestus*, indicating the room had been the depot captain's quarters. Inside, scattered papers and empty food containers drifted in the dark. The captain had not taken time to clean before leaving. She wondered which cityship he was on now. *Mining would be a valuable skill.*

As if reading her thoughts, Captain Apep yelled from his location three doors down. "That's where the big boss slept. I heard old Capt. Heph retired and planned to enjoy himself on the cityship Hathor. Now, can you please come over here and help me open this?"

Kaia pulled Captain Hephaestus's door shut and floated down the hallway.

The captain pointed to the circular handle. "It's stuck. No one has opened it since we abandoned the constructor." He grabbed the right side and motioned for her to pull up on the left. The handle inched open.

She could feel the gears starting to remember their purpose. It only took a quarter turn for the lock to release.

Captain Apep pulled the hatch open and looked inside the constructor. Yellow foam protruded through rips in a worn red pilot's chair that was turned around, facing the door. Behind it, a dense arrangement of buttons and analog readout displays covered every surface.

Kaia floated past him and pulled herself inside. "Wow, it's like a museum."

She ran her fingers over a panel of switches. She looked at the large, dark square near the front. "This viewscreen looks even more out of date than the one in the tugship. Did they not have holoprojectors onboard?"

He squeezed into the tiny space with her, shining his light at the conduits on the ceiling. "What you're looking at is the meteorite shield. It's just a window, not a viewscreen, if you can believe it."

She could.

"Scientists didn't invent viewscreens until several cycles after this baby was manufactured." He followed the wires snaking out from the panel. "Hmm, one of these must carry the power for the controls."

She looked at the multicolored bundle. "How can you tell which one?"

"I'll follow the cables to the back and see if any of them are hooked up to something that looks like a battery."

Kaia nodded and sat in the pilot's chair. She reached under the seat and pulled up on the first lever she found. The swivel lock released, and she pushed her arms against the wall to turn and face the front of the constructor. "This looks like it would take a lifetime to learn to fly," she said, attempting to decipher the relationship between hundreds of control buttons on the console and foot pedals that covered the narrow floor in front of her.

Captain Apep pulled the door off a compartment and stuck his hand inside. "Most of those levers control the construction arms. We won't need them."

Kaia heard the clink of a handle being pulled down and an electronic whir.

"Besides," he said. "There are way fewer buttons on this thing, or all of our ships combined, than there are species on Nu. My learning to fly them all pales in comparison to what you've memorized about biology, Kaia. Give yourself some credit."

The cockpit flashed to life. Multicolored dials and small displays of indecipherable data surrounded her. Captain Apep shut the hatch when the life support system hummed and began pressurizing the cabin.

He pulled himself to the front and looked over Kaia's shoulder. "I learned to fly with controls like those," he said, pointing to the three red levers in front of her.

"They're all yours," she said, pulling the lever under the seat again and swiveling around. She reached for a handle on the wall and pulled herself out of the chair. He took her seat and scooted it back.

Kaia held onto the seat back and looked over his shoulder.

"It has control power, but let's see if it has fuel," Apep said.

She marveled at the analog gauges. "I don't think I've ever been on a ship with liquid fuel engines."

"I haven't in at least ten cycles myself. It is primitive technology, but it has its advantages." He pointed to a round display with a full, green line. "They don't need to be recharged, just refilled." He tapped the gauge and the indicator stayed near the top. "This constructor has more than enough fuel. They can't come close to keeping up with a lightdrive though, so we'll need to dock them with the *Meridian*." He pressed down on the habsew's glyphpad. "Ra, we found a constructor with plenty of fuel."

"We're way ahead of you, sir," Ra responded. "Look out your window."

Captain Apep pointed to the buttons next to the right armrest. "It's one of these…"

He pressed a long, white one at the top. A metallic clang reverberated through the cramped cabin as a narrow slit grew in the blank front wall.

"I'm raising the micro-meteorite shield," he said to Kaia. The crack at the front of the constructor grew wider.

They watched as the thick metal plate slid into the hull, revealing three constructors floating in front of them. Bulbous fuel tanks dominated the small cabin section of the constructor ships. A set of robotic graspers protruded from the front, giving them the appearance of two-bodied insects floating through space. Two constructors did a flip, and their comms filled with the unmistakable hearty laughter of Mirk and Nef. Ra waved at them through his front window, looking somber as ever.

Captain Apep laughed. "Good work. Now let's get these beasts to the *Meridian* and head home."

Kaia looked out the window, past the blue flames shooting out from the backs of the constructors. A corner of the depot's superstructure dominated the view. The *Meridian* was visible just beyond the cube. Its tubular body, habitat, and bridge rings looked tiny—even feeble— compared to the massive depot.

Kaia's thoughts returned to the captain's earlier cryptic conversation, which still confused her. She whispered. "So, why did you ask me that about Councilor Hegira?"

He shrugged and looked down. After a few seconds, he looked up again, his brows pinched together. "Let's talk about it later. I promise to explain myself."

The constructor veered into the side of the depot.

She welcomed the distraction and pointed to the control levers. "What, can't figure out how to fly this thing?" she asked with a smirk.

Captain Apep narrowed his eyes at her, but she could see he was holding back a smile. He kept his eyes locked on hers and reached up for the center lever. The constructor pulled away from the docking port, sending Kaia toward the wall.

"You'd better hope I know how to fly it. These old beauties are all manual."

She put her elbow out just in time to stop herself from hitting the side and shrugged. "That's a shame. I was hoping the autopilot might have a better personality than the current one."

# CHAPTER 4
# PORCUPINE POINT

## MATHERAN, MAHARASHTRA, INDIA - 2034 CE

The diesel locomotive whirred and chugged, pulling the creaky train up the steep mountain to Matheran. Worn metal railcars squealed as they rounded the first of many switchbacks. Louise sat in the next-to-last car, smack in the middle of a group of screaming kids on a field trip. Sweat ran down her head and dripped onto her lap. She reached into her pocket and grabbed a handkerchief to wipe her forehead. The kids bantered on, oblivious to the heat. Louise leaned back on the wooden bench seat and fished through her bag to pull out a folder stuffed with academic papers.

She skimmed the first one to see if it was worth reading. The title was "Living in the Great Dismal Swamp: How Escaped Slaves Lived Free in the Pre-Civil War South." An interesting take, she knew, on the resilience of humans in terrible environmental conditions, but not related to her upcoming presentation about the relationship ancient cultures had with their land. She thumbed to the next paper: "Mayan agricultural practices lead to societal collapse."

*Perfect*, she thought, and settled in for the ride up.

The paper was a lengthy analysis of the ecological effects of the ancient Maya in Central Mexico. Its author hypothesized that the Maya had over-farmed their land. He argued that the irrigation canals and cleared forests made food production more susceptible to extreme drought. When the drought came, it led to famine and, ultimately, to the fall of their entire civilization. Louise thought it was plausible, but something about it did not feel right. How could people sophisticated enough to build entire cities not understand how to manage water? Her trip to the Maya ruins at Uxmal gave her confidence they were smarter than this author portrayed them to be.

She looked up at the kids in the train car, who had quieted down, and noticed they did not look local. Their skin was lighter, their eyes narrower, and their hair curlier than the indigenous population. *Are they refugees?* She decided they were by the way they stared out the windows. They would have never seen anything like these mountains if they were from an island. The thought spurred an idea for her speech.

"The next generation will not get to see the world firsthand as we can now. Travel creates environmental destruction. Fifty years from now, children will only have virtual reality simulations of the rest of the world," she said, scribbling in the margin.

The train rounded the next turn and entered a small clearing. The kids all yelled in excitement. She looked up from the paper and out the window toward the valley. Horizontal bands of bright green vegetation alternated with layers of black volcanic rock. The effect made the hills look like a life-sized topographical map. Late afternoon sunbeams shone between the jagged peaks, casting dramatic shadows onto the fields below.

"Wow indeed," she whispered under her breath before turning back to the paper.


She didn't notice that the train had pulled into Matheran until it jerked to a stop. The diesel locomotive continued to puff black smoke into the air. A light rain fell on the station's corrugated steel roof, adding to the noisy atmosphere.

Louise stepped out of the small rail car and stretched her back.

Vendors were hawking all sorts of goods to the Westerners, from fruit to sunblock and hats. She caught movement above her and looked up. A monkey leapt from a tree onto the canvas roof of a mango stand. The weary old woman manning the stand yelled and poked the roof with a stick, but the monkey crawled down the support post and grabbed a mango undeterred. It scampered back into the trees, drawing a crowd of more monkeys, who screeched at the successful shoplifting.

"Those are bonnet macaques," said a young boy with a wide smile.

Louise smiled back. "They're brave little critters."

He threw his arms out to the side. "One time, I saw mister monkey pull the hijab off a woman because it was banana print!" He giggled.

Louise kept an eye on the monkey and pulled her bag in closer to her body, remembering she had a couple of candy bars from the airport in it.

The boy watched her team unloading crates of drilling equipment. Sweat drenched their clothes, despite the cool mountain air.

"Where are you going with that stuff?" he asked.

"A campsite near Porcupine Point," she replied.

"You need a ride? I'll take you there!" he said, pointing to a rusty two-person rickshaw.

She smiled at him. "I don't think that is big enough. There are seven of us, plus a lot of equipment. We'll get a car. Thank you, though."

The boy laughed. "No cars allowed in Matheran! Only the ambulance, and it always gets stuck in the mud."

Louise grimaced. "*This* place is going to host a conference?" she whispered to herself.

"My friends can help your friends!" the boy offered.

He pointed to a group of even more boys, each with rickshaws of their own. They watched his conversation with the American woman with looks of anticipation. She knew they had high hopes of garnering fares of their own.

Louise smiled and gave a thumbs-up. "That would be wonderful."

The boy smiled in return, placed his hands together, and bowed. "I am Arjun."

"Nice to meet you, Arjun. My name is Louise."

The boy yelled to his friends. They leapt over to help unload the rest of the equipment. Louise put her hands on her hips and turned to her team. Everyone looked exhausted.

"Looks like we'll all get a break before the real work begins," she said.

The group of students hung back as the boys carried the crates and cases to the rickshaws. When they finished loading everything, she went to Arjun's cart and settled into the seat behind the boy.

Gravel crunched under the rickshaw wheels as Arjun and his friends pulled them along. Louise marveled at their sure-footedness, despite their shoes with holes worn through the sides.

The campsite was farther than she had anticipated. Worried about the kids tiring, she asked Arjun, "How are you feeling? Do you need a break?"

He turned and laughed.


The last twenty minutes of the trip to the campsite were steep, and the boys slowed down, panting.

"Stop right here, please. This is perfect," Louise instructed.

Arjun lowered the rickshaw poles to the ground in front of a worn wooden sign indicating Porcupine Point was about one hundred feet ahead.

"You are camping here?" the boy asked, wiping his face on his shirt.

Louise stepped down from the rickshaw. Evening sunlight filtered through the trees. She inhaled—it smelled of flowers and campfire smoke. She clasped her hands and smiled. "Yes, this will do."

The other boys stopped and unloaded the crates. The team got to work setting up camp and preparing the small drilling rig. Louise was eager to get Alan's project work out of the way.

The boys gaped at the odd-looking equipment. Louise picked up the heavy drill bit and handed it to Arjun.

He almost dropped it, surprised by its weight. "What is it?" he asked.

"Tomorrow, we will take this drill and make a deep hole in the ground to see its layers and how old they are," she answered.

"There is only dirt. Why are you drilling?"

"It is only dirt on the top. Come over here. I'll show you," she said.

Louise led them up the path to the overlook at Porcupine Point. A great plain stretched beyond the mountains. Puna's skyline poked through clouds in the distance. She pointed to a small, striated mound rising from the valley.

"See those black stripes on the hill? They are different layers from different times on Earth. And each one is ancient lava," she said.

"A... volcano?" Arjun asked, shirking away.

She shook her head. "Not quite. This entire area had cracks in the ground where lava came up. Just imagine Matheran covered in lava!"

A few boys exchanged sideways glances, and she thought she heard one whisper: *"That gori is crazy."*

Arjun gave them a dirty look. "I have never seen lava in Matheran," he told her.

She nodded. "You're right. There are no holes like that anymore. It happened when the dinosaurs were alive and stomping around, eating each other." She made a deep growl and held her hands out like claws.

The boys giggled and pretended to be dinosaurs with her. As she laughed with them, she noticed one snuck away and sat down with his legs pulled tight into his chest.

"Are you okay?" she asked in a raspy dinosaur voice.

The boy pulled his legs in closer. "Will the drilling make a big lava fountain happen again?"

Louise lowered her hands and crouched down to him. "No, no, of course not. Our drill is much too small for that."

The boy loosened his arms and crossed his legs. Louise guessed he still felt unsettled at the thought of his home being covered in lava.

"Why do you need to drill?" he asked.

She pointed to the east, toward the skyscrapers of Pune. "In a few hundred years, that city may be one of the few places people can live. The weather will be too bad everywhere else. Volcanoes can change the climate when they erupt, but they are much too small to make it happen as long as we need, so we need to study and learn more."

The boy tensed up again.

"Oh, we won't have to do it soon. It will be many, many years away. There is no reason to be scared." She sat down on a long bench and patted the seat next to her. "Come, sit."

He joined her, and they looked out over the deep green landscape streaked with dark horizontal cliffs.

She took a deep breath. "This is a wonderful place, and it is only this beautiful because of what happened so long ago. You have a very special home. The only place like this in the whole world. You should feel very lucky to see this every day."

The sun was setting, shining deep orange light over the valley. They all sat still and admired the view. The fiery sunset glinted off Pune's towering skyscrapers. She shuddered. If she looked on with pessimistic eyes, it looked like flames engulfing the city.

Arjun turned to her. "I like this place the way it is now. I hope it stays nice forever."

Louise smiled and kept her thoughts to herself. *Nowhere stays nice forever.*

# CHAPTER 5
# RETURN

## MERIDIAN - AD CYCLE 48

Enki watched the last crew member, Dr. Khnum, leave the bridge. They had left the asteroid belt and were on their way back to Nu. Though they had no tugships, the captain assured them that the constructors could do the work. First Officer Ra stayed behind to monitor their return, and Enki decided to continue his own work on the bridge. He pressed the glyphpad, and a progress bar appeared on his viewscreen. While he waited for the simulation to finish, he looked up at the ring of compressed starlight filling the bridge viewscreen. He leaned back, peering around a support column.

Ra's back was straight as his hands glided over the helm's glyphpad, his eyes darting between the output graph and sensor readings. Enki felt the *Meridian* move to the right then settle back onto a linear path.

Turning back to his screen, Enki saw the progress bar creeping up to 7% completion—it was going to be awhile before the new simulation was ready. He smoothed the wrinkles from his habsew, adjusted his hood to make sure the babels sat over his ears, then made his way to the helm.

When Ra looked up, their eyes locked. Enki slid his hands into his pockets. "Hello, First Officer Ra."

Ra flashed a smile. "Hey, Enki. As I've said before, you can just call me Ra." He looked back to the helm's viewscreen.

Enki dipped his head to peer at it too. "Ra, what are you working on?"

"I'm monitoring our path and adjusting the output to steer us around any asteroids or comets the sensors pick up. Each deviation also means I need to speed us up or slow us down a little bit to arrive back at Nu at the right time." Ra tilted his head toward the geology console and back. "Whatever you're calculating over there must be intense to be taking so long."

"I am running alternate simulations for the impacts."

Ra narrowed his eyes and scratched his head. "I thought you were sure they would work."

Enki pulled his hands out of his pockets and lowered his palms toward the floor to reassure Ra. "They will, they will. As long as things go according to plan."

Ra leaned his hip against the console. "You're running simulations in case something goes wrong?"

"Yes. I am creating an algorithm that can simulate various contingencies."

A crease spread across Ra's forehead. "Do you *expect* something to go wrong?"

"No, I do not," Enki said, "but I liked your idea of automating different plans ahead of time. And the eruption failure taught me to prepare alternatives in advance so that we may act with expediency in case of any troubling developments."

Ra nodded once. "That's a lot of words to say that you want to be prepared."

Enki cringed a little inside, but Ra continued, "Which is not a bad idea." He turned back to the helm and leaned in to the viewscreen. He moved his finger up the glyphpad a fraction of a cubit, and the *Meridian* sped up. "A lot can go wrong if we aren't paying attention."

"It can," Enki said, keeping an eye on Ra's screen. They were one tiny space rock away from being smashed to pieces at light speed. He caught movement out of the corner of his eye.

They both turned around to see Mirik and Nef coming climbing down the ladder.

Ra held his hand up to them. "Hey! Good to see you two."

Mirik jumped down to the floor, skipping the last two rungs.

Nef descended one rung at a time, rolling her eyes at Mirik. "Showoff." Her feet hit the floor and she strolled over. "What are you two doing? You look more anxious than a couple affis hiding from a hungry nathus."

Enki looked down, while they shared a laugh.

Mirik pointed to Enki. "This guy seems even more uptight than Ra."

Nef nodded in agreement. "I would not have believed you if you'd told me that was possible."

Enki's eyes darted to each of them. *Are they joking with me?* He started to open his mouth but decided against it.

Ra cleared his throat. "Nothing wrong with a little caution. Do either of you want another failure on our hands? I mean, we might not even be in this situation if Councilor Horus had listened to Enki the first time around."

Mirik hunched his shoulders and shook his head. "You're right."

Nef raised her forearm over her chest and bowed. "Sorry for teasing, we're thankful that you're so careful, Enki."

Enki returned the respectful gesture. "Thank you."

"I'm sorry, too," Mirik said, crossing his chest. "I guess we're lucky you know what you're doing."

Enki mustered a polite smile. "No apology is necessary."

Ra leaned back on the helm's glyphpad. "So, is Pakhet going to be the fourth pilot?" he asked.

Nef shook her head. "No, Captain Apep said he was going to, and of course insisted he pull the largest crystal."

"Captain Apep?" said Ra, with a glint of amusement in his eyes.

Mirik patted Ra's back. "Yeah, it's gonna be just like the good old days!"

Nef chuckled. "I don't think any of us would survive those days at this age!"

Enki winced as they burst into raucous laughter that echoed around the bridge.

Ra held up his hand to try and get back to business, but broke out into laughter again with a wheeze, which only made them all laugh more.

Enki tried laughing with them, but the weak attempt came across as apathetic at best. He gave up and tried a casual lean back on the console as he had seen Ra do many times. He felt the console, put his hip against it, and crossed his arms, then began sliding backward. His arm shot out to steady him, narrowly missing the *Meridian* control glyphs. He tensed as panic spread over his body. *Did they notice?* No more laughter came, so he assumed no one did. He leaned away from the glyphpad to stand up straight.

*Maybe I should ask a question.*

"So, you all worked together before the project?" he asked.

Mirik wiped his eyes with his sleeve and nodded. "We did. I met Captain Apep on a refugee ship after they deconstructed Tremva, when we were both kids. Then the two of us met Ra and Nef at a support group picnic in Puna for families who used to work in the shipping industry."

"Yes, all of our parents worked in oceanic shipping," Ra explained.

Mirik lifted an eyebrow. "Oh, your family worked, Ra?"

"Owning a company is work, too, Mirik," Ra said, dismissing the jab.

"I'm just messing with you. Sometimes I can't manage myself, let alone manage an entire company of workers."

"Hold on," Nef said, looking up for a moment. "I remember that picnic. That was when Captain Apep made us all play zoo, right?"

"Yep! I was the phara," Mirik said.

Ra's eyebrows shot up. "I remember Apep insisted on being a zookeeper."

"That's right, he sure did!" Nef chuckled and pointed to Mirik. "And

I remember him stealing your stuffed affi, telling you pharas couldn't have pets!"

"Yes, and the little guy has been with him ever since, see!" Mirik pointed to the upper edge of the console where the ratty old stuffed animal stared back at them. "I let the captain have it, though, after what happened to his real one when the Council deconstructed Tremva…"

Their wild gestures ceased as the storytelling energy drained from the room. Enki watched them all look toward the floor, avoiding eye contact with one another for a moment.

The geology console beeped, and Enki leaned back to get a look at his viewscreen. The progress bar read 100%.

"Ah," he said, turning to Ra. "I need to go start the next simulation."

"Hold on. What are you simulating over there?" Nef asked.

"The impact model has many more variables than the eruption. Based on chaos theory, of course."

Mirik and Nef exchanged confused glances.

Enki tried again. "Each calculation cycle takes time, so I am creating a database of alternate trajectories and impact sites to accommodate any uncertainties that may arise."

Ra put his hand on Enki's shoulder. "What Enki is saying is that he's planning ahead so we can act fast if something goes wrong."

Enki blushed. "Yes, that is correct. Thank you."

Mirik put his arm around Ra. "Say, does your friend here know about the plan?"

"I'm working on the plan," Enki said.

"Not that plan, Enki. What happens after it," Mirik said.

"After it?" he asked, not understanding what he was missing. "Nu will recover; there is no other plan."

Ra pushed Mirik's arm off his shoulders. He glared at Mirik. "The captain hasn't had time to speak to Kaia yet, but when he does, he wanted Kaia to be the one to tell Enki."

"Oh, sorry," Mirik said in apology.

"Tell me what?" asked Enki, his brow scrunched in confusion.

Nef put a hand on Enki's shoulder and nodded toward the geology station. "Like you said, Enki, can't be too careful." She crossed both arms over her chest and bowed. "You'd better go check that simulation."

"But—" The console beeped again, and Enki took a hesitant step backward. "Okay, I still want to hear about this other... plan." Then he turned and strode back to his console.

Ra glared at Mirik again.

Mirik leaned over to him, "Odd bird, isn't he?"

"But thanks to him, you can bet we'll be ready for anything," Ra responded through gritted teeth. He crossed his arms and locked eyes with Mirik, then Nef. "You two best get going."

They looked at each other, then said to Ra in unison. "Yes, sir." They bounded up the ladder and off the bridge like scolded children.

Ra went to Enki's console and watched him copying the number matrix over and over, adjusting variables as he went and starting new simulations. He finished tapping four new coordinates on the glyphpad and held his palm down to start the calculation.

"Don't you already have the final impact sites?" Ra asked.

"I am now simulating alternative options."

"I see," Ra said, watching the incomprehensible calculations flying past on the viewscreen. "So," he began, deciding to bring up the other reason for his lightdrive settings algorithm. "Do you remember what I was working on when we met? In the shuttle?"

"An algorithm to provide more granular control of time dilation," Enki replied, raising his head.

First Officer Ra nodded. "Yes, in part. Do you know why?"

"In case we needed it for..." then he remembered the algorithm's other feature. "Your simulated lightdrive output exceeds what we need for any impact plan." He thought for a moment then said, "I have other ideas."

First Office Ra invited him to guess. "And they would be?"

"Well, I know from the crew file that your family is on the *Hathor* cityship, but since it is not going to Duat, you must not be close with them. The file also indicated you do not have a partner, or children, and from what I have observed, all of your friends appear to be on board the *Meridian*."

Ra chuckled. "You're good, Enki. Keep going."

"I do not think you plan to stay on Duat."

"And what, then, am I planning?"

"You are planning to travel through deep time."

"To where?"

Enki turned away from his console to face Ra and crossed his arms, too. "Do not worry, I will not tell Kaia. But I assume you are planning to return to Nu after our simulations show our climate repairs are complete."

First Officer Ra's arms fell to his sides. "Wow, Enki, you're beyond good. You are a genius."

"So, I am correct?" Enki said with a slight grin.

"You're more than correct. You are spot-on," Ra raised a finger, "with one very large exception."

"I have a suspicion there, as well," Enki suggested.

"By all means." Ra waved his hand.

"You are going with Nef and Mirik."

Ra clapped his hands together three times then patted Enki's back. "Yes. Most of us are, Mirik, Nef, Thoth, Khnum. We all plan to leave Duat and travel millions of cycles into the future until whenever your simulation shows Nu will be habitable."

Concern spread over Enki's face. "What about the councilors? Captain Apep? Why doesn't Kaia know about this?"

"The captain plans to tell Kaia, but not the councilors, yet." Ra sighed and looked to the empty helm. "Captain Apep is still thinking about it all, though. His mother and sister are on the *Montu*, as I'm sure you know. It would be a tough decision for him to leave them on Duat."

"Yes, that makes sense." Enki grew somber.

The console beeped again, and they looked at the viewscreen.

*Simulation Complete.* Enki pressed start and swirled his finger to scroll to the end results. A vibrant green planet shimmered back at them.

"Was there a reason you did not ask me if I wanted to go with you?" He turned to First Officer Ra. "I may want to see this for myself."

Ra was taken aback. "We all thought you'd want to remain with Kaia, and we assumed Kaia would go where Hegira goes."

"Kaia has been very good to me when others were not, yes." Enki sighed. "But I do feel as though I am in her shadow."

"Well," Ra offered, "her shadow is cast by the light shone on her by Hegira. Don't assume that will last forever." He heard a footstep on the ladder and glanced behind him. "Speaking of..." He cleared his throat. "What do you think about the plan, Enki?" he whispered.

"I will think about it, but for now, I need to find out how many millions of cycles Nu will need to recover, so you can enter it into your lightdrive optimization algorithm." He smirked at Ra.

"That sounds good," Ra said as Enki dragged his fingers across the glyphpad in search of his answer, while the rest of the crew climbed down the ladder and took their stations.

# CHAPTER 6
# DIAMONDS

## MERIDIAN – AD CYCLE 107

Captain Apep felt refreshed as he descended the ladder onto the bridge. The rest of the crew seemed not to notice; their eyes trained on the viewscreen section in front of each station. Pakhet stared at gauge after gauge, most hovering in the yellow zone. Every few seconds, one would spike, causing a whirlwind of finger movement on her glyphpad to compensate. Enki, the lone science officer on the bridge, swiped away on his own glyphpad. The captain couldn't quite tell what he was working on but always assumed it was something very important when there were so many numbers on the screen.

First Officer Ra turned when Apep's foot clanged on the last rung. "I was beginning to wonder if you were coming."

The captain stepped up beside him and looked at the main viewscreen. "I wouldn't miss it."

The glowing ring on the main viewscreen still appeared motionless, but he could feel the ship humming with photonic acceleration. He passed the observation platform and nodded to Councilor Hegira on his way to the helm.

He whispered to Ra, "What's she doing here already?"

"Who?"

Apep nodded to his right. Councilor Hegira's eyes remained focused on the viewscreen until she noticed them and smiled.

Ra glanced back. "Beats me. I figured she would be somewhere scheming with Councilor Horus, as usual."

Captain Apep tried to stifle his laugh by looking away. He snapped to attention when he noticed Kaia coming down the ladder.

She stepped off and gave him a curt nod as she passed.


Kaia made a beeline to the geology console and saw four simulated crystals on Enki's viewscreen. They rotated to match the arcs he drew on the glyphpad.

She noticed his eyes were red. "How long have you been awake?"

He leaned in toward the viewscreen and moved his hands faster.

"Enki? Hey, snap out of it."

He jerked to a stop and rested his hands on the bottom of the console. "Sorry, I have been working on an algorithm to automate the impact simulation, so we can determine the optimal impact angle and location for each of the four crystals based on new data."

"Didn't you already do that?"

He nodded quickly, a little too quickly, she thought. "Yes, the results remain positive. I have not examined the nanomech modifications, but Councilor Horus assures me..." he trailed off and looked back to Councilor Hegira seated one station over. Councilor Horus now sat next to her, the two whispering to one another.

Councilor Horus looked up and scowled. "Enki, I told you their capabilities. Now stop questioning me."

Captain Apep strolled down the center of the bridge walkway. "Is everything okay over here?" His eyes moved between Enki and the councilors.

"Fine," Enki said, turning back to his console.

Councilor Hegira raised her chin. "Captain, shouldn't you be manning the ship at this critical time?"

He motioned back to the helm. "First Officer Ra has it under control." He offered Councilor Horus a viewpad. "I thought you might want to see the sensor configuration Pakhet is recommending. It will allow us to gather data from your nanomechs as they work."

Councilor Horus yanked the glyphpad from Apep's hands and swiped up. "I'll be studying this data until I die!"

Captain Apep raised his eyebrow. "Promise?"

Kaia decided on-the-spot that she could never reach Apep's level of disrespect toward the Councilors, even though it also kindled something towards them in her, Hegira in particular.

Horus looked back down at the viewpad. "I always outlive my adversaries, boy."

Captain Apep bowed. "It was a joke, Councilor. I'm sorry." He stepped out of the aisle and over to the mission console. "Hello, Kaia."

She felt her face flush. "Hello, Captain."

He addressed Enki. "How is Nu looking with your new simulations?"

Enki swiped the crystals away. He drew a circle, and the simulation appeared. "The result remains unchanged. The climate will stabilize between sixty and seventy million cycles from impact. We should add more biological data to gain precision, since the ecosystem affects habitability as well."

Captain Apep cleared his throat. "It sounds like we're still on track, then?"

Kaia nodded. "We are."

"Excellent."

First Officer Ra called over from the helm. "You'd better come here, Captain. We are almost home."

Captain Apep bowed to Enki. "It looks like the time is near," he said. "I have Ra bringing us to the edge of the phase two asteroid field so we can deploy the nanomechs. Will you be able to confirm the eruption is over at that distance?"

Enki nodded. "Yes, sir."

"Good."

Captain Apep held out his hand for Kaia to follow him to the mission console.

She brushed it away. "I can walk fine now, thank you." She nodded to Enki as she passed him. "We'll catch up later, okay?" she said, but saw he was already too absorbed by his work to hear her.

At the mission console, Kaia slid her left foot into the right-side loop on the floor.

"That one is all yours," she said, pointing to the open loop on the left.

"Thank you," Captain Apep said as he slid his right foot in, "for letting me use my own station."

"You're welcome," Kaia said, acting as though she just gave him a gift.

Ra raised his hand again. "We are dropping from light speed in three, two..." He drew a semi-circle on his glyphpad, and the bridge darkened as the starlight ring faded on the viewscreen.

Ra's countdown reached one, and the stars began to snap back into place.

The crew held on to their stations as the *Meridian* trembled. Kaia swore she could see the support beams flexing inward. On her left, Captain Apep braced himself against the console.

Ra clenched his teeth, then said, "Sorry, the shaking is worse than I expected. The lightdrive is running in reverse at full strength to slow us down, but I checked the power level multiple times, and we should be okay. As long as—" A bang ricocheted around the bridge.

"Report," Captain Apep ordered.

Ra glanced at the structural integrity monitor. The dial crept to the edge of the red zone. "I suspect it is one of the shuttle docking mechanisms twisting under the strain."

"Do we still have them?"

"Yes, sir," Ra said. "Three shuttles and four constructors docked."

"Good." Captain Apep held down the comm. His voice boomed over the noise, "Beginning final deceleration. Arriving at the phase two asteroid field now."

The ship groaned, along with the crew as it lurched to a stop. Councilor Hegira let out a yelp.

"Zero," First Officer Ra said with some hesitancy.

Kaia's mouth fell open in disbelief. She'd seen the asteroid field from afar, but it was even more beautiful up close. One hundred diamond-shaped asteroids stretching into the blackness of space. "It's… beautiful," she gasped.

Captain Apep clasped his hands behind his back. "Still takes my breath away, too."

"Excuse me, Kaia," Enki said, breaking her brief meditation. "I already have readings from the surface of Nu."

Kaia held her eyes shut for a moment to transition back to the mission, trying not to worry that something else had gone wrong. "Has the eruption stopped?"

"It would be better to show you. Captain, may I?" Enki asked, pointing to the main viewscreen.

Captain Apep nodded, and Enki swiped all the way up on his glyphpad.

The remains of Puna filled their view. A huge black scar split the city in two. "As you can see," Enki said with authority, "the eruption finished earlier than the model's prediction."

Kaia felt her pulse quicken. "Are we too late, then?"

Enki pointed to the graph on his viewscreen. "No, but 107 cycles have passed and the tipping point toward runaway cooling is fast approaching."

Councilor Horus clapped his hands once. "We had better get my nanomechs to work, then!"

"Are they ready?" asked Kaia.

Councilor Horus mumbled something under his breath as he went to the mission station. He drew a symbol on his glyphpad, and four circles appeared next to an enlarged nanomech bristling with drilling and grinding equipment. He began to release them when Councilor Hegira held her hand up in front of him. "That is Kaia's order to give, Horus."

"Thank you, Councilor," Kaia said with a nod. "Captain, everything is ready." She pivoted to Councilor Horus. "Release the nanomechs."

"I thought you'd never ask," he said with a sly smile.

Councilor Horus swiped up on his glyphpad to jettison four solid gray orbs from the front of the *Meridian*. He used both hands to draw four solid lines to guide them to the asteroids. Each sphere began dissolving into millions of granular bits.

Cloud-like fingers reached out from the swarms. The tiny machines reorganized into several streams flowing through the asteroid field. They pushed the small stones toward one another in four obvious clumps. Dust clouds expanded out where the asteroids met, and the nanomechs wasted no time beginning to merge them at the atomic level. They watched in stunned silence as the scale of their plan became evident.

Patterns in the dust reminded Kaia of the superstorms that swirled over the surface of Nu during storm season. Her heart grew heavy as her thoughts wandered to her parents, as they often did. Her eyes met Councilor Hegira's at the back of the room.

Councilor Hegira gave an approving nod and leaned back in the shadow of a support beam. A tingle swept up Kaia's neck. She thought of Captain Apep's question: did she trust Councilor Hegira? She looked back to the councilor's silhouette. *Why didn't she tell anyone about the other plan in the first place?* she allowed herself to wonder for the first time.

"Look!" Pakhet shouted. "You can already see the shape of one crystal!"

Enki tapped the upper right corner of his glyphpad, and the feed of the smallest asteroid filled the main viewscreen.

Kaia took a step back from the console to take in the view. "It's beautiful," she said as the mirror-smooth point poked through the top of the cloud.

Councilor Horus clasped his hands in front of his robe. "Quite impressive, isn't it?"

"Yes, it's more breathtaking than I imagined," Kaia said. "This is my first time seeing the little machines in an act of creation rather than destruction."

"Deconstruction, you mean," he corrected her.

She ignored the comment. "I've studied many swarming life forms on Nu, and it's hard to imagine these are machines and not a mass of living creatures."

Councilor Horus bowed his head and appeared to examine some floor tiles as he spoke. "I will admit a fair amount of their behavioral programming came from your biological research published in the journals."

Kaia smiled at this rare admission of credit. "I'm glad it was useful." She put her hands on her hips and looked right at Horus. "You know, some people might say old academic research was better left to the dusty halls of scientific history," she said.

Councilor Horus remained silent, but his eyes narrowed, betraying his irritation at her quoting one of his interviews. His voice softened as he spoke. "Perhaps we should work together more often."

She nodded, "Of course," and kept a smile to herself, content that he received her message and was hopeful that he would start to trust her. "How long do the nanomechs need?"

"No more than a day," Councilor Horus said. He turned to the captain. "By this time tomorrow, they will be ready for the constructors to haul them into alignment for impact."

"Looks like we're off to a good start, then," Captain Apep said. "Everyone, you're dismissed. We have a big day coming up, so get some rest!"

The crew all bowed and headed toward the ladder to exit the bridge. Kaia and Enki lingered behind, eyes still on the viewscreen.

Captain Apep sidled up next to her. "Hard to look away, isn't it?"

"It is magical," she said.

He nudged Kaia with his shoulder and gestured to the ladder. "Do you have time to continue our conversation from the depot?"

She considered it for a moment. Did she want the distraction of wondering whether she could trust Hegira? She thought again about the councilor's mysterious unveiling of the backup plan. "Enki wants me to fine-tune the simulation with biological data. Meet me in the lab, in say, two hours?"

He bowed. "I will see you then," he said and turned toward the ladder.

Enki shuffled over to Kaia. "Am I to assume you will be busy until the nanomechs finish combining the crystals?"

She crossed her arms playfully. "Enki! You don't miss everything after all, do you?"

"I miss nothing. I merely ignore uninteresting things." He looked down for a moment then shrugged. "And *most* everything is uninteresting compared to my studies." He smirked as he returned to his station.

Kaia glimpsed the captain's feet disappearing into the corridor and tried to tamp down that fluttery feeling in her stomach. The conflicting feelings were becoming annoying, though she could not prevent a smile from crossing her face.

# CHAPTER 7
# REDACTED

## BIOLOGY LAB - AD CYCLE 107

Kaia sat alone in her dark lab, bleary-eyed from spending the hour staring up at a projection above the table. The data matrix from Enki's impact model hovered in the air. His simulation showed that the climate would recover and stabilize, but the ecosphere's recovery timeline was still not clear. It would not matter to the plan, but Kaia wanted to know.

Enki had highlighted the data fields she would need for a refined simulation. But the data was proving hard to find in the *Meridian*'s archives. She searched every scientific publication from the last two hundred cycles and found little in the way of useful research. A spinning glyph appeared in the air, and she tapped to start another search, this time including unpublished research. She leaned back and lifted her arms in front of her, clasped her hands, and stretched her shoulders as she waited. The system beeped. A single item flashed at the top of a long empty list.

She leaned forward and tapped the glyphpad. The document's title page appeared.

·  ·  ·

*Multiple Impact Option to Reverse Climate Change.*
   *from Month 3, Cycle 2042*

*Promising, but old,* she thought and looked to see if she knew the author, but there was a black mark through the name. "That's odd." She swiped down to the next page and skimmed it. The words appeared ragged, like a bad scan of an actual document.

She read the first line aloud. "Our research revealed the crater to be twice as large as earlier studies assumed. Having combined this information with fossil data, we have high confidence that the impacts stabilized the climate and life flourished after the mass extinction." Her eyes widened as she continued to read. "I understand the notion of renewal through destruction is unpopular but may be necessary. If we are to save ourselves, to save our home, we must not exclude the impact plan option."

*This is it,* she thought. *This is the plan the Council rejected, the same plan they are now enacting.* She swiped through the pages and arrived at a familiar data table embedded between the paragraphs.

"This is almost identical to the model Hegira shared," she marveled. She double-tapped the glyphpad. The projection zoomed in to the data points gathered from the fossil record.

"It's all here," she said, scrolling through the data fields. "Biodiversity, habitats, populations, speciation, evolutionary rate."

Who removed these numbers from the impact model? The data was irrefutable. The climate would recover, evolution would continue, and life would go on. She wracked her brain for explanations while she selected the biological data points and swiped them over to Enki's updated model.

"Now…" Kaia tapped the glyphpad and watched the system lock the data in place.

"Start simulation?" appeared across the center.

There was a knock at the lab's door. She swiveled her chair toward the sound. "Come in."

A sliver of light appeared, followed by a metallic squeal. The door did not budge.

She got up and jogged over. "The door sticks!" She grabbed the handle and leaned to the side. Nothing. "Can you help?" she called to the person on the other side. A pair of gloved hands appeared in the opening and held onto the door. "Now," she instructed.

The door slid open with a bang. Captain Apep stood there with a concerned look. He leaned his arm against the doorframe. "I wanted to talk about our conversation in the depot, because I had a talk with the crew after we returned with the constructors, and—"

"Without me?"

He lowered his arm. "Well, not the whole crew. Everyone except you, Enki, and the councilors."

"What was it about?" she said, feeling her faith in him wane.

He put his hands in his habsew pockets. "Look, I've known them for a long time. They trust me. They had questions about the plan."

"I have more answers about this plan than you do, Captain," Kaia said, crossing her arms and giving him a stern look.

"You do, but..." he struggled to find the words. "They had questions about what happens long after the impact plan."

She looked back to the lab table and the projection. "I'm trying to find a way to show them that."

He pulled his hands out of his pockets. "They are curious to know what it will be like, though. Will there be forests again, animals, more superstorms?"

Kaia felt the weight of their question.

Captain Apep hunched down and tried to take some pressure off. "It's not on you, Kaia. They're not your crew."

"But that's tens of millions of years from now. We'll all be dead—" The glyphpad beeped. She glanced back at the screen, still waiting to start the simulation.

Captain Apep rubbed his forehead. "Saved by the beep. We can talk about it later if you want. What are you simulating, anyway?"

She faced the projection. "I'm refining the post-impact ecosystem simulation to answer the very question the crew asked you."

He held his hand through the doorway, palm up. "May I see?"

She nodded. "Of course."

He stepped past her to the projection. "Where did you find this?" he asked. "I thought you were missing a lot of the biological data. This looks complete."

She took a seat in front of the glyphpad. "Yes, we had enough data to know the plan would work. But," she tapped the pad, and a progress bar appeared, "we didn't know precisely *when* the recovery would be complete or *what* the climate would be like."

He watched the progress bar creep along. "Where did you find the missing data?"

She gestured for him to have a seat. He pulled out the stool next to her and sat with one arm resting on the table.

She turned to face him. "I found it in an unpublished research paper. One an earlier Council rejected."

"Rejected?"

"Yes, and someone redacted the author's name. It contains a model like the one Councilor Hegira provided. However, it had more biological data based on the fossil record. I think someone removed the data and tried to hide the research itself."

"Why?"

She shrugged. "I was asking myself the same thing. The best I can come up with is that it is just too much. The Council had a hard-enough time convincing society that an eruption and small impacts would work. This," she gestured to the paper, "might have given the Resistance more fodder to question why we would kill almost every species to save only a few. It would have been downright traumatic."

"Will be traumatic, you mean," he reminded her.

She looked at the progress bar. 25%. "Yes, but it's our only option now."

"I agree." Captain Apep leaned closer to her. "About what I asked you about in the constructor," he said just above a whisper.

She nodded for him to go on.

"Have you given it any thought?" he asked.

She sighed. "I have no reason not to trust Councilor Hegira."

Captain Apep looked down, trying to hide his dismay.

"But—"

He raised his head back up.

"I want to know why you asked," Kaia said carefully, testing the words with herself as much as with him.

"I do not trust her," he said without hesitation.

"Why?"

"I question her motives, Kaia. She only cares about herself, about her personal legacy."

Kaia shook her head. "That's not true."

Captain Apep took a deep breath and held it for a moment. Then he exhaled and she felt his eyes trying to cajole her into believing something she could not. "Some people care about others only because they like the adoration that comes along with it."

Kaia wondered if he was still talking about Hegira, or if he was suggesting she herself liked the adoration.

He leaned forward. "Kaia, I'm sorry, I know how you feel about her. I... I remember your parents' message. It was about change, yes, but it was change through education, through empathy—not through force. Councilor Hegira only understands force and coercion."

Kaia felt her cheeks flush and thought her eyes could burn a hole right through him. She raised her voice, "Councilor Hegira is the reason we're all still *alive*. She took me in and gave me a platform to continue the work my parents started. Councilor Hegira is doing the right thing."

Captain Apep clasped his hands and lowered his head to the floor again. "You can do the right thing the wrong way."

Kaia scoffed. "Why would you say those things about her?" she asked, beginning to feel stupid for allowing herself to let him in.

Captain Apep opened his hands, ready to offer a compromise, she assumed. "Can I tell you a personal story?"

Kaia studied his face. Whatever he was about to say, he believed it. She sat up straighter and crossed her arms. "About?"

He cleared his throat. "About how Councilor Hegira killed my father."

# CHAPTER 8
# CORE

Alan made it to the ship's railing in the nick of time. His stomach lurched, giving its shrimp dinner back to the ocean. The *Finality* was a huge, stable ship, but the subtle rocking was too much. He gathered himself and took a big gulp of water from his dented canteen. Thankfully, his bright floral print shirt was still clean. "I'm okay!" he yelled, waving to the crew.

Daxia ran over. "Is something wrong, Dr. Pearce?" She got closer and lowered her voice. "You don't look so good."

"I look better than this evening's shrimp."

She flinched. "Excuse me?"

"I threw up, Daxia. I threw up the shrimp dinner."

"Ohhh," she scrunched up her face. "Sorry I asked."

He wiped his beard and felt thankful when his hand still felt dry.

They both rested their arms on the railing and looked out to the horizon. The western sky glowed a faint orange as darkness crept up from the east. A slim crescent moon rose as the sun set over the Arabian Sea.

She pushed her hair behind her ear and sighed. "I'm going to miss these adventures with you, Dr. Pearce."

He smiled. "Why? You'll be on to bigger and better things! I'd give anything to be able to dig on the Yixian Formation."

She smiled. "I still need to pick a topic for my PhD thesis, though."

"Don't worry about that," he waved away her concern, "something will come to you."

"I know. It's more than that, though."

"Your father?"

Daxia stuttered, "Y-yes."

"He'll be okay. You'll keep him young working out there on the Yixian."

"His mind is slipping, but I hope you're right."

Dr. Pearce turned and leaned back against the railing, taking in the ship's deck. The derrick rose from the center of the ship like a drab Christmas tree. A group of roughnecks swarmed the rig, shouting unintelligible instructions to one another as the drill hummed.

Daxia turned around, too, and looked up just as the noisy rig ground to a halt.

Dr. Pearce chuckled. "Looks like they could use some help. If the PhD doesn't work out, there's always oil!"

She gave a one-shoulder shrug. "You laugh, but I'm sure they get paid more than most PhDs."

His smile slipped. "You got me there."

A man in a blue Tyvek suit looked over in their direction. He yelled something back to the crew, and the rig started turning again.

"Got it, sir!" someone yelled.

The man jogged over. His high-and-tight haircut speckled with gray would not have been out of place in a military uniform. "You two must be the scientists. My name is Jim Giles. First things first, put these on," he said, handing them hardhats, safety glasses, and radio headsets with hearing protection.

Dr. Pearce and Daxia took them and put each piece on. He held out his hand, then thought, *my first introduction should not include half-digested shrimp,* but in the interest of avoiding an awkward explanation, he shook Jim's hand anyway. Besides, he was pretty sure that shrimp was not the worst thing this fellow had touched today.

"We are indeed the scientists. Nice to meet you, Jim. I'm Dr. Pearce."

"Nice to meet you, too." The man moved his hand to Daxia. "The crew calls me Seagraves. I figure you can as well, so as not to confuse anyone," he added.

Daxia took his hand and shook it. "I'm Daxia Ling."

Seagraves smiled and rocked forward. "Right on. Nice to meet you, Daxia." He flashed them a big, confident grin. "I run the drill rig, but the one you need to talk to is still over there. One second." He whistled to the crew.

A wiry man came jogging over. He brushed rust brown hair to the side of his forehead. "What's up?" the thin-lipped man asked. His skin was so pale it seemed to glow through its grimy coating.

Seagraves gestured to Daxia and Dr. Pearce. "You should meet the scientists."

The man shook their hands. "Nice to meet you. Taylor here, but you can call me Notrees like every'n else round here." He turned halfway back to the drill rig. "Guess'n Seagraves here told y'all I'm in charge of making sure your core gets up?"

Daxia shook her head. "We didn't get that far."

Seagraves rocked on his feet with the waves. "I run the rig, Notrees handles the samples. Easy peasy."

Dr. Pearce held up two fingers. "A couple of things."

"Yes?" Seagraves nodded.

"One, how much longer until we have the core?"

Notrees chimed in, "The supervisor said five minutes, tops."

"Two, where in the world did your names come from?"

The two men looked at each other and chuckled.

"We figured you'd know from the accent. Texas is where in the world," Notrees said. "We're both oilers, but when the great West Texas oil fields dried up, we decided to work on our sea legs."

Dr. Pearce's brows rose. Although that was an interesting tidbit of info, he still had no idea what the names meant. He turned to Daxia to see if she looked more clued in than he did.

"I think Dr. Pearce was asking why those names?" she clarified.

"Oh, sorry 'bout that. I get stuck on our verb-y-age."

"What Notrees was trying to explain," Seagraves said, "is that they are the towns we grew up in. Seagraves is about sixty miles southwest of Lubbock, Texas."

Notrees nodded along. "S'right. And Notrees is twenty-five miles west of Odessa, but it's a blink-and-you'll-miss-it kinda place."

Daxia leaned forward. "Wait, you aren't joking? Someone named a town Notrees?"

The man nodded.

"As in no trees?" she clarified.

"Sure did. Not a dang tree in sight, neither."

Everyone shared a hearty laugh.

"What's funny?" Notrees feigned offense. "My family just got to work. Namin' towns takes time, ya know."

Daxia smiled and shook her head. "I can understand that. I study dinosaurs, and there are more than a few with names that could have only come from Captain Obvious."

"Like what?" Notrees asked.

"Like the *Sinosaurus magnodens*."

"Bless you," Notrees said, pretending to hand her a tissue.

She laughed and pretended to take it. "Its name means nose shaped like a sinus and big teeth."

"Where's that critter from? Maybe the person who found it is kin!"

Daxia shook her head. "I doubt it. A man discovered it while digging in the Yixian Formation."

He stared at her blankly.

"That is a fossil bed in China," she added.

"Ah, yeah, no kin of mine been there before." Notrees looked back to the rig. "Well, better skedaddle before Seagraves here decides to bury me at sea like 'is name says."

Daxia extended her hand to the man, and they shook. "Nice to meet you, Notrees."

Notrees jogged back to the rig and started barking orders.

Seagraves crossed his arms and looked to Dr. Pearce. "So, I hear this research of yours has something to do with the climate?"

Dr. Pearce fumbled with his hands. "Yes, but it's nothing to do with oil or carbon dioxide emissions. We're not trying to gather dirt on oil companies or anything. We're researching a plan to—it sounds funny when I say it—but to save the world someday."

"Well. I would say it's still pretty ironic."

"How's that?"

Seagraves laughed. "You're trying to save a world damaged by oil, on a ship whose only purpose is to find more of it to burn."

"The irony isn't lost on me." Dr. Pearce looked up at the rig just as it slowed to a stop. "Maybe this ship will also be part of the plan to save it."

# CHAPTER 9
# FATE

## BIOLOGY LAB - AD CYCLE 107

Kaia leaned back and analyzed Captain Apep's stern expression. He was serious. *He believes Councilor Hegira killed his father,* she thought. A chill traveled down her spine.

She averted her eyes and looked around her lab for a moment, then stared back into his eyes. "What do you mean, she killed your father?"

Captain Apep sat up straight on the stool and put his hands on his knees. "I mean just what I said."

"She would *never* do something like that." Kaia saw his face cloud. Something had happened, that much was obvious, but there was no way she believed it involved Councilor Hegira. And yet again, that chill passed through her.

He looked down then met her eyes. "Did you watch the deconstruction of Tremva?"

She checked again on the progress bar on her viewscreen. *47%*

Turning back to the captain, she straightened in her stool and said, "Yes, it was only a few days later that…" She turned away again.

"Kaia, that was a difficult time for both of us. We both lost important people at such a young age."

A squeak from the back of the lab interrupted them.

Kaia jumped from her stool and headed toward the cages along the back wall. "It's feeding time," she said.

"Let me help you."

She could hear the crinkle of Captain Apep's suit as he got up to follow her.

Kaia stopped in front of a shelf to retrieve a bin of brown pellets.

"Here." She handed it to Captain Apep. "These are for the affi. I'll take care of the nathus." She went to a cold storage cabinet and pulled it open. A misty vapor rushed out.

Captain Apep held the container up to his face and tilted it. The granules rolled over one another with a light swoosh.

Kaia pulled out a small clear bag of mushy red chunks and closed the door. "Those are dehydrated plant capsules." She held up her own bag. "And this is preserved meat. Nathuses are carnivores."

"Hm," he said, examining the capsules up close. "I always fed my pet affi table scraps."

"Why doesn't that surprise me?" Kaia pulled a tab to rip open the meat packet. "They're wild animals, you know."

Captain Apep bent down to the affi cage. "I know. My father got me one for my birthday when I was a kid." He put his hand on the latch and paused. "It didn't live long, though."

Kaia shot him a disapproving look.

"It didn't die because I did something wrong," he tried to explain.

She scoffed. "Keeping it as a pet was wrong."

He opened the latch, and the affi came out from its hiding place in the small log. It squeaked at him.

"Almost, little one, almost." He pulled out its food bowl.

The affi stood up on its hind legs, revealing its furry white underbelly. Its pointed nose twitched, sniffing the air. The food clinked as Captain Apep poured it into the metal bowl. He placed it on the pine bedding and closed the door.

The affi ran over on all fours and picked up a small piece of food, then another, and another, until its cheeks puffed out. It let out one more squeak, then ran back to the log.

Kaia looked down and saw him kneeling in front of the cage. He impressed her with how well he connected with the little creature. "I'm sorry, I only meant…"

"No need to explain. You spent your life trying to educate people on the importance of wild species."

She pulled the food tray out from between the bars of the nathus's cage and dumped in the chunks of meat. The nathus came out from behind a plant and made a chirping sound. She slid the food tray back inside, and the nathus ran over. It wasted no time, chomping down the meat without chewing.

Captain Apep stood, mouth agape, watching the nathus eat. "Someone sure was hungry."

It looked up at them and narrowed its eyes. A small growl turned into a miniature roar.

Kaia motioned behind them. "Let's let him eat in peace."

They returned to the lab table. The progress bar still hung in the air. *72%*

Captain Apep let his hands rest between his thighs.

Kaia crossed her arms low across her lap. "I believe you left off at the Tremva deconstruction."

Captain Apep looked concerned. "Are you sure you want to talk about this?"

"You, and everyone else, already know my story. I'd like to know yours."

He rubbed his thighs and began. "My memory starts with holding my mother's hand as she carried Helena, my younger sister you met, in her other arm. Our father explained we needed to leave our apartment soon because it was Deconstruction Day in Tremva. I looked out the window and asked him why there were so many airships outside. He explained we were the first of many Jacana cities to be deconstructed, and that the airships were recording the event to make sure that the next cities would know what to expect."

She leaned against the table. "I watched the recording of that day over and over at the wildlife observation facility. Even at seven cycles old, I never understood why they broadcasted it to the whole planet. It scared everyone, including me. As if uprooting everyone's lives and relocating to Puna wasn't scary enough."

"If you ask me, scaring everyone was Councilor Hegira's intent."

Kaia pulled her crossed arms up higher and felt an involuntary twitch in her jaw. She fought back her need to lash out and go on the defensive. She could at least hear him out.

Captain Apep studied her for a moment. "Hegira addressed us before it started, you know. She said we wouldn't have to go hungry any longer, which hit home for my family. My father lost his job a cycle earlier and we were struggling. She also said that in Puna, there would be no more flooding because we would be much farther away from the rising sea. I still felt scared about moving to Puna, though. I'd overhear my parents and their friends talking about the crime, about the garbage, and about what citizens did to refugees like us."

"There was some truth to those stories," Kaia admitted with regret.

"At the time, my father reassured me that my life would be better in the bigger city. He told me I had a bright future. He truly believed the Council would take care of us, no matter what happened."

He looked down and took a deep breath.

Kaia noticed his lips were quivering. She reached out and patted his knee.

Clearing his throat, he looked up, a hard glint in his eyes this time. "I didn't know those would be some of the last words my father said to me." He swallowed and said again, "That the Council would take care of us... My father trusted them, he trusted her—Councilor Hegira—right up to the end."

Kaia felt a strange combination of anger and anxiety muddying her thoughts. She still didn't understand what happened to his father. How was Councilor Hegira involved? But the direction his story was taking fostered a keen sense of dread in her.

"I-I don't understand, Captain. What happened to your father?"

"The deconstruction killed him, Kaia."

She gasped. *The man on the balcony.* "The man that died... was your father?"

He nodded and seemed to struggle to say more.

Kaia leaned forward. "Captain, you don't have to tell me this now. I had no idea."

He gathered himself and sat up straighter. "I'm okay. Yes, that man was my father. I'm sorry, I haven't told anyone about this for many cycles. Mirik, Nef, and Ra are the only ones onboard who even know my connection to the Tremva deconstruction, other than the Head Councilor herself."

Kaia's heart felt heavy, for the captain, and for herself, as selfish as it seemed. For some reason, she knew that when this story was over, things wouldn't be the same for her. But she took a deep breath and forced an encouraging smile onto her face—for him. She had to keep her mind open. She needed to be ready for whatever he was about to say. "Go on," she urged.

"Like you, I was seven cycles old, and I remember stepping out of my building with my habsew on and seeing people everywhere. I looked down the street to the waterfront where the massive cruisers waited to take us across the sea to Puna. I was holding my pet affi while my parents tried to tighten the seals on my sister's suit. She was squirming, as scared as I was, but as the oldest, I had put on a brave face. As I looked around, I could see fear and anxiety on everyone's faces. It was sad, seeing all these people with their entire lives crammed into three stacked green crates, waiting for movers to take them away from everything they knew. That was it, you know. The Council gave every family one large container and two small ones. If it didn't fit in the containers, it didn't go."

Kaia narrowed her eyes. "You had to fit all of your things in there? For a whole family?"

"Yeah, but we lived in a small unit so it wasn't too difficult. Families with more were forced to leave a lot more behind."

"That's unimaginable."

"It was, though everything seemed in order for us until I heard someone yelling in front of a building down our street. A man was arguing with his wife over which of four extra boxes should go into an already-overstuffed crate. He kicked an empty box in our direction. It hit our crate and knocked one of the small containers off the top, which crashed to the ground and spilled our stuff onto the street. That startled my pet affi and it ran straight back into our building. I was frantic. I yelled for it to come, but it disappeared into the atrium. It turned into quite a scene, with the neighbors arguing, me yelling, my sister crying, and with my mother trying to quiet her."

"It couldn't have been easy for anyone. I'm sure tensions were running high," Kaia said.

"Just when it couldn't get any worse, a line of huge movers came roaring down the street. Resettlement officers stepped out and barked orders at everyone to load up. I turned to my dad and started crying, too. I didn't want to leave my affi behind. He put his hand on my helmet and said he would get it. My mother begged him not to. She said we could get another affi when we got to Puna. I was having a meltdown. My father hugged me and said he would be right back, then ran inside our building after it."

Kaia noticed tears forming in his eyes.

He swallowed a lump in his throat. The urge to reach out overwhelmed her. She scooted her stool closer and rested a hand on his knee.

"He sounds like a good dad," she whispered.

The captain held his eyes closed for a moment and took in a sharp breath. "He really, really was." He reached up and wiped under his eyes. "But the resettlement officers were not as nice. When they noticed we weren't boarding a mover, they grabbed us by the arms and dragged us toward the one stopped in front of our building. We were the last ones to board. But I screamed that we couldn't leave without my father. The officers shoved me up the steps and shut the door. They said more movers would come before the nanomech initialization."

Kaia's head was spinning with images from that day. It all seemed so heartless now. "I've never heard that side. Councilor Hegira always stressed how sympathetic and understanding the officers would be. They received training just for that purpose."

"Training?" Apep scoffed. "I don't know what kind of training they got, unless it was an advanced degree in cold indifference."

Kaia's shoulders sagged. She felt questions rising to the surface but needed time to think before saying more.

Captain Apep tapped the table. "I boarded the mover with my mother and sister. It carried us and about one hundred other refugees to the shipyard. I looked out the window as we passed by empty street after empty street. The city's energy had vanished. It felt post-apocalyptic, which I guess, at that point, it was."

Kaia remembered the vibrance of the street she grew up on in Puna, kids running from backyard to backyard behind the dense rowhomes. Then the climate turned and made it impossible to play outside. She remembered how it felt to look out the window at the desolate neighborhood sidewalks and imagine she was the only kid left in Puna.

"When we arrived at the shipyard, they herded all of us into the ocean cruisers. My family was one of the last on the movers, so we were the first off and able to choose our own cabin. The resettlement ship must have been a repurposed luxury liner. Only the wealthiest could have afforded our room's view. I slid open the door and walked onto the balcony. Our ship passed the smaller boats being left behind in the harbor. Tremva's skyline was dark but still beautiful in the evening light. Our building was easy to spot because it was the third tallest. I noticed movement on one of the upper floors, squinted a little, and recognized my father standing on the terrace 150 stories up. He was waving and holding my affi, which now looked calm. Right after I spotted him, I heard the first alarm pulse. I yelled for him to get downstairs, but of course he was too far away to hear me. My mother and sister heard me yelling and came running out to the balcony. I pointed at our building, and my mother gasped and covered her face. Helena didn't quite understand what was going on. My mother did, though, and rushed to the comm in our room. The ship's captain answered and told her he would get a message to the Council right away."

Kaia swallowed hard, wishing for a moment that she didn't have to hear the rest.

A sharp edge crept into Captain Apep's voice. "The cruiser's captain called our room and said he had delivered the message to none other than Director Hegira herself."

The words knocked the breath out of Kaia's lungs. She squeezed her eyes shut, imagining Councilor Hegira faced with a decision to delay the deconstruction or have a person's death broadcast to the whole world. Her stomach dropped with this newfound knowledge. Kaia knew better than anyone how much Councilor Hegira understood the value of martyrs to rally people around the Council's plans.

Captain Apep asked, "Are you okay?"

Kaia felt the blood drain from her face. "Yes, sorry, please go on."

"Well, there isn't much else to tell that you haven't already seen in the recording. My mother and sister and I huddled on the balcony. When the alarm stopped, we watched as the nanomechs spread out to deconstruct everything in their path, which included our building. My father didn't panic, though. I guess he realized it was too late. The last time I saw him, he was falling into the dust, accepting his fate."

Kaia's eyes filled with tears as her mind replayed the scene in her mind, and then her own parents' last moments. They could have delayed the deconstruction to save Apep's father. But they, no, she— then Director Hegira—decided to make an example of the humble man falling to his death for the greater good, for the Council's mission to save the world, but it backfired and anger toward the Council grew. Did her parents know they would become martyrs for the Council's cause, like Apep's father became to the Resistance?

She remembered seeing the photo of Apep's family at the museum on her viewpad back at the wildlife refuge, before the storm swept her life away. She remembered the little boy, too, little Apep, and that long ago she'd worried about him. "I'm so sorry, Apep." She tried wiping the moisture from her eyes.

This time, it was him leaning forward to comfort her. "It was a long time ago. The memory almost feels more like a story I heard, not like something that happened to my family."

The captain's eyes were teary, so she knew that wasn't quite true and that he was playing it down for her benefit.

"Now you know my story. I know the truth is hard to hear." He pulled his hands away from hers and wiped a tear from his cheek.

"What happened after the deconstruction?"

"As you know, Councilor Horus's nanomechs did not touch organic material, so we were able to retrieve his body and carry out the traditional cremation. You weren't even able to lay your parents to rest. I can't imagine what it's like to not have that closure, to not be able to mourn their loss. To know that they're still out there... somewhere."

Kaia remembered the pomp and circumstance of the Council ceremony with two empty caskets. "I mourned. I am still mourning. You just... you move on, Apep." She looked at him anew, this man was full of surprises. "Your mother and sister are lucky to have you."

"I'm lucky to have them. And if Ra's calculations are correct, it won't be very long before we're reunited on Duat."

Kaia nodded.

Captain Apep shrugged. "We're still here for it, aren't we?"

"For what?"

"The greater good," he said with a weak smile.

The glyphpad beeped. They glanced up at the projection. *Simulation Complete.*

Kaia turned to the welcome distraction, but her hand hovered in the air just above the glyphpad.

He looked at Kaia. "Well? Aren't you going to find the answer to your question?"

She turned back to him, trying not to let their newfound tragic connection overshadow the task at hand. "What if the simulation shows we will fail?"

"How could it?" he asked.

She spun back to the projection. "Someone tried to hide the data I used. I'm not sure why, yet."

He shrugged. "That doesn't change the fact that your simulation is complete."

"You're right. Let's find out when Nu can support a civilization again." She tapped the glyphpad.

Their heads shot back as soon as they saw the number.

*66,190,237 cycles* hung in the air.

They looked to one another, wide-eyed, then back to the projection.

"That's about what I expected, but it's still hard to imagine," Kaia said.

"Do you have plans for then?" Captain Apep asked.

Kaia turned to him, dumbfounded. "Plans for what?"

"For 66 million cycles in the future," he said with a sly smile.

She wrinkled her brow. "Yes. I plan to be dead."

He held his hand over his stomach and laughed. "I may be crazy, but remember I said the crew was asking me questions about, you know, *after?*"

"Um, ye-es?"

He laughed. "I'll cut to the chase. The crew wants to come back after this plan."

"Come back?"

"Yes," he held up a hand. "When Nu is ready, of course."

"What about Duat?" she asked, not sure where he was going with this line of questioning.

He shrugged. "We'll still go there first, drop off the Councilors and any crew members who have changed their mind and maybe even pick up anyone who wants to come. I really hope my mother and Helena want to join us, but they were never as adventurous as me. Either way, we'll say our goodbyes if necessary and come back to Nu."

She thought about the impacts. The world would still be volatile, changing, even dangerous. "How will you know when it's safe?"

"Simulations, like the one you're running now, should be able to tell us, I think."

That was only true to the extent that the simulation was accurate, she worried. "We'll need to travel millions, maybe even tens of millions of cycles into the future. So much can happen between now and then."

He rocked his head back and forth. "You'll need to ask First Officer Ra for the details on that. He says it's possible, something about approaching the speed of light even closer than we did this time around."

She narrowed her eyes, unsure what to make of it. "What would we do there?"

He leaned forward and stared into them. "We can start over, Kaia.

Live off the land like our ancestors did. Guide sustainable development, without all the baggage of Council politics and entrenched ideologies. Not to mention the planet itself. Lush, clean, full of life. Wouldn't you like to see it?"

She imagined the green world from Enki's simulation. Her mind spun with possibilities. The jealousy of her colleagues exploring the destination planets faded to the back of her mind. "Of course I would, but—"

"Good." He sat back and tapped the table. "The crew is already excited about returning." The gleam in his eyes dulled, and he grew somber. "Can you promise me one thing, though?"

"I haven't agreed to anything yet," she said, though admitted to herself it was more interesting than Duat.

"Actually, I need two promises," he started, "about Councilor Hegira."

She now knew he was full of surprises, and not always good ones. She crossed her arms again to prepare.

He softened his voice. "It's just, I see how she treats you, and it bothers me. I know she tells you to rise above your past. She tells everyone that, not to dwell on our past lives and to be our own person."

Kaia pursed her lips. "I am my own person."

Captain Apep sighed. "You are, but she likes to make you the face of her agenda because everyone knows you. We all grew up with you, seeing you on all the Council announcements about the Dawn Project. She knows everyone likes you." He paused and lowered his voice. "Kaia, everyone loves you. But," he looked back down and shook his head, "she uses that love. She hides behind it."

"Why would she do that?"

He clicked his tongue. "That's the thing about her. You won't see Councilor Hegira's plan until it is too late."

Kaia still said nothing.

Captain Apep's eyes softened. "All I'm saying is don't let her keep you under her thumb. You don't have to do whatever she wants. You can... No, you should, have a plan of your own. Others will listen to you. There's more than one way to achieve any goal. Please, listen to your gut at least as much as you listen to Hegira."

Captain Apep's glyphpad beeped, and First Officer Ra spoke through his comm. "Captain Apep, please come to the bridge. The crystals are almost complete."

"I'll be right there, Ra."

"Good, and bring Kaia with you," he said with a snicker. "You are with Kaia, right?"

Captain Apep ignored him and looked at Kaia. "Anyway, that's why I asked if you if you had plans," he nodded to the projection, "in about 66 million cycles."

She was not sure what to say but was finding it hard to resist. Councilor Hegira promised her a fresh start, but there would be challenges on Duat. She knew the Council would need her to support their agendas, despite Hegira's assurances to the contrary. A future on Nu, without the Council, seemed more than a little interesting. She uncrossed her arms and said, "I'll consider it."

Captain Apep rose from the stool. "I'm looking forward to it," he said. "See you on the bridge?"

Kaia smiled in return. "I wouldn't miss this for the world."

The door squealed as he pulled it open. He lingered in the doorway and turned to look her in the eyes one more time before stepping into the hallway.

Her mind raced through the possibilities, the opportunities to start again. When the door slammed shut behind him, she snapped back to reality.

They were about to decimate their home planet in a desperate attempt to save it.

Kaia looked up at the projection. *66,190,237 cycles.*

The heaviness in the pit of her stomach was in direct conflict with the buzz of possibility in her mind as her growing feelings for Apep roared back. She still needed to process everything.

*A new world*, she thought, is what could be ahead for her on Nu, her home. The possibilities filled her mind and began settling into the unknown with Captain Apep.

# CHAPTER 10
# DISTORTION

## ARABIAN SEA - 2034 CE

Daxia made her way over to a touchscreen near the drill rig as the *Finality's* crew brought up the core. There was a buzz of excitement in the air.

Dr. Pearce joined her and let out a long, gurgling burp. He adjusted his hard hat and pulled the headset microphone over his mouth. "Sorry, still not all settled down there," he said, rubbing his stomach. "How is the drilling going?"

She pushed the safety glasses up higher on her nose and frowned. "Disappointing, so far. It's been layer after layer of brown granite."

"At least we won't have to report it to the council if nothing turns up! They already question everything I do. This will be one less thing for them to reject me on." Dr. Pearce looked at the screen and pointed to a blue dot pulsing over a white background. "Is that us?"

She nodded. "Yes, it's a little hard to make out where we are in relation to the depression on the seafloor. Here, let me show you a better view." She tapped a menu on the screen.

Topographic lines appeared as the map zoomed out. The contours of the 350-mile-wide Shiva anomaly came into view.

"The captain did an excellent job placing the ship. We're right over the center," Daxia said.

Dr. Pearce dragged his finger sideways to get a better look at the western edge of the seafloor's jagged slope. "It's the perfect spot to drill. If this is an impact site, we'll know it soon." He rested his hand below it and leaned in for a closer look.

The screen shut off.

"Hey!" Dr. Pearce said, smacking the wall. "What is with these machines. Daxia, can you pull that back up, please?"

Daxia smiled to herself. When it came to the big stuff, like how to fix climate change, he was one of the most brilliant scientists she knew, but the little stuff—like remembering to pay a phone bill, or how to set an alarm clock, or how to work on a computer? Well, he was hopeless. "We need to get you some lessons."

He laughed. "Why would I need those when I have a fresh pool of students to do it for me each year?"

Raising one eyebrow, she moved him out of her way. "What did you do to it anyway?"

"This *contraption* just turned off. I didn't touch a thing!" he maintained.

Daxia touched a button below the screen, and the image reappeared. She looked at him like someone helping their aging parent. "You pressed the off button when you leaned in."

"It's a conspiracy against old folks like me," Dr. Pearce huffed.

Nearby, Daxia saw one of the drill crew saying something to the man next to him over their radio headsets. They laughed and looked away.

Dr. Pearce's brows furrowed. He cleared his throat and said, "Yes, well, the thousands of hours of research in Mexico with *sophisticated hardware and laboratory models* lead me to believe this Shiva structure below us is at least three times as big as the Chicxulub crater."

He glanced back to the men, but their radios must have been on another channel as they focused on the drillstring tube containing the core.

Daxia tapped the screen to redirect his attention. "Do you want to go over to take a look?"

He rubbed his stomach. "I'm not feeling settled yet. I think I should stay here."

Daxia frowned. "Suit yourself," she said. "I'm going to go watch the crew bring up the next core." She walked over to the railing that encircled the drill cutout at the center of the ship.

Dr. Pearce continued studying the contour lines on the zoomed in image. The Shiva structure was oblong with ill-defined, worn side ridges that made it difficult to find the true center. Whatever it was, it had to be ancient. "No wonder it took so long to find it. It doesn't stand out much, especially for an impact crater if that's what it is," he said out loud.

He tapped to turn on an overlay of Earth's tectonic plates. The western edge of the Indian plate ran right through the Shiva structure. All the underwater landforms around the boundary appeared stretched.

*Why didn't this occur to me until now?*

He facepalmed. It was Geology 101 that India was once a small continent. Tectonic plate movement over tens of millions of years carried it until it collided with China. The collision drove land high into the sky and created some of the tallest mountains on Earth—the Himalayas, home of Mount Everest.

"Daxia! I need you to work your magic again!" he yelled.

She ran over. "Uh oh, what is it this time?"

He waved in the direction of the screen. "See this? Everything in this area appears stretched, including the Shiva structure. It looks like it could be tectonic movement."

Standing next to him now, she leaned in for a closer look. "You're right, it does."

Notrees's voice popped onto the radio channel. "The next core is about fifty meters from the surface!"

"Good, good! Keep it coming!" Dr. Pearce replied, waving his arm at them without taking his eyes off the screen.

"Daxia, can you rewind time on this map? Simulate India moving back to where it was?"

She was already on it, swiping around and tapping menus Dr. Pearce did not know existed. She finished changing the settings and pressed play. They both leaned forward in anticipation.

India slipped away from China and the Himalayas sank to a flat coastal plain. A widening waterway formed between the two landmasses. The underwater topography contracted, while the coast of India remained similar to the present day. Slowly but surely, the Shiva structure became more circular. Its low ridges in the center rose to match those at the edges.

"Wait. Right there, look!" Dr. Pearce shouted.

Daxia tapped the spacebar to pause the simulation.

Dr. Pearce pointed to the topography and lit up. "I knew it! It's circular now. Look at the edges. It's a perfect circle!"

She shook her head in awe. "Incredible."

"It has to be a crater. Distorted now, but still a crater."

A horrible screech filled the air.

Even with headsets on, they all covered their ears as the rig ground to a halt.

Notrees and two crewmen lugged a large plastic tube up the stairs. He pulled his headset down around his neck. "Something looks different with this one, figured you'd want to see it."

Dr. Pearce raised both hands above his head. "Well, don't just stand there! Get it down to the lab!" he barked.

He turned to Daxia. "We need to check for shocked quartz! And check the composition for—" He paused, unable to think straight. *Could this really be another crater?* His mind felt like a mini-tornado, and he raised a hand to his temple in an unconscious attempt to steady it. *The council is going to be certain I'm crazy now.*

Daxia spoke up, finishing his thought for him. "And check the composition for iridium?"

He felt his face split into a wide grin. *This was big.*

Moving back to the crewman, Daxia pointed them toward the

stairway leading into the ship. She looked back to Dr. Pearce. "You coming?"

He nodded, and she bounded down the stairs after the crewmen with the core. Turning back to the screen, he squinted and rubbed his chin. The circular landform filled the screen, staring back at him like a giant eye. He leaned in closer, and the giant eye winked out. Darkness!

He cried out, "Daxia, help!"

# CHAPTER 11
# OUT OF THE BLACK

## MERIDIAN - AD CYCLE 107

Kaia's feet touched the bridge floor. She looked around to figure out why everyone was so quiet. When she glanced up at the main viewscreen, her mouth fell open. She squeezed her eyes shut and opened them again. Four *Meridians* were looking back at her. "What is happening?"

Captain Apep kept his eyes on the ships and tilted toward Enki, who was standing at the mission console next to the helm. "Ask him."

They all watched as the ships moved in unison, then disappeared, only to reappear at a different angle.

Enki grinned and clapped his hands together, looking from the viewscreen back to the crew members. "It is the crystals! They are reflecting views of the *Meridian*."

Kaia saw them then: giant crystal-shaped rocks rotating in space. Now that her mind knew what they were, each angle, each edge was in stark relief. The surfaces appeared as smooth as mirrors. The nanomechs transformed one hundred small white asteroids into four gargantuan, perfect octahedrons: each half with four angled triangular sides pointing to a perfect point at both ends.

Councilor Horus stood up and clapped. "I knew they could do it!" He jabbed in Captain Apep's direction. "I told you the nanomechs would work!"

Councilor Hegira joined in the applause, still seated. "Good work everyone, and thank you, Councilor Horus."

Captain Apep turned to him. "Yes, congratulations, Councilor Horus. Your nanomechs outperformed our expectations."

Councilor Horus held up the viewpad and drew a circle above a diamond. He tapped, and it beeped in recognition.

The surface of the crystals appeared to move, a cloud forming around each one. The dust began to solidify into four large orbs above each crystal.

"My nanomechs self-replicated more than I could have dreamed." Councilor Horus stepped toward the viewscreen. "We haven't had this many nanomechs since the deconstruction days." He turned to the helm. "We must take them with us."

Captain Apep seemed mesmerized by the crystal shapes.

Councilor Horus put his hands on his hips. "Captain?"

Captain Apep stood up straight and answered in an official-sounding voice, "You're right, Councilor. Our mission isn't over yet—we may still need them. Open the cargo bay doors."

Each sphere moved toward the *Meridian*.

"Thank you, Captain." Councilor Horus walked back toward the wall. He sat next to Hegira but shifted his body away from her as subtly as possible and lifted the viewpad to his face. A scan of the crystals appeared on his screen. A tiny sphere sat in the heart of each crystal. Not the crystal forming nanomechs this time, but the special ones he had created earlier. "Your job will begin later," he told the nanomechs sitting in suspension.

"Excuse me?" Councilor Hegira said.

He jerked around to look at her. "Apologies, Councilor. I did not mean your job. I meant…" he looked at the tiny hidden spheres again and hoped they would survive impact.

"What did you mean then, Horus?"

He squeezed the viewpad's edge and it shut down. "The crystals. I meant the crystals will begin their job soon." He smiled.

Councilor Hegira pursed her lips as she regarded him. She wore a look that hovered on distrust. It was familiar to him. If only people understood that he always had the greater good in mind, maybe not *their* greater good, but… oh well.

Looking away, Horus noticed that the crew was standing still, astounded by the sight of the crystals. He raised his voice. "Well, come on, Captain. We didn't make these things to sit there and look pretty. Let's get the crystals moving!"

His words seemed to do the trick, as one-by-one, the crew went back to work. Pakhet scanned the data on her viewscreen. Even from where he sat, Councilor Horus could see nothing but green on the various indicators she was analyzing.

At the geologist's station, Enki spread his fingers on the glyphpad, zooming in to the simulated Nu. Four red circles marked each point of impact. He zoomed in farther, taking note of their coordinates on the glyphpad. "Captain Apep?"

"Yes, Enki?"

"I am sending the coordinates to First Officer Ra. It is critical that all four crystals strike at these precise locations and at the specified angle and velocity."

"Understood," the captain replied. "And Enki, congratulations to you, as well. So far, so good."

"It is too early to say with certainty," he replied, "but thank you, sir."


At her station, Kaia accessed her post-impact ecological simulation to update it based on the precise measurements of the actual crystals and the precise impact locations from Enki. She saw the final number remain at 66,190,237 cycles and turned to Enki. "Sixty-six million cycles is hard to imagine, isn't it?"

"No, I find it quite easy to imagine thanks to the simulations," Enki said.

Behind them, Kaia noticed Councilor Hegira stand up, steadying herself on each console as she made her way to the helm.

"Here, let me help you," Kaia said and jogged over.

"Thank you," Councilor Hegira said. "I never can get used to the gravity in this place."

Captain Apep turned to greet them. "How can I help you, Councilor?"

"Have you programmed the course into the constructors?" Hegira asked.

Captain Apep cocked his head. "Yes and no."

"Don't be coy with me, Captain."

He softened his stance. "I mean to say we have charted the course for each impact," he looked at Kaia, "but the constructors do not have autopilot."

"No autopilot?" Councilor Hegira asked.

He shook his head. "Afraid not. They will do the job we need them for, but they are manual control. First Officer Ra, Mirik, Nef, and I will each be piloting a constructor."

"Did you say you're going to tow one yourself?" she asked with concern.

He nodded. "Yes. We will get them up to speed then cut the cord and return to the ship." He looked over at Enki. "We've already run the simulation. The asteroids should have enough momentum to continue without the extra acceleration of a constructor."

"He is correct," Enki said, looking up from his work for a moment.

Kaia tried to push away the thought of Captain Apep and the others hurtling toward Nu with a giant asteroid crystal as cargo. "Which crystal are you going to tow, Captain?"

"The largest one," he said. "All those years as a pilot will come in handy."

Kaia looked down and fidgeted with her glove.

"Don't worry. It is perfectly safe," he said.

*Sure, it's perfectly safe,* she thought. She flashed a brave smile.

Captain Apep stepped back from the helm. "Councilor, Kaia, sorry to leave you here, but I need to get to work."

Councilor Hegira bowed. "Of course."

Kaia gave him a once over. She felt like she was seeing him in yet another light. Not just a captain, but a leader, out there with his team, at the forefront. And a mighty handsome leader at that.

He held out his hand. She took it and walked with him to the ladder.

Facing her, he held up his other hand. "So, are we on, in 66 million cycles?" he whispered.

Kaia took it and looked up into his eyes with a coy smile. "Yes," she said, the word jumping out of her mouth. "I'll come with you."

"Are you sure?"

"I'm sure," she said.

And then his arms wrapped around her, and her heart flip-flopped. Someone from the crew whistled; Pakhet, she thought, but no matter. Kaia could not stem the rush of emotions, excitement tinged with anxiety and other feelings she would need to sort out later.

Captain Apep winked at her then motioned to Ra, Nef, and Mirik to follow him up the ladder. Kaia watched them and imagined a future on Nu, before the Jacana ruined it. The simulation couldn't do it justice now that the future would include Captain Apep.

She made her way back to the mission console and caught a concerned look from Councilor Hegira. *Did she overhear?*


Everyone kept their eyes on the bridge viewscreen as four yellow constructors left the *Meridian* and moved toward the crystals. Captain Apep, First Officer Ra, Mirik, and Nef aligned each ship to the apex of each crystal and fired grapplers just below the top point of each stone. Ripples ran up and down each line, causing the crystals to swing around when the constructors began to move.

Kaia felt like a ball of nervous energy. It would have been hard to watch before, but imagining a future on Nu with Captain Apep made the risk almost unbearable.

Pakhet, now at the helm, pressed the comm to the pilots. "Tighten up the lines or you'll lose control!"

Kaia saw Captain Apep's constructor move erratically in response to the swinging crystal and held her breath.

"Pilots, we better listen to Pakhet," he warned. "Let's reel them in!"

The four pilots winched in the towlines, and the rocking reduced to a shudder.

Mirik said, "I think I'm going to be sick."

"You were always sick!" Nef said with a chuckle.

Ra's voice was stern, "Now is not the time, you two."

"Sorry, yes, sir," they replied in unison.

"Thank you, Ra," Captain Apep said. "Now, begin gentle acceleration."

Each of the constructors jolted to a standstill once the lines were taut and the connections secure.

"I'm good now," Mirik said.

"Me too, sir," Nef added.

"Ra?" Captain Apep asked.

"Ready, Captain," he replied.

"Okay, let's fire up those boosters!"

Excited murmurs rose from all around the bridge as the crystals began to move.

Kaia joined Enki at his console. "I hope we're doing the right thing," she said.

"We are doing the only thing we can to save Nu," he reassured her.

Kaia looked away from the mission console to the helm. Pakhet was standing wide, both hands on the helm glyphpad, and her eyes locked on the viewscreen as the crystals passed the moon, Iah.

Pakhet placed her hand on the glyphpad and dragged up. An almost imperceptible change in the gravity caused everyone to rock back the moment the ship's thrusters engaged.

Satisfied that Pakhet had the *Meridian* under control, Kaia looked back to the main viewscreen and saw the four bright crystals framing Nu. Gaseous plumes shot from the back of each constructor as they built enough momentum for the crystals to continue on, so Captain Apep and the others could break away and return to the ship before impact.

The familiar arrangement of continents became clear as Nu grew larger on the viewscreen beyond the crystals. It was almost peaceful, she thought. Four flawless, shining crystals floating in space, gliding toward the planet. But her logical side knew it was a contradiction.

Destruction was at hand.

She shifted her weight and rested her hands on the console, watching Professor Thoth and Dr. Khnum work for a few moments. Khnum was rocking back and forth on his heels, at ease with the readings on his screen. Kaia assumed no one's heart rate or stress levels had risen enough for him to encourage them to slow down.

Thoth traced the perimeter of his glyphpad, causing it to glow in the center. He then tapped the center and the glow faded. A small red light illuminated on Kaia's console.

"I initiated a recording," Thoth said.

The word 'recording' triggered an instinctual fear that Kaia forced to the back of her mind as she tried not to look at the red light. The same round red light she'd seen on the console of her parents' shuttle so many years ago. She heard rustling from the Council viewing platform behind her as Councilor Hegira prepared to say something.

"Thank you, Thoth. This is a historic event that all Jacana should see one day," the councilor said.

Kaia heard a slight quiver in Councilor Hegira's voice and remembered the daunting difference between the simulation and real life. She turned to smile at her and could have sworn she saw tears welling up in Hegira's eyes. This time, they would save Nu.

Councilor Horus, however, could not have looked more bored. He leaned to the side of his chair, resting his head in one hand, and tapping the arm rest with the other. She remembered his impatience during the initial drilling for the eruption, too. It was the pinnacle of his career, yet here he was slouched in his chair. She assumed he would perk up again once the crystals drew nearer to Nu.

There was a creak on her right. Kaia looked over to see Enki rocking back and forth at the geology console, waiting for sensor data to appear in the empty bar charts and line graphs on his viewscreen.

"Is everything still okay?" she asked.

Something flashed on his screen, then he swiped left. She squinted to get a better look when it began to fill with bright charts. Ascending and descending lines flew to the right on the graphs. Bar charts sprouted from the X axis like blooming skytowers as data poured in from their sensors.

"Well, Enki, what does it say?"

He studied the same graphs at his station for a moment. "As I predicted," he told her. "May the data and I join you?"

Kaia asked, "Are we too late?" as Enki's fingers swiped up on the glyphpad.

"No, we are just in time," he confirmed.

She closed her eyes and took a deep breath. The lightdrive hummed through her feet. She'd never noticed it before.

"Kaia," Enki said, his voice seeming to float into her awareness. "Kaia, I think you need to see this. Now that we are closer, the sensors detected an anomaly."

She opened her eyes and exhaled. "What is it?"

"This is—" he paused and spread his fingers over the glyphpad to zoom in farther, "it is something different."

On the viewscreen, Kaia saw the familiar gray mass of Puna's urbanization was now a black stain of cooled lava. Something else caught her eye, a white spot just off the western coast. She pointed to the strange island. "What is that?"

"That," he emphasized, "is what I wanted you to see. I do not know, and we are too far to zoom in more. The sensors are showing it is organic."

Kaia moved in for a closer look but only saw a fuzzy mass.

"If it is organic, send it over to Dr. Khnum for life form analysis, and maybe Professor Thoth can squeeze some more detail out of the sensors. You need to stay focused on the final details for the impacts."

"Of course." He tapped the upper left corner of his viewscreen. A circular diagram of the bridge appeared on his glyphpad. "Dr. Thoth, Professor Khnum, Kaia has requested your analysis of an organic anomaly off the western coast."

Professor Khnum's youthful voice replied, "Thanks, Enki. We'll get right on it."

Kaia nodded to them across the bridge. "Thank you." She looked back down at Enki's viewscreen and tensed when Captain Apep's voice came through.

"Everything still okay with the impacts?" he asked.

She leaned close to Enki and whispered, "Do we tell them?"

Enki shook his head. He leaned toward the comm. "Captain, the impact velocity and four locations remain accurate."

"Excellent, Enki. That's excellent."

Kaia held down the upper right corner of the glyphpad to open the comms up to the whole bridge. She heard a click and then Captain Apep's voice over his constructor's engine. "Pilots, did you hear that?"

"Yes, sir," First Officer Ra replied. "Enki, I am in position, and the crystal is near peak acceleration heading for Nu. Mirik, Nef, are you ready as well?"

"Ready," they replied in unison.

Another click, then Mirik's voice. "I hope whatever we left alive down there has run for the hills!"

Kaia winced but ignored the comment. She was about to tell Enki she was going back to the mission console but saw him preparing a post-impact data table for the real data that would come soon. She glanced back to the viewscreen for a moment, then went to the empty spot next to Pakhet.

"Everything is on track," Captain Apep assured the crew. "Pakhet, I am showing only seven more minutes of acceleration before we can cut the crystals loose. Can you confirm?"

"Yes, confirmed," Pakhet acknowledged. "I'll activate the docking stations now."

"Thank you," he said and clicked off his comm.

Kaia stood behind the mission console, watching the countdown with her arms crossed.

Pakhet said, "Great work, Kaia. It's nice for something to go according to plan for once."

They exchanged smiles and watched the four crystals shimmering dead ahead on the viewscreen.

A clang sounded around the bridge. Kaia leaned back to look behind Pakhet. Professor Thoth was running toward them, arms raised.

"Kaia, wait!" he yelled.

She scrunched up her forehead in concern, "What is it?"

"Something is..." he bent over and rested his hands on his knees. "Something is very wrong," he said between ragged breaths.

Councilor Hegira and Horus scooted forward in their chairs.

"Say again, Professor?" Councilor Horus said.

Thoth stood and gestured to the mission console. "Kaia, may I?"

She stepped back. "Yes, be quick," she said, eyeing the countdown.

He stepped over to her console. She felt her eyes widen as he brought up an image of the white spot below. It was no longer a single spot, but dozens of perfect white rectangles in concentric circles.

"How... What... It looks like a city, laid out like Puna, but smaller," she said.

"And look at this," he said, displaying the sensor readings. The biomass indicator soared to the top of the chart.

Kaia gulped and looked right at him. "It can't be. Those are—"

"Refugee tents," Councilor Horus finished for her.

Dr. Khnum approached from behind. "Yes," he took a place beside them, "They're standard issue habitat tents."

They all stood dumbfounded. Kaia heard more footsteps and saw Enki marching forward. He looked at the screen, slack-jawed like the rest of them.

Councilor Hegira broke the silence. "They can't be habitats." She dismissed the image with a wave of her hand. "Must be some kind of sensor echo."

Councilor Horus scoffed, "Of course it is. We left nothing, no one behind." He glanced at Hegira.

Kaia read the bridge's datestamp out loud. "AD Cycle 107."

Enki stepped closer. "That is not possible. No tents could survive the elements that long."

"That's why I don't think they've been here for over one hundred cycles," Professor Thoth said.

Dr. Khnum shook his head. "They haven't. Professor Thoth, next set of readings, please."

Professor Thoth swiped left.

Dr. Khnum cleared his throat. "As you can see, the life readings are Jacana. A few other species mixed in, some nathuses, some affis, but mostly Jacana."

"Impossible," Councilor Horus said, unwilling to believe. "Put that image on the main viewscreen. Now!"

Kaia drew a circle. She looked around the bridge and saw every crew member's eyes widen even farther as the image resolved with perfect clarity now that the *Meridian* was closer to Nu. Her mind struggled to find an explanation. It looked like a Jacana settlement.

A blaring proximity alarm broke her focus.

The helm's viewscreen flashed bright red.

Pakhet yelled, "Sensors show something coming around from the other side of Nu! Something big, approaching fast!"

"Put it on screen!" Hegira commanded.

The settlement faded, replaced by an image of the fourth crystal shining against the blackness of space with a sliver of Nu's brown surface filling one side of the main screen. A huge dark bulk appeared over the horizon. The round shape moved toward the crystal with tremendous speed as it emerged from behind Nu. Kaia noticed the odd black streaks marring its surface first.

Professor Thoth said, "It looks like an asteroid."

"Oh no," Pakhet replied, "no, no, no, it can't be."

"Pakhet, what is it?" Kaia asked, trying to remain calm.

"It's an asteroid alright, but look—"

Pakhet zoomed in and gasped. Unmistakable steel scaffolds arched over the craters on its surface. Jagged spires poked out from under the domes of broken glass. A blue glow grew from the back as the asteroid accelerated toward the smallest crystal.

Kaia recognized it now.

*A cityship.*

Councilor Hegira stood and yelled, her voice echoing off the curved main viewscreen. "What is that doing here?"

Everyone stared up at the viewscreen, unable to comprehend what they were seeing.

"Someone answer me!" Councilor Hegira yelled.

Kaia rushed over to the helm where Pakhet stood, mouth agape. She pressed the top right of the glyphpad, and a list of comm signals appeared. An unregistered signal was blinking at her. She pressed it and demanded, "Identify yourself!"

Nothing.

The damaged ship was nearly the same size as the fourth crystal on the viewscreen, and still drawing closer. Kaia merged the channels together, so Captain Apep and the pilots could hear what was happening.

A garbled message pierced the silence. "Surely you—"

Static filled the channel.

Then the gruff male voice came through, clear as day, "recognize the *Montu?*"

Kaia swirled around and saw Councilor Hegira's face burn bright red.

"Captain Set!" the councilor yelled.

He let out a deep belly laugh. "Well, hello, Head Councilor."

Captain Apep clicked through. "Set, what are you doing here?"

Kaia zoomed in on the cityship. It was accelerating toward them.

"Ah, Captain. I am pleased you are here to watch. A pity your precious *Meridian* won't be able to maneuver these crystals for impact."

Kaia zoomed back out. The cityship showed no sign of turning or slowing down.

Captain Apep's voice cracked, "I am not on the *Meridian*, Set."

"Nice try, Apep." The *Montu*'s lightdrive roared behind Set's voice.

"I am in a constructor," Apep said between gritted teeth. "How did you think we're moving the crystals? You know these old things don't have autopilot."

"A constructor?"

Kaia heard the confusion in Captain Set's voice, his tone creeping higher.

"No matter, we've been listening in." Set's voice grew firm again. "And don't worry, Captain. We evacuated the *Montu*, as I'm sure you've realized by now. It wouldn't serve my purpose to ram a ship full of people into you. They're all on the surface. I assume you found the settlement?"

*A settlement*, Kaia repeated in her mind.

Captain Set let it sink in, relishing in their shock, Kaia assumed. He cleared his throat. "So, tell me, Captain Apep, which constructor are you in?"

Enki turned to Kaia. A bead of sweat ran down his forehead. He froze as a roar filled the bridge comm and ricocheted off the bare walls.

Councilor Horus fell back into his chair.

"What on Nu is that?"

"Look!" Pakhet shouted, pointing at the viewscreen.

Ra yelled over the comm, "We can't let you do this, Captain Set!"

Kaia covered her mouth to stifle a shriek.

The tip of a crystal shot onto the viewscreen and slammed into the leading edge of the *Montu*. A crack hundreds of cubits wide snaked down the cityship toward the lightdrive. Its blue glow continued pushing and pushing. Kaia's throat clenched shut as First Officer Ra's constructor swung to the side, unable to compensate for the impact and the immense power of a cityship lightdrive.

Captain Apep yelled to him, "Ra! Disconnect the towline now!"

The growing crack reached the *Montu*'s engine. Its blue glow faded. A bloom of white debris flew from the thrust cone. A series of smaller explosions traveled up the lightdrive's photon chamber, destroying the ship compartment by compartment.

"Detach now, Ra!" Captain Apep repeated.

A constellation of debris bloomed outward at phenomenal speed, just missing Ra's constructor as it broke away.

Captain Apep's voice steadied. "Ra, get out of there. Return to the *Meridian*."

"You don't have to ask me twice," Ra replied, breathless.

The captain then yelled through the comms, "Pakhet! A piece of the photo-turbine is heading straight for you. You need to move!"

Through the main viewscreen, Kaia saw a ragged cylinder headed straight for the *Meridian*.

Pakhet reached down with both hands and swiped down hard on the glyphpad.

Kaia gripped the mission console so hard her knuckles turned white. "Hold on!"

Everyone gripped the handrails for impact. Councilor Hegira sat back down just as the *Meridian* rocketed backward to avoid the wreckage as it zoomed past, missing them by less than a few cubits.

Pakhet exhaled and looked to Kaia, her eyes like saucers. "That was close."

"Thank you, Pakhet." Kaia looked around. "Is anyone hurt?" she asked, regaining some semblance of her composure. She saw nods from each crew member that told her they were trying to collect themselves, too.

Enki approached the mission console and zoomed in on the location of the collision. "A fragment of the crystal survived, but…"

"What is it, Enki?" Kaia asked.

He looked up to double-check the trajectory. "It is heading for Iah."

"The moon?" Pakhet asked.

Kaia saw him nod with some hesitation. She looked straight ahead. "Thank you, First Officer Ra, and thank you, Captain Apep."

"No time for that," Apep replied. "We need new orders, Kaia."

She looked to Enki. "Will this work with three crystals?"

His hands moved faster than she had ever seen before as he entered new data. He swallowed hard. "I need to update the simulation."

She could tell by the intense focus that he had an idea. "Hurry, Enki."

"We don't have much time," Captain Apep added.


Kaia heard First Officer Ra's footsteps as he rushed down the ladder to the bridge. He stepped up to the helm.

"Pakhet, thank you." Ra looked at her, then at Professor Thoth. "I need you two to check the ship's systems to make sure we did not sustain any damage," he instructed.

They both nodded and returned to their stations.

First Officer Ra waved his hands over the glyphpad. The main viewscreen switched to show the three remaining crystals. He pressed down on the open comm. "Docking was wild with only one operational thruster, but I made it and am back on the bridge, Captain."

"Good," Apep responded. "Now, Kaia, Enki, we need that new plan."

Kaia's eyes darted over to Enki, whose hands were dancing over the glyphpad as data flew by on the screen above. "We're working on it, Captain."

"Thank you." His tone turned stern. "Captain Set?"

Static, then Captain Set chuckled. "Yes? I told you no one was onboard the *Montu*, did I not?"

"Why are you here?" Captain Apep asked.

Set laughed again. "I believe you meant to ask why I am *not* somewhere else? Duat, perhaps?"

"The *Meridian* was to meet you on Duat, so we could be there for the colony!" Captain Apep yelled.

Captain Set's voice turned formal. "I always intended to return."

Councilor Hegira interrupted him, "You were not to return! No one was to return!"

"Ah," Captain Set began, "but that is where you are wrong. I knew the eruption would fail because a little birdie shared the plans for the nanomechs. I made some…" Kaia could hear him licking his lips, "shall I say, adjustments."

Kaia felt the blood drain from her face.

Councilor Horus stood and yelled, "You sabotaged my work!" He turned to Kaia. "I told you my calculations were flawless," he yelled, then looked beyond her to Enki. "It was Captain Set!"

Enki stopped and looked at Councilor Horus, an apology in his eyes. Then he resumed his work, channeling that apology into a solution. She saw the tight, puzzled look on Ra's face bloom into realization as another explosion from the *Montu* drew his eyes back to the viewscreen.

Ra leaned on the glyphpad. "You—you pushed the lightdrive faster, didn't you? Dilating time to arrive before us, assuming we wouldn't be back for five hundred cycles as we originally planned. When you knew—"

"When I knew our descendants could stop the *Meridian*? Stop the impacts, so our people could survive? Yes."

Ra shook his head. "You could have killed everyone onboard, Set."

"Well, there were some unfortunate... *accidents* when a couple of photon cells melted down and leaked radiation. We only lost a few habitation units, though," Set said as if he were recounting his moves during a board game.

Kaia gasped. She joined Ra at the helm and pressed down on the private channel to Captain Apep. "What about your mother and sister—"

Captain Apep said through gritted teeth. "Captain Set, you cannot stay on Nu."

"It's too late. I'm sure you've seen our new city on the Isle of Alanis? Governor Krishna named it Dvaraka. Beautiful, isn't it? He has planned out quite a faithful re-creation of Puna, minus the skytowers, but we'll build those again, too, one day."

Councilor Hegira growled from her chair. "Set, we will not let you stop the mission."

There was a loud bang from Captain Apep's comm—Kaia was pretty sure he'd just slammed his fist into the constructor's console.

"Why, Set? Why have you done this? Even if we stop, no one can survive down there. The planet is going to die."

"We will not just survive, we will thrive! I know what you're planning to do with those crystals. I know you will not kill your family. That's right, Apep, they are alive on Nu. And we both know they're all you have left."

A message flashed on the mission console and Enki ran over. *Simulation Complete. Run?*

Pakhet shouted, "Look at that!" and pointed to the main

viewscreen. Kaia looked up as a sparkling white cloud appeared over Iah's horizon. The fourth crystal turned to dust from the impact. *And then there were three.*

Enki tapped her shoulder. He looked at her with uncertain eyes.

"Run it," she said.

Enki began fast forwarding through the simulation. Only three bright flashes this time, but the dust lingered in the atmosphere far longer as the planet burned.

The entire crew held their breath, hoping to see a spot of green as the simulation progressed.

*Please, please,* Kaia willed it with every cell in her body. They'd come too far to fail now.

# CHAPTER 12
# SHOCKED QUARTZ

## ARABIAN SEA – 2034 CE

Daxia rushed to the lab below the ship deck, eager to analyze the core. It could hold the key to completing the impact model. She opened the door and saw Seagraves directing Notrees to lower his end of the four-foot tube onto the center table. The plastic casing slipped out of the steel drillstring, sounding like nails on a chalkboard.

She winced and covered her ears.

"Notrees, be careful!" Seagraves chided.

"I ain't a technician! If they wanted careful, they shoulda gone with professionals not greasemonkeys," Notrees scoffed.

Daxia went to the opposite side of the room. She switched on several pieces of lab equipment along the counter on the back wall then returned her attention to the table. The work light's metal arm creaked as she pulled it down from the ceiling and turned it on. A bright white light glared off the tube containing the core sample.

Seagraves put his hands in his pockets and leaned against the opposite wall. "Need anything?"

"Where can I find a hammer and a chisel?" she asked, concentrating on the sample.

Seagraves tapped the metal table. "Underneath here."

Daxia knelt and opened a cabinet door; an avalanche of tools fell onto the floor.

"Sorry," Seagraves grumbled. "Notrees is supposed to keep things organized down here."

Notrees threw his arms up. "Hey! No one even told me about this little side project until we were on top of it!"

Daxia picked up the tools one by one, placing them back in the cabinet as she searched for the hammer and chisel.

"A-ha!" she said, right as Dr. Pearce walked through the door. She stood and set the hammer and chisel on the table.

Dr. Pearce pointed to the still sealed plastic pipe. "Having trouble getting it open?"

Seagraves uncrossed his arms and put his hands in his pockets. "Sorry, we don't use this lab often, so it isn't set up for this kind of analysis."

"It's no problem," Dr. Pearce said. He stepped up to the table and adjusted the light so it shone on the pipe's center. "Daxia, why don't you do the honors?"

Daxia held the chisel against the pipe and took one swing with the hammer. It cracked in two, both halves clanging on the table as they fell to the side. The muddy stone cylinder shimmered under the light.

"Great job," he said to her, then turned to Seagraves and Notrees. "Thank you for bringing this up safely."

"It's what we do," Seagraves replied. He leaned over the core and rested his palms on the table. "So, what is it you're looking for here?"

Notrees just shook his head. "Every core looks the same to me." He wiped his hands on his pants. "I'll be in the mess hall if you need me."

"Thanks again," Daxia said as he stepped out of the lab.

Dr. Pearce leaned over the sample, too. "The layer should be right about," he reached out and ran a clean towel along the sample, wiping away a layer of mud, "here."

The beginning of a chalky gray layer appeared. He continued to clean the mud off until the layer ended, returning to featureless brown rock.

Daxia pointed to the counter behind Seagraves. "Please hand me the sample tray?"

He picked up a square white tray from a pile. "This too?" he asked, holding a dental pick.

"Yes," Daxia said and reached out as he handed them to her.

Dr. Pearce pointed to the center of the gray layer. "This spot should do nicely."

She scraped some material onto the tray. "X-Ray, right?"

He nodded. "All metallic elements."

She opened the top of the XRF spectrometer and placed the sample tray inside. When the lid locked, she selected the metals option on the touchscreen and pressed start. The machine whirred and clicked, irradiating the sample and recording the energy emitted. "We should know whether there is iridium in the layer in just a few minutes."

"Good." Dr. Pearce used the small tool to pick up a small flake of brown stone from just below the gray layer. He sat on a stool in front of the microscope. "I'm going to take a look for signs of impact myself."

The corners of her mouth rose. "You don't trust the machine?" Daxia said, her tone dripping with sarcasm.

"Very funny," he replied.

He pulled out a small glass slide and dabbed the flake onto it.

"That *machine* isn't going to tell us what happened to the rock, just what's inside it," he said, then added, "And that depends on if it decides to work."

Seagraves chuckled. "I take it you don't care for computers much?"

Dr. Pearce turned on the microscope's light, inserted the slide, and put his eye to the eyepiece. He turned the lenses to find the right magnification level.

"Dr. Pearce has disappeared into his work," said Daxia. "But yes, to say he hates computers would be an understatement."

Seagraves smiled. "I sympathize. I remember when we told the drilling machines what to do, but now I feel like they're giving me the orders. Drill here. That's too slow. That's too deep. The warning lights nag non-stop!"

Dr. Pearce pulled back from the microscope and squinted, then switched to a higher magnification.

"What do you see?" Daxia asked.

He leaned back and sighed. "Nothing." He spun around on the stool to face her. "It's just silty clay. No trace of shocked quartz like we found in Mexico."

She frowned. "Are you sure?"

He slumped, his face drooping in disappointment. "Either it isn't a crater or, Seagraves, your microscope is broken."

Daxia pulled the microscope toward her. "Wait." She pressed a button on the base and looked through the eyepiece. "Now look."

Dr. Pearce spun back around and gasped. "What did you do?"

She pointed to the button. "You didn't turn the autofocus on."

Seagraves guffawed. "A digital microscope, your favorite kind, I'm sure."

"Very funny," Dr. Pearce said and switched to his other eye. He slapped his thigh. "Daxia, come here. You've got to see this."

Daxia rested her elbows on the counter next to the microscope. "Did you find it?"

She caught Dr. Pearce's smirk as he rose off the stool and waved his hand toward the eyepiece. "See for yourself."

She sat and peered into the eyepiece. White spots flecked the gray stone. She increased the magnification. Each spot was filled with microscopic striations. "There is at least twice as much shocked quartz here as at Uxmal!" She jumped up with a squeal.

He crossed his arms, satisfied. "There's no doubt about it. Something subjected this layer to a massive amount of pressure."

Daxia glanced over to watch Seagrave's reaction, but he was scraping off some of the gray layer with a toothpick and putting it on his tongue. "It doesn't taste like anything," he declared. He wiped it on his pants. "I think it looks like ash. Are you sure it isn't volcanic?"

Dr. Pearce grimaced. "It could be, but," he pointed to the lab equipment, "that contraption is called an X-ray fluorescence spectrometer, or XRF for short, and it will tell us the composition of the layer. If we see lots of iridium, it has to be an impact."

"Iridium?"

"Yes, most asteroids are made of iridium," Dr. Pearce explained.

Daxia turned her attention to the XRF spectrometer and watched the progress bar fill up.

Dr. Pearce continued, "They pulverize themselves on impact, then get mixed in with the dust they kick up."

Seagraves gave a quick nod, which Daxia interpreted as a partial understanding but not wanting Dr. Pearce to stop the lecture.

The XRF spectrometer beeped.

Daxia read the alert out loud. "Analysis complete." She tapped the message, and a bar chart appeared. She felt Dr. Pearce move in to look over her shoulder.

"What is the tall bar rising over the others?" he asked.

She could, but also could not, believe her eyes. "Iridium."

"It's true—" Pearce stammered. "It's really true."

Daxia nodded. "We have shocked quartz, just like the samples from Chicxulub. And according to the analysis, this sample has even more iridium than the samples from Mexico." Daxia noticed him starting to sway with the ship. "Are you okay?"

He braced himself against the counter. "Just a little lightheaded. This is the moment I've been waiting for…"

She held his elbow.

Seagraves rushed around the lab table. "Dr. Pearce, please sit down."

"Yes, yes, I should," he said and sat on the stool Seagraves pushed under him.

The color returned to his face.

"Congratulations, Professor," Daxia said and patted his back. She was excited for herself, but more for Dr. Pearce. She knew how much this meant to him. It was more proof that his theories were right.

He looked up at her with awe. "I could scarcely imagine the Chicxulub impact, let alone one as large as this."

She looked back at the XRF spectrometer and tapped the bar representing iridium levels. "This is odd," she said.

"Let me guess," he said, his voice growing irritated. "We calibrated it incorrectly and that is actually just some iron?"

Daxia ignored the comment and tapped the screen again. "It says there is a match in its database."

He perked up. "A match? We have found this iridium before?"

"In Ukraine."

Seagraves raised an eyebrow. "Ukraine?"

Dr. Pearce rubbed his beard then stopped and looked up. His face turned pale once more. "That other crater, the one with the same iridium." The name popped right into his mind. "The Boltysh crater, isn't it?"

She nodded, sensing they were onto something—a discovery that would extend far beyond the Shiva crater.

Seagraves raised his hand to ask a question. "Sorry, but what does that mean?"

Dr. Pearce's mind wandered off in thought, so Daxia looked up to Seagraves. "It seems impossible, but the craters could be related."

# CHAPTER 13
# IMPOSSIBLE DECISION

## NU ORBIT - AD CYCLE 107

Kaia put her arm around Pakhet. They watched a milky white shock wave from the lost fourth crystal encircle the moon. Pakhet's voice quivered, "What are we going to do now?"

Kaia patted her back and pointed to the viewscreen. "We still have the other three crystals. Enki will figure something out."

He was running a new simulation. His finger swirled to the left then tapped the glyphpad to pause it. Kaia thought she saw green appearing on the continents, but it was hard to tell from the helm. She told Pakhet, "Go, please keep an eye out for more debris."

"I w-will," Pakhet replied then returned to her viewscreen.

Kaia pursed her lips and stepped away to join Enki at the mission console. It was a promising sight. She could make out greening continents in the simulation. "Does this mean three impacts still work?" she asked, the tension seeping from every pore in her body. She scanned his face for any trace of emotion. But he showed none, other than his furrowed brow.

"Kaia," he said, nodding. "It can still work."

She raised her heels off the ground and clapped her hands. "Everyone! The plan will still work."

"Kaia, wait," he urged.

But she couldn't help herself. She grabbed his shoulder. "I knew you would find a way."

"It is not that simple."

She noticed his shoulders slump and stepped back. "What is it?" She looked up at his viewscreen. The planet was green with life, more than she had ever seen. "I don't understand. I can see the recovery myself."

Enki looked her in the eye. "It won't come without a price, Kaia."

There was a thud behind them, and Kaia turned to see Councilor Hegira raising her hand to whack the chair again.

"Speak up, Enki," Councilor Hegira ordered.

Everyone turned to look at him again.

"Hey," Kaia said, "it's okay, explain."

He shuffled his feet and mumbled, "Three crystals can be successful, but..."

Kaia put her hand on his shoulder. "But, *what?*"

"It will require more speed, more powerful impacts, and—" he looked up at the viewscreen, "it may take more... sacrifice."

Kaia frowned. "Enki, we've all sacrificed so much already. What could be worse?"

He said nothing, just looked up at the three crystals on the main viewscreen. Kaia glanced around the bridge; everyone was focused on the image as well.

Enki spread his fingers on the glyphpad and zoomed in closer. To the three points of red flame at the end of the towlines.

"The constructors?" Kaia asked, with relief. Who cared about the constructors, anyway?

Kaia saw him nod almost imperceptibly.

"So, we have to sacrifice the constructors. That's not a big—"

"Kaia," First Officer Ra interrupted.

She faced him. He was rubbing the back of his neck. His gaze wandered around the bridge, then he spoke.

"I don't think Enki means *just* the constructors."

Kaia's stomach clenched in the thick silence that permeated the bridge. Her mind replayed the conversation with Captain Apep, his pride in the power of old, *manual* Jacana technology.

She looked up at the viewscreen and focused on Captain Apep leading the way.

*The constructors do not have autopilot.*

Her knees were about to buckle. Her heart pounded in her ears, and she squeezed her eyes shut.

*There must be another way.*

*The pilots!*

*The captain!*

*All the people on Nu!*

When she opened them, Enki was staring up at a map while moving his finger over the glyphpad. A small red dot followed the motion around the open sea.

She leaned in to grab the edge of the console for support. "Are those the impact locations?"

He nodded. "I am trying manual adjustments to check the simulation. Maybe…"

"Maybe what?" she asked impatiently.

Enki studied the new data. The simulated temperature graph continued to fall, flatlining below zero degrees. He lifted his finger and dropped his arms to his sides.

"Nothing else is working," he said, looking down, shoulders slumped.

He closed his eyes then opened them and looked straight at Kaia. "The only way to make it work with three crystals is to generate enough power that they impact at full speed."

"Okay. And?" Kaia asked, waiting.

"That means the constructors must pull each crystal all the way to the moment of impact."

She looked up at the viewscreen even though she did not want to see. A gray dot near the former city of Leneum, Enki's hometown, marked the now-impossible impact site of the fourth crystal. She reached up, rubbed her forehead, and took a deep breath. She moved her hand over the top of her head and down to the back of her neck.

Councilor Hegira smoothed out her robe and said, "Kaia, this is still your mission."

Kaia felt the whole crew watching her, waiting for orders.

Captain Apep's voice echoed around the silent bridge. "Can someone please tell me what is going on over there? Do we have a new plan or not?"

Kaia's eyes met First Officer Ra's.

Ra pressed down on the comm. "We're here. And we're working on it." He turned back to the viewscreen. "What is the status of your ships?"

"Mirik, Nef, report," Captain Apep ordered.

Kaia thought Mirk sounded out of breath. "Crystal two remains under control. But I'm not sure for how long."

"Come again?" Captain Apep asked.

"My fuel tank is leaking," he clarified. "I think I took a hit from the *Montu's* debris."

Captain Apep sighed. "Nef, status."

"Crystal three is also still under control," Nef said with a hint of apprehension.

Captain Apep reported back to the bridge. "Ra, we're still able to maneuver. Kaia, what should we do?"

She stepped away and up to the Council platform. "Councilor Horus, can your nanomechs help? Maybe program them to steer the constructors by swarming the electronics?"

He looked over to Councilor Hegira, who nodded for him to answer.

"They could, but I would need to reprogram them and," he nodded to the viewscreen, "there is not enough time."

Nef's voice crackled onto the comm. "Captain Apep, Kaia, Nu is getting mighty large out my window. I need to know what we're doing."

A deep voice boomed, "I know what you should do."

"Captain Set," Kaia growled.

"Kaia, you know your plan will fail," his voice rasped. "Might I suggest you turn back?"

She responded sharply, "You cannot survive down there even if we call this off."

"We will do what we must," he replied.

"Nu will become a frozen wasteland! We've run the simulations, Set."

Captain Set's tone was clear. "I swore to protect these people. Entire families are depending on me. We're doing what is necessary to protect ourselves. Besides, our simulations show it will be hundreds of cycles until the weather—"

His voice cut off. Kaia looked to First Officer Ra, brows raised.

He gave her a curt nod. "I jammed his signal. We have heard enough from Captain Set."

Kaia was thankful for that.

Captain Apep spoke again. "Enki, where do the impacts need to happen now?"

Enki looked to Kaia for guidance.

"Tell him," she said, walking toward his station.

"Hurry!" Captain Apep's voice crackled, exceeding the comm system's bandwidth.

Enki pulled his shoulders back and looked straight ahead. "Nef's crystal needs to impact the sea halfway between Puna and the north pole. Mirik's must hit the ocean between the northern and southern continents in the western hemisphere. Captain Apep, yours—"

"Wait!" Kaia interjected. She looked at the red dot representing the largest crystal's impact site, Captain Apep's crystal, as she spoke. "We have to find another way."

"Ra, send those coordinates to Mirik and Nef so they can line up their trajectories," the captain ordered.

"Yes, sir. Sending them now," Ra replied.

Kaia took a deep breath and leaned her palms on the console. "Captain," she started but struggled to find the words.

Captain Apep's voice softened. "Kaia, I know what you're going to say."

She shot Enki a look.

His shoulders rose, and he said, "I did not tell him anything."

"Kaia," Captain Apep began, "We planned for four crystals. Now we only have three." He exhaled into the comm. "And those three will need to strike with more force to produce the same effect."

She didn't respond.

"Enki, am I right?" asked the captain.

Kaia turned and glared toward First Officer Ra, who looked down sheepishly. Fortunately for all of them, the lump in Kaia's throat prevented her from speaking. *He told Captain Apep.*

Enki sheepishly said, "Yes, Captain. The constructors need to pull the crystals at maximum speed toward the surface. Nu's gravity will not accelerate them fast enough to produce an effective impact."

Kaia turned her glare on Enki. She pushed him aside and took over the mission station. "Enki is going to work on other options, Captain." She turned to the back wall where Councilor Hegira was watching from the raised platform. "The Council put me in control of this mission. We will find another way."

Captain Apep clicked back on. "Is there any hope for the *Montu*'s refugees?"

Enki joined Ra at the helm.

Ra answered, "I am afraid not, Captain. The climate will crash if we do nothing. They will not survive."

They watched Kaia move her fingers over the glyphpad to rearrange impact sites, keeping her eyes on the simulated temperature. The line dived below zero every time.

Captain Apep sighed over the comm, "Kaia, it will be okay."

Her voice held firm. "Captain Apep, maintain orbit, do not descend."

"Kaia, we need to fulfill the mission."

"I said, *do not descend*. That is an order," Kaia commanded. She heard a creak and spun around.

Councilor Hegira stepped away from her chair and down off the platform. She placed her hand on Kaia's shoulder. "Kaia, you must give the order."

*"No,"* Kaia said, jerking her shoulder away from Hegira's hand. "I will not." She pointed to Enki. "He can simulate another solution."

Enki walked back to the mission station and stood shoulder-to-shoulder with Kaia. "I have tried everything." He looked up at the map; a sheen of sweat had appeared on his brow. "I am afraid Councilor Hegira is right."

Kaia reopened the comm channel. "Pilots, how much fuel do you have?"

"Barely enough to accelerate to the speed in Enki's plan, let alone cut and run all the way back to the *Meridian*," Captain Apep replied, the resignation clear in his voice.

"Me either," Mirik said.

"Same here," Nef added. "Mine is already in the red."

"We can find another way," Kaia insisted, a queasy hot-cold feeling descending upon her. "You don't have to do this."

"Kaia," Captain Apep said gently, "we knew the danger when we signed up for this mission."

"Enki, can we create new crystals?" she blurted.

He shook his head. "It will be too late. The tipping point, remember?"

Councilor Hegira spoke up. "Kaia, you must give the order while there is still time."

They all looked up to the scene before them.

The three remaining crystals reflected the surface of Nu, the surface they would change forever. The towlines slackened for a moment as the pilots maneuvered the crystals into position before the final acceleration.

She turned her head to face Councilor Hegira, "I am not going to order them to their deaths and kill tens of thousands of innocent colonists."

Councilor Hegira frowned. "I understand, Kaia. I too have had to watch people die due to my decisions. Sometimes sacrifices are necessary for the greater good."

Kaia saw Enki standing still, waiting for her decision like the rest of the crew. She turned back to Councilor Hegira. "Don't lecture me on sacrifices, Councilor."

Hegira stood straight and smoothed out her robe. She looked to Councilor Horus for support, but his eyes stayed glued to the floor.

"Kaia, my dear." Hegira's eyes softened, and she bowed. "We all remember your father's last words." She clasped her hands. "Think about what he would want you to do."

Kaia felt a lump rise in her throat as the words came back to her as clear as if she were seven years old again, stuck on the shuttle flying away from her parents. She imagined the same invisible hand steering her to a future where she did not want to go.

Except this time, the invisible hand was visible.

*Hegira.*

Kaia squeezed her eyes shut to fight the emerging truth.

Her father's words echoed in her mind.

*You can save the world from us.*

She turned to the console and took a deep, shaky breath. "Captain Apep, I am not going to order you to do anything."

The crew gasped.

Enki faced her, asking softly. "Kaia, are you sure?"

Her eyes settled on the tiny dot of light in front of the largest crystal. "Captain Apep, do you remember what you asked about who I trust?" She turned to Councilor Hegira, eyes ablaze. "I-I see the truth, now."

"Kaia!" Councilor Hegira yelled. "You must give the order!"

Kaia turned away from the councilor and waited for a response from the pilots.

Captain Apep's somber voice reverberated around the bridge. "I'm glad you see it, Kaia. You are in control. Your future is yours, and yours alone."

Kaia gathered her thoughts and stood as straight and tall as she could. One by one, she looked at each crew member. She spoke with renewed strength, despite feeling like something was breaking inside.

"This is not *my* plan. This is not *my* mission. It is *our* mission. It is for all Jacana and for all the life that might flourish again on Nu."

Then she glared at Councilor Hegira. "My father did not say I should do it alone."

Councilor Hegira glared back. "Don't be weak, Kaia. The decision is yours to make, now make it."

Kaia turned and held down the comm. "Captain Apep, what do *you* want to do?" The wetness in her eyes spilled over. A single tear rolled down her cheek.

"Kaia," he took a deep breath, "I know what we *need* to do. And given what's at stake, I think most everyone, even the people in the settlement down there, would do the same."

His voice was steadfast now. "Mirik, Nef, you with me?"

Nef's voice was taut. "Always, sir. This mission is bigger than any of us."

"Why not? I have nothing better to do," Mirik quipped.

"Well, that settles it then. The three of us just became a critical part of the plan to save the world. Kaia, make sure it counts."

"We will, Captain," she said, choking back more tears.

"Pilots, you all have your new coordinates. Are you in position?" he asked.

"I'm looking straight at the ocean and am ready for a good swim," replied Nef.

Mirik sang his response: "Back to the sea, I can't wait to be. Riding a wave, as the world I save."

Kaia could hear Captain Apep's strained chuckle, then he continued, "Let's rev those boosters."

# CHAPTER 14
# CONCENTRIC

## ARABIAN SEA – 2034 CE

Dr. Pearce felt a rush of excitement and turned toward the laptop on the counter. "Daxia, can you pull up the satellite image of the Boltysh crater?"

She opened the mapping application and entered the coordinates from the XRF spectrometer. Farm fields filled the screen. She zoomed out and tilted the image. The crater's rim was only visible in a few spots on its northeast edge. The rest had weathered away millions of years earlier.

"This is another crater?" Seagraves asked.

"Yes, also very old," he said.

Seagraves whispered to Daxia, "What am I missing?"

"Look at the edges of the image," she explained. "See the small hills that form a semi-circle?"

"Ah," he said, leaning forward to get a closer look. "Maybe? It's very faint."

She nodded. "Much smaller than the Shiva crater below us."

Dr. Pearce pointed to the screen. "Daxia, take it back in time like you did up on deck."

She pressed a few keys. On the screen, the hills began to rise from the land, undoing tens of millions of years of erosion to transform back into a crater rim. Then a smaller, second rim appeared inside the first.

"Check out the structure," Dr. Pearce said, pointing to the double circles.

A flat blue surface rose from the bottom of the crater, accentuating a smaller circle within the larger rim of the crater.

"What's happening to it?" Seagraves asked.

Daxia noted the sea level graph at the edge screen. "There were no glaciers anywhere on Earth when this impact happened, so the sea level was much higher."

Seagraves asked, "The whole area was underwater?"

She nodded.

"Yes." Dr. Pearce said, stroking his beard, watching the double-ringed Boltysh crater vanish beneath the waves.

He took a closer look at the evidence of impact. "Daxia, turn it back until we can see the rings again." He slapped the counter. "Unbelievable! Look at that!" He leaned away to let Daxia see. He saw her eyebrows rise and knew she understood.

"It looks just like the—" She turned to him. "No, it can't be. Can it?"

He clapped his hands together like an excited child. "Add the image of the Chicxulub."

She flipped through the menus until the Yucatán Peninsula appeared on the screen.

Dr. Pearce asked, "Now, take us back to the same time as you did for the Boltysh."

"The ocean, it's going to—" said Seagraves.

Dr. Pearce interrupted him, pointing to the screen. "Just watch."

The Yucatán disappeared beneath the water, leaving two concentric ridges peaking above the waves.

Dr. Pearce rubbed his hands together. "Yes, very good, Daxia. Now, combine both images and enlarge the Boltysh crater to be the same size as the Chicxulub."

She overlaid the Boltysh on top of the Chicxulub and scaled it up.

Their mouths fell open at the same time.

Daxia brushed a lock of hair back from her forehead. "How could this happen?"

Seagraves replied, "They're the same. But what is that Chicxu-whatcha-call-it we're looking at?"

Dr. Pearce and Daxia chuckled.

She explained, "It's the Chicxulub crater in Mexico. It's at least five times larger than the Boltysh crater, but they look the same otherwise. See the double rings?"

"I thought all craters looked the same?" Seagraves asked.

"No," she said, "there are many factors, such as the velocity, angle of impact, even the shape of the asteroid."

"Wait!" Dr. Pearce exclaimed. "Daxia, how far back was the timeline when you ran the simulation of the Boltysh crater?"

She clicked back to the tab. "66 million years—the same age as the Chicxulub crater. But that's…"

Dr. Pearce felt a rush of adrenaline. "Impossible. They couldn't have been created at the same time." Goosebumps spread over his arms.

Daxia spread her fingers over the computer's touchpad to line up the images side-by-side.

"Whoa," Seagraves said.

Dr. Pearce turned to him. "Do you see something else?"

Seagraves nodded and pointed back at the screen. "Those double circles make them look like a set of eyes."

Dr. Pearce squinted at the images and saw it, too.

"And wet rings of land from the surrounding ocean… it's almost like they've been crying," Daxia said.

Dr. Pearce stared into the two eye-shaped craters on the screen. "What secrets are you two hiding underneath the waves?"

# CHAPTER 15
# LASTING EVIDENCE

## NU ORBIT - AD CYCLE 107

Nef steered her constructor down toward the gray sea. She imagined her father on the deck of a freighter captained by Apep's father on the very same water below.

*That is where I belong, too.*

She glanced down at her fuel gauge. Near red.

She swallowed hard and nudged the accelerator forward. The constructor jerked as the towline tightened, pulling the crystal down with her. She felt the momentum build as her speed increased and pushed the accelerator to full. *Faster.*

There was a brief flash of firelight outside the window. The constructor pierced the atmosphere and hazy orange clouds zoomed past the window. Nef looked straight ahead. She could make out individual ocean waves as she descended.

Faster still.

In her mind's eye, Nef's father stood behind a freighter's deck railing, waving as it rode the swells. He raised his hand in a salute, then lowered it and smiled. *I am proud of you, Nef.*

Nef smiled in return as the constructor slammed into the waves, cracking the window to darkness.



Mirik looked out the constructor's right-side window and fought back tears. A jet of brown rose over the horizon. *You did it, Nef.* He tapped the fuel gauge. It fell below half a tank. "Captain Apep, I have just enough fuel left."

"Mirik, it has been a pleasure," Captain Apep replied, his voice solemn.

"Likewise, Captain." Mirik's voice cracked as he pushed the accelerator forward. "Hey, you know the stuffed affi I gave you after... Tremva?"

Mirik heard the captain clear his throat. "It's sitting on the helm of the *Meridian* right now."

"I bet it can fly that rust bucket better than you," Mirik ribbed. The constructor rattled as it entered the atmosphere. He tightened his lap belt and held on to the seat.

"Only because I taught it everything it knows," joked the captain.

Mirik's last thought was of how much he'd miss working with the captain and the rest of the crew.

And then there was nothing.



Kaia looked away as two cones of water and rock gushed high above the clouds. The ocean raced away from the impact sites, revealing wounds on the seafloor. Her spine tingled—even the smaller crystal left a crater larger than anything the Jacana ever created. The surrounding atmosphere turned brown with sediments thrown into the sky. Kaia thought of Nef and Mirik, and her heart clenched.

Councilor Hegira sat back on the platform, crossed her legs, and leaned to the side. "Stay sharp. Everyone."

Councilor Horus was silent for once, sitting in rapt attention.

Training her eyes on the viewscreen, Kaia asked, "Enki, readings?"

"Particulates are increasing." He watched as more data poured in. "Kaia, it-it appears to be working," he said.

She closed her eyes and gave a status update. "Captain Apep, Nef and Mirik were successful." There would be time later for all of them to grieve. Right now, she had to be strong.

The crew watched the sea slosh back into the craters with unimaginable power, filling both the inner and outer rims, leaving a scar of concentric circles rising above the waves. Kaia tilted her head. The shape was… familiar.

Under different circumstances, the double rings could have been an artistic impression of the layout of Puna, their last great city. The city's urban plan was now part of the crust of Nu itself, and there it would remain for tens of millions of cycles.

She whispered under her breath, "There will always be evidence of us. Ours is a story carved in time."

# CHAPTER 16
# DISBELIEF

## ARABIAN SEA - 2034 CE

Dr. Pearce continued to stare at the evidence in disbelief as the two craters stared back at him from the computer screen. He was numb. "This isn't possible," he said.

Daxia crossed her arms and stumbled backward. "I can't believe it either."

He tapped the counter. "Pull up the sonar scans from the Shiva crater."

She opened a new tab on the computer. A multicolored elevation scan replaced the Boltysh and Chicxulub craters. He saw the faint, eroded oval shape on the sea floor—the Shiva.

"Now, please run us back in time again," Dr. Pearce said.

Daxia pressed the spacebar. Dr. Pearce stroked his beard again, while Daxia chewed the inside of her lip. They watched as the oval became a circle.

"Nothing yet," Dr. Pearce said.

"Wait, look!" Seagraves pushed his arm between them and pointed toward the inside of the ring. A circle formed inside the Shiva crater's rim. "There it is again, a second ring."

Dr. Pearce sat up straight and swallowed hard. "Daxia, pull up the Boltysh and the Chicxulub one last time, in elevation relief."

The two multicolored elevation scans appeared on top of the Shiva crater.

"And you're sure these are correct? All three are different craters?" Dr. Pearce asked.

Daxia's dark hair rushed back and forth over her cheeks as she nodded. "Yes, each one is a different crater."

Dr. Pearce scanned the numbers around the outside of the screen but had no clue where to look. "Daxia, when does the computer say the Shiva crater looked like this?"

She moved the cursor to the menu and selected the timeline display. "It makes no sense." She stepped back and turned the screen to Dr. Pearce.

He leaned forward, squinting as he studied the data. "Sixty. Six. Million. Years."

# CHAPTER 17
# FINALITY

## NU ORBIT - AD CYCLE 107

Enki checked the data and turned to Kaia. "The readings are as I simulated."

Kaia fidgeted with the end of her habsew sleeves. A sense of dread prowled the boundary of her consciousness, but she hardened her focus and kept it at bay. "Good. That's good."

A dot appeared on the map above Enki's console. "Captain Apep, about your impact location…"

"Go ahead, Enki."

Enki hesitated and looked at Kaia.

She put a finger up for Enki to wait. *I'll tell him.*

Enki nodded once and looked down.

She cleared her throat and steeled herself for what she was about to say. "Captain, your impact will occur off the western coast of Puna."

The comm clicked on and off twice, but there was no word from Captain Apep. Then a gruff voice, "Where the *Montu*'s refugees are living?"

"Yes," she said.

Loud static filled the comm as Captain Apep exhaled into the microphone. "I know the answer to this already, but are you sure?"

Kaia took a few steps and stood next to Enki at the mission console. She studied the coordinates for the third time and saw the future temperature graph stay above critical freezing for tens of millions of cycles.

"I'm so sorry, Captain," she said. "Captain Apep," she started, feeling the tears well up, blurring her vision. She grabbed the edge of the console for support and whispered, "I want to thank you for everything."

"No, thank you," he said. "And, Kaia, remember what I said. The next steps are yours to decide. Do not dwell on the tragedies of your past or they will destroy your future."


Captain Apep's gaze darted around the cockpit. Every warning light flashed red. The engineers did not design constructors to handle a load as large as the crystal at this speed. He took a deep breath. There was a chime from his console. He looked down at a green dot pulsing on the screen to his left—a message from the surface. He pressed the signal indicator.

Two figures in pressurized habsew suits appeared. A tall, young woman held the arm of a shorter, stooped figure, steadying her as their ship bobbed in the ocean swells.

"Apep? Is that you?" the short one asked.

Captain Apep closed his eyes and choked back tears.

"Yes, Mother, Helena, it is me."

He closed his eyes and bit his lip, hoping he was having a nightmare. But when he opened them, his mother and sister were still there on the viewscreen, waving and smiling. His mother's hand moved to her heart. "We're so glad you're okay. We saw explosions in the sky."

Helena squinted to the east. "There was thunder in the distance, and now there is a glow on the horizon." She looked back at the camera, almost straight into his eyes. "Apep, what's happening?"

He took a deep breath. "I'm afraid our original plan for the Dawn Project failed. Our mission to save Nu is not over."

She pointed to the sky and cried out, "What is that? A square ship? It looks like it's shining."

Flames ringed the front window as his constructor hit the atmosphere. He could feel the heat radiating into the cabin.

Helena gasped. "It's on fire!"

Captain Apep felt a chill on his face as tears ran down his cheeks. The island that held his mother and sister lay off to the right side of his window. Flames licked the glass as he blasted toward them.

"Apep? Why are you crying?" his mother asked.

"The fire in the sky is..." his throat constricted as he choked back more tears. "It is me."

The constructor groaned as the crystal punctured the atmosphere behind it.

"Oh, thank you, Apep! I knew you'd bring another cityship back to save us!"

"Mother, Helena, please forgive me. This is—there was no other way—a final sacrifice is required to save our world."

His sister looked back up at the fireball, then back at the camera. "Apep, what are you saying?"

"There is no time to explain. I love both of you very much," he replied, and pushed away the viewscreen.

He could not watch.

He heard his mother step toward the camera. "Apep, I am so proud of you."

In front of him, he could now make out individual rows of colony tents and the crowd gathering at the makeshift central plaza. He channeled thoughts of his father falling calmly into the dust. Twenty cycles after Tremva, he felt more connected to him than ever before.

*I understand. You knew what needed to happen.*

Captain Apep took his hands off the controls to wipe away the tears.

*I do too.*

. . .

Kaia stepped up to the helm next to First Officer Ra. "Point the *Meridian* toward the final impact site."

He reached down and tapped the thruster controls until the final crystal sat at the center of the main viewscreen.

"Thank you," Kaia said. She turned to Pakhet at the ship's systems console. "Access the comm feed being sent to Captain Apep's constructor." She saw Pakhet's hesitation. "We all need to know the price we're paying to finish the mission."

Pakhet scooted closer to the console, head hung low and tears welling up in her eyes. The *Meridian*'s crew let out a collective gasp when the video feed appeared on the helm's viewscreen. Pakhet wrapped her arms around her body and groaned.

*Montu* refugees, Captain Apep's mother and sister included, crowded the colony's plaza. Many fixed their fearful gazes on the blazing fireball approaching from the sky above.

Most of the crew shirked away from the viewscreen, unable to watch.

Kaia caught a look from Enki. He clenched his jaw and kept his eyes open with her. She tightened her grip on the edge of the console. Her neck stiffened with resolve—she, too, would not allow herself to look away.

Enki stepped over and put his hand on her shoulder. Together, they watched flames pour off the leading edge of the final, largest crystal. Captain Apep's ship looked like a tiny dot of fire ahead of impending destruction.


Captain Apep pushed himself back in the constructor seat and sat up straight with his hands back on the controls. The island below beckoned him forward and he pressed on, full throttle. There was a crashing sound on his right. Before he realized what was happening, a small silver sphere shot through the constructor's window. Flames rushed in behind it and burned his skin through the suit. An immense force pulled him sideways until his consciousness faded.

· · ·

The *Meridian*'s bridge seemed to shake with a roar so deep it caused the speakers to crackle and pop. The crew shielded their eyes as a blinding white flash filled the viewscreen.

Kaia was first to look up. She saw most everyone still had their faces buried in their hands, many leaning over their consoles in terror.

Enki lowered his forearm from in front of his face and raised his eyes to the viewscreen.

"It's over," she said, loud enough for everyone to hear.

One by one, the other crew members looked up, wiping tears from their faces. Kaia drew a circle on the glyphpad, and the viewscreen adjusted to the bright light from the explosion below. Cloudy streaks formed a circle, as if running away from the impact, terrified of the carnage. A massive shock wave dwarfed the previous two, generating a dust storm that spread over the entire hemisphere. Plumes of rock soared beyond the atmosphere and into space. The eruption shafts around Puna reopened. Fiery fountains of lava poured onto the surface through the hole the crystal punched through the crust of Nu itself.

The seafloor around the impact laid bare, but the water came rushing back in waves two hundred cubits high. They crashed together then rippled back toward the land once more, scouring away every remnant of the once lush coastal ecosystems. Chunks of Nu's crust that had blown into space began falling back. Their fiery trails slashed through the atmosphere. Everywhere they hit the surface, dead forests burst into flames. It grew to become a global fire that, according to Enki's simulation, would burn for many cycles.

Behind her, Kaia heard Councilor Hegira's robe crinkle. She turned and saw the councilor stand up and clap three times, pausing between each strike. "Thank you, everyone."

Hegira bowed to Councilor Horus, but his eyes stayed locked on the viewscreen. "And thank you, Councilor Horus, for your years of dedication to nanotechnology. We could not have done this without it."

Councilor Horus did not turn to acknowledge her.

The glowing destruction on-screen accentuated the creases on Councilor Hegira's face, and Kaia saw it then; a slight curl at the edge of her lips, as if she was struggling not to smile.

Kaia felt a rock in the pit of her stomach—this was the true Councilor Hegira. In theory, focused on the greater good, but also willing to pay any price to achieve those goals. Captain Apep's words floated to the surface.

*You can do the right thing the wrong way.*

Kaia knew that they were all part of the decision, but as she looked around the bridge, it was clear that the crew felt devastated by the enormity of the sacrifices they had witnessed.

No one could stomach the loss of so many Jacana lives.

Councilor Horus met Kaia's eyes then looked up at the viewscreen. "Thank you, Hegira, but you must mean to thank more than nanomechs," he said, trying to coax out a shred of empathy from her.

Councilor Hegira scoffed, "I already thanked the crew. What more would you have me do?" She stepped off the platform, making her way toward the ladder leading off the bridge.

Kaia felt a seething anger rise in her chest and clenched her fists. *This is not over.*

Pakhet fell to her knees and covered her face. Dr. Khnum and Professor Thoth rushed to her side. Together, they wrapped their arms around one another and let their tears flow.

Enki stood by Kaia's side at the mission station, his feet planted in the floor loops, staring straight ahead. There was still work to do. He reached down and drew a jagged line on the glyphpad then dragged it to the right. The geology station, two consoles away, lit up. Sensor readings flooded onto its viewscreen.

Kaia stiffened her neck, still fighting her instinct to look away as their planet suffered. Millions of living creatures, Jacana and wild, vaporized on impact. The rest would drown, suffocate, or die of starvation in the coming cycles. She tried to remind herself that Captain Set doomed them the moment they left the *Montu*, but it was little comfort. She crossed her arms over her chest and held on so tight her knuckles turned white. The three final wounds her people would inflict upon their home poured destruction over the surface.

Tears streamed down her face as a flood of emotion consumed her.

But she willed her body to stay standing. And it did.

Kaia forced herself to watch the world die.

# CHAPTER 18
# THREE TIMES

## ARABIAN SEA - 2034 CE

"This is so exciting! Three impacts, at the same time, 66 million years ago. I can't believe it!" Dr. Pearce exclaimed, raising both hands in the air.

Daxia nodded and said, "The Council is really not going to believe it... It's unprecedented."

She watched Seagraves sulk away from the counter and cross his arms.

"Sounds like a pretty bad day to me," he said.

Dr. Pearce turned to her. "Do you realize what this means for your field of study, Daxia?"

She furrowed her brow. "This is for geology, Dr. Pearce, not paleontology."

Seagraves spoke up. "Take it from the oil guy—paleontology and geology aren't so different."

"You're right. Oil is just dead plants and animals," she acknowledged.

Dr. Pearce put his hand on her shoulder. "This discovery has a big, dare I say," he waggled his eyebrows, "*impact* for you."

Daxia rolled her eyes. "You can't help yourself, can you, Dr. Pearce?" She closed her eyes and shook her head.

Dr. Pearce smirked and shrugged. He put both hands back on the counter. "Now, I'm still curious about something." He rolled the stool over to the XRF spectrometer and studied the pie chart dominated by one silver slice. "Based on the amount in this sample, the Shiva asteroid must have been about 98% pure iridium."

Daxia joined him at the machine. She returned to the bar chart and pressed the iridium bar again to look at results from the Boltysh crater in the system's library. "And so was the Boltysh."

"I bet we'll find the same thing if we run the samples from the Chicxulub crater, too," he said.

"I suspect you're right," she pulled the laptop over to get a better look, "but that in and of itself may not be unusual. Haven't astronomers seen multiple impact events before?"

Dr. Pearce nodded. "Yes, the most recent was Shoemaker-Levy 9 in 1994."

"Now wait," Seagraves said. "I'm pretty sure I would have remembered learning about multiple asteroids hitting us."

Daxia explained. "They weren't on Earth. Shoemaker-Levy 9 was a comet ripped apart by Jupiter before impacting the gas giant."

"I see where you're going. It's a great idea, surely the Council will support the research." Dr. Pearce looked back at the three identical craters on the screen. He jumped from his stool and headed to the communication panel next to the lab door. "I need to call Louise and tell her all about this!"

# CHAPTER 19
# RUNNING AWAY

## MERIDIAN - AD CYCLE 107

Kaia's vision blurred with tears, thinking of all the Jacana who gave their lives for the Dawn Project. All the Jacana who died before she was born from famine, disease, and the third great war fought over their dwindling resources. Squeezing her eyes shut offered no relief either, as a kaleidoscope of scenes flashed in her mind. Green fern leaves carpeting the floor of a forest. A pack of nathuses scampered between the trees, chasing prey. A gray rain began to fall, the plants withered, then one nathus remained. It chittered as it looked for something to eat among the decaying foliage. Skeletal animal remains and rotting tree trunks covered the land as it dried out. There was a deep, distant rumble, then a wall of fire swept across the land, vaporizing the nathus in an instant.

She fought to push away the image of everything she knew fading away. Her once lush planet was dying before she was born, but she remembered the photos on the nature projectors. Jungles, grasslands, and shimmering blue seas, now gone for millions of years because of the Jacana... Because of her.

Exhaling, she looked at Captain Apep's ratty stuffed affi, sitting on the helm. She felt her throat constrict and let a deeper realization set in —the lump in her stomach grew even heavier. She was the reason Captain Apep was dead. The reason the families from the *Montu* were dead. They were innocent: their only crime was allowing Captain Set to bring them back to the only home they knew. And she could understand why. It wasn't a crime at all.

Her last conversation with Captain Apep clawed to the surface through the thick guilt that weighed her down. She pictured his warm smile and gentle eyes, his pleading—in his gentle, sincere way—for her to be the leader her parents would have wanted after it was all over. She took a deep, ragged breath, and remembered Captain Apep's last words to her about Councilor Hegira: *"You won't see Councilor Hegira's plan until it is too late."*

Bare facts lay disconnected in Kaia's mind. The rejected research paper, the preventable death of Captain Apep's father, Hegira's constant encouragement to her to educate people on the importance of the Dawn Project. Her subconscious began arranging and re-arranging them to find the pattern, the connections. She sensed it was on to something and left it to its work. Right now, she needed to focus.

Kaia's blood coursed through her veins, hotter than the fires that raged on Nu. She wiped her nose and dried her face with her hand. She stood up; her fists clenched by her side.

"This is not over," she whispered under her breath.

Enki pulled on her sleeve. "Kaia?"

She realized that this torrent of emotion might have frightened him. She needed to be strong, for him, for the crew. For Captain Apep and her parents. She forced the tension from her face and turned to him. "What do we need to do now?"

He pointed to the geology station. "I heard the captain advised you of..." he paused and glanced at the main viewscreen, "the alternative plan for the crew... after all of this."

"You knew?" she asked, brows raised.

"First Officer Ra told me."

"But we were not going to do that until after we arrived at Duat, so the ones who were leaving again could say goodbye."

Enki whispered, "Kaia, there is no *Montu*, and we cannot know if any other cityship will succeed. I do not mean to sound callous, but I ran a new simulation based on the sensor data to confirm the results you found in the lab." He swiped his finger all the way across the mission glyphpad. The simulation appeared in front of them. Nu was green and blue, alive, and fully recovered.

Kaia shook her head in awe. It was hard to reconcile the fireball Nu on the viewscreen with the healthy Nu in the simulation.

Enki pointed to his screen. "Based on real-time readings from the impacts, the recovery should take around 66 million cycles, just like your earlier results."

She sighed and squeezed her eyes shut for a moment. *I wanted to build the future with you, Apep.* She shook her head to snap out of it. Now was not the time for wandering thoughts.

Enki looked over to engineering, where First Officer Ra was helping Pakhet to her feet. "Ra says it will be difficult, but the lightdrive can take it."

"How difficult?"

"He is concerned about rogue planets and uncharted stars on our course. So, he recommends we stick close to home."

"Our course?"

Enki nodded. "We will have to cover a lot of ground to build up speed. It will be safer to orbit the sol system instead of venturing outside. We need thousands of orbits, but we can get moving fast enough to travel that far into the future."

"How fast?"

He pointed over to the helm. "Look at the top speed."

She glanced over and read *99.9999999999999999923% sol.*

"Well, are you up for it?" She turned to face him. "If you have doubts, say them now."

Enki nodded to Horus on the viewing platform. "What about the councilors? We need their approval, do we not?"

She felt the fire in her eyes. "This is still my mission, and we need to see it through."

Enki said, "I would never turn down the opportunity to see geological change over such an immense timescale."

She nodded. "I'll take that as a yes." She turned back to the helm. "First Officer Ra? Are you sure the ship and lightdrive can handle that speed?"

He nodded. "Yes, but only just."

Kaia took a deep breath, unsure of what to say.

She felt Councilor Horus brush past her on his way to the biology console. He pulled something up on the console viewscreen. She squinted to make it out. It appeared to have the numbers *1,298 of 8,000* next to an image of a nanomech unlike any she had ever seen.

He swiped down on the glyphpad, and the image disappeared. He came toward them, his face wrinkled in either dismay or confusion, Kaia wasn't certain which.

"Did I hear something about returning in 66 million cycles?" he asked.

Kaia stiffened and was about to put her foot down when he spoke up.

"Because," Horus said with a smile, "I would also like to see the results of our work."

Where Kaia expected to feel defensive, she felt only surprise. She did not care why he was eager to go along with the plan but was glad he did.

"Kaia, we must leave now, right?"

She nodded. "Soon, yes."

"Then, with all due respect, we'll need a captain." He bowed to First Officer Ra. "Ra is next in rank. It should be him."

She remembered Apep saying that too, *because Ra's father paid off Councilor Horus.* Still, there was no one more qualified than the inventor of the lightdrive itself. "Does anyone disagree?"

Kaia looked around at each crew member again, seeing no challenges. "Captain Ra, set a course for 66 million years into the future." She noticed a smirk playing at the edges of Horus's mouth, but she didn't have time to analyze it right now.

"Enki, broadcast these events to the other Jacana among the stars."

"Kaia, are you sure?"

His question gave her pause. "They need to witness what we've done, so we never need to do this to another innocent world."

Enki gulped, "But, all of it? Destroying the colony, too?"

She started to second-guess sharing the story. The thought of so many people giving their lives for the cause, most without being given a choice. Then, she thought, the project had a tragic beginning, why should it not have a tragic end? Nothing about what her species had done to the world was for the better, until now.

"Yes, Enki. Share the whole recording. The Dawn Project must leave scars on our people as deep as the ones we left upon our world."

Enki broadcasted the recording to the stars.

Kaia felt his hand on her back, and she could not fight it anymore. The destruction on Nu, the memories of Captain Apep and of her father's last words. The words that led her to play a role in these tragic events. She collapsed into his embrace and sobbed. Her tears splashed onto her suit. Reflected in them were the fires that burned on the viewscreen.

Captain Ra spoke up from the helm. "We will not forget these sacrifices. Our plan will work. It must." He pressed a line on his glyphpad.

The lightdrive hummed to life and began the journey, sixty-six million cycles into the future.

*AD Cycle 107*
*AD Cycle 391*
*AD Cycle 708*
*AD Cycle 1,142*

# CHAPTER 20
# ORIGINS

## ARABIAN SEA - 2034 CE

The deep past raced through Dr. Pearce's mind as fast as the phone hopped between satellite connections from the ship to Louise's phone at Porcupine Point in Matheran.

A click then, "Hi, Alan, how are you? I hope you aren't too seasick."

He tried to contain his excitement. "Honey, you're never going to believe what we've found. We have proof that..." He paused; he didn't know where to start.

"While you're thinking, let me tell you what I found here in Matheran," she said.

"Okay, yes, go ahead."

"The team tells me that the eruption that created the Deccan Plateau was two distinct events. There are two layers, not one."

He furrowed his brows and rubbed his beard for a moment. *Two?*

"You still there?" she asked.

He broke his silence. "And I'm guessing you found iridium-laced rock sandwiched between the eruptions. Right?"

"Bingo! Everywhere we drilled there is a big ashy band between endless black igneous rock. The first eruption was much smaller, while the second was four times as big. It is hard to say how much time passed between them."

"The K-Pg boundary layer," he said, fading into thought.

Louise continued, her voice rising, "Alan, the K-Pg is not only present, but the students also tell me it's the thickest ever found! It's over twenty inches from top to bottom."

He held his hand over the phone's receiver and looked to Daxia and Seagraves, who had their heads down, studying the core sample. "They found the K-Pg there, too. The layer is the thickest I've ever seen!"

Daxia rushed over. "This is an even bigger discovery than the Chicxulub." She smiled at Seagraves across the room.

"Literally," Seagraves added.

Dr. Pearce didn't even register the joke. He struggled to process the scientific discoveries they made in the last hour.

He turned back to the phone. "Louise, there is still so much to do. So many unanswered questions!" he said, looking at the three craters.

Louise sounded tentative. "Like what?"

"Daxia?" he said. "Can you put this thing on speaker?"

Daxia reached up and pressed the button labeled *Speaker* and said, "You can hang that up now."

He set the phone down on the wall receiver. "Can you still hear me, Louise?"

"I can, and I'm on pins and needles over here, wondering where you're going with this."

Dr. Pearce nodded to the stools. "You two are going to want to take a seat," he said to Daxia and Seagraves.

He spread his arms wide and began. "Three asteroid impacts happening at the same time as one of the largest volcanic eruptions is threading the needle."

Daxia furrowed her brow. "How could the eruption be related to the impacts?"

He shook his head. "I wouldn't go that far yet, but..." He rubbed his hands together. "First, a little geology lesson. Sixty-six million years ago, India was surrounded by ocean, closer to Africa than it is today. Plate tectonics pushed the whole subcontinent north on a collision course with what is now Asia. Its path took it right over the Réunion hotspot."

Louise interrupted. "The same hotspot the Climate Council is considering for their volcanic eruption plan?"

He nodded with excitement.

Daxia cleared her throat. "Dr. Pearce, she can't hear you nod."

"Oh, yes, yes, Louise, the very same one. The flood basalt eruption spread out to an area twice the size of," he looked around the room, and his eyes settled on Seagraves, "Texas."

Seagraves laughed. "Texas is an awful big place, Doctor."

"It is," Louise agreed.

Dr. Pearce explained, "The first one might have just covered the panhandle, but the second one? Well, that one covered two entire Texases with lava flows. Fire fountains must have shot up all over the place from the cracks created by this asteroid impact, spilling even more magma and forming a huge plateau. The eruption would have created dirty thunderstorms that sent lightning to the ground. Everything within a thousand miles would have been incinerated."

The mental image appeared to stun Seagraves as he took it all in.

Dr. Pearce swelled with satisfaction. "Humans have never witnessed destruction on that scale."

Louise asked, "Do you think the other two impacts would have also caused volcanic eruptions near their impact sites?"

He looked up in thought for a moment, then concluded, "It's possible."

Louise added, "And I'm sure the Climate Council would want to learn as much as they can about life after this eruption they're planning. That's your ticket, Alan. And keep the name Shiva for this crater, because Shiva is the Hindu god of destruction and renewal."

"Destruction and renewal... I like it. It's like Picasso said. You know that quote?" he asked.

"Remind me?" Louise said.

He punched one hand with the other. "Every act of creation begins with an act of destruction."

.   .   .

The three double-ringed impact craters stared back at him from the computer screen. "But another question is bothering me more…"

He walked over to the laptop. "Most impacts don't form craters with this double-ring structure." He nodded to the screen. "What if these three asteroids not only struck at the same time but were also the same shape?"

Daxia stood and joined him at the computer. "That's a stretch, even for you."

"But look," he said, pointing to the concentric circles. "How else could we explain these identical rings?"

Daxia sighed and conceded, "It is an interesting proposition."

"Al-an," Louise began, "I know you like the impact theory, but don't you get any ideas. Stick to what the council will fund."

He scrunched his face just thinking about how frustrating it was trying to fit his discoveries into the mold of something the council could tolerate.

Daxia tapped his shoulder. She pointed to the screen. "Do you think the Deccan eruption was affecting the climate before these impacts?"

He knew the look on her face. It was the spark of a student who had just found her calling. He smiled. "There is no doubt that this affected the climate. If I recall, the die-offs started even before the eruption, right?"

She nodded. "Yes, and while the eruptions and impacts are interesting, none of it has anything to do with what started the mass extinction, unless…" she began to wonder.

Dr. Pearce put his hands on his hips and ventured, "I bet the animals living before it could tell us." He watched the spark in Daxia's mind catch fire and spread, consuming her thoughts with more questions; questions he predicted she would spend her life answering.

"We do know cataclysmic climate change followed these three asteroids crashing into Earth."

Daxia shifted her eyes back to Dr. Pearce. "And finished off the mass extinction that was already underway." She looked over to the core lying under the light on the table. "And so, now we know."

Seagraves swiveled his stool toward the table. "Know what?"

Daxia and Dr. Pearce exchanged a knowing glance.

She grinned. "The dinosaurs. We know what killed the dinosaurs."

Dr. Pearce raised a finger. "It's more than that, though!"

She nodded. "We also know what created the conditions that made it possible for mammals to evolve. The climate in the years after these impacts would have been awful for reptiles, but it was survivable for rodents like our mammalian ancestors." She held her left hand up flat and used the fingers from her right to make a running motion over it. "They were nothing but little furry things scurrying along the forest floor."

Dr. Pearce followed along. "Yes, Daxia. We can explain where we came from. We can explain how the world ended for dinosaurs and was reborn for us. A climate perfect for a species like ours to evolve." He looked down and shook his head, smiling.

Seagraves bobbed his head in wonder. "There's nothing this cool in oil drilling. Is this the kind of stuff that every paleontologist works on?"

Dr. Pearce laughed. "No, but the best ones do." He looked at Daxia with a sense of pride.

The fire of discovery flashed in her eyes. She stood up straight and said, "The Yixian, it has fossils from before the impacts."

"I think you've found your PhD thesis topic," he said.

She grinned again. "I'll be able to prove this all happened, without a doubt!"

Dr. Pearce looked back at the gray line on the core.

They all gathered around, and he said, "We're looking at the geological relics that prepared Earth for the dawn of humanity."

# CHAPTER 21
# DEEP TIME

## MERIDIAN – AD CYCLE 31,489,250

Kaia stood at the small window in her lab, looking out at the passing star trails. They moved by so fast that some appeared as an endless line. She imagined herself piloting a constructor as it pulled a crystal down deep through the layers of Nu, straight to its fiery core where Captain Apep was waiting. Her eyes teared up at the memory of him. The looks that lasted just a little longer than necessary, the warm eyes as he showed her around the bridge. Her rational mind was more powerful, though, and the images changed to the constructor vaporizing into trillions of molecular flecks upon impact. Her body would join the swirling dust, sentenced to hundreds of cycles of chaos before settling into the layer of ash thick enough to become part of the geological story of Nu. It would soon separate the Jacana's past from the creatures of the future.

*A boundary between worlds*, she thought.

She leaned back from the window and moved her head from side to side to stretch her neck. If she wanted to see her work through, she needed to stay in the present to make sure no one else would be sacrificed in vain. *So many lives*, she thought. Captain Apep, Mirik, Nef, all the *Montu* refugees. They weren't the first, but she hoped they would be the last.

A thought surfaced in her mind. What was it Councilor Hegira had said about the deaths?

*I, too, have had to watch people die due to my decisions!*

Hegira's reproachful finger seemed to point all the way to the present. She remembered the way Hegira's eyes glowed with fury as she uttered the last two words.

*My decisions.*

Kaia's thoughts snapped to Captain Apep's question. Now she asked herself the same thing. *Why did I ever trust Hegira?* The naïve feeling wavered as more questions filled her mind.

*Why did Hegira bring me onto the project as a child?*

*Why did Hegira make me relive my parents' deaths over and over?*

*Why didn't the Council evacuate us before the storm?*

She was suddenly aware Councilor Hegira would have seen the storm's path.

*Why weren't my parents rescued?*

*Why wasn't Apep's father rescued?*

Darkness consumed her thoughts as the ultimate question settled in her mind.

*Did Councilor Hegira kill my parents?*

There was a knock at her door.

Kaia shuffled away from the window, shaken.

All she could manage was a simple, "Come in."

"Hi, Kaia," Enki said, poking his head through the crack in the door. "We wanted to stop by—"

"We?"

Ra stuck his head out from behind Enki and said, "How are you, Kaia?"

"Hello First Offic—" she felt her throat tighten, "I mean, Captain Ra, sorry. I'm fine."

He raised his palm. "It's okay, Kaia."

Enki leaned against the doorjamb. "We were checking to see if you wanted to join us for some food."

She couldn't remember the last time she'd eaten, but also didn't feel like it right now. "No, thank you, though."

Enki waved his hand down the hall. "Kaia, please, you need to eat."

She looked back through the window at the compressed starlight flashing past. "I keep replaying his final moments in my mind. Doubting myself, doubting the decision to pursue this plan from the beginning. But I know the sacrifices were necessary."

Enki stepped inside and joined her at the window.

She saw his shoulders tense. "It was noble," he said. "And because we sent the recording to all the remaining Jacana, no one will forget their sacrifice. All Jacana will speak their names with the deepest gratitude. Everyone will know the story of how Captain Apep, Mirik, and Nef saved the world."

She sighed. "You're right. Let's get something to eat."


Enki devoured everything on his plate before Kaia's cup of soup had time to cool.

"Someone was hungry," she said.

Captain Ra said, with one eyebrow raised, "I'll say."

Kaia swirled her spoon in the hot liquid and looked up at the ship's chronometer as the cycles flew by.

*AD 31,489,259*

*AD 31,490,473*

*AD 31,492,621*

"It's only been a day since Captain Apep gave his life, but it has been 11.5 billion days on Nu. Sometimes I wonder if I should have studied physics instead of geology," she mused. "I still have a hard time wrapping my head around how it all works. How a lightdrive can make time go slower for us, while the universe outside continues at normal speed."

Captain Ra nodded. "Well, I *know* the science, and some days, even I still find it hard to wrap my head around." He smiled at Enki. "I felt the power of what we were doing when I saw the entire eruption had cooled in what was just a few hours for us."

. . .

Enki swallowed a bite and licked his lips. "It took about 107 cycles, or forty thousand days."

"Yes, I know." Ra looked back to Kaia. "Studying and simulating time travel doesn't do the real thing justice."

"I'd be happy if I never saw another simulation again," Kaia tried her soup, but it was still too hot.

Enki leaned forward with his elbows on the table as Kaia and Ra ate. "It is not disaster-preventing backwards time travel I wish we had, but it is compelling, nonetheless." He studied his plate, and Kaia thought he might pick the last bits of food from the fork, but he continued, "I wish I could watch what is happening right now on Nu. Most geological processes occur so gradually that you cannot see them. But if I could watch it at the speed it is moving, I would have a whole new perspective of how everything works on Nu."

Kaia ate another spoonful of soup then rested her spoon upside down beside the bowl. "Your simulations aren't sufficient?"

Enki cocked his head to consider it. "They are exquisite, but none of our simulations compared to watching the eruption or impacts in real life. So, I can infer that entire geological process would also blow my mind."

"You're right," Kaia chided, "none of your simulations almost killed us."

Enki leaned in and waved his hands in the air. "The simulations of what is happening on Nu right now only show planet-wide events, such as the transit of landmasses above the mantle or broad changes in climate. But the resolution is poor. I can only imagine watching individual ecosystems change, the volcanic eruptions initiated by the impacts. Or," his hands stilled for a moment and he looked right at Kaia, "even the evolution of animals."

Kaia rested her hands in her lap. "You're right, Enki. Evolution from one species into another only happens over large amounts of time. I can witness subtle variations in live creatures in my lifetime but never anything like the vast transformations we see in the fossil record. Those changes are lost to time."

"And some of the geologic changes happen even slower than

evolution," continued Enki.

Kaia smiled when she saw Captain Ra hanging on Enki's every word. It was nice seeing his formal demeanor give way to a more approachable one.

Enki flung his arms to the side with more enthusiasm than she'd ever seen. "Just imagine you are in an all-glass spaceship orbiting Nu. Right now! Never mind that it is not feasible for us to see it with our own eyes, just stay with me. So, you are in this all-glass ship that is moving through time at the same rate as us. No, let us say it is even faster. Each minute you spend standing on the ship, you are seeing 100,000 cycles passing below on Nu. The geology is changing right before your eyes. In the first ten seconds, you see the impacts' dust clouds beginning to dissipate. Light is reaching the surface for the first time in thousands of cycles. It would look much the same as it did when we left, except, if you can believe it, more dead."

Kaia felt her eyes grow moist and looked down.

"Oh, I apologize. Poor phrasing," Enki said.

She looked up. "No, it's okay." She pushed the dark thoughts aside.

Enki made a circle with his hands. "The atmosphere is gray. The oceans turn brown from rain washing the loose dust off the continents. Now, there are little patches of green on the land. We will focus on one. We would see it spreading. It keeps growing, joining with other growing green patches. Over thousands of cycles, green is covering an entire continent. Sure, it is moss and grasses, not much forest, but it is life starting anew. The same event is happening on every landmass. You are witnessing the recovery of Nu's primary ecosystems in just the first few thousand cycles."

Enki paused and noticed Captain Ra staring at him with a wide smile. He smiled back and kept going. He was just getting to his favorite part.

"If we speed things up a little bit, you can see bright white ice sheets forming on Nu's polar regions. A cold air mass is developing above them. The ice begins to expand farther down from the north and south poles, pulling moisture from the oceans. Less water in the sea means you can see more land. The forests are now growing outward from freshwater rivers, covering new land as fast as it appears."

Kaia interrupted, "Do you think the wildlife on Nu would be back by now?"

He shook his head. "Not yet. Things are just getting started. The land itself has healed. The climate is stable, and the continents are beginning to move and change shape. During our time, Nu had twelve great landmasses, all of them in motion over the molten layers below. Our vantage point on this imaginary ship lets us see things faster, though. You could watch them drift across the surface like huge cargo vessels over the ocean. Entire ecosystems are riding on their backs. Geb, the smallest continent, the one Puna sits on, is racing toward the top of Nu. But another landmass is in its way."

Captain Ra looked up at the ceiling in thought then back to Enki. "They told us about that at school, but I never thought about what it would be like if I could watch it move. The only reminder we ever got that we were not stationary was the occasional groundshake."

"Oh yes, that is one reason the plan to drill through to the magma below it was possible. The land below Puna is, or I guess was, thin compared to the other landmasses. There was a mantle plume below it, which is what was sending Geb moving across the ocean at a rate many times that of other landmasses. You would see it moving fast from our hypothetical ship. It is even stretching out a bit as the leading edge moves ahead. In fact, it is moving so fast it may lose pieces of itself on its march to the north. In just a few seconds, you see Geb collide with the much larger landmass in its path. There is no dust because it is happening gradually on Nu, but to you, it looks like a grand collision. The land on both sides buckles and bends into jagged ridges. These ridges become the largest mountain range Nu has ever seen. The peaks continue to rise into the sky for tens of millions of cycles. The forces that pushed Geb will try to plow their way through an entire continent. But my favorite thing to witness is happening far to the west of Geb."

Kaia looked up at the chronometer again. *AD 39,267,384* whizzed by as Enki was talking. "How far west of Geb?" she asked.

Enki lowered his voice in a show of respect. "Near the phara breeding grounds."

She closed her eyes for a moment, trying to imagine the forest and wetland thriving instead of dying as she remembered it. "Go on," she urged.

Enki nodded. "Okay, but the breeding grounds are just a small section of it. The five great landmasses have pushed farther west. However, they are not colliding with another landmass. They are forcing a great section of land under the ocean to move below them, back toward the core of Nu. This subduction causes my favorite thing to form, volcanoes. Lots and lots of volcanoes. A volcanic mountain chain will run along the western edge of the two continents, stretching almost two-thirds the length of Nu. You could watch eruption after eruption happening up and down the chain as the land sinks under the ocean. The ground above is buckling and building more mountains as it runs over the top of the other plate. Not mountains as large as the ones north of Geb but still breathtaking. Now, back to where your parents worked. They were on the coast of a narrow sea between two of the western continents, right?"

"Yes," she swallowed hard, "the strong current through it brought warm water up and caused storms." Her voice cracked with too much thought of death. "The worst storms on Nu plagued our station, wildlife refuge number seven."

Enki took a deep breath and continued with the difficult topic. "Well, if you were in this time-warping ship looking down on Nu, you would see that narrow sea drying up about a minute after our impacts.

"Why would it dry up?" Captain Ra asked.

"It is a combination of the land rising due to another tectonic plate moving under it and the falling sea level due to icecaps forming. Wildlife Refuge No. 7 is no longer a lush coastal rainforest, but an expansive grassland."

Kaia felt the memory pass and leaned back in her chair to consider the possibilities. "No narrow sea," she pondered. "So, what would Nu look like now? I mean, overall?"

Enki held up his hand counted off on his fingers. "It will have fewer landmasses, maybe six. Eight at the most. I know that Geb will have joined with the larger one for sure, and lower ocean levels will reveal connections between them. There are also more mountains, which means there are more diverse climates than in the world we knew. There are likely rainforests, grasslands, wetlands, and deserts. Perhaps we will see some of each on every continent."

Kaia smiled at the thought. "The climate when it was our planet was too similar everywhere—too hot and dry. When it started to change, it meant that animals everywhere suffered as well. If you're right, and it has more diversity now, it will take a lot more damage to destroy everything as we almost did."

He nodded. "Much more." They all three sat in quiet contemplation.

She looked up at the chronometer. *AD 65,120,472.* "Our trip is almost over."

Enki jumped out of his chair. "Time to go home!"

# CHAPTER 22
# REVOCATION

## UNIVERSITY OF CHICAGO - 2034 CE

Daxia reached up to the globe on Dr. Pearce's shelf and ran her fingers down the mountainous spine of North and South America, the American Cordillera. The longest mountain range in the world, much of it volcanic, thanks to the subduction of the Pacific plate.

Dr. Pearce held a manila envelope high above his head. "Yes!" he shouted.

Daxia turned away from the globe and sat down on the other side of his desk. "I still can't believe you force people to mail things to you."

He pretended to growl at his computer, then sat the envelope down next to a stack of papers, picked up his phone, and called Louise. The phone rang once, then clicked.

"Hel—" she began to say.

"Louise, it's here!" he blurted out.

"What is?"

"The paper. I mean, the notice of publication for the asteroid impact plan after my appeal!"

"Wait for me, Alan. I'll be there in two minutes for the grand opening!" Louise said and hung up.

Daxia beamed a smile from across his desk. "Dr. Pearce, this is so exciting!"

He sat down and held the envelope in front of him. He traced his finger along the paper and read it aloud: "United Nations Climate Council, Publishing Department."

"It didn't take them long to change their mind about your work," Daxia said.

He nodded. "I assume they liked what we found at the Shiva crater because it leaves no room for dissent. It must have been the impacts *and* an eruption, not the eruption itself, that stabilized our climate 66 million years ago."

"Can I see?" Daxia asked.

He slid it across the desk. She picked up the envelope and held it up to the window.

"Hey, no peeking," Dr. Pearce joked, reaching across the desk to pull it out of her hands.

He looked down at the rest of his mail and shuffled through it. He pulled out a tri-folded piece of paper and handed it to Daxia. "Read this if you need something to do while we wait for Louise to get here. You'll get a kick out of it."

"What is it?"

"That would spoil the surprise."

She unfolded the paper and read the header, "The International Order of Extraterrestrialism." She raised her eyebrows. "What is this?"

"Keep reading," he urged.

"Dear Dr. Pearce, Your ancient meteor impact research has come to our attention, and we would like you to submit it for canonization," she dropped her hand to her lap and laughed in disbelief. "Canonization?"

Dr. Pearce laughed with her. "I know! Can you believe it? Check out the third paragraph."

She skimmed the letter. "We feel your work substantiates the cornerstone of our belief system—that extraterrestrials shaped and guided the evolution of life on Earth. We consider your research to be a revelation of sacred knowledge." She stopped reading and burst out laughing harder than before. She held up the paper and shook her head. "This is a real religion?"

He smiled. "It would appear so. Now read the rest, it gets better."

She lowered the paper and continued.

"In addition to the inclusion of your research, we are pleased to offer you the rank of Prophet of Verities. Your work is revealing ancient secrets we believe to be true. We would like to offer you $2,000,000 USD to continue your work. We do have one condition to send the funds."

"Oh." Daxia looked up and quirked a brow at Dr. Pearce. "They have *conditions*."

"What religion doesn't?" he quipped.

She continued, "You must allow our order to be the sole publisher of your future discoveries." Daxia's mouth fell open. "They're offering you two million dollars for exclusive publication?"

He nodded. "But granting sole publishing rights to a religious organization? That would be academic suicide."

"As if working with them at all isn't bad for your career?"

"*Touché*, Daxia."

She leaned on the arm of her chair. "So, what are you going to do?"

He chuckled. "Nothing, of course. They're just a bunch of ancient aliens nutjobs. I've always steered clear of that stuff." He held up the envelope from the UN Climate Council. "Besides, two million dollars is nothing compared to what the Council has at its disposal."

Dr. Pearce heard the telltale creak of the office door as it flew open and Louise rushed in. She made a beeline to where Alan sat behind his desk and leaned down to give him a big hug. "I'm so proud of you." She followed it with a peck on his cheek then went and sat in the empty chair next to Daxia.

He leaned forward. "I want to thank you both for sharing such an important moment with me." He picked up the sealed envelope from the Climate Council. "I could not have done this without you, Daxia. No one can manage a research team as well as you." He looked to Louise. "And my dear Louise, you have always been by my side, believing in my work when others did not." He put his hand over his chest. "Thank you both from the bottom of my heart."

Louise blew him another kiss, then urged, "Open it!"

Dr. Pearce pulled the letter opener out of his desk drawer and slid it across the envelope's flap. He glanced up at Louise and Daxia. They both had the biggest grins he'd ever seen from either of them.

He pulled out the single piece of paper, set the empty envelope down, then unfolded the letter and began to read.

"Dr. Alan Pearce," he looked up.

Daxia and Louise were leaning in, waiting to hear the good news.

He cleared his throat. "The United Nations Climate Council Geology Committee thanks you for your dedication and lifetime of work to helping preserve the natural ecosystems of Earth. Your unconventional research and your unconventional theories have proven invaluable as we plan for the future."

Daxia began to clap, but stopped when Louise cleared her throat.

"Go on, dear," Louise said.

Alan continued, "We deliberated over this decision longer than any other prior decision. I regret to inform you"—he tightened his jaw—"that we are removing your research from our future budgets."

He huffed, already feeling his eyes burn.

"We will also retain rights to your recent work in Mexico and India. We will not be publishing it at this time." His heart seemed to drop straight into his lap. The paper fell from his hands, and his face felt hotter than an iron.

Daxia picked it up and asked, "May I?"

"Go on," he said, waving it away. "Read it for yourself."

She took the paper and read it in silence.

Louise reached her hand across the desk, and he leaned forward to meet it. "Oh Alan, I am so sorry."

He sighed. "I finally went too far for them."

Daxia shook the letter. "But they said they appreciate your non-conventional theories. This doesn't make sense..."

He looked down. "It isn't that simple. My research pointed to a plan that is politically impossible to carry out. No one wants to hear we may not be able to change course fast enough to counteract the damage we've done. It would feel like we were giving up."

He let go of Louise's hand and knocked on the table. "It's over."

"Alan, this can't be the end," Louise urged. "The university could fund your work, or another government, perhaps. You've never given up without a fight."

He reached down and opened a desk drawer. He pulled out a small stack of papers and sat them on his desk.

"What are those?" Louise asked.

"Rejection letters from journals," he said. "I've tried everything."

He reached toward Daxia, and she handed him the letter. He set it down on top of the pile and flattened it out.

"There is nothing left," he said, looking down at his lap.

"No, Dr. Pearce," Daxia said and looked at Louise. "You have not tried everything." She held up the letter he'd shown her earlier and waved it back and forth.

He shook his head. "I can't take their money. It would be career suicide."

Louise snatched the letter from Daxia's hand. "Can't take whose money?"

"Read it yourself," he said.

She skimmed the letter. "Two million dollars? Now that's the definition of unconventional."

"That's an understatement," he said.

Louise scolded him. "Now hold on, they are not the only people who believe this, you know. There are some well-respected anthropologists in my circles who think we don't know the whole story of how human culture evolved."

He scoffed at the notion. "You don't need to make me feel better, Louise. Not understanding the full story is a far cry from thinking ancient aliens helped us."

She nodded once. "I'll give you that. It leans more on pseudo-archaeology than hard evidence." She looked back down at the paper then said with renewed resolve, "But they'll give you two million dollars."

"The field would shun me," he said. "And they might take Daxia down, too."

He heard the chair squeak as Daxia squirmed in it. "Don't worry about me," she said.

"But dear," Louise turned to her, "he has a point. Your career is new, this could—"

"No, it's not that." Daxia looked to them both. "Remember? I need to go back to China. My father needs me."

Dr. Pearce raised his hands and drummed them on his desk. "And you get to dig on the Yixian Formation. It should be easy for you to keep your academic distance from all of this!"

Daxia pressed on, "I'll be fine, Dr. Pearce. You're on to something here. You need to keep your research going."

He leaned back in his chair and gazed up at the ceiling, thinking about the offer. It was a fact that he trusted and respected these two women more than anyone, and they were saying he should go for it. He pointed to the letter in Louise's hands. "Hand that over, please."

She gave it back. "What have you got to lose?"

"Nothing," he said. "Nothing at all."

He sighed and read the header out loud, trying hard not to chuckle. "The International Order of Extraterrestrialism."

Louise waggled her eyebrows. "Has a bit of a ring to it."

# CHAPTER 23
# REPETITION

Kaia and Enki watched Ra speed down the corridor ahead of them to the bridge. His hands and feet seemed to know just where to grab and just where to push off to keep him moving at a quick pace.

"Sorry!" he yelled back to them. "I need to make sure Pakhet has the lightdrive ready."

"Go ahead!" Kaia returned. She tugged on Enki's suit to slow him down as he passed her, too. "Wait," she said. "What if the impacts didn't work?"

"The plan worked. I anticipated a multitude of scenarios and included those in my calculations. 99.99% of them were successful."

Her face pulled tight. "And the other .01%?"

Enki tilted his head downward. "One cannot rule out the chance of a confounding variable over sixty-six million cycles."

"66 million cycles..." her voice trailed off for a moment. "I wish I could have seen the creatures that evolved and went extinct in that span of time."

"Do you recall my favorite mineral?" he asked.

"Iridium?" she looked up for a moment then back at him. "No, it was kohl."

He nodded. "Kohl is interesting because it is a stone consisting of the life energy of dead plants and animals from millions of cycles earlier."

"Your description makes it sound good because it is natural. Nature can kill just as fast as Jacana technology, though."

"Yes, though it would not have been so dangerous if we left it alone. But it stores energy so well that we built our entire civilization around the utilization of that energy. It helped us progress. Too bad it took us so long to realize that burning it was killing us," he said.

"And then too long to act on it when we did figure it out," Kaia added.

Enki stopped and held his hand up, making circles as he spoke. "Plants and animals die and then turn to stone. We mine the stone and burn it. The act of burning the life energy of long-dead organic matter then begins to kill live plants and animals on Nu."

She stopped with him.

"I have never thought about it that way—as a very long cycle."

"It is, and a terrible one," he added.

"Well, I don't think anyone will make that mistake again," she said, remembering the ten commandments.

They were nearing the bridge, and Kaia's mind turned to the possibilities of what they might find on Nu after so much change.

She stopped and turned to Enki just outside the doorway. "Do you think any creatures from our time survived?"

He shrugged. "Perhaps, though, the odds are against most every species you studied. They are more likely to be dead and turned to stone, or rather kohl, by now," he said.

"And so, the cycle goes." She made a circle with her hand.

He chuckled.

"What's so funny?" she asked.

He smiled. "That means your animals are my territory now, being rocks and all."

She laughed for the first time since Apep's death, thanks to Enki's earnest attempt at humor.

"You're right," she said. As she prepared to open the hatch to the bridge, her heart thumped in her chest. She stopped short again. "Can I ask you something?"

He grabbed the handrail and floated next to her. "What is it?"

"We're about to find out if our plan—" she began. "No, I'll cut to the chase." Kaia looked at him straight on. "Do you trust Councilor Hegira?"

His face scrunched in puzzlement. "What do you mean?"

"Do you trust her judgment… that she knows what to do?"

He looked away. "She outranks us, Kaia, so we must do as she says. How is trust relevant?"

Kaia sighed; he did not understand. She took a different approach. "Do you trust me?" she asked.

He turned back to her. "Of course, Kaia. Everyone trusts you."

"Why? You haven't known me that long."

"That is incorrect, Kaia. We all grew up hearing your story. We knew you were part of this project for the proper reason. Not for fame, or money, but to save the world."

Kaia's chest expanded with pride for the first time.

"If I may ask," Enki said, gesturing toward her with an open palm. "What is the reason behind your question?"

She looked out a porthole in the corridor. Compressed starlight shimmered along the metal walls around them. "I'm a little afraid of what we're going to find, and what I might need to do."

Enki reached out and touched her shoulder. "Kaia, you inspired all of us when we were young. You were one of us; we wanted to join you, to help you. We still do." He looked away then back at her. "People do not follow others they do not trust."

She smiled. "I needed to hear that more than you know."


The bridge was full of quiet work. Kaia heard fingertips scraping on their glyphpads as everyone prepared for arrival.

The flurry of quiet activity reminded Kaia of just a few days ago when they learned that the eruption failed. She looked at the two chronometers on the bridge as she walked to her station. One displayed the current date on Nu, and the other showed the date on the ship. The difference was staggering. A few days had passed on the ship, but it was AD Cycle 66,187,885 for Nu. Enki was also looking at the chronometers. They slid their feet into the loops on the floor in front of the mission console and braced themselves in anticipation of the final deceleration.

Captain Ra was to her left at the helm. He was chewing his lower lip as he studied the main viewscreen. Councilor Horus stood over his shoulder, pointing at something, but Ra seemed to be ignoring him, keeping his eyes on the ring of starlight in front of them. She looked past the helm toward the ship's systems console. Pakhet towered over it, back straight, feet shoulder-width apart, hands clasped behind her back.

"Hello, Kaia," a familiar smoky voice came from behind.

It was Councilor Hegira sitting on the platform. The shadow of a support beam crossed her face.

Kaia nodded and turned her back on the councilor.

"Ignoring me will not bring him back," Councilor Hegira said.

Captain Ra clicked over the comm. "Winding down the lightdrive, now."

Kaia pulled her shoulders back and crossed her arms. She looked up at the viewscreen and focused on the familiar dark void ringed with starlight. The circle of light began to widen while the blackness shrank, and within seconds, she could make out individual stars. The ship creaked as it came to a full stop and the darkness snapped away.

Captain Ra held down the comm. "We are back. I am going to maintain this position. Nu's orbit should bring it across our viewscreen any moment."

The activity of the bridge ceased as every crew member trained their eyes on the left edge of the screen.

Professor Thoth gasped. "Over here!" he yelled. His arm flew up, and he pointed at the section of the viewscreen in front of his console.

Kaia turned to see along with the rest of the crew. A faint glow grew near the edge of the viewscreen, bathing Thoth's console in pale blue light.

Kaia leaned forward. "That must be it."

Enki leaned forward, too. "It is."

"Is that…" she felt her stomach knot, "blue smog?"

"No," Enki shook his head. "Not smog, haze. That is the atmosphere," he explained. He glanced down at his glyphpad and drew a square.

The haze gave way to a solid blue arc. The viewscreen glowed brighter as the arc grew larger. She gasped and covered her mouth, staring in awe.

Enki's eyes widened. "Is that a landmass?" he asked, pointing to a solid green patch entering the edge of the screen.

She nodded, lowering her hand. "It has to be."

The crew watched in rapt silence as their home came into view.

They left behind a planet covered by a dingy gray ocean, with twelve large landmasses and green bits of dying forests.

Kaia couldn't believe her eyes. It was a completely different world. "Captain Ra, double-check the coordinates."

The captain's voice cracked as he spoke. "They are correct. The orbit matches Nu's."

"It doesn't seem possible," she said, unable to take her eyes off the luminous blue planet that sat at the center of the viewscreen.

The sea was bright blue. The atmosphere was a rich mix of natural storm systems and clear air. Below the clouds was an unrecognizable arrangement of continents. Pure white ice obscured the southernmost continent, while great forests, deserts, mountains, and plains covered the rest.

A majestic mountain range curved along the north edge of Geb, where plate tectonics had pushed it north, sending it crashing into another landmass just as Enki described.

Kaia pointed to where new continents rotated into view from the west. "And look over there!" The north and south continents were farther apart but separated by a tiny land bridge that straddled the equator. A few gray streaks were visible on the mountain range that ran the length of each continent.

Enki grinned. "Those are ash clouds. It's the volcanic mountain range. And look up there, the narrow sea is gone!" he exclaimed.

A smooth green texture had taken the place of the gray water. "Is that the grassland?" she asked.

"It appears so," Enki said. "It looks healthy."

They stood, marveling at the creation in the wake of their destruction.

Kaia felt tears welling up. "I've never seen so much life. No living Jacana has seen Nu so alive." She pulled her gaze away from the screen and looked around to each crew member on the bridge. Their eyes twinkled with hope. She walked around in front of her console, toward the main viewscreen, wishing she could reach out and touch her home.

"Apep, it worked," she whispered, with her hand over her heart. "We saved everything."

Enki joined her. "It-it is just like I imagined!"

"There must be more life than I could ever hope to study," Kaia said as she surveyed the diverse landscapes.

Enki put his hand on her shoulder. "This is a success beyond our wildest dreams."

She leaned back and turned her head toward Captain Ra at the helm. "What do the biological sensors show?"

Captain Ra took a step over to the mission console and studied the chart. He smiled. "Life, Kaia. Life is everywhere, on every land mass and of every shape and size."

Councilor Horus clucked. "Kaia, you're going to be very busy." He nodded at the viewscreen. "Excellent work."

Kaia turned to Enki just as he turned to her—his eyes were as wet as hers. They smiled and fell into an embrace, with the rich green and blue planet on the viewscreen creating a stunning, living backdrop.

The rest of the crew gathered around Kaia and Enki in a huge, tearful group hug while Councilor Hegira and Councilor Horus looked on. Kaia could not have dreamed this much happiness was possible, given the still-fresh heartbreak and anguish.

The air was thick with emotion.

Kaia let go of Enki but kept her arms on his shoulders.

"We did it, my friend," she said, her face warmed by her tears.

He looked to the screen with eyes full of hope. "And to think we failed only days ago."

Kaia wiped her eyes and nodded.

*And that Apep gave his life.*

She kept the thought to herself as she marveled at the world below. A world more alive than any of the destination planets. She took in the joy on the bridge and wondered what the colonists on the other cityships had found. Did they have this much cause for celebration?

She let her mind wander ahead through the steps of setting up a new colony on this pristine planet. Days passed wandering its landscapes, collecting samples, observing new animal behaviors. In the evening, they would gather for dinner to share what they'd learned. Each day would be an encyclopedia of new discoveries, but then her mind went deeper. Troubling thoughts rose to the surface. They would be the only Jacana, and their only medical doctor, Dr. Khnum, was the oldest of them. There would be moments of extreme loneliness and anxiety, she knew. Then the last of her excitement melted away when she remembered what was missing—Apep. Captain Apep should be here with them, with... her.

Captain Ra returned to the helm and was tapping at the glyphpad. "Kaia, Enki, what do you make of this?"

Kaia pulled herself away from the viewscreen and went to the mission console. "What is it?"

Captain Ra narrowed his eyes, scrutinizing tiny red dots on the updated map of Nu. "The sensors are picking up fires on the surface."

Kaia leaned in for a closer look. "Could be lightning strikes?"

Enki leaned in for a better look at their locations. "No, the clusters are not in forests." He zoomed in on one such cluster on the northern end of the second largest continent. "See?" He pointed to the screen. "This is a desert, but there are several concentrations of fires."

Kaia noticed something else on the screen. Lines, too straight to be natural. She felt her heart jump. "How big are the fires?"

Enki zoomed in on the largest cluster and froze; only his mouth moved. "Too small to be natural."

"Captain Set?" she asked as her body tensed.

Captain Ra shook his head. "Impossible." He nudged Enki aside and closed the map to glance at the radio spectrograph. The lines were flat. "No transmissions." He flipped back to the map. "Unless they aren't using electronics, these fires can't be from other colonists."

Kaia tapped, and the dot clusters disappeared, leaving the straight lines connecting dark spots where they had been. "What are they?"

Captain Ra shook his head. "Professor Thoth may be able to squeeze more data from these images.

The other crew members began to make their way back to their stations.

"Professor Thoth, can we join you at your station?" she asked.

He nodded.

"Captain Ra," Kaia started, "why don't you go back to the helm, and Enki, you stay here. I'll go investigate with Dr. Khnum and Professor Thoth."

"Of course," Ra replied.

As Enki headed to the systems console with Kaia, Professor Thoth leaned in and whispered, "Kaia, I hope you know that this is still your mission as far as I'm concerned."

"Thank you."


Kaia stood next to Professor Thoth, who was pointing at a zoomed-in image from the surface.

"What are you seeing?" she asked.

He clicked his tongue and crossed his arms. "It doesn't make sense."

"What doesn't make sense?"

"There can't be any Jacana roads left, but that sure is what these look like to me. And there's more," he said, uncrossing his arms. He zoomed in farther. "There is movement along the lines. And where the lines end," he panned up to the end of one line, "you can see these clumps of smaller lines divided by stone boxes."

Kaia waved Enki over.

He jogged around the empty side of the bridge, past the council table.

She pointed to the stone shapes. "What do you make of these?"

Enki narrowed his eyes. "They are too linear to be natural formations."

"What are they, then?" Kaia asked.

Professor Thoth's eyes widened. "They look like... No, they can't be."

"What?" Kaia pushed.

"They look like prehistoric Jacana ruins."

"That is not likely after 66 million cycles of geological forces," Enki said.

"Captain Ra?" Kaia said over the continuing din of excited conversation.

"Yes?"

"We need everyone's take. Let's put this up on the main viewscreen."

"Understood," he said and motioned for the crew and councilors to quiet down and look up.

Professor Thoth transferred his camera feed to the main viewscreen. He pointed to the horizon.

Kaia noticed Councilor Hegira squinting, trying to see what they were commenting on.

Then her mouth fell open. "Ruins," she said. "Those have to be Jacana ruins."

Kaia nudged Professor Thoth. "Access the biological sensors."

He drew a long rectangle with small lines in it, and a bar chart appeared on his screen. One bar flew to the top of the chart.

"Impossible!" Kaia said.

Councilor Hegira raised her voice from across the bridge. "What kind of life?"

Kaia turned toward the council platform and shouted, "Complex! Complex life is all over the ruins, and whatever they are, they are not Jacana." She looked up at the main viewscreen again then turned to Enki. "I don't know what to make of this, do you?"

He cocked his head and stepped toward the console. "May I?" he asked, gesturing for Professor Thoth to step away.

Kaia knew that look very well. *He has an idea.* "What are you looking for?" she asked.

"You will see." He zoomed in on the northern region of the continent. A desert gave way to a great forest that stretched across the middle.

Enki zoomed in farther to reveal even more geometric lines. "They are everywhere," he noted.

Kaia felt her mind race. "Impossible." She looked back to the council platform and noticed Councilor Horus staying quiet. And with a very suspicious look on his face. *He knows something,* she thought.

Councilor Hegira stood, her face red with anger. "We deconstructed every city, erased every trace of ourselves. The ruins of Puna and Set's colony could not have survived the impacts, much less 66 million cycles of change! I need answers, now!"

A smile spread across Councilor Horus's face. He stood up. "Kaia, please join me at the mission console." He waved his hand toward it.

She exchanged glances with Enki and went toward the councilor.

They both arrived and he nodded down to the glyphpad. "Please zoom in on those shapes for me."

She heard footsteps and saw Enki coming to join them. The images appeared on the mission console's viewscreen, and Councilor Horus inspected them.

"These are not Jacana," he said. "Our ancestors did not build so small with stone, and the nanomechs would have recognized even natural stone as touched by Jacana and deconstructed it."

Kaia stepped back and stood in front of the council platform where everyone had gathered. Councilor Horus clasped his hands and stretched his fingers over the console.

"Let's have a closer look on the big screen," he said as the bridge filled with yellow light from the desert view on the main viewscreen. He zoomed in even farther and tapped the console to enlarge the image, then panned around the region.

Kaia noticed hundreds of straight lines on the ground.

"Look," Councilor Horus said, keeping the image focused on one section where a long straight line terminated in another clump of small, dense lines. "Something is moving in there."

Kaia shook her head slowly. "It has to be colonists. I've never seen wildlife make anything like this. Their movement appears to be within the lines."

Councilor Horus panned the camera farther up. The lines lead to a large open space. There was colorful movement everywhere as the odd bipedal creatures moved about the area. He locked the view and faced the group.

Kaia caught the slight prideful grin that he seemed to be fighting.

He clasped his hands in front of his robe. "This is a new civilization."

She felt the realization in her bones. Dr. Khnum and Professor Thoth whispered something about more Jacana.

Horus nodded backward toward the screen. "But these are not Jacana. The life-form readings prove it. Yet this appears to be an open-air market, much like the ones our ancestors created." The camera panned over table after table. Each one held only a few items. "It does not look like there is much for sale, though," he remarked.

Kaia observed the movements of individuals as they approached the mercantile stalls. Others left with items in their hands and moved on to the next one.

Councilor Hegira's voice interrupted Kaia's thoughts. "Pakhet."

Pakhet faced the councilor.

"Please check the ship's sensors for electromagnetic emissions from the surface."

Pakhet looked to Kaia then Captain Ra.

"I already checked," Ra said. "There is nothing."

Kaia noticed Councilor Horus fidgeting.

"No electricity yet, though. Hm," he said.

Kaia's eyes grew wide. "But if they are like us..."

Enki placed his hand on her shoulder as they watched the activity below.

She continued, "If they are like us, what would stop them from destroying Nu again? Their society will industrialize. They could repeat the cycle." She shook her head in sadness, staring at the bipedal creatures. "Right now, it looks like they are starving."

Dr. Khnum stepped to the side of his workstation to get a closer look at the viewscreen. "They need our help."

Captain Ra checked the food storage levels. "We don't have enough food to help that many. In fact, we do not have enough to last six months since we won't be going to Duat."

Kaia, Enki, and Councilor Horus swapped ideas as the rest of the crew watched the creatures.

"No!" a voice shouted above the excited chatter.

Everyone turned to see Councilor Hegira rise from her seat, the light moving around the outer edge of her headpiece as she stood.

She put her hands on her hips. "We must eradicate them."

Kaia felt her blood heat and put her hands on her hips, matching Hegira's pose. She met Hegira's eyes with fire in her own. "Absolutely, not. This is my mission. I will decide what orders to give."

Councilor Hegira stamped a foot. "Your mission was to save Nu." She gestured to the viewscreen. "You've done that. Good work. Now the *Council* must prevent these creatures from destroying it all over again."

"There has been enough death," Kaia said, crossing her arms tight. She shook her head at the councilor. "There will be no more."

Councilor Hegira pointed right at her. "You! You have already proven yourself incapable of making the tough decisions. You miss the big picture. You are afraid to do what is necessary to keep this planet alive. You value the life of these," she waved her hand to the viewscreen, "these *creatures*. Do you honestly believe they're more important than the future of Nu, the planet countless Jacana gave their life to save?"

Councilor Horus took a step forward. "Councilor Hegira, I think you may be getting ahead of—"

Hegira gestured to Kaia, spitting out her next words with venom. "Are you going to listen to this *child*?"

Horus shook his head. "I am merely suggesting we not jump to conclus—"

"This is just like you, Horus, always wanting to find the truth. You still have not learned that people don't like the truth. Sometimes, you must create your own. You knew the eruption would fail, but you almost believed in it to satisfy your own ego."

He winced and shirked away.

Kaia looked from one to the other, her mind a confusion of thoughts. "What do you mean you knew it was going to fail? Captain Set admitted it was he who sabotaged—"

Councilor Hegira hissed, "Oh, he sabotaged it alright, but where do you think he got our plans? How did he know what to do? I'm telling you it wasn't ever going to work."

"You still knew," Kaia repeated.

"Of course I knew," Hegira insisted. "It is ridiculous to think a bunch of lava from a single spot was going to make a long-term climate shift. A bunch of small impacts were never going to work either, but it was palatable, Kaia. And it did wonders getting the research funded."

"It. Was. You," Kaia felt numb. She pointed at Councilor Hegira. "You hid the original impact model. I found the paper," Kaia blurted out. "The one you tried to hide."

"I did what someone had to do, Kaia," Councilor Hegira replied. "Do you think anyone would have left the planet if they knew it was going to take total annihilation to start a recovery? Captain Set's Resistance would have overthrown the whole Council!"

"You don't know that. You didn't even give the people a chance to make the decision!" And then Kaia realized what this meant. If they had time to plan the larger impact, Apep and the others might still be alive. Kaia's heart turned cold. She clenched her fists at her side to keep from lashing out. "Captain Apep, Nef, Mirik, everyone from the *Montu*. Their death is on you, Hegira!" she cried.

"That was not my intention. Captain Set sealed their fate when he rammed the fourth crystal." She remained unphased. "Sometimes things don't go according to plan." She walked toward the console. "I'll finish this myself. It's nothing a few nanomechs can't deconstruct."

Councilor Horus raised his hand. "Now, Hegira—"

"Now, Horus," she replied in a controlled voice, eyes narrowed.

Councilor Horus slumped against the console, gaze toward the floor.

Kaia raised her hand and pointed into Councilor Hegira's face. "You killed them all. You killed Captain Apep's father. And you killed my parents. Now you want to murder an entire species! How many others did you kill for this project?"

Councilor Hegira raised her hands, palms down, to ease the tension. "Kaia, I didn't plan your parents' death. It was just an opportunity."

"An opportunity?!" Kaia yelled.

The crew gasped.

"Yes, my dear. One that we capitalized on for the good of the Dawn Project. Support was waning and Captain Set's Resistance was swaying public opinion in ways we'd not thought possible. But everyone adored Ory and Rhea Badra. I realized it could change the tide of public support if a climate tragedy took them. And Captain Apep's father, well, that was an accident, and had he been following instructions, it would have never happened. Though it turned out to be a benefit. People saw how serious we were about the evacuations."

She waved at the lush green planet below. "Think about it, Kaia, we could not have achieved all of this without those tragedies."

Enki went and stood by Kaia, putting his arm around her. He glared at Councilor Hegira. "You mean you could not have done it without Kaia, the Dawn Project's poster child. You knew people would not help you after what you did to Apep's father, but they would help an orphan."

Councilor Hegira raised her voice. "The project needed to succeed! A few lives is an acceptable price to pay."

Kaia crumpled in Enki's arms, sobbing.

He pointed at Councilor Hegira. "There were other options!" His finger aimed at Councilor Horus. "And you! You ignored them because lining your pockets was easier than funding the science."

Councilor Horus kept his head down and looked away.

Councilor Hegira ran her hands over her robe. "Such naivety. Our society would never change. Captain Set's Resistance saw to that. No one was going to make the lifestyle changes necessary to prevent these drastic measures. Nu was doomed."

The rest of the crew waited in rapt silence as they watched the exchange.

Kaia stood up straight and wiped her nose. She bowed to Enki and whispered, "Thank you." She pulled her shoulders back and stomped toward the council platform. Fists balled. Eyes narrowed.

Councilor Hegira stumbled backward at Kaia's advance, tripping over the edge of the raised platform. She fell, catching herself with her elbows, and looked up.

Kaia saw the fear in Hegira's eyes. She leaned over her. Their expressions locked on one another. "You will pay for this, Councilor. I will make sure of it."

She turned to the engineering station and saw Pakhet's tall frame standing at attention. "Pakhet, will you please escort the councilor to her quarters?"

"I would love to," Pakhet said, glaring. She grabbed Councilor Hegira's arm and dragged her off the platform and toward the ladder off the bridge.

Kaia returned to the mission console. Her skin tightened as the tears dried on her face.

Councilor Hegira turned right as Pakhet pulled her into the corridor. "Kaia, the world will not survive another intelligent species! You must terminate them! Remember what your father said, Kaia! You can save the world from us, and now, from them!"

Kaia's eyes burned with a vengeance. "You will never use those words to control me again. Get her out of here, Pakhet."

Pakhet yanked Hegira so hard her headpiece hit the doorway and fell to the floor. Kaia walked over to the headpiece. The blue light still circled its edge. Her foot came down hard.

Smashing it.

The light blinked out.

She held it up with both hands and ripped it in two.

Dr. Khnum and Professor Thoth cheered. She tossed the pieces behind her and returned to the helm, determined.

On the viewscreen, the Jacana-like creatures were packing up their meager market as dusk settled over the village.

"Dr. Khnum, Professor Thoth, what do you recommend?" she asked.

Dr. Khnum answered first. "We need to study them before doing anything."

"I concur," Professor Thoth said with a small bow.

Kaia stood up straight. She looked to Councilor Horus. "You went along with Hegira's plan when you knew it was wrong."

"I did what I thought was necessary."

"Necessary to save Nu? Or necessary for yourself?"

He shirked away from her words without responding.

Kaia clenched her jaw.

Everyone waited with bated breath to see what she would say next, except Enki.

He joined her again at the helm and whispered, "Horus can still help us... the nanomechs can..."

She chewed her lip for a moment and closed her eyes. Her shoulders relaxed, and she turned to Horus.

"Councilor, please assist Dr. Khnum and Professor Thoth in the investigation."

He nodded and looked away. "Very well."

Kaia said nothing more. She took another look at the viewscreen. The beautiful blue planet, her planet, her home. She could not let another ecological disaster happen.

Everyone stood up straight, waiting for her to speak.

*They trust you,* she remembered Enki saying.

She looked back at the viewscreen. "We need to learn as much as we can about the creatures below. Their intelligence means we can teach them. We can reveal a better way."

*The Dawn Project is not over.*

# REVELATION

ACT THREE

# REVELATION

## HIDDEN TRUTHS OF OUR ANCIENT PAST

# A.W. DAVIDSON

# CHAPTER 1
# STARVATION

## SAQQARA - YEAR 12 OF DJOSER

King Djoser sat restlessly in his sedan chair as four sweat-soaked men carried it to the front of the stone plaza. His starving people's somber faces stared back at him. He looked up to avoid their gaze. *Gods, if you're there, please help us,* he prayed. But the desert sun shone bright in the clear blue sky. No goddess was watching, no god was intervening, and he knew it.

The four men sat the sedan chair down and the crowd rushed forward. Djoser stepped down to greet them. His caramel brown torso glistened with an oily sheen, like the broad gold necklace draped around his neck. He adjusted his white tunic higher around his waist and made his way to the royal dais. Advisors surrounded him as he wove a path through his people. A group of mothers pushed their children in front of him and pleaded.

He knelt down to a young girl and took her hand, placing it over her distended, starving belly, and bowed. His heart felt heavy, knowing the food would not last long, and full of hope that his influence over the real gods, if they existed, would be enough to save these children. He stood and bowed to their parents, then continued ahead, ascending the short stairs to the top of the royal platform.

Djoser turned to face his worshippers gathered between the stone columns. He squinted, accentuating his already sharp facial features, and listened for his advisors' sandals to stop scuffing against the stone floor as they took their seats behind him. He raised his arms, and everyone in the plaza dropped to their knees and bowed to him. They believed that their god, that *he*, Djoser, possessed the power to save their families and improve the lives of this gathered mass of dirty, poor, and starving humanity. He felt guilty, knowing the truth.

*I have no magic.*

Djoser heard his advisors quarreling under their breath behind him. They debated for hours, every day. Seven years had passed without the annual flooding that brought water and nutrients to the farmland along the riverbanks. The kingdom was in a dire situation. For all his power as ruler, Djoser, the divine of body, the bringer of stability, was powerless to help his people. The climate was beyond his control, despite what his subjects believed.

Each advisor had a different theory for why the gods had forsaken his kingdom. Maybe they were being punished for bad deeds. Maybe there was a new god that Djoser had not recognized. Or perhaps they did not sacrifice enough goats during the last harvest moon. He was tired of listening to them.

He lowered his arms and motioned for his chief advisor to join him.

"Imhotep," Djoser said. "You know you are the only one I trust, and you know the gods cannot help us."

Imhotep clasped his hands and tilted his head down. "I am in favor of numbers and knowledge. I'm afraid we do not have enough of either to help us understand why the floods will not come."

Djoser's chest swelled as he took a deep breath and looked past the crowd toward the river and the desert lands beyond the edge of Saqqara. Three puffs of black smoke dotted the horizon.

Imhotep explained, "There are rumors of rebellion in the outer villages. I expect it will arrive in the city before long. We need to act soon to maintain the peace."

He nodded and Imhotep bowed, returning to his seat at the back of the dais. King Djoser spread his arms wide and spoke.

"People of Saqqara, I hear your prayers. Your time of suffering is near its end. The river will soon flood once more, and you will experience a bounty unlike any you've ever seen. I am merciful and will release grain from the palace stores and distribute it to each family. Your stomachs will be full until the next harvest."

Cheers erupted from the crowd, but he heard his advisors whispering amongst themselves.

"These difficult times serve to make us a stronger people." Djoser raised his hands toward the sky. "Ready your tools and beasts for the planting season. The flood will come soon! Now, go!"

The crowd pumped their fists in the air and shouted his name as they left the plaza. Everyone spread the news as they paraded through the city's narrow streets.

Imhotep stamped forward. "Depleting the grain stores is," he hesitated to say it, "inadvisable."

Djoser watched the last few people leave the plaza. "The people are starving," he said as he turned to his court. "I have no choice."

The high priest began to say something, but Imhotep stepped between the two men.

"I think," Imhotep began, "that he wishes to say the temple stores do not have enough grain to feed everyone for long. We will all starve."

He took another step toward Djoser. "It could be the end of us all. The end of everything we have built. Our city will fall into anarchy."

"Look around!" Djoser said with a sneer. "We are already losing control. Our society is approaching a breaking point. Releasing the temple stores will buy us time to understand the origin of the flood." He looked straight at Imhotep. "I am sending you south to learn what we can do to bring it back."

Imhotep bowed. "You have more faith in me than I have in myself. I hope you have not misplaced it."

Djoser smiled. "You are a good observer. You will save us. I have already prepared a caravan for the journey. Go, Imhotep, join them at the southern gate. Leave at dusk when the desert heat subsides."

"Of course," Imhotep replied. "Thank you for your trust in me." He exchanged a nervous glance with the high priest, then descended the royal platform.

As Imhotep passed through the city market, he heard the usual shouts of bartering over cloth and the bleating of livestock. He also noticed many of the merchants did not bother to set up covers over their stalls like normal. Instead, they spread a meager selection of grains out on reed mats under the evening sun. Djoser's decision to release more from the storehouses would give the impression of plenty, a *false* impression, he knew.

Imhotep met the caravan's soldiers at the stables near the gate. He avoided glances from the starving, sunken-faced slaves as they loaded grain baskets onto the camels. It was more food than they had seen in years. He rested his hands on his stomach and felt guilty for his well-fed appearance, but knew that people needed to believe Djoser's powers took care of his royal court advisors.

The lead soldier adjusted the reins on his camel. "We're going south, yes?"

Imhotep nodded.

The man asked, "How will we know when to stop?"

"When we find the source of the great river."

The soldier rubbed his chin. "It will be a long journey."

"That is why we must leave now," Imhotep said, tightening his robe. "And it is cooler to travel at night!" he yelled and waved the men to follow him.

The wooden gates creaked open as the caravan headed south out of Saqqara. The din of voices and animals faded as they moved into the quiet stillness of the desert.

He noticed the first stars on the darkening horizon. They had a different quality out here, he thought. Beyond the city walls, they were precise pinpoints of light, not the fuzzy, faint dots obscured by the smoky haze that hung in the air around the palace. It felt good to be in the desert again. There was a chill in the air as the last of the sunlight faded. Imhotep pulled a blanket over his shoulders and settled into the soft rhythm of the soldiers' footsteps on the desert sand. He did not miss the bustle of the city. Out here, his mind was free to wander, and tonight it wandered toward the gods.

Imhotep remembered when his father spent an entire week's worth of grain to purchase a lamb, only to sacrifice it to the gods in hopes they would return it tenfold during harvest. It seemed odd to him at the time, and downright futile now that he understood their many gods did not listen. Even King Djoser, a god among the people, was a regular man, no different from himself. Being close to the benevolent king, though, helped him understand the role of spirituality. It brought order to society. Order brought stability, and stability enabled their civilization to grow wealthy and powerful. Still, he could not help but wonder if there was another, deeper truth to the god stories as he looked up at the stars.

The stillness was shattered when a soldier yelled, "Imhotep! Behind you!"

Imhotep turned to see a stone ax spinning through the air straight for his head.

# CHAPTER 2
# PLATONIC SOLIDS

## UNIVERSITY OF CHICAGO - 2035 CE

A loud bang ricocheted around Alan's office. He ran over to the two-foot-wide glass cylinder in the corner by his window. His jaw clenched at the sight of a four-inch red dodecahedron at the center of a round depression in the brown clay at the bottom. The high-speed camera beeped that its memory was full. He bent down and pressed delete on its screen. There was no point in keeping a recording of yet another failure to model a mini double-ringed impact structure.

Alan mumbled under his breath. "I'm running out of asteroid shapes." He spoke a little louder as he opened the hatch and pulled out the dodecahedron. He held it up to the light of the window. "Maybe it was the angle of impact?" He kicked the base of the machine. "Or maybe it's you! I should have used that Order of Extraterrestrialism money to buy a proper air gun firing cylinder instead of saving it for the long haul."

The machine's compressor let out a sad squeal as it released the leftover pressure.

He did his best not to regret the decision to call in a long overdue favor from a colleague in the forensics laboratory at the University of

Illinois. The man lost a bet to him over who would get tenure first. Dr. Alan Pearce won by a mere two months and had saved the favor for decades before he decided this research was worthy of it. Or, that he was that desperate.

"What do you want with that old firing chamber?" his friend had asked when he phoned him.

"Trust me, you don't want to involve yourself in this research," Alan explained, leaning back in his squeaky chair.

"You know, I can help you set up a computer model. It would be a lot easier. That's how we all work these days."

Alan rolled his eyes—a computer was the last thing he trusted with this research. "No, thank you, the firing chamber will do."

"Say, if I may ask, is this about your project for the UN Climate Council?"

Alan did his best to mask the contempt. "I am no longer working with the council."

"Okay, well, we haven't used it in years, but you're welcome to it. It's in the pharmacy building's basement."

"Thank you. Does 2 PM tomorrow work?"

"That sounds good. And Alan, I hope you find what you're looking for with this impact stuff. The Council really needs you back in the fold. The regulations they're discussing... people won't like it."

Alan responded simply with, "I'll see you then and there."

Alan looked again at the air gun module on the top of the firing chamber. His eyes followed the cable snaking down to the air compressor on the floor.

"Let's go again," he told it.

He set the dodecahedron down on a side table littered with several other red models of basic shapes, then walked over to the machine. The clay crater was already leveling back out. His phone rang just as he was reaching in to speed the settling along. He wiped his hands on his pants and picked up the receiver.

"This is Dr. Alan Pearce," he announced.

A man on the other end of the line laughed. "It sure is Dr. Alan Pearce! Whew boy, am I glad I got a hold of you!"

The man's voice was unmistakable. Alan asked, "Jim? I mean, Seagraves?"

"You got it!" the man said. "You can stick with Seagraves."

"How in the world are you doing?"

"Well, get this. I got a new line of work," Seagraves said.

"Oh?"

"Yep, I thought about it some after meeting you and Daxia and decided drillin' oil wasn't for me anymore."

"Well, that sounds nice."

"I didn't want to contribute to our problems." His voice grew more serious. "Thought maybe I could help do something to help them instead."

"Well," Alan said as he sat down in his chair. "That's great, just great. What, if I may ask, did you decide to do?"

"It's kind of a long story."

"I've got a few minutes," Alan said.

"Nah, I'll keep it short." Seagraves cleared his throat. "So, I remembered what you all said about dinosaurs and the asteroids and all that. I thought it sounded cool; study some asteroids, do some drilling. Like in the movies, you know? Maybe I would get to go to space or something."

Alan tried to stifle his laugh. "Yes, that does sound fun, I suppose..."


Concise wasn't how Alan remembered Seagraves, so he grabbed something to fidget with from his shelf. His fingers danced over the rock samples and other baubles from his travels with Louise. They settled on a cold metallic surface—it was the small award that came with his original grant to research the Chicxulub crater in Mexico, before the Climate Council defunded him. The trinket was pure iridium, just like the asteroid they hoped he would find. He picked it up and rubbed it in his hands as Seagraves rambled on—something about being told he didn't have the experience to go into space.

"Just imagine my surprise," Seagraves said. "It turns out they don't need people to drill on asteroids. They have enough of them already working on Gigantia. But I found somethin' way cooler, I think." He paused for dramatic effect.

Alan took his bait. "And what is that?"

"The other part of what you and Daxia said." He paused again. "Dinosaurs!"

He could hear Seagraves's knee slap his own knee.

"Dinosaurs?" Alan asked.

"Yep, dinosaurs! I found out you don't need anything, no degree in paleo-something, to go digging them up."

"Well," Alan began, "it is better to—"

"Oh, oh, I know, don't worry. I am hooked up with a good group of people. Some of them are the same kind of scientist as Daxia."

"Paleontologists," Alan finished it for him. "That's great, Seagraves. Lots of good dig areas in Texas."

"Oh no, Dr. Pearce, I'm not in Texas. I never want to go back there if I can help it. I'm in South Dakota now, digging around with the Black Hills Institute in Hill City."

"Wow! Seagraves, that is great. They're a good bunch of people. Great little museum, too. It's a real shame what happened to them with the T. rex in the 1990s. What was her name now?"

"Sue," Seagraves said. "They still talk about that like it was yesterday! How that ol' girl ended up in Chicago for millions of dollars. They're still out there trying to find another skeleton."

"I hope they do," Alan said.

"I'm sure keeping my eyes peeled. Just imagine what it would be like to find one!"

Alan nodded. "The find of a lifetime, that much is true." He looked over to the firing chamber. The clay was level again and he was eager to get back to work. "So, Seagraves, it has been good catching up, but I am in the middle of an experiment."

"Of course, I did have a question for you, though, about Daxia."

"Go ahead," Alan said, unsure where this was heading.

"So, I'm out there one day walking this ranch near Belle Fourche. We've had a bunch of rain out here the past two weeks. So, the river was—"

*Any day now, Seagraves,* Alan thought as he moved the metal Council award to his other hand and kept rubbing it.

"Never mind, the rain doesn't matter," Seagraves said, catching himself in a long story. "A rancher found something interesting where a flood cut away a big ol' slice of the riverbank in his pasture. He called us right away, and they sent me to check it out. There was a big line in the rock right above it, and I recognized the color right away. That layer you were looking for on the *Finality,* the line that separated our time from the dinosaurs' time."

"The Cretaceous-Paleogene boundary layer, the K-Pg."

"Yeah, that was it. Anyway, this thing is something else. And get this, there are weird marks in the rock around it, almost like feathers. Did dinosaurs have feathers?"

Alan sat up. "Feathers? You need to tell Daxia. She's digging in China studying avian evolution as we speak."

"That's why I called you. Can you put me in touch with her?"

"Of course!" Alan said, unable to contain his excitement. "I'll have Louise email you all her information. You might remember that computers and I aren't friends."

Seagraves laughed. "I sure do. I think Daxia would love to come take a look at what we've got. It's a real head scratcher."

"I am certain she will."

"Great! Well, it was good catching up with you, Dr. Pearce."

"You can call me Alan, and yes, it was great to hear from you, too."

"Don't be a stranger!"

"Nor you. Goodbye, Seagraves."

"Bye, Alan!"

.   .   .

Alan hung up the phone and grinned from ear to ear. He knew this is what Daxia needed. She was still trying to settle on a specific topic within avian evolution for her PhD, and as far as he knew, no one had studied a bird fossil from North America.

He stood up and put his award back on the shelf. He gazed at the laser engraved seal of the United Nations, with its two olive branches cradling the world. Below the seal, it read: *Climate Council*. On another facet, the words *"For our Future"* were etched into the shimmering surface. He shook his head then paused. *The shape.* A perfect equilateral octahedron, like two pyramids stuck together at their base, eight sides in all. He'd never noticed it before, but he did now, because he'd thought of nothing but different shapes for the past two months.

"Now, you're one shape I haven't tried yet," he said to the small octahedron. "And maybe I should," he made sarcastic air quotes, "For our Future—and for my own well-being." He smirked at that last part and grabbed the award again.

He walked over to the cylinder and tipped the air gun off the top. The silver octahedron slid easily into the barrel. He lowered the air gun back into place and leaned down to the floor to flick the power on to the air compressor. It chugged to life, reverberating around his office so hard that dust kicked up from the bookshelves. Alan picked up his mug and took a sip of coffee while he waited for the compressor to finish. *That is such an awful noise,* he decided. The compressor whined as it neared four thousand pounds per square inch of pressure then shut off. He set the mug down over a timeworn, ring-shaped stain on his desk.

He walked back to the cylinder to press record on the high-speed camera mounted outside and took the air gun control in his hand.

"Here we go again." He closed his eyes and jammed the fire button down.

A loud bang made his ears ring. He opened his eyes to see the cylinder had cracked, and silvery dust poured out of it.

"Nooo!" he yelled and fanned the grimy cloud away.

He opened the side panel door and blew inside. The dust cloud dissipated. He looked at the clay bottom and almost fainted.

Two concentric rings that had escaped him over for a year stared back. The same two rings that consumed every waking moment, and even his dreams, now lay in front of him.

"They're perfect," he said, unable to believe his eyes alone.

He reached inside the chamber and ran his finger over them. Dust coated his fingertips. Then, he remembered where it came from.

*The award. An eight-sided crystal.*

"The asteroids were octahedrons!" He stood and looked around his office at the fine layer of silver dust coating everything. "My very own K-Pg layer!" He brought his fingers together and smooched them, releasing the kiss into the air.

The camera beeped. *Memory full.*

He leaned down to it and was careful to press replay instead of delete. The playback started. The silver octahedron moved into the frame. Its bottom tip pierced the clay, creating a wave that emanated outward as more of the crystal sank into it. The widest part struck with a ferocious force that rippled out and back just as the top tip disintegrated on full impact, leaving behind two perfect concentric circles. *No,* he thought. *Two ripples, frozen in time.*

Alan felt lightheaded. He had the answer to his question. His mind raced, grasping for what it could mean.

# CHAPTER 3
# ABDUCTION

## MERIDIAN - AD CYCLE 66,192,364

Kaia gathered the remaining crew around the Council table on the bridge. It was time they decide the fate of the creatures below. She stared down the table, past Enki and Captain Ra on her right, and Professor Thoth, Dr. Khnum and Pakhet on her left, and right at Councilor Horus. He wavered on whether to take Councilor Hegira's now-empty seat. He saw Kaia watching him, straightened up, pulled the chair out, and sat. He was in his finest attire, which meant he was going to try and persuade them of something, she knew.

She rested her hands on the table and leaned over it. "Thank you, everyone. Dr. Khnum, Professor Thoth, and Councilor Horus have some information to share about the creatures below, and I wanted us all to hear what they have to say. Remember, it is clear from their level of sophistication that these creatures have existed for thousands of cycles already. We need to use this conversation to plan what to do about them. We should not make hasty decisions."

With that, she sat at the end of the table and gestured for Dr. Khnum to begin. He was starting to stand when Councilor Horus's chair scraped across the floor.

"Excuse me," the councilor said. "I think my general observations should come first." He searched for the right starting phrase, "They set the stage, so to speak." He bowed toward Dr. Khnum. "If you don't mind, good doctor."

Kaia looked to Dr. Khnum, who shrugged and settled back into his chair.

"Go ahead, Councilor," she said.

Councilor Horus tilted his chin upward.

He waved his hands wide and began. "The *Meridian* is a science vessel before all else. Its purpose, and our purpose, is to study Nu and save it from further destruction. We have made considerable progress toward this goal. Now, I argue that our mission is not over."

Pakhet jeered, "We don't need the setup, Councilor."

Kaia caught a fleeting flash of anger cross his face, but he continued.

"Now, the climate is stable. And yes, life is flourishing below. However, the presence of this new species is cause for alarm. They are intelligent enough to build a civilization."

He pressed a button on his wrist, and an image of the market appeared on the holoprojector at the center of the table. The image zoomed out to show the whole city. It was a dense network of narrow streets and two-story structures. He zoomed out farther. Barren fields lined the banks of a great river flowing through the heart of the city.

Councilor Horus pointed to the brown vegetation. "As you can see, there is nothing to harvest. Enki's climate model shows this should be the flood season. Those fields should be green with crops. The people, and yes, they are a 'people' are starving. Their bodies are malnourished and unable to fight disease."

He zoomed in on a group gathered around a small figure lying on the ground. "Their young are dying."

Kaia watched as the group knelt. She heard a sniffle and saw Pakhet look away from the projection.

Councilor Horus tapped his forearm glyphpad and bowed. "Thank you. Now, Dr. Khnum?"

"Please," Kaia said, and gestured for him to stand. His formal suit's chest featured a red mortar and pestle, communicating his status as a physician.

"I have taken an oath to save people's lives, just as we all have taken an oath to protect Nu's ecosystem. We've done that, Nu is alive. However, I am afraid my job may have just begun," he said, pressing the glyphpad on his wrist.

The projection zoomed to an open space in the city with a hole in the ground at its center. Several creatures gathered around it.

"I would like to share a few things I have learned after spending the day observing this particular spot from above. I believe it is a waterhole of some sort. First, they are bipedal like us but with a shorter stature. Based on the number and ages of individuals per dwelling, they appear to live in familial units with children remaining with their parents until adulthood. Unlike us, they birth their young without the need for an incubator. Their skin has no natural covering for temperature regulation as ours does," Dr. Khnum explained.

The image zoomed in to show two of the creatures standing next to one another. Their hands waved as if they were talking to one another. A third was heaving a wet clay vessel from the hole in the ground. They all wore white cloths around their midsections. Some had another cloth wrapped around their heads.

Dr. Khnum pointed to the image. "You can see that they do not require the constant protection of a habsew to exist in their natural environment. No doubt a testament to Kaia and Enki's climate engineering. This region, and most others, appear stable and hospitable."

He bowed to Kaia and then to Enki.

Kaia suspected he and Councilor Horus were about to make a proposition. Neither of them was ever so warm. She returned his bow with a grateful nod but recognized disingenuous pandering when she saw it.

Dr. Khnum zoomed the image back out and continued, "Their medical knowledge is very primitive. I have witnessed numerous deaths from apparent diseases of the digestive tract and skin afflictions.

We eradicated similar ailments thousands of cycles ago for our people. These problems are worsened by malnutrition."

The image panned to a parcel of land just outside the city's border. A geometric grid of disturbances covered the ground.

"This is where they put their dead. Our scanners detected traces of rare minerals, like yellow nebu, buried with some of the bodies. This, along with the various sizes and qualities of their dwellings, leads me to believe they have a stratified society with upper and lower classes. Sadly, many of these graves are fresh," he looked to Kaia, then to Pakhet, "and contain children."

Kaia looked away.

He sighed a heavy sigh and said, "These are a dying people, not dissimilar from the early Jacana who struggled with famine."

The councilor stood. "Thank you, Dr. Khnum. You can have a seat now."

Kaia caught Dr. Khnum glancing at her as he sat.

Horus tapped the table. "We also learned a few things about their food supply. He zoomed the image back out to show the whole city and the great river next to it.

"This is an agrarian society. The early Jacana experienced a similar transitional time before complete urbanization. We settled down and began to consolidate into villages when we discovered that plants sprouted from seeds. We harnessed that ability and created agriculture to feed our growing population. We can tell they've cultivated food along the riverbank for thousands of cycles by looking at abandoned farmlands farther south. This means they have settled and are not a nomadic people. However, I did find traces of nomads in other regions on Nu."

He moved the image to a field of muscular, four-legged creatures. "They keep great herds of a large, docile animal to pull plows over the fields."

The scientific description of a domesticated farm animal elicited a chuckle from Captain Ra. Kaia tapped her foot, trying not to show her impatience at Horus's slow build to his recommendation.

Horus cleared his throat. "I have not witnessed overt aggressive tendencies toward other members of their species, but these brief observations limit our ability to understand them. I suspect they war over resources with one another, just as we did at this stage in our development. We have found abandoned settlements spread across the land, some burned and in shambles. We can only guess that it may be due to brutal fighting."

The image zoomed out away from the creatures in a field until all of Nu was visible. He became more animated when he said, "Larger scale observations reveal that they appear to fill the same niche in the ecosystem as we once did. This is the most exciting discovery we have made." The image of Nu turned dark.

He swiped over his forearm, and the image showed bright sensor readings dispersed over the surface of Nu. The picture unfolded into a flat visualization.

"They have spread to five of the seven continents. They are developing in the same way that we did. As we know all too well, this trajectory will lead to a problem in the future. For now, they do not seem to have extensive knowledge of kohl. However, all the evidence suggests that they will, and—"

Pakhet interrupted. "They haven't found it yet, because we used it all! We should be glad it is gone."

Kaia watched Enki's reaction as he absorbed what Pakhet said. She could tell he knew where Horus was going based on the particular way Enki's eyes seemed to look past the person speaking. He turned to face Pakhet.

"That's not true, Pakhet," Enki said.

"Yes, thank you, Enki, please explain," Councilor Horus encouraged him.

Enki rested his arms on the table and leaned forward. "There is more kohl now than there was before."

Pakhet shook her head. "That's impossible. We used so much of it already."

Enki raised his eyebrows. "Kohl is nothing but dead plant and animal matter compressed into stone or fermented into liquid over time. In some conditions, it takes a mere few hundred thousand cycles."

Pakhet leaned back. Kaia could see she wasn't quite getting it by the way she was squinting.

Councilor Horus raised a finger. "Enki, please continue. Explain why that information is important."

Enki looked incredulous. This was basic science, for him.

"Our plan to reset the climate on Nu also killed over ninety percent of the life there. Now, all that dead organic matter has had sixty-six million cycles to transform."

Pakhet's face turned white. "And..." she trailed off.

Enki nodded. "There is more kohl now than our greediest Jacana industrialists could have dreamed of," he looked around at the rest of the crew.

Councilor Horus clasped his hands in front of his body. "Thank you, Enki. So, as you can see, the need to intervene is greater than ever. Our ultimate mission could still fail."

He made firm eye contact with Kaia. "Nu is still in great peril."

She saw his proposal as plain as day, now. "And what do you suggest we do, Councilor?"

"I recommend Dr. Khnum, Professor Thoth, and I visit the surface at once. We can teach this fledgling civilization. Our knowledge can guide their development in a sustainable direction."

Dr. Khnum leaned forward. "Now wait, Councilor. That is not what I recommended. I said we *may* need to intervene, not that we should do so now."

Professor Thoth turned to him. "But it sounds to me like you can save their lives."

The chatter around the table grew. He met Kaia's stern expression. "With your blessing, of course."

She narrowed her eyes. "No, not yet."

Councilor Horus scoffed. "Time may be of the essence!"

"Not yet," she repeated. "You would be gods among them," she stated matter-of-factly.

Councilor Horus conceded the point with a tilt of his head. "It is possible. But they will listen to what we say. Gods or not, it is important that they listen to us. We can prevent a future disaster on Nu."

Kaia sighed. "Dr. Khnum, you sounded more cautious. What do you recommend before we attempt such a thing?"

"Well," he said then looked to Councilor Horus, who nodded for him to continue, "we need a more in-depth analysis of their physiology. We need to ensure we will not make them sick, or they us."

Councilor Horus smacked the table. "Preposterous. Jacana medical technology is superior in every way. We can cure anything that ails them, or us."

Dr. Khnum shook his head. "I cannot confirm that without more study."

Councilor Horus tried pleading, "Kaia, they will aspire to be like us. We can teach them to live in perpetual balance with nature. To not be a cancer upon Nu as we once were, as our ten commandments make clear."

She sat up straight. "Or," she offered, "they will aspire to be just like us. Their ambition to be like the 'gods' will lead to a resource-intensive society. They will need energy to keep growing. That thirst for energy will lead them to discover kohl, maybe even faster than our ancestors did. They will learn of its power, of its energy, by witnessing our technological superiority. Even though we no longer use kohl, we could not achieve what we have without it."

Councilor Horus seemed taken aback by her dissent.

She looked straight at him, her shoulders stiff and authoritative. "This is still my mission. I will consider your plan, but it is not your decision. Dr. Khnum and I will continue the analysis." She looked around at the rest of the crew.

"We must all decide if we are to become gods."


Councilor Horus stormed down the hall of the habitat ring toward Councilor Hegira's quarters. He knocked once, and the door slid open half a cubit.

"What is it?" Councilor Hegira asked.

He huffed, out of breath. "Kaia is delaying!"

She sighed and slid the door the rest of the way open. "Come in and have a seat, Horus," she said and waved toward the sofa on the opposite wall.

He stepped past her and sat down. "Look here," he said, pointing to the image projected above a small table in front of the sofa.

"Wait a moment, I need to put my babels in. I can't understand a word you're saying," she said and headed toward her desk.

He admired its luxurious woodgrain. It was just like the Council table on the bridge. A small metal box lay on top, and she opened it and pulled out two babels then stuck them in her ears. He'd never noticed it before, but without her usual circular hat, her gray plume was thin and stringy down the sides of her head.

She ambled over to the chair across from the couch and settled into it. "Now, what were you saying?"

He decided he didn't need to show her and shut off the projection. He leaned back and threw his arms in the air. "Kaia is delaying visiting the creatures and there is nothing I can do about!"

Hegira tapped the chair's armrest. He didn't understand why she wasn't more upset. Her chest rose as she inhaled and looked him straight in the eye. "You did it, didn't you?"

"Did what?"

"Them."

"I don't—"

She glanced up at the ceiling, then back at him. "Don't be dense. I'm talking about the creatures. You created the creatures with your nanomechs. I'm not sure how, or when, but the odds of a species like us evolving a second time were… Well, the odds are vanishingly low."

He decided no answer was the best answer and looked down, sulking.

Councilor Hegira shook her head in disappointment, then leaned forward and pointed her finger in his face. "This is all your doing. You need to take care of it."

"But Kaia wants—"

"Forget Kaia!" Hegira shouted. "She knows nothing. She is just a child. A child who would be nothing but another climate orphan if it weren't for me."

Councilor Horus felt a tightness in his chest as he thought of what they had done in the name of the Dawn Project. "Hegira, that isn't true. You know, I've had some time to think, and, well, it wasn't right, what we did."

She belly laughed. "Now? You want to talk about this *now?*"

He held up his hands to calm the tense situation. "I'm just saying she has…"

"What, Horus?"

He met Hegira's eyes. "I think she has risen to the occasion. We can't write off her contributions to this project."

"Her contributions to this project? Are you suggesting she's the one who came up with that impact plan? She wasn't even born when the earlier Council rejected it!"

"But she convinced the crew…"

Hegira smacked her chair's armrest. "Kaia had nothing to do with it."

"All I'm saying is we wouldn't be here without her, and you know it," Horus said, trying to keep the peace.

"And where is that, Horus?" She waved her arms around the room. "This doesn't look like a scenic view of Duat, or even a suite on the *Montu*. No, this," she pointed at him again, "this is your doing. Captain Set couldn't have ruined our plans if you hadn't convinced me to negotiate with that terrorist!"

He sank back in the chair.

She crossed her legs. "You need to go clean up this mess."

"Yes, Head Councilor," he said, eyes on the floor.

"Go to my desk, second drawer on the right."

He stood and walked over to it. The drawer slid open to reveal a tiny gold cube. The weapon of choice in the third great war.

"No," he said. "I can't do that to them. Blasting the surface with radiation would also harm Nu again. It would put our entire mission at risk. Those creatures have done nothing wrong, Hegira."

She glared at him. "You know they will. You created them in our image, Horus. They will do as we have done."

He looked down at the cube and picked it up. "Kaia isn't going to—"

"Are your babels broken, Horus? I said, forget Kaia."

He slid the gold cube into the pocket of his robe and walked back to the couch.

Councilor Hegira softened her tone. "I know it will be difficult, but you must."

"I know," he said. "I will." He rose from the sofa and walked toward the door. Turning back at the last moment, he said, "It's still wrong, you know. What we did to Kaia's parents. To Kaia, herself."

He stepped into the hallway, and the door slammed shut behind him.

"What was that?!" someone yelled from down the hall.

Horus turned to see Professor Thoth. He shrugged. "Her door must be malfunctioning. You know how shoddy the construction on this ship is."

Thoth stepped out of his quarters and into the hall. "You can say that again. What were you two talking about?"

Councilor Horus thought about it for a moment. "I was just making sure she was comfortable." He saw the skepticism in Professor Thoth's eyes.

"Pakhet has been stopping by with food," the professor said.

Horus nodded. "Yes, the councilor is fine." He saw a flash of orange light come from inside Thoth's quarters. "What was that?"

"The video feed," said Professor Thoth. "I'm keeping an eye on a few of the creatures that left the city. It looks like they're carrying a lot of food with them, for some reason."

"Show me," Councilor Horus instructed and followed Thoth back into his quarters.

An aerial view of Nu hung in the air above the desk. The creatures walked in a line, heading south, away from the firelight of the city.

Professor Thoth sat down in his swiveling chair. "Check this out."

He spread his fingers over the desk glyphpad and zoomed in. "There are more creatures now!"

Councilor Horus leaned in for a closer look. "Amazing."

"Hold on," Thoth said, sounding concerned. He zoomed back out. At least a dozen shadowy figures carrying torches made a beeline straight for the caravan.

Councilor Horus felt his heart break. One of the creatures threw something toward the first creature in the caravan. The rest extinguished their torches in the sand and began to beat the others with them.

Professor Thoth shot to his feet. "It's an attack!"

Horus's thoughts went to the gold cube in his pocket, and he repeated Hegira's words. "They are like us," he said. "They'll fight with one another until they run out of resources and ruin Nu."

Thoth shook his head. "I don't believe that for a second. We need to try what you said, Councilor."

Horus turned to look at him. "What I said?"

Thoth nodded and ran to a shelf beside the door. He pulled off a well-worn book and held it up. "We can teach them everything they'll need to know. I mean, these words are a couple of hundred cycles old at this point," he said, flipping through the pages. "But it's plenty to get them started."

Horus let himself feel the growing excitement. Councilor Hegira told him to go down and take care of it. She did not say that his only choice was to use the cube, did she?

"And!" Professor Thoth grabbed a plaque off the shelf. "We can leave them the ten commandments, just like you suggested."

There it was, that feeling. The rush coursed through Councilor Horus, just like in the early days of planning the Dawn Project. He remembered the thrill of changing the world.

He stood up tall, resolute, and said, "Let's get to a shuttle, now. I know what we need to do."

.   .   .

Imhotep turned his head back and ducked as the stone ax sailed past his face. He cinched his belt and ran. The men behind him yelled, and he heard the clang of their blades striking stone weapons. He dared not turn back and headed away, off the road, toward the distant glow of Saqqara.

A scrubby shrub caught his foot, sending him hard onto the sand. Imhotep coughed and opened his eyes, wiping his face as he rose onto his knees.

"We are fools," he whispered, reaching for his canteen and collecting his breath. He swished the water around in his mouth to get rid of the gritty feeling between his teeth.

"Yer muss be Imhotep," a deep voice said from behind him.

Imhotep froze. A dark blur delivered a hard knock to his head. The sand squeaked underfoot as a shadowy figure stepped around him. He smelled sour beer on the man's breath.

"Yessss," the man said, "it is youuu."

Imhotep tried to speak but struggled to breathe as the man grabbed him by his necklace and dragged him back toward the caravan. He kicked at the man's legs and yelled for help.

The man laughed. "No one to helpsss you out heeere." He dropped Imhotep and kicked sand in his face.

Imhotep rubbed it away and looked up to see more angry men attacking the caravan. There was a sickening crack and the man laughed again. His mind fogged—he realized something had hit him on the head. He slumped forward as the bandits continued their assault. The snap of bones breaking filled the air, followed by the gurgling of men choking on their own blood. His demigod status in their superstitious minds is all that protected him from certain death, Imhotep knew. The attackers threw the caravan's equipment into the sand.

They were only after the food, he realized. They gathered all they could carry and ran off.

Imhotep tried to get up but could not move his arms or legs. He rolled himself onto his back. He looked up at the night sky, preparing to take his last breath.

*The stars shine even brighter in silence.*

His thoughts drifted to the stories of the gods, who so many believed determined the fate of his civilization. He closed his eyes and whispered to the stars.

"If you are real, I beg for your help." He licked his dry lips and closed his eyes. "Many lives are in jeopardy. We will be set back for generations if society descends into chaos. We all want peace and prosperity, but we do not yet know enough to create it. If you are listening, please, help us."

He opened his eyes one last time and saw a new star appear in the night sky. The pinprick of light grew larger. A blazing tail formed and expanded before his eyes.

His consciousness slipped away as the hands of God cradled him, carrying him into a beam of light.

# CHAPTER 4
## FALCON

### SAQQARA - YEAR 12 OF DJOSER

Even with his eyes closed, Imhotep could feel warmth all around him. He felt better than he had in a long time. *What happened?* he asked himself. *A journey.* He was traveling with a caravan to find the source of the great river's floods, but they did not travel far. There was an ambush. Bandits killed everyone. King Djoser's people would starve.

Imhotep opened his eyes and sat up, then started spinning in the air. He saw he was in a glowing white room. The light seemed to be coming from everywhere. There was a small, dark square on the wall. He pushed with his feet and floated toward it. It was a sensation unlike any he had ever felt. He looked down at his tunic. It was moving in a strange way over his body. He suddenly recognized the undulations and his eyes told him he must be underwater. Afraid he was drowning, his body gasped for air but had no trouble filling his lungs.

A soothing voice distracted him from the panic. It spoke his language but had an unfamiliar accent. The voice assured him he was safe, and everything was going to be okay. He looked to the dark square again as his breathing slowed. It had been featureless moments ago, but now it contained a carving of a strange face. The person had on a broad, striped cloth descending from just above the eyes and wrapping around the top of the head before draping down the sides. Then, the carving moved and started to speak.

"Be calm, you are not in danger," the man assured him.

Imhotep stopped flailing and focused on the man in the square. "Please, help me."

"We already have. Others of your kind hurt you, but we healed your body."

Imhotep reached up and touched the back of his head. *It doesn't hurt anymore.*

The man in the square asked, "Do you know where you are?"

Imhotep remembered the desert, the ambush, and lying on the ground, unable to move. His voice shook. "I remember a star growing larger and wrapping around me. Am I inside it?"

"Yes, in a manner of speaking," the man said. "You are inside a ship that travels in the sky with the stars."

"If I am on a ship, why am I also in the water? How can I breathe in the water?" Imhotep pointed down to his free-flowing tunic. He heard the man saying words he could not understand.

"How do you explain gravity to a species that thinks the sky is made of water?" the man seemed to ask someone Imhotep could not see. "Imhotep, that is your name, right?"

He nodded.

"You are not underwater. Ships in the sky do not move through the water."

Imhotep was looking at the square with the small man moving inside. He saw another figure behind the man, gesturing to him. The other man was floating, too.

"Who are you?" Imhotep asked.

"I am Horus, and this is Thoth," said the man in front. "Do not worry. We will tell you everything soon. Let us help you home first."

The one named Thoth said, "We are almost there. Please remain calm and do not fight the heaviness."

Just as Imhotep was about to ask what they meant; he felt a light pressure on his back that spread to the rest of his body. He moved toward one side of the room and bumped his head against the wall. His body seemed as though it was growing heavy as stone. The sensation intensified and tugged him down to the wall feet-first until he touched the floor. He looked toward the two men in the square and noticed they were no longer floating either.

The men disappeared, replaced by a brown image with a dark, wavy line running through it. The dark line was getting thicker. Imhotep felt heavier and more steady on his feet now. The image in the square transfixed him. He started noticing other details in the picture. Dark spots dotted the brown areas. A thin green band surrounded the line. The line grew even larger, and he remembered that this ship was in the sky. He gasped in astonishment when he realized what he was seeing.

He was far, far above the great river. The dots were villages; the largest mark was Saqqara. His city became larger and larger in the square. *We're falling toward it.*

Streets now filled the square, and he could see its citizens running in panic. Everyone rushed toward the temple plaza.

The sky ship stopped its descent and drifted over the city. Imhotep could see the roofs of homes and stacks of pottery lining the private courtyards. Women looked up and shooed their children inside the tiny dwellings.

"This is what the falcon sees," he muttered to himself.

Horus's voice boomed in the room again, "That is truer than you realize."

"Where are we going?" asked Imhotep.

"To the place everyone is running toward," the man responded.

"The temple—that is where they are running. The people are afraid of this sky ship," Imhotep said, more than a little afraid, himself.

"We will not hurt anyone. The temple is close. Will your leader be there? We need you to take us to your leader."

Imhotep was wide-eyed. "He will be there. His name is King Djoser."

"Good, we are almost there," Horus said.

The image in the square stopped moving, and everything in it grew bigger again. The crowd parted to make way for the falling ship.

The ship rocked as the image in the square became nothing but sand. An odd whirring sound filled the white room. He turned around and saw three blue lines materializing on the wall. They lengthened until he realized it was a door; the blue was the sky outside. It was folding down, unlike any door he had ever seen. He raised his arm to shield his eyes from the bright desert sun.

People surrounded the sky ship, yelling prayers over one another. The door opened fully, resting on the sand below the ship. He left the room and stepped down the ramp created by the door. The familiar cool sand was warming in the morning light. The crowd fell silent.

They recognized him, a few bowed down before him. Imhotep's eyes were adjusting to the sunlight when he saw a man walking toward him through the crowd. *Djoser.*

Imhotep lowered himself to his knees and pressed his hands together in front of him.

"King Djoser, please forgive me. I have failed. Bandits attacked the caravan." He looked up but saw Djoser walking right past him, toward the sky ship.

He stood and followed Djoser up to the edge of the ramp. They both froze. Two towering figures descended from the dark interior and into the light. Their clothing shimmered in the sun. Where there should have been a face there was only a dark, shiny rectangle. Djoser stepped out of the way as the figures continued down the ramp. Imhotep stumbled backward, and Djoser helped him up. They stood next to one another, slack-jawed, as the taller of the two figures spoke.

The voice came from a small box on the person's stomach. "My name is Horus." He bowed.

"And I am Thoth," the other man said and bowed even deeper.

Horus took a step closer to Djoser, and the crowd screamed. Men with spears appeared from nowhere and pointed them at the two shiny figures from the sky ship.

"We come in peace."

There was a tense standoff as Djoser considered their appearance. He turned to Imhotep.

"Is this who attacked you?"

Imhotep shook his head. "It was bandits, not them. They came from the sky at night. They saved me. The bandits injured me, but I was healed in their ship," he said, feeling the back of his head one more time. He then bowed forward. "Thank you for returning me."

Djoser turned back to them. "Have you heard our many prayers?" he asked.

The one called Horus turned to the one called Thoth and whispered something. Thoth shrugged and Horus looked back at Djoser. "You are starving, dying. We know you need help."

Imhotep's heart sank when he saw the deep ribbed torsos of his people, shoulders sticking out like bony shelves, thin upper and lower arms separated by elbows like knots on a sapling.

Horus bowed. "Thoth can teach you many things, important things."

Imhotep looked at the sleek black skyship with its two pristine, glimmering occupants. He leaned over to Djoser. "We must accept their help," he whispered, glancing at a young starving child.

Djoser nodded to his left, and a contingent of warriors lowered their spears and approached Thoth. "This one, Thoth, must go with Imhotep." He waved Imhotep forward. "Record the knowledge at once."

Thoth turned and began to go back up the ramp.

"Stop!" Djoser yelled.

A warrior burst forward and held a spear at the throat of Thoth's habsew. Thoth froze. "I," he gulped, "I brought you a gift."

Djoser grunted, and the warrior backed off. Thoth went inside the shuttle and came out with a bundle wrapped in a fine cloth. He handed it to Imhotep.

Imhotep took it in his hands, surprised by its weight. He opened the cloth and saw strange sheets of a thin material with symbols and lines covering it.

"I do not understand," he said.

Thoth said another strange word. "It is papyrus. It holds ancient knowledge. Helpful knowledge."

Djoser grabbed it from Imhotep and leafed through the pages. He handed it back. "Pah-py-rus."

Thoth nodded. "Papyrus." He turned to Horus. "They do not have such a word, so the babel is letting our language straight through."

Djoser raised his hand to silence Thoth. "You must go with Imhotep to the temple." The soldiers raised their spears again.

Imhotep stepped forward and waved Thoth toward him. "This way, follow me."


Horus watched Thoth avoiding the spear points as he followed Imhotep through the crowd toward a sturdy stone structure alongside the plaza. He returned his attention to Djoser.

"We are here to help. Your great river has not flooded yet."

He saw Djoser narrow his eyes and took that as a yes.

Councilor Horus clasped his hands in front of his habsew. He glanced at the sensor readings in the upper right of his helmet visor. Everything indicated clean, breathable air. *Now is the time,* he decided.

The warriors raised their spears higher as he lifted his hands to the sides of his head and pulled the helmet up.

The crowd shouted. Horus looked to Djoser, who was doing his best to stay strong, composed, but even he looked weak at the knees.

The creatures stood in rapt silence.

Two screeches came from high above the scene. Horus looked up and saw a feathered creature soaring over the plaza. A warm smile spread over his face.

"Something of us survived, after all."

# CHAPTER 5
# SPARROWS

## YIXIAN FORMATION, JINZHOU, CHINA- 2035 CE

Daxia spotted cute little birds flying from tree to tree at the edge of the excavation. It was a hot day, even for this part of northern China. The last few months of digging on the Yixian Formation had been at least ten degrees warmer than normal, but the humidity made it feel like twenty. As soon as she landed in Jinzhou, she got a chin-length haircut. Her longer dark hair was perfect for Chicago winters but would have been miserable in this weather. She brushed it behind her ear and heard shuffling footsteps behind her.

Her father clutched his cane with one hand and rested his other on her shoulder to steady himself. "When does the next school group come through?"

She looked down at her phone. "They should be here any minute," she said.

Her father was eighty-two years old, but he still held the position of principal biologist at the Áoxiáng Native Bird Sanctuary. His level of dedication, over fifty years in the same job, was difficult for her to imagine. She reached into a small plastic bag and pulled out a handful of seeds. Several sparrows flocked to the ground in front of them, seeming to know what would happen next.

She laughed as the small brown and white creatures chirped and jumped in anticipation. "These little guys are smarter than they look."

Her father smiled and gestured for her to throw the seeds. She did, and the sparrows chirped even louder than before.

"Chairman Mao hated that sound," he said. "I was just a boy when he initiated the Four Pests Campaign. The government put sparrows in the same category as rats, mosquitoes, and flies. Such a shame; they're delightful little creatures. I was so disappointed to see my comrades killing or abusing them when told to do so."

Daxia watched as small fights broke out over the remaining seeds. "Not only are they delightful, but they're useful."

"Mm, yes," her father agreed. "When Mao told us to drive them out, twenty million of us starved. Sparrows loved to eat locusts. Without the birds, huge swarms of them attacked our fields and ate our food. Maybe we deserved it. What we did was terrible."

"The Great Chinese Famine..." Daxia said and trailed off as the sparrows dispersed, leaving empty seed shells on the ground. She smiled; her father's love of these feathered creatures was an inspiration. It was no surprise to him that Daxia chose to study them and their origins. Birds were a much older type of animal than humans, but evolutionary biologists knew little about their lineage, which reached back to the time of the dinosaurs.

Her father shuffled his feet as he turned toward the hills and shielded his eyes from the sun. She joined him. The skyline of Jinzhou rose in the distance. Broken windows interrupted the smooth surface of many buildings. The population had boomed but was decreasing now due to a water shortage. Many buildings fell into disrepair as their tenants moved out.

He scanned the yellow and gray grassland that blanketed the Yixian Formation's hills. "This view used to be full of green, full of life. I fear another Great Chinese Famine is in our future," he said.

Daxia nodded. "There is still no trace of rain in the forecast. The drought cannot go on much longer without consequences."

"Perhaps we will turn into skeletons like the ones you study."

The Yixian fossil beds were ground zero for paleontologists interested in avian evolution. They yielded more feathered fossils than anywhere else. Daxia often joked that Darwin was studying a tiny twig on the bird tree of life with his finches, while she was planning to one-up him by discovering the entire trunk. There would be no discoveries today, though. It was a day for tours, for attempting to inspire the children to care about paleontology—to win the uphill battle for their attention against the better-than-reality virtual worlds inside their video games, all so they would care about animals that died 125 million years ago.

Daxia's father pointed to a school bus that was rounding a hill in the distance. "There they are. Good luck. I'll be in my tent."

She rolled her eyes. "Leaving your daughter all alone with the kids?"

He smirked and hobbled away.


Chao, the first boy off the bus, marched up to Daxia and began incessantly questioning everything she said. "But how do you know they had feathers?" he asked again.

It was only the first stop on the school group's field trip, and Daxia had already had enough of this boy's questions. His shirt featured Captain Cordova. She had no doubt Chao could beat every game level alongside the virtual captain, defending Earth against the evil bug-eyed aliens from planet Thulen.

*How are fossils supposed to compete with that?* she asked herself. She looked away from the exposed rock face and over the rolling hills dotted with paleontologists excavating the rich fossil beds. It was relaxing to imagine the lush forest that covered this land when the fossils were living animals.

Daxia did her best to channel an elementary school teacher's voice while answering Chao's question. "Well, we know about the feathers because we have found a protein called beta-keratin in the fossils. Today, bird feathers have a lot of beta-keratin, too. That is one big clue that these small dinosaurs may have evolved into the birds we know today," she said, smiling through her teeth.

"That still doesn't look like a dinosaur to me!" he said, pointing to a jumble of fossils in the cliff.

*This boy is relentless,* she thought. "Let's go to the next spot in the dig, and then you can tell me what you think. How about that?"

The boy looked satisfied for now, so she waved her arm for the children to follow her toward a large tent.

As they approached, Daxia held her finger to her mouth to quiet the children. "Now, what you are about to see is 124 million years old and one of only five discovered in the whole world," she told the group.

They all stopped fidgeting. She opened the flap and ushered the children inside the dark tent. A single light was shining on a small sheet lying on the smooth bedrock. They formed a semi-circle around the spot, and Daxia began a story.

"124 million years ago, this area was a dense forest with a small creek running through it. Imagine it is late afternoon. The weather is much cooler than it is today. Thick clouds are hiding the sun. There are bugs everywhere, crawling all over everything. Strange sounds fill the air between the trees. Screeches, howls, and growls like nothing you have ever heard."

Chao tried to create a new growl, but it sounded like an angry fox.

Daxia looked right at him and said, "There are many big creatures out there, some that might think you are a snack."

He stopped, and several of the children in the group shrieked.

Daxia continued, "There is a chirping in the distance. Then several more. It sounds like a group of twenty or thirty small creatures, all coming toward you. You get down on your knees and stay quiet to watch them. They move closer, hopping over fallen trees and calling out to one another. One jumps up on the log at the edge of the creek. He is standing on two legs and chirping into the air that he's found something interesting. His beady eyes are looking at a spot on the ground. His family enters the clearing and starts to dig in the ground in front of the log."

Her phone vibrated, and she reached down to silence it.

"They've found a huge nest of delicious bugs in the ground. There was more than enough to feed everyone in his group—a giant buffet for the whole family. The rest of them run over and start eating all the bugs as they crawl out of the nest. Everyone is so happy squeaking and eating that they don't notice the rain. The creek starts to rise, then overflows its banks and surprises everyone. The water is up to all of their little knees, and the leader squeaks for everyone to run. He leaps off the log in the wrong direction and lands right in the deep part of the flood."

Her phone interrupted the story again. Through the fabric of her shorts, she held the power button down to turn it off.

"The water is too powerful for such a small creature, and he cannot swim. The current is pulling him farther away from his family."

A couple of children whimpered, scared to hear what would happen next. Chao crossed his arms and rolled his eyes at them.

"He squeaks to them to save him, but there is nothing they can do. His legs are wearing out, and his head dips below the surface of the water as he disappears downstream. The rain stops a few hours later. The flood is over. His family looks for him, but he was buried under thick mud. No one will see him again until today, 124 million years later."

Daxia leaned into the circle of light and removed the small cloth. "Here he is, take a look."

All the children leaned in closer. In the middle of the circle was a tiny skeleton, only eight inches long. Its arms were spread wide, as if it had frozen in a stretch. There were familiar looking indentations just below the arms.

"Are those feathers?!" Chao yelled.

"Yes, we believe they are," Daxia replied. It was nice to see him zone in to something real.

"But why did he have feathers?"

"Well, we aren't sure," she replied.

Chao flapped his arms. "Could he fly?!"

She shook her head. "We don't think so. The forest this little dinosaur lived in was cool. The feathers might have helped keep him warm," she said.

"It looks like a baby T. rex. How do you know it isn't a baby T. rex?!" Chao asked, this time louder.

"Well, this little guy died 124 million years ago. T. rex is a much newer dinosaur, about sixty-four million years younger. But want to know something interesting?" she asked.

Chao nodded.

"T. rex and this little dinosaur are relatives," said Daxia. "Over millions and millions of years, this little dinosaur evolved into T. rex. And a lot of other different dinosaurs. We call this kind of dinosaur a theropod. They were some of the smartest ones around."

"Woooow," he murmured, still gawking at the tiny skeleton in the circle of light.

It surprised her Chao and the other kids were amazed by the small creature. They pointed and chatted to one another. The wind outside picked up, and the tent's flapping made it even noisier. Daxia took the moment to check her phone and see why it had been buzzing. Caller ID showed she had a missed call and voicemail from a South Dakota number in the US, thousands of miles away from Jinzhou, China.

She pressed play on the voicemail and held the phone to her ear.

"Hey-o Daxia, at least, I hope I have the right number for Daxia Ling. This is Seagraves, from the *Finality*. Dr. Pearce gave me your information; I hope that's okay. I gave up the oil drillin' business and ended up digging for dinos. Didn't want to make our problems worse anymore, you know?"

She smiled, remembering his enthusiasm and genuine interest when he realized the core sample he helped them get was important to Earth's history.

"Anyway," he continued, "I'm working as a fossil scout for the Black Hills Institute in Hill City, South Dakota, and boy howdy, have I scouted something super cool. A rancher found it after a torrential rain, thought it was weird, and called us. I think you're going to want to see it. Check your email. If you're up for it, I'd be more than happy to show you the real thing, feathers and all. Hope to hear from you soon and see you in South Dakota!"

The message intrigued Daxia. Few paleontologists found feathered dinosaurs outside the Yixian Formation in China. The kids were still chattering among themselves and pretending to be small dinosaurs, with an argument over who would be drowned and buried in the flood. She looked back to her phone and opened her email.

*Hey Daxia,*

*This is Seagraves. I left you a voicemail, too. A rancher named Alex Bullock sent us a photo of a skeleton he stumbled upon this past weekend after a big rain. His ranch is right on the Hell Creek Formation fossil beds near Belle Fourche, north of the Black Hills here in South Dakota. We at the Black Hills Institute (and museum!) are way out of our league on this one. Check out the attached photo. What do you think? Please come see it. The trip is on us at the institute!*

*Your friendly recovering greasemonkey,*

*Seagraves*

She clicked on the attachment. *Most fossils discovered in the Hell Creek formation are only half as old as those in the Yixian,* she thought. It downloaded, but she struggled to understand what she was seeing. A gust of wind made the whole tent shake and bend, but it soon subsided. The children fell quiet for a moment, nervous, but were still more interested in the skeleton than the wind outside. She zoomed in on a dark patch of rock in the photo and gasped.

There were unmistakable striations in the rock near the fossil. The delicate bone structure looked similar to the small skeleton in front of her. It had to be a feathered dinosaur. If she was right, this would be a historic first. Her brain ran wild through a list of the things she needed to do as soon as possible before she could get to South Dakota.

She pocketed her phone and looked down at the long-dead fossil. "There is more to you than meets the eye, isn't there? What else do you have up your sleeve?" she asked. She could have sworn the small fossil was smirking in reply.

A frantic woman burst into the tent. "Children! Come, hurry up! We must go!"

Daxia led them through the canvas door, careful that none stepped on the specimen. "What's wrong?" she asked the woman, a chaperone on the field trip.

The mother pointed toward Jinzhou. Some children screamed; others froze in terror.

Daxia looked up and gulped. Her stomach worked itself into knots.

A dust storm loomed large over the city. The wail of distant sirens filled the air. Red dirt soared into the sky four times higher than the tallest skyscraper. The buildings, the whole city, disappeared into the roiling wall of dust. Such storms were a regular occurrence during the record-breaking drought, but this was the largest she had ever seen.

Her father reappeared next to her. "Daxia, come. We must get to the trailer. The tents will not be safe."

She was paralyzed with fear. A bolt of lightning shot from the storm to an abandoned building. Sheets of glass exploded from its side and fell to the streets below. She watched as the storm engulfed the city.

*This is our future.*

# CHAPTER 6
# THE MISSING FLOOD

## SAQQARA - YEAR 12 OF DJOSER

Councilor Horus walked into the temple and found a few of the creatures gathered around Professor Thoth. He was showing them a book in the early morning light. He scanned the faces of the group. They seemed well-fed compared to most of the ones he saw when they landed.

He told Thoth, "They look eager to learn."

"Yes, these individuals are fast learners, much faster than young Jacana," Professor Thoth said, pointing to the small group of representatives from the palace. "They appear to be a type of leadership. Perhaps something like the royalty of early Jacana civilization. The one we saved, Imhotep, is particularly smart." He nodded to the man wearing a smooth head covering that resembled a habsew helmet without a viewport.

"He seems to be the one in charge of the day-to-day affairs, while Djoser appears to be the leader of this civilization."

Imhotep stepped forward and introduced himself officially. "Greetings. I am Imhotep, Chancellor of Djoser. I act as the

Administrator of the Great Palace. I am also a builder, Chief Sculptor, and Carpenter."

Councilor Horus stepped forward and bowed. "Very pleased to meet you." He turned to Professor Thoth and smiled. "You appear to have things covered here. Djoser invited me on a tour."

Thoth swept his gaze over the eager group and sighed. "It's going to be a long day, isn't it?"

"I imagine so, yes," Councilor Horus said as he ducked out of the room.

Councilor Horus and Djoser strolled alongside the riverbank. The ruler told Horus stories about the annual flood that fed his people, but he explained that it had been lower than normal for the last seven cycles, and sometimes it had not come at all. A full contingent of soldiers followed behind, separating them from the throngs of people trying to get a peek at the visitor from the sky.

Djoser pointed to a dry channel cut perpendicular to the river. "We use these canals to tame the great flood. Water should be flowing through this one, but the river is too shallow to reach it."

Horus stood at the edge of the canal, examining a narrow stairway carved into the soft bedrock. "Where does this carry the water?"

"There," Djoser said, turning to face a nearby field of knee-high yellowing grass with meager heads of seeds crowning the stalks. "The canal separates into smaller ditches to bring water to the emmer wheat."

"How high is the water supposed to be flowing at this time of year?" Horus asked, noticing many different water marks on the canal's stone walls.

Djoser gestured toward the steps. "Come, I will show you."

Councilor Horus followed him, careful not to slip on the narrow steps designed for much smaller feet.

Djoser strode up to the wall and pointed to a dark, linear stain just above his waist. "Here," he said. "It is darker because the great flood also brings dirt from faraway lands."

*And replenishes the soil's nutrients,* Councilor Horus knew. "I understand."

He wandered toward the river and stopped at the end of the canal. The river lay at least a cubit below the bottom of the canal. He glanced back at the water stain and scribbled a few glyphs onto his forearm glyphpad. *Double-check the water volume back at the shuttle,* he reminded himself. Something stirred in the water.

He knelt and saw large ripples moving toward him. The disturbance moved closer and then faded. Whatever made them had moved deeper below the surface. He leaned forward, trying to get a better look, when the surface rose up to meet him.

Djoser grabbed onto Horus's robe and pulled, shouting, "Do not go to the edge!"

Councilor Horus fell back on his haunches and felt Djoser pulling him away just as a splash of white water erupted toward him.

A terrifying growl echoed off the canal system's bare walls. A narrow mouth full of long teeth stared back, hissing.

Horus stood up and backed away to get a better look at the creature from a safe distance. It was very long, longer than he was tall, and covered in tough, lumpy skin. He recognized it right away. It was a sobek.

The same dangerous amphibious animal that he remembered seeing at the Puna City Zoo. He even remembered the plaque next to its enclosure. "Biologists believe the sobek evolved at least 100 million cycles before us. This resilient species has survived more cataclysms than we can comprehend."

He bowed with deference and whispered, "Hello, old friend." Horus couldn't help but chuckle at its continued existence. "Not even we Jacana could end you."

The creature closed its mouth and slid back into the water. He knew it would stay just under the surface, waiting patiently for its next opportunity for a meal.

"Horus, we must go." Djoser crinkled his face then continued, "We must prepare for the feast to celebrate your arrival. It will begin at *sol* down."

*He's using our language,* Councilor Horus noted.

Djoser gestured toward the steps leading out of the canal.

Councilor Horus went up first and saw the crowd had thinned out as they headed back to the temple plaza. The pressure became palpable at that moment. If he failed, these people would starve. They would eat the last of their food reserves in celebration of Jacana contact, only to die soon after.

He reached down to pat the gold cube concealed in his robe that Councilor Hegira ordered him to use. If he failed, he knew what he needed to do to ease their suffering. But, his pocket was empty.

*The cube is gone.*

Panic spread through him. He looked back to the canal bed. *The sobek, the water, it must have fallen out,* he realized. This civilization, the largest and most advanced their sensors showed on all of Nu, would be snuffed out if the water level remained too low to get to their crops.

He thought about what to do next, and his mind settled on a plan.

*I must choose my nanomech design with great care.*

# CHAPTER 7
# BOOK OF THOTH

## SAQQARA - YEAR 12 OF DJOSER

Warm late afternoon light poured into the stone room. Professor Thoth stretched his neck, unsure how many more questions he could take. Of all the advisors gathered around, Imhotep was the keenest to learn. Thoth had to admit that he admired that insatiable thirst for knowledge.

The group of Kemites, as he learned they called themselves, had a crude glyphic system similar to early Jacana cultures. It was little more than stylized scratches on stone tablets and made direct translation difficult. The marks needed to be more robust for abstract concepts like "oneself" or verbs like "feel" if they were to ever read the Jacana textbook on their own. He drew three Jacana glyphs: a wavy line representing 'river', an outstretched hand, then a new one he invented that looked like the round flat bread he'd seen the Kemite's eating.

He pointed to each glyph and spoke out loud, "River, give, bread."

Imhotep interpreted it right away. "Yes, we need the river water to grow crops to eat."

"Very good," Thoth said, smiling. "We call this method of writing rebus. You can write more complex ideas using sounds, because everyone knows them when they see it. You can preserve knowledge, or history, in glyphs rather than relying on spoken stories."

Imhotep drew two more symbols while Thoth watched. First, a flat-bottomed boat, outstretched hands like Thoth's, followed by a starburst, then a man bowing. At the bottom of the column, he drew an eye but added an angled line off the bottom of it. Thoth could not believe his eyes.

It was a shuttle with the landing gear and ramp down.

He raised his eyes to Imhotep.

The Kemite bowed. "This is how I will begin my story." He held the quill to each glyph, starting at the bottom. "The ship brought knowledge carried from the stars and we are thankful."

He wasn't sure how to respond, it was astonishing. "Yes, you understand."

Thoth forced down a nagging feeling of dread and pieced together a rough dictionary by asking Imhotep to tell him what each spoken word represented, listening to the babel, and drawing a corresponding Jacana glyph on the blank papyrus. By the time he had the basics down, Imhotep was already taking notes in Jacana glyphs. Thoth could tell he understood how these more detailed symbols could be used to express complex thoughts, even to record entire histories.

Imhotep turned the book a few pages forward to a map of the night sky. "Stars?" he asked.

Professor Thoth nodded. "Yes, but you will need to create your own. We created this map sixty-six million cycles ago, and the stars have moved since then."

"They move?"

"Everything moves, Imhotep. And many of them are not stars, like the sun. Some are groups of suns, many millions of them."

Imhotep ushered another advisor over. "This is our star gazer. He will update it for us." The man bowed.

"Very good," Professor Thoth said. "Horus and I must return to the stars soon, so examine this map and learn the notations. You will be able to track the seasons better by creating a map like this for yourself."

He mused to himself that creatures who fill similar niches in their environment must develop in similar ways. There was no other explanation for the similarities between these people and his ancestors.

"Now," Thoth said as he turned a few more pages forward. "Knowledge is important, but you cannot do anything with it if you do not keep track of your society."

Imhotep looked up at him, puzzled.

"You must count each person," Thoth continued. "The count will tell you how many baskets of grain you need to grow each cycle. You can predict problems if you track all of this. You can understand how your city works in a new way." He pointed Imhotep to the glyphs used for record keeping.

Imhotep looked up at the professor. "I understand, we will need much more papyrus."

"Yes, you will."

"But the river flood has not come this year. There are too few reeds to make enough papyrus to copy this book."

Professor Thoth sighed. He looked around at the faces of the men. Their bright eyes sat in front of those big, energy-hungry brains. "I have more of this book." He turned to Imhotep. "You can keep this one, but," he closed it and brushed the dust from its cover, "you must protect it."

Imhotep bowed. "We will."

"I'm serious," he emphasized. "It is imperative that you keep this safe. Nothing must happen to it. You will need this knowledge as you grow. Without it, you may perish."

Imhotep whispered something to two advisors, who dashed away and returned with a carved stone box. He lifted the bound book and placed it inside.

"This is a model for the box that we will bury Djoser in when he departs our realm," Imhotep explained. He removed a chisel and hammer from his waist and began to chip away at the stone lid. The professor smiled as Imhotep carved the Jacana glyphs he'd learned.

Imhotep held it up after he finished. "We will protect this

knowledge from the sky gods for all time." The gathered advisors cheered and bowed to Thoth.

Kaia's words echoed in his mind—that knowledge may only accelerate their evolution and destroy the world faster if not approached in a thoughtful manner. Thoth knew right away that this was not thoughtful, and the evidence was right in front of him.

The professor lost his fight with the feeling of dread as a primitive man in a primitive society called him a sky god while holding a carving aloft that read:

*The Divine Book of Thoth*.

Professor Thoth dashed through the crowd still gathered between the temple and the shuttle as the sun set on their first day. A few of the creatures sat together in groups on blankets spread over the ground. He walked up the ramp and saw Councilor Horus alone in the cargo bay, staring at a projection spinning in the air above the console. He knew manipulating something, anything, was always an activity Councilor Horus enjoyed.

"Hello, Professor," Councilor Horus said, not turning away from his work. "King Djoser and I had a good, long talk about what he needs to do about this unfortunate situation." He swiveled the chair to face Thoth and rested his arm on the console. "And I promised him I could deliver what he requires: a flood."

Professor Thoth took a seat across from him. "We have to go, Councilor. We have already shared too much."

"Nonsense, boy." Horus waved him off and turned back to the image on his screen, a nanomech orb, and zoomed in on an individual machine.

"Now, let's see. You won't be needing those polishers," he said to the projection.

He reached up and plucked them off its tiny rectangular body. He perused over a few more components in the library.

Professor Thoth saw a long list of drilling attachments. "What are you doing, Councilor?"

"Finding water, of course," Horus said. "I need to know the bedrock composition before I can choose the right drill." He swiped the nanomech away and leaned forward to scan through a list of sensor readouts.

"I'd work your way back through the river's tributaries first," Thoth said. A map of the great river appeared, with Saqqara indicated by a small blue dot.

"Thank you, Professor," Councilor Horus said and examined the map. A tap on the glyphpad added a water flow indicator. Tiny arrows indicated the river current's direction as Councilor Horus panned in the opposite direction, deeper into the continent to find the source.

Professor Thoth thought the map looked like a tree turned upside down. Numerous thin fingers of water combined at different points at the bottom of the map, adding their contents to the widening river that flowed north. "You're creating a flood?"

"Yes, one of these channels must be the primary source," Councilor Horus said as he zoomed in on a dry canyon. "There, look."

Thoth noticed ripples carved into the rock. "It doesn't look as though it has been wet for quite a while, though."

"Very good, Thoth. Where did your water go?" he asked the canyon in the projection.

Another swipe turned on an overlay that displayed underground reservoirs detected by Enki's geological scans. "There it is," Horus said as he began scanning the composition of the rock surrounding the buried water. The projection chirped as the scan completed. It was now displaying a chart of the density and hardness of the stone. Horus rubbed his hands together. "Sandstone. This should be easy."

Professor Thoth squirmed in his habsew.

Horus chose two jagged drilling appendages for the nanomech. They snapped onto its body. The image zoomed out, and the lattice of connected nanomechs became visible once again. It continued to zoom farther out until the structure appeared as a single small orb.

"That should do it," he said, leaning back in his chair.

Thoth wrapped his arms around himself. Despite the warmth outside, he felt a shiver.

"Now, Professor, everything is going to be fine. We came down here to help them. And we will."

Thoth shook his head. "But Kaia is right: we'll become gods."

Councilor Horus conceded with a shrug. "But, my boy, we can be gods who only help those who help themselves."

Thoth didn't understand.

Horus continued, "You taught them things today, right?"

Thoth nodded.

"All we're going to do is kick-start them—give them a little leg up. Then they will have what they need to run things on their own." He turned back to the projection. "I must orchestrate the perfect timing during the feast this evening."

Thoth squeezed himself. *This is not good.*

# CHAPTER 8
# SUSPICIONS

## BIOLOGY LAB - AD CYCLE 66,192,364

Kaia knelt down to the crates along her lab's back wall. "How are we doing in here?"

The male nathus crouched on two legs, ready to pounce, as if it were stalking some small prey in the forest. It squawked and leapt toward the edge of the cage as she passed. She stopped and frowned. It squeaked and sprung back to the far wall of its crate.

"I know, little guy, it is stressful to be trapped on this ship," she said, trying to calm it.

The nathus looked up from cleaning its feathers and crept toward the bars of its cage. It seemed to plead with her. The realization of what they'd done was beginning to settle in.

Nu was a home they both shared. She knew it was still the same planet they left all those cycles ago, but everything had changed. On their Nu, destructive storms pounded the surface; temperatures were off the charts, and the air was unbreathable without a habsew's air filters. It was dying, but it was still home.

The world was now unrecognizable. Entire continents had moved. Puna, once in a valley on the subcontinent of Geb, had joined with another landmass to the north. Unimaginable landscapes carpeted the continents, separated by bright blue oceans teeming with life. There were vast green forests full of creatures, and even the deserts were more alive than most of the ecosystems in her time. She put her finger through the cage. The nathus leaned forward and rubbed its head on it, cooing.

"It's still home. It's still there, and more alive than ever. There may still be a place for us with its new inhabitants." *That's what I came here for*, she told herself, and moved toward the affi's cage.

There was a knock at the lab's door.

"Come in, Dr. Khnum. We can get started," she said. She left the cages and made her way to the lab table.

She could hear Dr. Khnum groaning as he tried to pull the door open. "Lift first!" she yelled.

He grunted and the door slid right open.

Kaia tapped the empty stool next to her. "Let's get to work, Doctor."

He took a seat. "Where should we start?"

She accessed the simulations Enki set up earlier based on the biological data she provided. "I would like to figure out which animal from our time these creatures evolved from."

"Good idea," Dr. Khnum said. "We can use that to make assumptions about viral and bacterial pathologies that could affect us both, and perhaps about how to help them."

Kaia shot him a look.

"I mean," he stammered, "if we decide to intervene at all, of course."

She nodded and looked back up at the list of simulations. "This is the simulation Enki updated with the latest data from our sensors," she said, pointing to the bottom of the list.

Dr. Khnum rested his hands on his legs. "Let's see it."

Kaia swirled her finger to the left on the glyphpad. "Remember, it's going to run in reverse, so we can see where they started."

He nodded.

An image of one of the two-legged creatures appeared.

Kaia leaned closer. "It is so odd to see skin exposed to the air."

"Mm, it is." Khnum nodded in agreement.

They watched as the creature's body morphed, growing shorter, more muscular. Its face also changed. The nose grew larger, and the mouth and jaw stuck out farther. Its eyes seemed to sink into its skull.

Kaia leaned back. "Look at its brow ridge," she said, dragging her finger across her eyebrows, "it's getting more pronounced."

Khnum squinted. "And its forehead looks to be getting smaller, curving toward the back of the skull sooner."

"Fur!" Kaia shouted, pointing to the arms and legs. "It's moving down the back from its head and covering everything."

They watched as hair crept over the smooth skin, even the edges of its face. And then the body began to slouch forward, diminishing its stature.

Dr. Khnum chuckled. "It's getting harder to believe they're related," he said.

Kaia agreed. "And look at its posterior."

He laughed harder. "A tail? They used to have tails?"

"It appears so, according to this simulation."

They watched as it continued to shrink overall, especially the skull. Kaia knew that meant the brain was also shrinking. They were getting close to its original ancestor from her time, she was sure of it.

"Oh," Dr. Khnum said as the creature dropped to all fours and small claws grew from the tips of its fingers and toes. "I see where this is evolving."

Kaia did too; it was the shape of the noise.

The creature's snout stuck out farther until it formed a point that whiskers then sprouted from.

The simulation stopped. A small, furry, four-legged animal floated in the air in front of them.

"And there we have it," she said. "An affi!"

"Were you expecting that result?" Dr. Khnum asked.

"I was," she admitted.

"How did you know?"

"Well, we evolved from the nathus. It fills a similar niche in the ecosystem as the affi does, but with an altogether different lineage going back at least a hundred million cycles. The climate was more friendly to the nathus during our evolution, cooler and wetter," she said, remembering the simulation of post-impact Nu. "The asteroids would have made it colder for longer than the nathus's feathers could handle. Meanwhile, the little affi can burrow underground and is covered with insulating fur." She stared up at it. "It had the best chances, by far."

Dr. Khnum rubbed his palms together. "Well, that's good. We know plenty about the affi's physiology. But I would prefer to have a DNA sample from one of the creatures to be sure."

Kaia heard him but noticed something more interesting in the bottom of the projection.

"Kaia?"

"Sorry," she said. "Something about this simulation is wrong."

"Why do you say that?"

She pointed to the chronometer in the lower right corner. "It says the affi should have evolved into this bipedal creature in 150 million cycles."

"That makes sense," Khnum said. "That is about how long it took us to evolve from the nathus. What's wrong with that?"

Kaia saw him freeze and knew he realized it, too.

He blinked. "Only sixty-six million cycles have passed, though."

"Correct." She looked back up and fast-forwarded the projection until it showed the bipedal creature again. "I could understand it being off a few million cycles, maybe even tens of millions of cycles. But over sixty million? Impossible."

"What could have caused them to evolve faster, then?"

She looked at the creature; its basic form was so similar to a primitive Jacana. "The timing is all wrong. How did a four-legged animal evolve so fast? It took the nathus one hundred million cycles to go from its quadruped ancestor to walking on two legs."

"Kaia?" Khnum started.

She saw something was bothering him. "What is it?"

"Do you remember how excited Councilor Horus was about going down to save them?"

The last meeting replayed in her head. "Yes, and did you see the nanomech he was looking at on the bridge after the impacts?"

Dr. Khnum's eyes widened. "You don't think he…"

She stood up. "We need to get that DNA sample. Now!" She raced out of the lab, down the lab ring hall, and toward the corridor leading to the bridge.

Kaia's feet found the ladder with ease, and she climbed down. Pakhet was keeping an eye on the ship's engine, while Captain Ra and Enki chatted away near the helm. She couldn't help but pause to admire Sol rising over Nu's largest ocean on the main viewscreen.

"Captain, Enki, Dr. Khnum, and I need a shuttle," she said as her feet hit the floor.

Ra looked to Enki, then to Kaia. "Can I ask why?"

"We think Councilor Horus did something unspeakable. We need a DNA sample from the creatures below."

Captain Ra turned to Pakhet. "Warm up the biology shuttle."

Pakhet nodded and got to work on the glyphpad.

Enki approached Kaia and said, "Are you sure going down is a good idea?"

"I don't think we have a choice now," she replied, seething. "We need to be discreet and do our best to observe without making contact."

Captain Ra crossed his arms. "What do you think he did?"

"Those creatures," she said then heard a clatter above her. She looked up to see Dr. Khnum hurrying down the ladder.

He was nearly out of breath. "Kaia! I can't find Professor Thoth. I was going to see if he could gather any more information, but he's not in his quarters."

Pakhet cleared her throat. "Captain?"

"What is it, Pakhet?"

Kaia saw her double-check the image of the *Meridian* on her viewscreen.

Pakhet stepped away from the console. "Captain Apep's shuttle is missing."

"Where is it?" Kaia asked, trying not to jump to conclusions.

Pakhet went back and scribbled a command on the glyphpad.

Kaia saw it before Pakhet had a chance to respond. The blue dot was right in the middle of the creatures' village. "Are they inside the shuttle?"

Pakhet shook her head. "No, but they can't be far from it. I'm still getting a strong signal from their habsews."

Dr. Khnum joined her at the console. "Based on Councilor Horus's galvanic skin response, he must be excited about something. But," he looked to the other readings, "Professor Thoth's heart rate and body temperature are elevated. He's anxious, very anxious, indeed."

Everyone's gaze darted to one another before settling on Kaia.

Her face burned, and her head felt like it was going to explode.

"Pakhet, bring it back as soon as they are both inside!"

# CHAPTER 9
# RETELLING

## SAQQARA - YEAR 12 OF DJOSER

Councilor Horus looked over the crowd from his vantage point on the royal platform with Djoser. The people of Saqqara dressed in colorful but dirty garments as they danced in the plaza. He smiled, noticing they celebrated just as the Jacana once did. Everyone seemed pleased to have full bellies after stuffing themselves on the temple's food stores. They even drank something like tekhit. The substance appeared to cause even more dancing and singing. He looked at the front of the crowd and saw Imhotep staring back, studying his every move.

The thick metal plates of Djoser's necklace clinked against one another as the leader turned to him. "It is time. Are you ready, Horus?" he asked.

Horus took another sip of the tekhit-like liquid, which burned his throat in a familiar, satisfying way. He held his hand over his stomach as it grumbled, hoping the tekhit would sterilize the odd food he forced himself to eat out of respect. A feeling of loose calm washed over his mind as he sighed a heavy sigh. "Yes, I am ready to share our story."

Djoser stood then raised his head high. He spread his arms wide, and the raucous crowd grew quiet.

"I have learned a great many things from Horus," Djoser told his people. He waved his hand toward Imhotep at the front of the crowd. "And Imhotep has recorded the knowledge of Thoth."

Councilor Horus glanced at the stone chair on his right. Professor Thoth looked to be doing his best to stay still, but his discomfort was obvious in the way he kept fidgeting with his golden robe.

Djoser sat and waved for Horus to stand and begin. "Now, it is time to share their story with you."

The councilor stood, holding firm to the chair until his feet felt steady under him. Tekhit always had that effect on him. He took a few cautious steps toward the front of the platform and looked up. Few Jacana had ever seen the pale light from Iah; there had been too much particulate pollution in the atmosphere. He admired the white surface cratered by billions of cycles of natural impacts that created a complex dance of circles. He bowed his head for a moment, knowing one of the craters was not natural. He never wished for Captain Apep and the others to die, but he was thankful for their sacrifice. They created this lush and pure world.

He lowered his chin and exchanged glances with some Kemites gathered below. The yellow light from the torches mixed with the moon's glow to brighten their eager faces. He pulled a small round box from his robe, set it down on the platform, and powered it on with the press of a button.

The crowd gasped and seemed to jump back in unison as the holoprojector lit up. A glowing blue and green model of Nu filled the air behind Horus. "This is your home. You are here," he said, pointing to a spot in the northeast region of the second-largest continent.

He felt sweat beading on his forehead while he paused to let them become more comfortable with the projection technology. His banded cloth, alternating between blue and gold, flowed down the sides of his babel hood. It looked regal, but it was too hot for a body warmed by tekhit, he realized. He reached down and adjusted the stylized eye necklace, a Jacana symbol for knowledge that he also used to conceal the babel speaker. Thoth warned him that it could not translate everything he needed to say because the Kemite language simply had no equivalent words.

The crowd's murmuring ceased. The fear vanished from Imhotep's face and turned to curiosity.

Councilor Horus began. "I am from a ship that travels the sky with your day star. The *sol*. The ship is full of others like me. A man named Ra, a dear friend of mine, flies the ship."

Every eye in the crowd was trained on the projection, where a double-ringed ship circled the planet.

Councilor Horus spread his arms. "We are from this world, like you. It was not full of life when we knew it." He pointed to the projection. The planet's colors grew dull. "A dying ocean covered its surface. Few of the great landmasses existed as they do today."

Djoser leaned forward. "Your world is, here?" he asked, pointing to the pale planet.

"Yes, it looks different now. We are from another time, and the world has changed, but it is our home, too. We call ourselves the Jacana and our home Nu." The name *Nu* slipped out untranslated, he noticed.

He then pointed to a small landmass on the projection. "We lived on one piece of land in the middle of the sea. We, and many more like us, lived in a single city. A mighty city. It was the last place on Nu that we could live."

He paused and zoomed the projection to a dead forest on the surface, "The world was dying. Many animals were dying with it, from the smallest mammals like the affi, to one of the mightiest Jacana ancestors, the phara." The animal names passed through the babel, too.

"Pha-ro?"

Horus tilted his head. *Close enough.* "A much larger relative of the *sobek* that you saved me from earlier," he tried to explain.

Djoser leaned forward. "The ruler of our river," he noted with a satisfied nod. "And your people were starving, as we are now? Even with the water to grow food?" he said, gazing at the gray ocean.

"It was something much worse than not enough food." Councilor Horus moved his hand up and down his body over the habsew, visible under his robe. "We could not live outside. These coverings were the only way to stay alive."

"These suits give you protective powers?" Djoser asked.

Councilor Horus half-nodded. "Yes. They gave us the power to go out into the world without fear. They helped us survive in the world, and survive one another."

He grabbed the necklace and pointed to the babel speaker. "We call this machine a babel." He heard the word *babel* straight from the speaker. "It allows us to talk to one another and to talk to you. Poor communications and misunderstandings resulted in many wars in our history."

Djoser looked confused. "It speaks for you?"

"No. We talk in our normal tongue, and it turns our sounds into ones that anyone can understand," Horus said.

"Did the gods give it to you because you were fighting?" Djoser asked.

Councilor Horus shook his head. "We created it. We had to move all our people to one city when Nu was dying. Seven languages came together in one city, and we needed to speak to one another to prevent the miscommunication that leads to violence." He swiped on his wrist glyphpad, and the projection displayed a city of skytowers; one rose far above the others. "We created it in this skytower."

"Gods built this tower?"

Horus shook his head again. *This is going to be harder than I thought.* "No, like the babel, we also created the tower, and many other things to make life better. It was our center of knowledge," he said.

Imhotep shouted a question from the plaza. "Where is this tower of the babel now?" he asked.

Councilor Horus swiped a finger forward on the glyphpad, and the ground below the skytower skyline began to glow bright orange.

"It no longer exists, nor do the rest of the skytowers. Nu needed to recover without us. We could not leave anything behind."

The city collapsed as fiery geysers erupted from the ground.

Djoser fell back in his chair and the crowd gasped.

Councilor Horus continued, "This was no way for us to live. We kept harming Nu, even when we lived in only one city. We destroyed it with our final actions, but our plan failed." The ruins of Puna smoldered in the air behind him. Several skytowers were still standing.

Djoser raised his arm and waved it through the air. "You say that this is Nu, but it is not dead. Is this plan a failure?"

Councilor Horus estimated that now was the time. He held down on the far right-hand section of the glyphpad until it beeped to confirm the nanomechs had activated. He turned back to Djoser. "We had another plan. We used our great knowledge to bring the planet back to life. Our plan created the world that you see today. The world that created you."

He drew a glowing symbol on the glyphpad, and the projection zoomed out to show all of Nu once again. "Our plan used four enormous crystals in the sky," he said as the four crystalline asteroids appeared in the space surrounding the planet. The image of crystals orbiting Nu captivated Djoser and his court.

"One of our people tried to stop us," said Horus. "His name was Set, and he was the captain of a ship called the *Montu*." Both names came out untranslated. He glanced to Professor Thoth, who shirked away from the story.

*It's too late, now.*

A burst of light dotted the projection, showing the *Montu* ramming the smallest crystal. "We lost one crystal to Iah." Horus heard the babel pronounce 'Iah' in his native tongue rather than translating it to whatever the Kemite word was for the moon. He noticed Imhotep repeating his mouth movements for the word.

Djoser watched as the smallest crystal slammed into the cratered white surface. He gazed at the night sky. "That is, I-a-h?" he asked, pointing to the moon shining in the night sky.

"Yes, that is Iah. And this is Nu. And this is a habsew." He pulled at his suit. Djoser repeated each word.

Horus was eager to keep the story moving. The projection resumed playing. The three crystals glided toward the surface. He pointed to the largest one. "A man named Apep was controlling this crystal." His name also ran through the babel unchanged.

The crowd all jumped back on their feet when the projection flashed.

The three crystals smashed into Nu. Three plumes of debris shot away from the planet into the space around it and fell back in a fiery rain.

Djoser gasped with fear but then leaned closer. "Why did this man, Apep, cause such destruction?"

Horus explained as a beige cloud shrouded the land. "It was not destruction. His actions brought new life over time. These crystals created a dust storm."

"Apep brought new life? A second life to Nu?" Djoser asked.

Horus considered the analogy for a moment, then nodded. "First, there was a very long darkness. Light could no longer reach the surface because of the storm. When the light returned, Nu was healed and ready for new life." *You must tell them what you did*, his tekhit-addled brain suggested. He let it slip.

"I created you from this darkness."

"Horus!" he heard Professor Thoth whisper through a clenched jaw.

Djoser sat for a moment, absorbing the story. "You can create life; you can create storms. Can you bring life to our river? Our city will die if you cannot save it."

"I created you, and I can save you, but," Horus paused. *You must teach them, not help them*, he remembered. "I can only save you once. You must use the knowledge we have shared. You must learn from us, learn from our mistakes. You must keep the story alive, so you do not destroy the world again," he demanded.

"We will do as you say," Djoser said with a bow from his chair.

Councilor Horus nodded in return as he heard a low rumble growing in the distance. "Another of our people, Khnum, a healer and a wise man, observed your great river from the sky and found the answer," he said, knowing he fudged the story a bit because he didn't want Enki to get any credit.

Djoser stood, looking to the meager river. Councilor Horus heard the sound but saw nothing.

Imhotep's mouth fell open first. "The flood!"

A deluge raced down the riverbed toward Saqqara. The crowd turned to face the river as well, and cheers erupted.

Councilor Horus heard Professor Thoth shuffling up behind him.

"Do you realize what we have done?" Thoth asked.

Councilor Horus grinned. "We have saved them. There should be no doubt in their minds that a quest for knowledge like ours is the only thing that can help them," he replied.

A heavy feeling filled his stomach, but he attributed it to the odd food. He stood next to Djoser as the flood waters filled the canals and spread out over the dry fields.

A wave of satisfaction washed over Horus; the nanomechs were able to release water from the underground reservoir. The city's inhabitants raised their hands in the air, ecstatic. More people poured into the court, cheering.

"Horus! Horus! Horus!" they chanted.

Djoser raised his arms to the stars. "The sky people told us the story of our world. They told us how it died and how to resurrect it. They created the world for us. Now, they have saved us from starvation. We must learn from them. We must never forget their wisdom. There can be life after death!"

Imhotep ran up onto the platform and lowered himself to his knees. "Praise Thoth!"

Djoser also knelt and waved his arms toward the councilor. "Praise Horus!"

The rest of the Kemites joined, all bowing toward the two Jacana now towering over the scene. A smile spread across Councilor Horus's face as he saw the plaza full of his creations, all on their knees, worshipping him.


Professor Thoth scuffed his feet on the ramp as they returned to the shuttle. "Councilor Horus, we have made a grave mistake."

Horus turned to scold him, "We have saved them. Nu will know life, know civilization like it has never known before. With our teachings, they will be more perfect than any Jacanan society could dream." He turned back and marched into the shuttle.

Professor Thoth shook a finger at him. "You did this, Horus. You created them. Now we have destroyed them."

"You need to calm down. They are—" Horus paused, noticing the ramp door closing behind the professor. "What are you doing?"

The professor spun around. "Nothing. That's not—"

The door clanged shut.

Councilor Horus took a seat in the cargo bay. "You may as well sit down, Professor."

"Why?" Thoth asked, stumbling forward as the shuttle began a rapid ascent. He caught himself on a bench and pulled himself up onto it.

Councilor Horus smoothed out his robe. "Because Kaia found us."

They heard the docking mechanism latch on and the seal hiss as the pressure equalized. Professor Thoth rushed to the door. The latch turned before he reached it.

Councilor Horus stood but quickly fell back in his seat when Kaia stormed in. He could see the fire in her eyes.

Her voice was sharp enough to pierce his suit. "I should throw you out the airlock."

She turned to Professor Thoth. "You, too, if Pakhet and Dr. Khnum didn't need you to run the ship."

Thoth scampered past the glare of his crewmates like a scolded pet nathus.

Kaia turned back to Councilor Horus. "What have you done?"

"I've saved them," he insisted. "And I have saved Nu."

"No! You have ensured Nu's destruction." she seethed.

# CHAPTER 10
# HYPERCANE

## UNIVERSITY OF CHICAGO - 2035 CE

Dr. Pearce took a sip of his coffee as he looked over the university commons while he waited for Louise to arrive. On normal days, the patter of rain against his office window comforted him, but it had been raining for days, and the pleasant sound turned grating. He looked into the distance toward Lake Michigan, its surface a chaotic stew of whitecap waves. Small, colorful spots were moving back and forth along the shore.

He squinted. "Are those runners?" he asked out loud. He shook his head at their incautious dedication. *Why would anyone want to run in this weather?* The wind picked up and pummeled another sheet of rain into the window. His watch vibrated, and he saw a severe storm warning issued by NOAA. He looked back toward the runners on the lakefront path. A gust of wind pushed a massive wave into the embankment, sending water twenty feet into the sky before crashing back onto the path. It flowed over the pavement, knocking one unlucky runner off his feet.

Dr. Pearce set down his coffee, ready to call for help when the man stood, brushed off his shorts, and resumed his jog. The watch vibrated again. Now, there was a flood warning for the Fox and Des Plaines rivers in the suburbs. *This kind of weather used to be rare,* Dr. Pearce thought as he took another sip of coffee.

He was halfway through his morning ritual, although he hadn't yet removed his sweater or sorted through his messages. Students streamed into the commons on their way to class.

*Why all the black umbrellas? There are so many other colors to choose from!* he wondered.

There was a knock at his door, and then it creaked open. He turned to see Louise gliding through, her coat sopping wet from the rain.

"Here, let me," he said, setting down his coffee mug and crossing his office to her.

He helped her remove her jacket without getting water all over herself, though plenty sloughed onto the floor when he hung it up on the coat rack.

She brushed the remaining droplets off the front of her sweater. "It's crazy out there."

"Yes, pretty late in the fall for a severe thunderstorm."

"Do you think it is related to Levi?" she asked.

"Levi?"

She shook her head and stepped toward a poster board covered with a haphazard arrangement of maps and data printouts of his asteroid impact research. "You haven't watched the news, have you?"

He followed her gaze to the trifold poster board leaning against the wall. "No, I've been working on that all week."

"This?" she said, pointing to the board. "It looks like an elementary school science fair presentation."

"It's all I had time to do before the Order of Extraterrestrialism conference in Raleigh later this week!"

Louise went to the shelf and moved a stack of academic journals from in front of his small television. She leaned over and blew the dust off the controls on the side then pressed the power button. "You've got to see this, Alan. There's no way that conference is happening in Raleigh now."

Alan watched as the screen flickered on. A man stood in front of a green screen, where the eye of an incomprehensible storm appeared. He assumed the man had been there for endless hours of nonstop coverage from the looks of his disheveled hair and suit jacket.

"Hurricane Levi… No, sorry," the meteorologist corrected himself, "Hypercane Levi has broken another record. We're seeing sustained wind speeds of," he gulped in disbelief, "300 knots." He looked at the camera wide-eyed. "Folks, that is over 350 miles per hour, with gusts approaching 400 miles per hour 50 miles from the center of the eye."

Alan fumbled for his chair behind him. His fingers found it, and he lowered himself. "Louise, this is unimaginable. It makes Superstorm Sandy or Hurricane Florence look like a Spring shower."

Louise took a seat on his desk, eyes still glued to the TV. "It may be hard to imagine but it isn't unexpected, Alan. Climatologists have been predicting a hurricane like this for over a decade."

The meteorologist zoomed out. "The scale of this storm is like nothing we've ever seen. And by we, I mean humans. No human has seen a storm like this."

The storm spun over the open ocean just north of the Dominican Republic. Its swirling arms stretched from the tip of Florida to the border of South and North Carolina.

"This is a 100-mile-wide F5 tornado, with F1 tornado strength winds stretching out 300 miles. The whole system is 600 miles wide and still strengthening."

Alan exhaled. "The models are so good these days. They must know where it is heading."

"Watch," Louise said, nodding to the TV.

"Now," the meteorologist said, making nervous eye contact with someone offscreen, "NOAA is recommending an unprecedented evacuation of the Eastern Seaboard over the next week." He tapped on the controller in his hand, and a red dot appeared in the center of Hypercane Levi's eye. It moved to the west, leaving a red trail behind it. The dot headed toward Miami, then turned north.

"It traces the coast all the way up to Wilmington, North Carolina, where we forecast it will make landfall." He pointed to the red line continuing across eastern North Carolina, "And then," the line jogged to the east at Norfolk, Virginia, "our simulation shows it will head back out into the open ocean until..." the line made an abrupt turn back to the west, straight for New York City. "A high-pressure system over the North Atlantic will push it back, and it will make a second landfall over the Big Apple."

Alan shook his head. "This is a catastrophe in the making."

Louise crossed her arms. "It is the first of its kind, but it will not be the last. Cyclones and typhoons in the Pacific are also getting stronger and are going to displace even more people in Southeast Asia."

Alan looked down, remembering the refugees at the airport in Mumbai. "Refugees are going to overrun Pune in no time."

She nodded. "There's something else I need to tell you." She turned the TV off as the announcer was describing the sixty inches of rain and twenty feet of flooding forecast for parts of the five boroughs.

"What is it now?" Alan said, feeling unprepared for more bad news.

"It's about the Climate Council."

"Not again," he said. "I'm not even affiliated with them anymore!"

She shook her head. "This isn't about *you*, Alan. It's about *me*."

He sat up in his chair. "Oh, sorry, it's just..."

"I know and understand," she said and reached over to pat his hand. "You remember my talk in Matheran, at the Relocation Committee conference?"

He wracked his brain, then nodded. He was almost afraid to admit it had gotten buried in the fallout of his excitement over the Shiva crater.

"Well," she continued, "Dr. Layton over at UCLA had something come up, so they asked me to take her place at the Global Climate Conference."

Alan jumped out of his chair. "Louise that's amazing!" He felt a wave of pride wash over him. "I'm sure your session will have the highest attendance of the bunch."

"Oh, yes," she cleared her throat, "I should hope so. It's the *keynote*."

He clamped his head with his hands. "The keynote?!" He wrapped his arms around her and squeezed hard, maybe a little too hard.

"That's the honor of a lifetime!" He backed away but kept his arms on her shoulders. "You deserve it so much more than the one last year by the guy talking about the future flood basalt eruption plan. We've got *real* problems with climate refugees right now, and you're leading the charge."

"Thank you, dear. I must admit, though, that I am nervous about one thing."

"No need!" he assured her. "You're going to do great."

"It's not that," she said. "You know I drive a hard bargain, even more so on short notice. The conference begins next Friday."

He nodded then paused. "Wait, did you? I mean, you got me on the *Finality* drill ship last time they asked you to speak. I can't imagine what you could have negotiated this time."

She shrugged and scooted off the desk. "I told them your research needs to see the light of day, even if it is," she made her way to the poster board, "controversial."

He put his hands in his pockets and walked over to her. He read the title plastered across the top of the display: "Too Perfect: The Post-Cretaceous Extinction Climate."

Louise reached up and held onto the paper with the title printed on it. "I think," she began, "these words will be a problem," she said, tearing off the *Too Perfect*. "Too perfect implies some kind of intent, like something did too good of a job."

"I'll concede that if it means my research gets presented at the conference," Alan said.

"Well, now, I wasn't quite that good of a negotiator."

"What do you mean?"

She chewed her lip for a moment, then turned to the window. "Remember how I said your research would see the light of day?"

He nodded.

"They'll let you set up out on the front plaza."

"The *plaza?*" he scoffed.

She turned back to the poster. "It's that or nothing, Alan."

He kicked the floor once then looked at the torn title section of the title. "Outside it is. But where is this plaza?" he asked.

"Giza," she said.

"Giza?"

She nodded. "Just outside the Grand Egyptian Museum. I hear the fall weather is great there, very mild."

He sighed, knowing that was as high-profile as his research was going to get.

"Alan, this is a chance," she reminded him.

"I know. Thank you."

She patted his back then looked at the poster. He watched her scan the images, the graphs, and the video loop of the impact on the electronic paper. A puzzled expression swept across her face when she noticed what the mini asteroid really was. "Is that your..."

He nodded. "It sure is. That's the award the Climate Council gave me when they first funded my impact research."

She doubled over in laughter. "I'm sorry," she said, still laughing. "You have to be kidding."

"I'm serious!" He couldn't help but join her and chuckled. "Who would have dreamed a perfect octahedron would be the only shape that could produce that kind of impact structure?"

"A perfect octahedron, huh?"

He nodded. "I tried everything."

She sighed, and her voice cracked from the laughter. "There's just one problem with that."

"What?" he asked, watching the crystal-shaped award slam into the clay over and over.

Her face grew serious. "Where would an octahedral asteroid come from? Let alone three of them?"

There it was. It stabbed him in the gut with the same ferocity as it had the first time he questioned it too. He knew it didn't make sense. "I still can't explain that for the life of me," he said. "And add to that, it had to be made of almost pure iridium." He went back to his chair and plopped down.

"What did you say?"

"There is no mineral that crystalizes in—"

Louise shook her head and interrupted, "No, the other part."

"It had to be iridium?"

"That word..."

"Iridium is the primary element in most asteroids."

"No, the other word. *Made,*" she emphasized. "I mean, there are no octahedral asteroids."

He nodded. "That's right, there aren't..." Then it stuck in his head, too. Something about that word, *made.* "They were *made,*" he said out loud. "MADE!" he yelled, unable to believe he was even considering that. He wiped his hand across his forehead and pushed back his hair.

He got back up and leaned in close to the poster board, examining the details of all three craters for the millionth time. "The crazy Extraterrestrialists might be right. Aliens!"

"Now, Alan, let's not go that far. There has to be some other explanation."

He tried to cool his jets but couldn't stop himself from jumping to conclusions. "We evolved because of these impacts. These three octahedral asteroids are impossible for nature to create." He looked Louise straight in the eye. "Someone *made* them." He looked down then right back at her. "What if this place was *made,* Louise? What if Earth was *made for us?*"

# CHAPTER 11
# MONITOR

Kaia and Enki bumped shoulders as they leaned over the mission console to study the images of the Kemites on the viewscreen.

"Sorry," she said.

Enki didn't seem to notice. "They have a lot in common with us," he stated.

"Why wouldn't they?" she said with a hint of anger. "Councilor Horus admitted he accelerated their evolution by designing DNA-manipulating nanomechs. One could even say he *made* the Kemites. They do differ from us in one important way that Councilor Horus could not have planned."

"Oh?" he said with one eyebrow raised.

"Their bodies appear to be more adaptable to different conditions," she said, looking up at an image Horus took from his little trip to the surface.

"What makes you think that?" Enki asked.

Kaia pointed to their clothing. "Well, this group lives in the desert, and they require very little covering. But this group..." She swiped to another image from land far north of the desert. "This group lives where it is a little cooler, and they appear to be wearing animal hides over more of their bodies."

She looked down at her habsew. "The insulating garments must help them regulate body temperature, but nothing like what we would need if we were somewhere that cold."

"Yes, our environment must be perfect, or we have to wear these habsews," Enki said as he fidgeted with his sleeve.

"Yes, in that way, they are even more successful than the Jacana. They may cover Nu even faster than we did."

Captain Ra stepped away from the helm and joined them. "How long do you think it will take for them to discover kohl?"

"Professor Thoth might know," Kaia said. "He is well-versed in Jacana history, though the thought of asking him makes my stomach turn." She looked across the main viewscreen toward the systems console. The professor's posture was stiff, and his face showed no hint of his youthful energy. *Maybe he's learned his lesson.*

"Professor Thoth!" she shouted across the bridge.

He froze and looked up from the glyphpad.

"We need to ask you a few questions. Please come over here."

Thoth backed away from the systems console and tiptoed over as if he were walking past a sleeping phara.

Captain Ra patted his back, and Kaia saw a glimmer of concern in Thoth's eyes.

She took a step toward him. "Professor Thoth, as much as I'd like to keep you in your quarters like the councilors, we still need you."

He placed his forearm over his stomach and bowed. "What can I do for you, Kaia?"

"Come closer," she said, waving toward the mission console. "Look at the viewscreen."

He weaved his way past Captain Ra and Enki to study the image on the screen.

"Where are these Kemites located?" he asked, rubbing his chin.

Kaia zoomed out. "Much farther north and east from where you and Councilor Horus visited."

"That explains the animal pelts covering their bodies," he said and leaned in closer.

Kaia watched the group trudge across a snow-covered meadow toward the tree line.

Enki joined him and stood on the other side of Kaia for a better look.

Professor Thoth pointed to a long stick in one Kemite's hand. "See that?"

Kaia squinted then saw what he was talking about. "What is it?"

"A weapon of some sort, I think."

The Kemites stopped and dropped to the ground. "There!" said Thoth. "Look!"

A four-legged creature covered in brown fur plodded along the edge of the trees. One of the Kemites stood and threw the stick at the fur-covered beast. The creature turned toward the Kemites and charged. They jumped up and began to run back across the snowy meadow. The creature stumbled, leaving a trail of blood pouring from the open wound where the spear pierced its hide.

The Kemites kept turning around to see if it was still chasing them, but it had slowed down, and they did as well. They pointed more sticks at the creature as it lumbered toward them. Two Kemites approached and jabbed it with their spears over and over until it stopped moving. The others rushed around the creature and jumped up and down, their mouths opening and closing.

Professor Thoth grinned. "They're celebrating a hunt. These are hunters." He put his back to the viewscreen and explained. "These are not Kemites at all. This must be another group. They probably call themselves something different."

Kaia put her hands on her hips. "There are groups all over Nu."

Enki added, "And they all seem to have unique attributes. Some hunt as these do, some farm, some live in mud huts, while others live in caves."

"As I would expect," Professor Thoth said, "if Councilor Horus designed them based on us."

Kaia's jaw tightened; she tried to stuff down her rage. "How long do we have?"

Professor Thoth looked at her with sorry eyes then turned to Enki. "How many are there?"

Enki went to the glyphpad and dismissed the sensor image. He accessed a global view. Millions of red dots appeared all over the planet. "Between 20 to 25 million. Accurate readings are impossible without a more detailed survey."

"Thank you, Enki," said Thoth. "That's all I need to know."

Kaia watched him take a deep breath. "Well, how long until they discover kohl?

"I would have said at least fifteen, maybe twenty thousand cycles if they follow our trajectory from this level of development."

She pursed her lips. "But…"

"But we intervened, so it may take less time."

"What did you tell them?"

Thoth swallowed hard. "Everything."

Captain Ra offered, "Maybe they will forget?"

"Unlikely," Thoth said, shaking his head. "I left them one of our books."

"Thoth!" Kaia yelled. "What was in it?" She saw his mind race through the pages.

"Record keeping techniques, energy sources, economic principles, geometry, geophysical sciences, astronomy, even some on rocketry and orbital calculations."

"Enki, get us an image from the Kemite city, now," she ordered.

Her jaw dropped when the image appeared on the viewscreen.

Sculptors were carving hundreds of Jacana glyphs on the naked stone walls of several buildings.

"You shared our language and writing with them, too, didn't you?"

Thoth's silence told her everything she needed to know.

Enki pointed to an open-air section of the temple structure. "Look at this." He zoomed in as close as possible.

They saw a large stone table with a book laid open, showing pages depicting three crystalline shapes with annotations on the geometry. One man leaned over the book, pointing to the data and gesturing commands to the others.

"That Kemite's name is Imhotep. He seems like a First Officer, second-in-command."

Kaia couldn't believe her eyes as she watched Imhotep sketch something with a feather quill on a blank sheet of papyrus and hand it to a man across the table. The man's clothes were familiar. A striped blue and gold head cloth, like Horus's, sat on the man's head, starting just above his eyes and falling over his shoulders down the sides.

She scoffed, "Councilor Horus left that behind, too?"

Thoth sighed. "I didn't know, but it looks that way, yes. That is Djoser, the ruler of this region of Nu."

However, it was Imhotep's sketch that had commanded everyone's attention.

A long line ran along the bottom of the papyrus. Two angled lines came out of the ground and intersected at a point near the top. Small glyphs noted angles and distance.

Kaia shook her head in disbelief. "They're building a crystal."

Enki cocked his head. "It looks like they are making it appear as though it is half buried in the ground."

Kaia agreed. "Like it is mid-impact."

Professor Thoth sighed. "That must be what it represents. They're memorializing the creation of their world."

Kaia put her hand on her hip. "What?"

Thoth explained, "The impact... They are building it to represent the moment of impact."

"You told them about that?"

He shook his head. "Councilor Horus did. He tried to instill respect for knowledge in them, but I think he overestimated their ability to assimilate the material. It was, perhaps, indistinguishable from the powers of a god to them. They may assume this shape can cheat death."

Kaia looked at him, puzzled. "Cheat death?"

"Councilor Horus told them our world was dying when we lived here, and that we saved its life with these crystals. It looks like Djoser is having this built as his tomb. We tried to bring them knowledge, so mythology like that which led the Jacana astray for far too long would not hold them back."

Kaia's arms dropped to her sides. "You gave them science and religion at the same time. At this stage of their evolution, the two could be in conflict for thousands of cycles!" She huffed. "We will deal with this later. Right now, we need to know how long until they discover kohl and use enough to damage Nu."

Thoth moved his mouth, but nothing came out.

"Thoth? How long?" Kaia demanded.

He clicked his tongue. "Seven, maybe ten thousand cycles?"

"That's it?" Kaia said in disbelief.

He nodded to the screen, and she understood. This new species had a head start.

She turned to Captain Ra. "The lightdrive, again?"

"Already on it," he said and headed to the helm to start the calculation.

She turned back to Enki and Thoth. "We need to track their progress while we're gone. As much as I want to trust your estimate, Thoth, I would rather be careful."

He bowed. "As would I, Kaia. Perhaps we could measure the atmosphere for increasing levels of pollution."

Enki shook his head. "Sensors aren't good enough for that, either. It needs to be something we can detect from a distant orbit, something that does not require visible light."

Kaia saw Enki go back to his mental drawing board then return. "We could monitor for artificial radiation as a sign they harnessed the power of the atom."

"What's your thinking there?" Kaia asked.

Thoth shook his head, "No, that would be too late. We need to catch them sooner. Once they learn that, it will mean exponential growth, and we may not arrive in time to stop them. They could have advanced far enough to shoot us out of the sky."

"Radio emissions?" he suggested.

Kaia looked at Thoth; it sounded good to her.

He rubbed his chin again. "Yes, but once they start, their signals could overwhelm our systems because we'll be traveling near lightspeed. We'll be inundated with many cycles of information in a few seconds. We need to leave behind something to record and alert us when they've reached that milestone."

Professor Thoth snapped his fingers and turned to Enki. "Your shuttle."

"My shuttle?" said Enki.

"Yes," Thoth said. "We'll leave it behind on Iah. I can program it to only send us a brief burst when it detects a specific threshold of radio emissions."

Kaia narrowed her eyes. "It will last thousands of cycles?"

"With the help of some nanomechs and sol power to keep it running, yes. There is no weather on Iah that could corrode the electronics."

"Enki?" Kaia asked. "Will you need your shuttle here?"

He considered it for a moment. "Perhaps, but if the nanomechs work, we can retrieve it when we return."

She pointed up the ladder to the corridor. "Thoth, get to work. Now."

He bowed, went to the ladder, and scrambled off the bridge.

Kaia made her way to the helm and filled Captain Ra in on the shuttle plan.

He shrugged. "I see why that would work." Kaia did not pick up a hint of mistrust on his face. "Thoth may be a professor, but he's only had that status for a couple of cycles, you know. He's twenty-some cycles old, still more kid than adult."

"I know," she said, remembering Councilor Hegira telling her she couldn't be a kid anymore at fourteen cycles old. "But he still made a grave error."

He nodded. "I hope that makes up for it," he said and honed in on her console. "He left you something."

She followed his eyes to a bundle wrapped in cloth on the biology console. "What is that?" she asked.

Ra shrugged. "He didn't say."

She jogged over to her console and examined the small package. The cloth was a coarse weave of thick, stiff, beige strands. Rough twine held the fabric closed, with a note tied in the knot.

*Hello Kaia,*

*Dr. Khnum told me you needed this for your analysis. It's not an entire planet of samples, but it's something, I hope.*

*Sincerely, Thoth*

She flipped the note over and saw a few more glyphs.

*I mean what is inside the cloth, not the cloth. Though, the cloth may be of interest to you as well. The Kemites told me it comes from an animal called a "sheep." They're cute, covered in white fluffy curled fur. They even made a new glyph for it.*

The drawing of a four-legged animal with a pointed snout and two horns on top of its head made her smile, because it made the sheep look like a cloud with a head.

Kaia set the note down and untied the twine. The cloth unfolded itself to reveal a braid of dark hair—and another note.

*The Kemites call this a "lock of youth" and they allowed me to witness their ceremony of removing it from a young boy as his body was beginning to undergo changes into adulthood. They believed it was a great honor to have a "god" take it back to the sky. I hope you find it helpful.*

She picked up the delicate sample and marveled at the tight braid held together by beads on each end. A surge of excitement coursed through her veins, and she wished she could run to the lab right now to begin her analysis. But there was more work to do first. She placed the sample back in the cloth and retied the string.

Enki stepped aside as Kaia rejoined him at the mission console.

"Captain, are we ready?" she asked.

"Almost."

"Good."

"Hello, Captain," Pakhet said as she climbed down the ladder. "The professor told Dr. Khnum and me about the plans then dashed off to Enki's shuttle."

Captain Ra acknowledged her with a nod then turned back to the helm to enter one final value into his time dilation algorithm.

"Hello, Kaia," Pakhet said when her feet touched the floor. "It looks like we're taking another light speed spin, huh?"

"This one will be very brief, less than an hour for us," Kaia said.

Pakhet went to the engineering console. "And how long on Nu?"

Kaia looked over to Captain Ra for confirmation. "Seven thousand cycles?"

He nodded. "Give or take. This will be so fast I may be off by a few decades."

"Understood." Kaia went to Pakhet and said, "I'm sorry. I didn't intend for you to be a jailer."

Pakhet laughed. "It's fine." She puffed out her chest and stretched her spine, towering over Kaia. "I look the part and am happy to play it. Someone had to put those two councilors in their place, and I'm glad you gave the order."

Kaia shook off her twinge of regret about locking up her former mentors. "How are they?"

"They're both doing well. Eating plenty, maybe a little bored, and are shooting me a lot of seething glares."

"That's understandable."

Another set of footsteps clanged as someone came down the ladder. Dr. Khnum made his way onto the bridge, followed by Professor Thoth returning, too.

Pakhet's mouth scrunched to one side, then she said, "There is one odd thing, though."

"What is it?"

"The councilors don't seem to be on speaking terms. I've been monitoring their systems, just in case, and they haven't said a word to one another."

Kaia wasn't sure what to make of this right now, but she filed it away for later consideration. "Thank you for telling me."

"Perhaps it's nothing," Pakhet said

Captain Ra cleared his throat and raised his voice. "Everyone ready?" he asked, glancing around the bridge as everyone went to their stations. "This is going to be a short trip, and we may need to move fast when we return. Kaia, can you please explain the plan to everyone?"

She flicked off the mission console's viewscreen so everyone could see her through it. "Professor Thoth believes the Kemites will take between seven and ten thousand cycles to discover kohl and use it to the point at which it will damage Nu. We're leaving Enki's shuttle behind to monitor them while we again travel at near light speed to return to Nu in seven thousand cycles. When we return, we will again plan to make contact, though their civilization will no doubt be much different, and perhaps even dangerous for us."

She saw nothing but resolute expressions. *They're still with me. Good.* "Captain Ra, please turn us toward Iah."

"Turning now," he said and placed both hands on the helm.

The *Meridian* creaked but held firm as the moon's white glow appeared on the edge of the viewscreen. The ship turned until the entire surface was visible.

"Professor Thoth, release the shuttle," Kaia ordered.

The crew watched as the silver saucer's autopilot took it past the main camera then down to the surface. It grew smaller and harder to distinguish the closer it got to Iah, until it vanished amid the gray rocks and craters.

Thoth clasped his hands behind his back. "The shuttle is in place, and the sensors will begin sweeping Nu three times a day."

"Thank you, Professor," Kaia said with a subtle emphasis and a glance at the bundle of cloth on her console. She saw him catch her extra meaning, and a faint smile spread across his face.

"Captain Ra, start the lightdrive," she said.

Everyone braced on the consoles as the ship turned to the blackness of space and the stars began to stretch on the screen.

Kaia took a deep breath. "We'll return as soon as we receive word from the shuttle. Stay sharp, everyone."

The lightdrive's now familiar hum reverberated around the bridge as a ring of compressed starlight shone like water.

# CHAPTER 12
# THE RANCH

## SOUTH DAKOTA - 2035 CE

Daxia pressed the parallel park button on her rental car's screen and let go of the wheel as it backed itself into a tiny space in downtown Hill City, South Dakota. It came to a stop and beeped that it was finished. She grabbed her bag and opened the door. The strong scent of pine filled her nostrils, along with the cool autumn mountain air. She crinkled her face at the mishmash of one-story buildings that lined the narrow main street through town. Several were boarded up with their torn awnings flapping in the breeze. A heavy door creaked open somewhere behind her, and she spun around, shielding her eyes from the mid-morning sun.

"Daxia! You made it!" a man said with an extra enthusiastic wave.

She recognized his captivating, energetic eyes despite the brown hair now reaching down to his shoulders.

"Seagraves, it's so nice to see you," she said and extended her hand.

He shook it so hard she did her best not to recoil. "I'm glad you're here." She looked up and down the street again. He let go and chuckled. "It's not much, I know, but we've got *this!*" he said, and spread his arms toward the building behind him. "The Black Hills Institute of Geological Research."

She waved up to the rusting sign hanging off the painted facade. "And museum, I see!" she said with a hint of sarcasm. *How nice could such a small museum really be?*

He wagged his finger. "Now, now. There's more to it than there looks. Come on in!"

She followed him inside. *No fresh air in here,* she realized as the pine scent gave way to the familiar dusty, musty odor that seemed to fill every museum in the world.

Seagraves tapped on the entry desk. "Just me today, so I guess your admission is free," he said with a smirk. "I need to go downstairs and finish packing up a specimen for shipment to the Field Museum in Chicago tomorrow. Won't be more than half an hour."

He tilted his head toward the doorway leading to the museum. "Go ahead and stretch your legs in there if you'd like. I don't know about you, but lots of time in airplanes and cars does a number on mine. We'll catch up on the ride up to Belle Fourche."

"Great," she said and watched him scamper down a set of stairs into the underbelly of the building. She figured she might as well take a look.

Daxia stepped up onto the main hall floor and her jaw dropped at the stunning collection. Cases full of fossils lined the walls all the way around a cavernous room. A raised platform with several skeletons filled the far wall. She realized the building used to be a theater, and now the only actors were skeletons frozen in time. Her eyes gravitated upward and locked onto the skull of a complete T. rex skeleton, which dominated all the smaller theropods in the center of the room.

"Wow," she said out loud, already impressed.

A sign that said *Start Here* and she strolled up to the first case. Slabs of reddish gray rocks leaned against stands; small arrows pointed at disturbances in their layers. *Cyanobacteria of the Archaean Eon, approx. 3.8 billion years old,* read one label. She'd seen photos of such specimens, but never a real one. The description explained that these fossils were from Western Australia and were some of the oldest ever found.

She moved on to the next case, and then the next. Each one featured fossils from every Earth eon, broken down by era then by period. There were lumpy stromatolites, delicate jellyfish, and thin worms, all preserved in rocks from the Precambrian era.

The next case focused on the Paleozoic, with its hard-shelled trilobites, insects, and more complex soft animals like squids. Here, mass extinctions killed off almost everything, twice, only for it to rise again until the next threat. The entire case ended with the largest such tragedy yet. The third mass extinction on Earth, separating the Permian period of the Paleozoic era from the Triassic period of the Mesozoic era. It was so horrific that scientists called it the Great Dying.

The specimens grew more recognizable in each case, with drawings of long-necked plesiosaurs swimming alongside beautiful, coiled ammonites, now all preserved in the fossils on display. Then a fourth mass extinction and into the next period of the Mesozoic era, the Jurassic, where the surviving dinosaurs took off and Daxia's work on the Yixian began. The museum even had a small specimen of archaeopteryx, a small, feathered, two-legged Avialae theropod from the late Jurassic, not all that different to the one she had been excavating a few days earlier. There were also a few fossils of ferns and palms from the period, clues to the climate that she knew she would have to feature in her PhD thesis.

The last period of the Mesozoic era, the Cretaceous, featured most of the dinosaur fan favorites, from the *Tyrannosaurus rex* and the velociraptor—*They had feathers, too*—all the way to the triceratops. Daxia was so absorbed in the story of life on Earth that she felt a tinge of grief at the end of this case. It concluded with the massive impact and the fifth mass extinction, the one she knew too much about from her time with Dr. Pearce.

An arrow guided her from there into a newer section of the museum. "The Age of Us" a sign above the door read. Inside, she saw fossils of woolly mammoths, saber-tooth cats, and other creatures Daxia thought might still be around if it weren't for humans. The exit of the exhibit featured pictures of industrial waste ponds and towers spewing smoke and filth into the atmosphere. A sign at the end read: *A Sixth Mass Extinction?* She shuddered. *Let's hope not.*

She realized the genius of the museum's design. It led a visitor through the unbroken chain of life on Earth, from the cyanobacteria some four billion years ago, all the way through every chunk of time on a geologic scale, right up to the point where humans evolved and began to change everything. A major bonus was all the educational facts combined with some of the best fossil specimens she'd ever seen in such a modest museum.

It drove home the point that life on Earth had persisted despite multiple near misses in each mass extinction. Then, finished by warning a sixth one was underway, and this one was because of us. That question mark, she knew, was a subtle call-to-action. Whether there would be a sixth mass extinction was up to us, the anthropoid apes who dominated the planet and left traces in the very layers of Earth. They even had a geologic epoch named after them—the Anthropocene.

*Brilliant,* she decided, but something stuck in her mind about the description of the impact at the end of the Cretaceous.

Daxia now knew the museum's description of the impact was wrong. It wasn't just the one asteroid that had created the Chicxulub crater in Mexico and ended the dinosaurs' reign, as the plaque read; there were three, and the Chicxulub crater wasn't even the largest. Her mind jumped to Dr. Pearce. It had been too long since they chatted. She knew he was trying to keep his distance because, last time they talked, he worried that his "crackpot" theories could tarnish the opinions of her doctorate panelists and threaten her chance at obtaining the degree she deserved. She wandered across the museum hall, under the towering T. rex and stepped back down to the entryway. There was still no sign of Seagraves, so she decided to call Dr. Pearce.

"Hello?" he answered.

"Dr. Pearce, it's Daxia. How are you?"

"Daxia! It's been too long. I'm great, just great. Now, please stop calling me Dr. Pearce. I'm not your advisor anymore!"

"I'll try to undo the years of calling you Dr. Pearce... Alan," she said.

"Good, now, how the heck are you?"

She felt a rumble and noticed a massive semi-truck drive by, spewing black smoke into the blue sky, staining the American flag that hung from a dirty chrome exhaust stack.

"I'm fine. I'm actually in the states, in South Dakota. Seagraves called about something he found here. I wanted to thank you for giving him my information."

"That's wonderful, Daxia! He didn't tell me a lot about it, but it sounded like something you needed to see, maybe even what will seal the deal on your doctorate."

"I hope so," she said and turned away from the window. "How's Louise doing?"

"She's great, even better than me. You should talk to her yourself; she's right here!" Daxia recognized the chair squeak and knew he was in his office. There was a click, and she was on speakerphone.

"Daxia?" a woman said.

"Louise, hello! How are you?"

She could hear Louise's smile through the phone. "I'm wonderful. I received some good news this morning from the Climate Council."

Daxia knew Alan hated talking about the council but wanted to know. "I heard you did great in Matheran, so I'm going to guess it's a speaking opportunity?"

"It sure is, Daxia!"

Alan chimed in. "It's a *big* opportunity, too!"

"Now, Alan, don't be boastful," Louise urged.

"How big?" Daxia asked.

Louise cleared her throat. "I'll be the keynote speaker at the Global Climate Conference in Egypt."

"Louise! That's amazing!" Daxia said, thrilled.

Alan added, "And they're letting her whack job husband go, too!"

Daxia laughed. "Don't cause too much trouble," she joked.

"Oh, I plan on it," he said and laughed in return. "Daxia, you should come, too! It would be wonderful networking for a PhD candidate. You might even find a great post-doc opportunity."

Louise added, "Now, Alan, I'm sure she's busy, and it's short notice since the conference is next week. Daxia, you're welcome to, of course, but I understand if—"

"I'd love to," she said. "My father is doing better, well enough to take care of himself for a couple more weeks after South Dakota."

Alan clapped. "It's settled then!"

"Daxia, I'll send you all the details. And don't worry about the ticket or accommodations, those will be on us."

"You don't have to do that."

"We insist," Louise said.

"It's the least we can do for all your help on the impact research, Daxia," Alan added.

Daxia heard Seagraves huffing and coming up the stairs.

"I'm heading out soon, but real quick: do you have any updates on those three asteroids? I know a museum in Hill City, South Dakota, that could use some newer information."

"I sure do," Alan said. "We can talk about it in Giza. Louise secured me a spot at the conference, sort of."

"You're serious?"

Louise chimed in, "It's on the patio of the Grand Egyptian Museum, outside the conference."

Daxia laughed. "I guess you take what you can get."

Seagraves popped out from the door at the back of the gift shop. "That raptor claw is shipped off to Chicago, so let's get going! I can't wait to show you the skeleton."

Daxia signaled for him to wait a moment. "Alan, Louise, I'd love to hear more, but I've got to run."

"This research isn't going anywhere," Alan assured her.

"Goodbye!" Louise and Alan said in unison.

"See you next week!" Daxia said and pocketed her phone. She pulled her bag up over her shoulder. "Let's go!"

. . .

Seagraves struggled to keep the wheel straight as his small rusted-out car bounced up the narrow dirt driveway leading to the ranch.

Daxia looked out the window with groggy eyes and saw nothing but grassland dotted with a few farm buildings. "This is Belle Fourche?"

Seagraves shook his head. "You missed the town a while back, sleepyhead."

"Sorry," she said, "jetlag."

"I hate jetlag." He slowed the car to a stop next to a white Ford F–150 truck parked outside a classic white farmhouse with overgrown landscaping.

Someone was moving around inside. They got out of the car and walked up the stairs to the wraparound front porch.

She looked to Seagraves. "I don't look like I'm from here, so let's leave this conversation to you."

"Oh stop, people around here aren't that bad. Besides, you'll be the one studying the big discovery on his land. You better get acquainted," he said.

"Okay, here we go." She took a deep breath and knocked on the front door.

A Western caricature appeared in the doorway, complete with a wide-brimmed hat and cowboy boots. He looked to be in his mid-fifties, face hardened from exposure to the elements. His dirty jeans and a button-up shirt were pulled together by the biggest belt buckle she had ever seen.

Daxia and Seagraves exchanged a worried glance until the man started to speak. "You must be here to check out my fossil. I was on a trip to Cody, Wyoming last time you came poking around in my pasture."

Seagraves pointed to himself, "Yes, I didn't see anyone so went on back to the site you described."

"Well, nice to meet you properly this time. And oh boy, let me tell you, this is the best one we've ever found. We always find interesting stuff in the cow pastures after big rains, but this takes the cake," he said.

The rancher went to the closet, pulled out a beige jacket, and grabbed his truck keys. Daxia had been expecting a dull, and perhaps hostile farmer. This man appeared even more excited than her and didn't seem to notice or even care that she wasn't "from around these parts."

"Y'all better grab your stuff and come with me. The fields will be muddy after last night," he said and pointed to their car. "That little jalopy won't make it ten feet."

Seagraves looked at Alex's truck and gave a thumbs-up. "Yes, sir! By the way, I'm Seagraves, and this is Daxia. She's the expert. I'm just along for the ride."

"Oh, oh yes, I'm so sorry. I forgot to introduce myself! Name's Alex Bullock. My great, great granddaddy settled Belle Fourche. I've always loved it here, 'specially the fossils. Would have gone to college and become a paley-onto-logist, but can't escape family roots that strong, you know?"

Daxia smiled, charmed by the rancher's authenticity, "Pleasure to meet you, Mr. Bullock."

"Oh now, none of that. It's just Alex. It is a pleasure to meet you as well," he said as he shook their hands.

They all squeezed into the truck's cab, sharing its single bench seat as it bounced along the rutted dirt road on the ridge. It was slow-going in the mud, but the prairie view was hard to beat. Daxia had never seen such a flat expanse.

Alex turned to Daxia. "You know, they say water used to cover this entire area. Is that right?"

Daxia nodded. "Pretty close. From about eighty to sixty some million years ago, this area was near the coast. The sea was to the west a bit farther. The land would have been a dense and swampy forest. Like wetlands along the Gulf Coast," she explained.

"I tell ya, that is fascinatin' stuff. Just so many things for ponderin' in the history of this great planet." The rancher shook his head in amazement. "Okay, almost there. It's not safe to drive up yonder. We'd get stuck in a hole, so we'll have to get out and walk the rest of the way. Now, you be careful when you get out, Ms. Daxia and Mr. Seagraves. Don't want you to slip and fall on a cow pie!"

They laughed right along with him.

The three walked through the tall prairie grasses to the edge of the ridge overlooking the valley. He led them over the rim and down onto a small ledge about halfway to the bottom.

Alex pointed to the solid rock wall beside the ledge. "They tell me this here is the very tippy top of the Hell Creek Formation. So, I guess that means it's, what, sixty-some million years old? Anything you find here is that old, right?"

Daxia studied the wall. "Yes, that is about right, between sixty-five and sixty-six million years, depending on which geologist you ask." She pointed to a gray line between layers of rock. "See this line? That is the K-Pg boundary. It marks the end of the dinosaurs."

"And it is the dust that settled out of the air from a big ol' space rock, they tell me. Is that still what they say these days?" the rancher asked.

Daxia looked at the line in the rock and thought back to the museum's description. She kept it simple, "We don't have the whole story, yet."

Seagraves added, "It's all over the Earth, and a single asteroid couldn't have stirred up that much dust. Also, most of the dinosaurs were dying out before the impact, so it's a mystery."

Daxia turned to him and smiled. "You *did* learn something from Dr. Pearce and me."

He laughed. "Yes, I sure did."

She lifted her chin in mock authority and turned back to Alex. "So, I'd love to see what you found."

"Oh right! This way," he said and walked a little farther along the ledge. He pointed to a collection of dark lines on the wall. "There it is. Beautiful, ain't it?" he said as he adjusted his hat.

Daxia walked up to the wall. This was unlike anything she had ever seen. Its size stunned her. There was no doubt this was avian as she looked at the skeleton encased in stone. Its legs appeared frozen in mid-run. Its knees articulated to the rear, unlike a human's but just like the specimens in the Yixian Formation. Its short arms were outstretched haphazardly to the sides.

She pointed to the legs. "The bone structure is so similar to smaller specimens. There are differences above the legs, though. It is much taller, too. I'd say almost 250 centimeters."

"How tall is that?" asked Alex.

Seagraves did the metric conversion in his head. "About eight feet."

"Whew-wee!" the rancher said.

Daxia continued, "This one looks more upright and slenderer, and there doesn't seem to be a long tail like most of the specimens I've found. Although it looks like there may be a vestigial one here," she said, pointing to the lower end of its spine.

Seagraves ran his fingers along the fossilized indentations of the feathers. "Just incredible. There is no question, these are feathers. I mean, right? It's covered in them. Even on the legs."

"They are, and big feathers at that. It has to be a new species," Daxia said. She pulled out her phone and snapped a series of photos that the software would stitch together into a single large image.

Seagraves walked past them both to the lower left side of the fossilized skeleton. "What's this? I don't remember seeing it last time."

Alex went over to join him.

Daxia finished taking photos and went to see what they were checking out. The two men were examining four large rectangles in a vertical row. They looked like fossils: gray and smooth in the brown dirt.

"I didn't notice these in your picture, either," she said, pointing to the shapes.

Alex put his hands on his hips. "Hm, you're right. I reckon the rain a couple days ago must've washed some more away," he said.

Seagraves pulled out a small pickaxe and began to peck away at the rock at the top of the line. Several more bones were lined up above, extending farther over their heads.

"What do you make of this, Dax?" he asked and motioned toward the shapes.

"They look like the vertebrae of something much larger than that one," she said, pointing back to the feathered specimen. "Try going a little higher," she instructed.

He used his pick to remove material at the top but only found empty dirt.

Alex leaned against the wall while Seagraves worked. "Could be nothin'. This area has fossils all over it. We find little bits and pieces of critters all the time."

A rumbling sound came from the rock face above them. Daxia looked up to see a small landslide tumbling down the wall and leapt out of the way just in time.

"Phew, that was a close one! Son, you gotta be careful when you're pecking at rocks like that!" Alex said, dusting himself off.

"Need some help there?" Seagraves asked, offering his hand to Daxia, who had fallen to her knees and stayed there.

She felt as if she had seen a ghost.

Seagraves followed her gaze up the rock wall where the slide came from. He went pale.

Alex lifted his hat a little and wiped his forehead. "Well, would you look at that! That sucker's mouth is big enough to eat us!" He replaced his hat. "I don't reckon there's ever been a T. rex found on our ranch before!"

Daxia went to the massive skull. She placed her hand on the lower jaw, careful not to disturb it. "It is so well preserved."

Alex shrugged. "There have been about twelve rexes found round these parts."

She looked back at the feathered fossil. "It doesn't make any sense."

Alex continued. "They find a lot of T. rex nests, too. All in pretty good shape. Ain't that unusual too?"

She nodded. "Yes, it is. Not as unusual as this feathered one, though. The climate here would have been too hot for this animal. Look here," she said, pointing down to a jumble of fossilized leaves. "These are all ferns and palm trees."

Seagraves added, "It would have overheated in a few minutes outside. Maybe it had a way to cool itself, like panting?"

"It must have," Daxia agreed. "I need to ask Dr. Pearce what this might mean." She put her hands on her hips and stared at the eight-foot-tall, feathered, fossilized skeleton in the rock. "Why have we never seen your kind before? How did you get here in Belle Fourche when your smaller relatives are in Asia?"

Alex grabbed his belt and hiked up his pants. "What do you reckon got 'em?"

"Got them?" Daxia asked.

"What killt 'em?"

She pointed back to the plant fossils again. "This type of fossil concretion occurs during a disaster. This could have been a landslide, or maybe a flood. Even a tsunami or a big storm, it's impossible to say."

Seagraves brushed some dirt away from the center of the skeleton. "Look at this," he said, pointing to a compact bundle of bones between the arms. "Is that what I think it is?"

Daxia could only stare in disbelief.

# CHAPTER 13
# APOLLO

Kaia rubbed her eyes. It had been almost half an hour since they left the shuttle behind. She glanced over to Captain Ra, who was still adjusting the parameters of his algorithm. The ring of starlight changed thickness with each data point he entered. Captain Apep's stuffed affi sat above her console, right where he'd left it before boarding the constructor, and no one on the crew had balked when she kept it for herself. On her viewscreen were a few short lines of glyphs, all the progress she'd made on the poem she'd started after they found the Kemites.

A small-brained affi witnessing the eruption under Puna would know something was wrong, Kaia thought, but could not have imagined it was a fateful event for its species. The affi was not the main subject of her studies on Nu, but she still understood quite a bit about them. They lived in burrows underground, coming out to forage for food on the forest floor. She had observed them sniff the air outside at the wildlife refuge. Smell was their primary sense. They were also skittish, running away to their home at the slightest hint of danger.

She paused and looked up at the symbols arranged in nine groups. *How should this end?* She re-read the last couplet she wrote:

*We left your world in ruins and fled to the stars.*
    *Little affi, you taught me the planet was now yours, not ours.*

She leaned forward and drew a new set of symbols, then leaned back and looked at the completed tenth and, she felt, final couplet:

*You came into your own, growing up, too,*
    *So now, little affi, it is time for Me to teach You.*

"Kaia, look!" Captain Ra's voice broke her contemplation. The *Meridian* screeched to a halt, throwing all of them into their consoles. She closed the poem and looked through her viewscreen. The ring of starlight snapped away. A small point of light was heading straight for them.

"Captain, what is that?" she asked as she ran over to the helm.

"The sensors picked up an obstacle and did a full stop on the lightdrive." He shook his head. "But now I don't see anything. Professor Thoth, anything from the sensors?"

Kaia saw him go pale. "Thoth, what is it?"

He looked up. "It's," he swung his gaze over to Enki. "It's the geology shuttle, coming straight at us!"

"Captain Ra, how long has it been on Nu?" Kaia demanded to know.

He looked at the time dilation calculation. "Only about four thousand five hundred cycles."

"Was there a malfunction?" she asked. "Pakhet, access its engineering systems. Check for anything unusual."

"On it," Pakhet replied and got busy.

The shuttle grew larger in the viewscreen as it approached. It came to a full stop just off the front of the *Meridian*.

"Whoa!" Pakhet yelled.

"I have something too!" Professor Thoth added.

"What?" Kaia rushed over to the engineering station.

Pakhet pointed to the viewscreen. "Something messed with its antenna. I'm seeing an emergency autopilot sequence was activated. The system thought the shuttle was in danger."

"Thank you, Pakhet, see what else you can find," Kaia said and jogged over to the Professor Thoth. "Enki, follow me!"

Thoth pointed at a graph on his viewscreen. "This shows the electromagnetic spectrum around Nu was flush with signals."

"Do they contain patterns?" Enki asked.

"They do, very complex ones. Wait, I think it is video."

Kaia shook her head. "The Kemites may be advancing much faster than anticipated." *Which also means they may have discovered kohl and are exploiting its energy to destroy Nu at this very moment,* she worried.

Captain Ra shouted from the helm, "Anything concerning? I don't want us to land in the middle of their version of a great war!"

Kaia yelled back, "We're still analyzing the data." She pointed to Thoth. "Work on decoding their radio signals, send the video recordings to the mission console, and send Enki any data that could give a clue as to the level of kohl pollution in the atmosphere."

"Yes, Kaia," he said.


The videos appeared on Kaia's viewscreen, but it was hard to tell what was happening from the recording's vantage point on Iah. She could only see portions of Nu at a time, and sometimes in the day or night depending on the orbital position. Her eyes darted around the screen, searching for clues to what was happening, but it was hard to decipher the flashing images.

Enki pointed to the glyphpad. "The system should be able to lock onto the outlines of landmasses and create a stable perspective."

"Good idea, thank you," she said.

He nodded and returned to organizing the atmospheric data at the geology console.

Kaia tapped the glyphpad, trying to remember the command. It came to her, and she drew two commands at a time. The ornate glowing trails reminded her of vines as they faded away. *That command is almost beautiful,* she thought.

The projection began to move faster than her eyes could perceive, but the occasional frame dropped below the projection into one of the two new spots her command had identified as the focus. She chose the Kemite city of Saqqara as the center point, but the city itself was too small to be visible from the surface of Iah with the shuttle's limited sensors. She looked at the most recent frames from each scene as the system extracted them from the main video. It was still hard to believe this was the same planet that she had called home. To her relief, everything still looked alive. The Jacana damage had not been repeated, yet. *The only traces of us are lava beds and ancient, eroded craters that the Kemites won't notice,* she thought.

The system beeped when it finished compiling the still frames into new videos. One new video file showed Nu during the day, while the other showed it at night. "Enki, Thoth, how is your data looking?" Kaia asked. She moved both new video files up to the main viewscreen.

Thoth answered first, "There are a lot of electromagnetic signals originating from the ground and a few more from space."

"Are they ours?" she asked, hoping another cityship had not returned.

"No, these are not Jacana. The patterns are different," he said. "I'm going to see if I can decode them. Give me a few minutes."

She walked over to Enki before playing the videos from Thoth. "Any sign of atmospheric change?"

Enki took a deep breath. "Yes. It is not good." He spread his fingers on the glyphpad to enlarge the gas composition chart. "Here are all the main atmospheric gases over the last few thousand cycles," he said, pointing to each smooth curve on the chart. He zoomed in farther at the right end of the graph, where two lines spiked upward. He sighed. "And here are just the most recent two hundred cycles."

Kaia lowered her head and closed her eyes before speaking. She looked back up. "The Kemites have discovered kohl."

Enki nodded. "Yes, they have. They are exploiting it faster than we did. At this rate, I estimate they have used sixty percent of the total kohl in only two hundred cycles."

"Are you sure?" she asked.

"I am certain. They are burning more each cycle, according to these readings," he said, examining the steep red line that angled upward on the chart.

"This is our fault," Kaia said through gritted teeth. Anger was her only response. Councilor Horus and Professor Thoth gave the Kemites knowledge that led to an ambition to consume kohl sooner and faster than they would have on their own.

Enki cleared his throat and pointed to the videos waiting at the mission console. "Why don't we check those out?"

Kaia took a deep breath.

Light bathed Nu's surface.

"I think we both know what to expect," she said when Enki joined her.

They could not see very much; the surface appeared static and unchanging. The Kemites did not seem to be doing any significant engineering of the surface itself. Kaia swirled her finger on the glyphpad to speed up the video playback, in the hopes they could see changes if time was more compressed.

The images flashed by, but it was still impossible to spot anything of consequence. It still appeared unchanged, still green, and alive. She thought that perhaps the Kemites had figured out how to use kohl without destroying Nu, despite what the atmospheric data showed.

Enki leaned closer to the projection. "Wait, slow it back down," he said. "There, look at the landmass in the northern hemisphere with an odd peninsula extending from its southern coast toward Saqqara's continent below."

Kaia slowed the video down and saw what Enki was pointing to in the northern section. "Those are forests disappearing."

"And fast," Enki added.

They watched as geometric green patchwork replaced the dense forests across the whole northern continent.

"Agriculture. They're cutting down the forests to grow food," Kaia said. "Just like the early Jacana did."

Enki gestured to the top of the viewscreen. "And look at the ice caps. They are contracting. There can be no doubt about it. Nu is in the early stages of a climatic disaster. The Kemites are following the same path as us," he lamented. Gray splotches spread over the green land around them like a flood. "Those must be Kemite cities expanding."

"I know how we can find out for sure." Kaia swiped the video away. A second video of the same hemisphere appeared, and she scrubbed through it until she saw artificial light.

It was hard to see in the video from the shuttle, but she could just make out the fires from the few Kemite cities below. "It captured this frame just a few cycles after we left."

She knew that Saqqara was not the only city, but there were more than they expected. Small communities dotted the entire region northeast of Saqqara. The light from the cooking fires of each household combined to create a glow that the shuttle could see. She sped up the video as Enki leaned over to watch the glowing masses radiate outward.

"They are multiplying fast," he noted.

"Yes," Kaia said and held her breath. The orange glows of the cities flashed to white. "Electric power. This is the point that their cities are lit by artificial light," Kaia murmured. "There is no need for fire when you discover the electron."

A few seconds later, the white lights spread to overtake the surrounding darkness. Arms of light branched out, their glowing tendrils connecting one hub to another.

"And they must be linked by roadways," said Enki. "Moving goods, and themselves, all over the land."

Kaia marveled at how soon the streams of light flowing between each city appeared.

They watched in silence as the white lights continued to spread all over the surface, touching and connecting every landmass. The Kemites dominated Nu faster than she could have dreamed.

Something odd flashed on the screen. All she could see was white, then what looked like a distorted reflection of the camera and Iah's horizon. Kaia swirled backwards on the glyphpad to rewind the video and drew a command that played it back in real time.

She and Enki jumped back from the viewscreen.

A habsew glove took up most of the frame, obscuring the surface of Nu below. The glove disappeared, and then the camera shook. Nu floated out of the frame and the shaking stopped. The shuttle's silver plating rotated into view, but it was upside down. A large, insulated wire ran from the bottom of the frame into a hole in the body panel.

"Someone tore the camera off," she said. "Someone from the *Montu* must have come back to mess it up!"

The view rotated back to blackness and then an odd, rounded reflection of the camera. She could make out the circular edges of the camera's lens and the cable that led back to the shuttle behind it.

Two thick white lines dominated both sides of the image and converged on the rounded reflection of the camera in the middle.

"Those are the arms!" Kaia said. "And there is the helmet!"

Enki squinted. "It looks like a crude habsew. That is not from the *Montu* or any other cityship. It does not even look Jacana."

Kaia yelled to Professor Thoth, "Get over here, Professor!"

He jogged over just as she noticed something. "Look at the symbols on it." She pointed to a small patch on its shoulder. A small blue rectangle filled one corner of the patch, dotted with white stars. Red and white stripes covered the rest of the patch. "I think we're looking at a Kemite," she said, noticing another symbol on the opposite shoulder. It was a blue circle with strange, rounded symbols on it. "They went from cooking with crude fires to electric power to space travel in just a few hundred cycles."

"Impossible," Thoth countered. "It took Jacana society thousands more cycles to come this far."

Just as Kaia spoke, the distorted reflection of the shuttle disappeared up into the habsew's helmet. "The helmet visor is opening," she observed. Their eyes grew wide as the confused face of a Kemite replaced the camera's reflection. "It looks like it's saying something! Professor Thoth, activate the babel on this video!"

He drew a square on the glyphpad with one arrow going in and another arrow coming out. Mirik exclaimed. "The audio analysis completed faster than I thought. It said there was a match in the babel data, which seems impossible."

"That's a mystery for another day," Kaia said. "Right now we need to know what's on this recording."

"Yes, I just need to sync it with the video," he replied, drawing on the glyphpad. "There, done."

Captain Ra, Pakhet, and Dr. Khnum all stood behind them in disbelief as the figure *spoke*.

"Houston, confirming contact on December 13, 1972."

"Roger that, Apollo 17. What did you find?

"It looks like a camera of some sort," said a voice from the habsew.

"Understood. Does it look Soviet?" asked Houston.

"No, but it is what we thought it would be, based on that old book the Nazis used to make the V2 rocket. It looks like it has been here for a long time," the voice said as a hand brushed white dust off the shiny exterior. "The ship back at 51 is black, right?"

"Affirmative, Apollo."

"This one is silver. It's like they tried to hide it on the moon."

"Well," the man on his comm said. "It is just where Big Bird said it would be. Let's bring it home."

"Roger that, Houston. The crew is working on attaching boosters to it for a return to Earth."

The shaky video revealed the Kemite was examining the shuttle from every angle.

"Houston, something is happening," the Kemite paused, startled. "Oh my God. It's powering up. The landing gear is retracting!" He dropped the camera to the ground.

The Kemite ran past the shuttle in slow motion. He waved to the two others. They joined him and bounced toward an odd four-wheeled vehicle. The camera shook as the ground fell away. They watched the suited figures grow smaller and smaller as the shuttle ascended.

"That was a Kemite," Kaia stated with confidence.

"His name appeared to be Roger, and he was speaking to someone named Houston," Enki said.

Captain Ra tilted his head. "Odd names."

Kaia shrugged. "Ours would sound odd to them, too, I imagine." She scrubbed backward in the video to see the face of the Kemite in the helmet. She looked at it for a moment then to the captain. "We need to head straight to Nu. And given the Kemites have achieved spaceflight, we need to be *very* careful."

She turned to Captain Ra. "Get us back."

"We aren't far, but I can't do it as fast as we might like. We shouldn't dilate time any more than necessary," he said.

"How much time will pass on Nu as we return?"

Ra estimated it in his head. "I'd say sixty, maybe seventy cycles."

Enki raised his hand. "That should put our arrival in the 2030s on their calendar."

Kaia whirled around. "How do you know that?"

Enki shrugged. "The Kemite said 1972, so some event must have reset their calendar much like the Dawn Project reset ours."

"Good catch. That may be useful. Thank you, Enki—"

"That wasn't all I caught," he interrupted her with a look of concern, which Kaia knew was rare for Enki.

"What is it?"

Enki paused; she could see he was afraid to say it.

"Go on."

"The Kemite mentioned a book." He glanced at Professor Thoth.

"Are you suggesting they still have the book?"

"It is only an observation, a troubling one, though, yes."

Kaia turned back to Captain Ra. "Get us back there now!"

"I'll adjust the destination to drop us off on the dark side of Iah. No need to come straight to their front door."

Kaia braced herself on the console, looking into the male Kemite's eyes. "Have you already destroyed Nu again with our help?"

The lightdrive whirred to life, shaking the *Meridian* as the stars in front of them compressed into a circle of light.

# CHAPTER 14
# KEYNOTE

## GRAND EGYPTIAN MUSEUM, GIZA - 2034 CE

Louise stood off to the right side of the stage, smoothing out her blouse while she waited for her cue. The auditorium was packed. Every seat was full, and people were even standing along the walls. She spotted Alan and Daxia waiting on the other side of the stage. *You've got this, Louise,* she could imagine Alan saying. Many of the world's leading scientists, economists, historians, and artists had traveled to Egypt for this conference. Earth's climate challenges would need the best and brightest to take humanity through the impending crisis, and many of them were in this very room.

A man approached the podium in the front of the room. "Distinguished ladies and gentlemen, welcome to Giza and the Climate 2034 Summit. It is my pleasure to introduce the United Nations Climate Council, Relocation Committee chair, Dr. Louise Pearce."

She took the stage. Everyone clapped as she walked into the spotlight.

"Thank you, thank you all so much," she said as she waved to the crowd. "I'm going to tell you now; I plan to keep this brief. I do not want to preach to the choir and would rather the choir broadcast our message to the world instead of huddling together in this echo chamber. We all know why we're here."

She stepped out from behind the podium. "We are experiencing another record-breaking year on every climate metric we measure. Earth is hotter, deserts are expanding, sea levels are rising, and ice cover is at an all-time low. Temperatures are fluctuating far outside norms. Just yesterday, it reached 75 degrees Fahrenheit at the South Pole, while Orlando, Florida in the United States fell below freezing in the wake of our first hypercane, Levi. A storm so massive it sucked the energy out of the entire Atlantic basin, from the edge of Tennessee to right here, in Giza. It decimated half of Florida and several other states. Miami and Jacksonville are gone. Savannah, Georgia, Charleston, South Carolina, Wilmington, North Carolina, and Norfolk, Virginia are no more. These areas will never recover. Natural features that could have protected us from future storms are lost as well. Fifty-foot-high waves eroded barrier islands from Florida to the Outer Banks in North Carolina. Now, let us take a moment to remember the lives lost, all 26,792 and counting.

A quiet hush fell over the auditorium. Louise swore she could feel a collective consciousness in the room as the horrific images of last week filled everyone's thoughts.

"Thank you," she said and looked up. "We must all promise to do more and to be better. Lives are counting on it. Humanity is being squeezed into ever fewer stable areas. Outbreaks of cultural violence, such as the recent one in Pune, India, where refugees are pouring in from all over Southeast Asia. Despite this, the world continues to consume fossil fuels at an ever-increasing pace. Our vehicles continue to use oil and gas. Our power plants continue to burn coal. We have the technology to do better. It is within our grasp to begin reversing these alarming trends. Trends that, if we don't stop them, will force us to change our lives in unprecedented ways. Now, I don't mean to condemn," she paused, "well, okay I do."

She smirked, and the audience laughed. "But you will notice that this year, we still do not have any world political leaders in attendance. No one came to listen to what we have learned in the past year."

Many in the crowd grumbled in disappointment. She went on to name names. Presidents, Prime Ministers, Party leaders, all complicit in doing nothing.

"The Paris Climate Accord, dissolved. Even worse, Climategate 2.0 started by the now confirmed-to-be-a-deepfake 'leaked' video of myself saying that: *There is no such thing as climate refugees'* when we all know that is not true. I'd like to point out that the video, paid for through a series of shell corporations set up by an American oil company, was entered into evidence by lawyers for refugees from the Maldives after their homes sank beneath the waves. Politicians, greedy corporations, and more sinister, shadowy forces are vying for our attention, and worse, vying for the facts. Who are people supposed to believe in these unprecedented times?"

Louise walked to the side of the stage. "But, this year, as I'm sure you've seen if you went outside this morning, something of a different, unprecedented variety has happened." She reached into her blazer pocket and pulled out a single-button remote control.

A staff member removed the podium from the stage. She held up the remote and pressed the button. The curtains behind the stage parted, and everyone in the crowd shielded their eyes from the bright light entering the auditorium. She spread her arms toward the widening view of the outside. "Let them ignore us now."

Shocked gasps rose from the audience.

The face of the Great Sphinx seemed to be looking into the room from across Al Ahram Street. A thin layer of white coated its striped head covering. The palm trees drooped under the weight of accumulating white powder. Behind it, in the distance, bright sunshine glinted off the icy slopes of the pyramids of Khufu, Khafre, and Menkaure.

When Louise turned back to them, a hush fell over the audience. "It is snowing. In Cairo."

Some attendees stood on their chairs for a better view.

Louise went on, "We know the Egyptians built the pyramids with a white limestone covering. This view may be the first time in thousands of years anyone has seen them the way the ancient Egyptians intended them to be seen. All because of an exceptional weather event, a snowstorm in Egypt, due to a hypercane on the other side of the ocean."

The excited chatter turned to a dull roar, and Louise had to raise her voice. "Next year, every leader in the world will want to hear what we have to say!"

The room erupted in applause, and she took a bow. "Thank you all very much for coming," she said, and then exited stage left as the crowd continued their standing ovation.

Alan swelled with pride and wrapped Louise in a big hug as the crowd filed past them, exiting the room.

"Great job, honey!" he said, squeezing her. He hadn't been this excited for her since the Climate Council first invited her to join the Relocation Committee.

Daxia adjusted her shoulder bag and said, "Yes, it was awesome. And, snow, in Egypt, it's wild!"

Louise let go of Alan. "Thank you, thank you both," she said. "Now, Alan, you'd better get set up while everyone is out there! And Daxia, if you think the snow is surprising, you should see Alan's poster."

He peeked into the hallway and saw people milling about in small groups. Everyone seemed to be riding on the high of Louise's presentation, too, as they waved their hands toward the museum's atrium windows. He picked up the folded poster board he had printed up before her keynote. "I'm sure the Council won't mind if I'm in the hallway instead of freezing my buns off on the patio, right?"

Louise laughed. "I'm guessing they would prefer you outside freezing, under the circumstances I think you can act like you got it mixed up." She shooed him and Daxia out the door. One attendee stopped to give her a high five on his way to the atrium.

Alan scoped out an empty area right next to the stairs leading down to the atrium. "That spot looks good," he said.

Louise agreed "It's perfect."

He set the poster down on the floor, now thankful he selected the wrong size and had the board printed almost as tall as himself. He held the middle steady and opened each side panel until it stood on its own.

Daxia read the title across the top out loud: "Perfect for Us: The post-Cretaceous Extinction Climate." She laughed and turned to Alan. "You're just egging the Council on with those first three words."

Louise rolled her eyes. "That's what I told him. I tore his first version off, but then he made it even more antagonistic."

"It's not like I need their funding anymore thanks to the Extraterrestrialists!" He smiled a mischievous smile. "Oh, Daxia, you have to see the recording, too," he said, guiding her to the black-and-white video loop of his final impact experiment.

She squinted as she studied the image then turned to him, laughing. "Is that the award from your original Climate Council grant?"

"It is!" He slapped his knee and chuckled. "*That* shape is what leaves a double-ringed crater."

"No, that can't be right," Daxia quipped. "I mean, the obvious problem is there are no octahedral asteroids."

He nodded to the side. "Though, there may be a natural process in space that creates octahedral crystals. We know volcanic basalts can form into hexagonal columns as they cool."

"I suppose," she said.

He saw her turn away to scan the crowd. Everyone was heading towards them, and he grinned, sure this would be his moment to get at least a few people to listen to his findings.

Alan spread his arms and began to say, "Thank you for—." Everyone left a wide berth around his poster as they passed, heading for the stairs down to the atrium. One man stopped and glanced at his poster. Alan took a step toward him, but the man sidled over to Louise and raised his hand to wave.

"Great job, Dr. Pearce!" he said, then shot Alan a derisive glance.

Louise offered a polite smile as she said, "Thank you."

The man gave the poster a once-over again and headed down the stairs.

Alan whined, "I don't think anyone is going to stop. They know who I am and don't want to read work funded by the 'ancient alien nutjobs.' In fact, maybe you two shouldn't be standing with me. Your reputations might suffer."

Louise slapped his shoulder. "Oh stop." She nodded toward Daxia. "I want to hear the other issues you see in Alan's crazy hypothesis."

"Me too," he said and pivoted back to Daxia, but she wasn't facing the poster anymore. Her eyes seemed glassy, staring off into the distance. He followed her gaze and saw the three-story statue of Ramses II at the center of the atrium lit by the afternoon sun streaming in through the floor-to-ceiling. They framed the Giza necropolis's three pyramids.

*The windows*, he noticed. They were shaped like interlocking pyramids, clear ones pointing up, tinted ones pointing down. He took a step forward and stood next to Daxia.

Alan blinked, hard. "Octahedrons," he said.

"Yes," Daxia replied, eyes fixated outside.

The clear upper half of the three largest windows perfectly framed each of the three pyramids. The shaded lower half mirrored the top's size but pointed at the ground.

His head spun back to the poster board. "It can't be."

Louise crept forward. "What are you two looking at?"

He grabbed Louise's hand and pulled her back to the poster. "Look, the octahedral asteroid, and then,"—he pointed at the window—"out there." He scrutinized her face as she watched the octahedron smashing into the Earth over and over, then back to the windows. His pulse quickened when her eyes widened.

*She sees it too.*

Louise closed her eyes for a moment then cocked an eyebrow. "Alan, be reasonable."

Daxia took a step backwards toward the poster, dragging her feet and not looking away from the window. She stopped and turned to Alan, then gawked at the poster.

Alan raised his hand and covered the bottom half of the octahedron diagram. *A pyramid.* His eyes moved on to the slow-motion video loop of his award impacting the dirt at high speed. The leading tip pierced the ground, and a rush of dirt flew up, funneled outward by the sloping sides. He leaned closer and tapped the electronic paper to pause the video right at the midpoint of the impact. The widest part of the octahedron was level with the ground, and he understood right away. *Three craters, three asteroids.* He looked back outside. *Three pyramids.* Alan squeezed his eyes shut and rubbed his temples.

"This is huge!" he yelled. "There's something here, there has to be!"

"No," Louise said in rapid retort.

Daxia held her finger up to the electronic paper video. "That's not all," she said and swirled counterclockwise to rewind the loop, then stopped after just a few frames.

She dragged her finger to the words on the crystal and tapped twice to enlarge them.

Alan froze. The Climate Council's inscription stared back at him, carved into the shiny iridium surface of his award.

"For our Future," he whispered.

He covered his mouth then wiped his forehead. "For our Future!" he yelled. The etching was more than an inspirational phrase, he knew it. "It was a message. Someone knows what happened!"

Louise shook her head. "This is crazy, Alan. Have those ancient alien Extraterrestrialists made you go mad?"

He looked back outside at the three pyramids out the window.

*Three octahedral asteroids.*

*Three impacts, and the world was reborn.*

*Three pyramids.*

"Someone has known what happened for thousands of years!" he yelled. "Someone told the ancient Egyptians, Louise!"

"Impossible," she said. "That's impossible."

"Look at them!" he said, pointing wildly out the windows. "A pyramid looks like a half-buried octahedron!"

Louise looked out the window at the three gleaming pyramids standing against a deep blue sky, then back to the poster board again. "There has to be another explanation, Alan."

He saw that flicker on her face despite what she said. She'd spoken before the thought fully formed in her mind. The knee-jerk reaction of an anthropologist throwing out a wild theory came before the measured response that he now saw. He could tell by the look on her face that she was beginning to understand what he was raving about.

Alan held up three fingers. "There were three impacts of three octahedral asteroids that reset a hot climate and made way for the stable, cooler world we have today."

Daxia stared at his fingers then looked up at him.

He heard the skepticism fall away in Louise's voice as she said, "The ancient Egyptians believed the pyramid shape held the power to help resurrect the dead."

Alan turned back to the view of the pyramids. "But, how? How could they have known?" he asked but saw Louise turned the other way, looking down the stairs. There was some kind of commotion. People were yelling in several languages.

Everyone was running toward the wall of windows.

He turned to Daxia but saw she too was now staring out the windows again, pale as a ghost.

"Daxia?" No response. He tapped Louise on the shoulder, "What is going on?"

Louise blinked. "Oh my stars, Alan. Look at the sky!"

# CHAPTER 15
# ADVANCED

## MERIDIAN - AD CYCLE 66,196,238

Captain Ra eased his hands up on the glyphpad. "We're just about there, everyone."

On the viewscreen, the compressed starlight began to stretch back to the center of the blackness. They all braced as the *Meridian* shuddered to a stop and the bridge went dark. The ship sat in space on the dark side of Iah as Nu loomed in the distance.

"What happened?" Kaia asked, looking around to make sure everyone was okay. The lights flickered back on.

Ra looked around the bridge, then to Pakhet. "Everything nominal?"

She nodded. "Lightdrive looks fine."

"Professor Thoth, is anything nearby?"

Thoth shook his head. "All clear."

Enki scrutinized the viewscreen. "From here, Nu looks the same as when we left it."

Kaia breathed a sigh of relief. "Yes, still plenty of green."

Captain Ra asked, "Professor, are there any traces of radioactivity in the atmosphere?"

"One moment," he said and examined a graph on his screen.

Kaia braced herself for the worst answer. That would be even worse than kohl, she knew. When the answer came, it left her chilled.

"There are traces of radioactivity everywhere. It is likely due to atomic weapons," Professor Thoth confirmed.

"How bad is it?" she asked, concern edging her voice.

She watched Thoth through his viewscreen as he examined a line graph of radioactivity.

He finally replied, "Not dangerous. Most detonations appear to be over eighty-five cycles old. Only two seem to have been weapons deployed above ground in populated areas. Most others were underground or underwater."

"Tests," Captain Ra said. "They discovered the power of the atom but have maintained some level of peace." He crossed his arms, impressed.

Pakhet stepped toward the helm. "What about spaceflight? Any vessels we should be worried about before we enter orbit?" Thoth shook his head. "Nothing in space appears weaponized. There are small outposts and many satellites, and one captured asteroid that they appear to be mining. There is nothing dangerous except a substantial number of derelict satellites and other debris we will need to avoid."

The *Meridian* maneuvered from behind the dark side of Iah, and Nu came into full view. Darkness covered half the planet as the light of a new day made its way across the surface. The glow of Kemite cities was visible in the nighttime half. The Kemites had indeed conquered Nu, and done so very fast by Jacana standards.

Kaia let out another sigh of relief. Nu still looked more alive than it had been when the Jacana had left it. "Enki, how is the atmosphere?"

He went to the geology station and pulled up readings from the sensors. "This is not good. They appear to be relying on kohl even more than when the shuttle left Iah. They will run out in a couple of hundred cycles, or less at this rate."

Kaia joined him at the workstation and drew a new command on the glyphpad. "Their climate is also already being affected. It is much warmer at the poles. The oceans appear to be a little higher, too. They are likely in the early stages of climate change. Judging by that storm system in the north, I'd say they are experiencing larger and more frequent storms, and extreme temperature swings."

Enki added, "The desert surface area has also increased by twelve percent since the shuttle instrument's last readings. They are less than one hundred cycles away from an irreversible sixth mass extinction."

Kaia shook her head. "They might be two hundred more cycles away from experiencing the absolute worst of it. But by then, they will need habsews to go outside as we did."

"They don't yet, though," Captain Ra said with a glimmer of hope in his voice. "There is still time."

Kaia rolled her shoulders back. "You're right. We need to make contact."

Enki and Thoth were already in the shuttle when Kaia arrived after changing into a fresh habsew in case Nu's air was no longer breathable. She marched right up to Professor Thoth. "You stay with us and let us do the talking. Do not speak unless we tell you to do so. Is that understood?"

He nodded.

"Good," she said, the authority clear in her voice. She dashed to the pilot's chair and buckled in around her suit. Enki sat next to her.

"I'll be the navigator. Let's find an appropriate spot to land this time." He zoomed the shuttle's display into Saqqara. "The region looks different to what it did during our last encounter." He circled a smooth white shape rising from the ground.

Kaia noticed it, too. "Thoth, you were right. They built a crystal in the desert, with tombs surrounding it. I doubt it resurrected any Kemites buried nearby as they planned," she said.

Thoth looked up in interest. "There is only one crystal?"

"Wait a moment," Enki said as he zoomed out and panned the map north. He turned to face the cargo bay. "How did you know?"

Thoth smiled when he saw what Enki had found.

Three gleaming white shapes rose out of the plain. A massive city stretched to the east of them.

"Councilor Horus told them there were three crystals. I assumed that they would build three, but I never dreamed they would build them with such precision," he said.

The sight shocked Kaia. "Not only the shape, but the color. They gleam just like the real ones did. How did they do that?"

Thoth shrugged. "I don't know."

Her mind lurched when she saw the largest crystal. A name escaped her lips. "Apep," she whispered.

"Wait," Enki said, "everything around them is turning white. The ground should be sandy, this is a desert." He turned on the heat overlay and pointed to a bright spot on the edge of the city. "There is a high density of Kemites in this structure near the crystals."

Kaia leaned in for a closer look. "You're right. The heat signatures show an arrangement of rows. Perhaps it is a large meeting of some sort."

Enki tapped the three crystals on the map. "This is where we need to go."

# CHAPTER 16
# SECOND CONTACT

## GRAND EGYPTIAN MUSEUM – 2035 CE

Alan followed where Louise's finger was pointing, through the atrium's wall of windows out to the three great pyramids in the distance. The snow covering made them glitter like crystals against the clearing blue sky.

"They're beautiful," he said.

Louise grabbed his chin and pointed his face to the right spot. "Not the pyramids, Alan. Over there, in the sky!"

Now, he saw it too. A sleek, black, saucer-shaped craft moved toward the pyramids. The dark shape darted unnaturally, as if scanning the area. It then slowed to a stop in the open space between the Great Pyramid of Khufu and Khafre's smaller one. Goosebumps swarmed over his arms and the hair on his neck stood on end.

"Impossible," he managed to utter.

A hush fell over the crowd.

Louise lowered her hand from her mouth. "Alan, Daxia, you're seeing this, right?" she asked and began to head down the stairs to get closer to the window.

Daxia followed as if drawn by the same magnetic force. "Yes…"

Alan felt his mind in a tug-of-war between the incomprehensible image outside and his determination to force the wild ideas flying around his brain to coalesce into something sensible.

The craft began to move again, this time coming straight for the building. His mind raced, zooming past all logic and rationality. It was all too much, too perfect a connection to let his usual skepticism run rampant. He bolted down the stairs and ran toward Louise and Daxia, pushing people out of his way.

"Kaia, a large group of Kemites is gathering at the front of the stone and glass structure. They appear to be gathering in response to our arrival," Enki said, circling a mass of dots on the map.

Thoth stood between the two cockpit chairs, marveling at how far this society had come. Skytowers, just a little shorter than the Jacana's, reached for the sky in the city not far from the crystals. He clicked his tongue. "I'm sure a shuttle landing is quite a sight for them."

Kaia put her gloved hands on the controls and looked out the shuttle's cockpit window. "We'll go to them."

She piloted the sleek shuttle between the two largest crystal monuments and descended toward open ground in front of the building.

"Do you think they know who we are?" she asked as she turned to Thoth.

He shook his head as he put a broad striped hood over it. "No, the monuments look weathered. I suspect they have forgotten about us, the deities that inspired them."

Kaia and Enki looked at each other and rolled their eyes. She turned back to him and jabbed, "How does it feel to be a forsaken god?"

Alan, Louise, and Daxia watched the craft hover above the open plaza in front of the museum for a moment. The crowd behind them murmured when the craft descended, and three pieces of landing gear began to lower from its bottom. A security guard in a yellow uniform stood in front of the door, shouting into the radio transmitter attached to his shoulder.

Alan couldn't believe his eyes. He thought back to all the conversations with the Order of Extraterrestrialists. So many crazy ideas, he remembered thinking as he thanked them for the funds. He'd read countless papers from pseudoscientists and lay historians about the real purpose of the pyramids. He always assumed they were wrong but couldn't say that and still receive his funding. Now, he knew.

The pyramids weren't power plants. They weren't spaceship landing pads. They were monuments, but not the kind archaeologists and anthropologists believed them to be. He foresaw a reckoning on the horizon between the pseudoscientists and the real ones. The image before him proved them both right, and both wrong, at the same time.

He chuckled at the insanity of it all as he watched a flying saucer land in front of the pyramids. It was all too much. Too much for him, and too much for the world, he knew. He decided to set every bit of nagging skepticism aside in that moment and rushed past the security guard and out the door.


Kaia looked straight at the Kemite faces on the viewscreen. No one was running away. "They're quite a brave species," she noted.

Thoth agreed. "Their eyes have the same curiosity I saw thousands of cycles earlier. Remarkable."

Enki reached up for the glyphpad and zoomed in on a few of the faces. "There is one difference, though," he said.

"I'm sure there are many differences, but which one do you mean?"

"The Kemites in this location had light brown skin, while the ones far to the north had pale white skin." He examined the faces on the screen. "Here we have many skin tones, facial structures, and differences in stature. The single group must have branched into different species."

Kaia shook her head. "That's not what happened, Enki. Think about our own species. Our ancestors moved around to different places on

Nu and adapted to our surroundings in superficial ways, like our schemochromes changing color to suit the environment."

He tilted his head to the side. "So how did so many colors end up in the same place?"

"They traveled, Enki. Remember? They've advanced enough to have spaceflight, maybe even shuttles like ours."

Thoth added, "I'm sure they don't call themselves Kemites anymore, at least not all of them," he said, nodding to the wide variety of creatures behind the glass.

Enki nodded. Kaia could see he understood, but still harbored a healthy skepticism. She hoped Enki could join her when making contact with them, but now she was worried he might say something to offend them by accident. Maybe Thoth was more suited to the role— plus, he had already worked with their ancestors.

She turned to Thoth. "Why don't you come outside with me?" Then to Enki, "While you keep the shuttle ready to go in case things don't go as planned."

"Do you have a plan?" Enki asked.

She looked back at the faces. "We plan to help them understand what they are doing to Nu and to help them stop."

Enki looked at her, deadpan. "I prefer plans to have more detail than that, but this is your mission, Kaia."

"Thank you," she said and got up from the pilot's seat. "Seriously, though, keep the shuttle ready to leave on a moment's notice."

"Wait, look!" Enki yelled.

She swirled around and saw a single Kemite burst through the door and run toward the shuttle. "Is he armed?"

Enki shook his head. "I am not detecting any weapons known to our systems."

Kaia wondered what kind of brazen creature would approach a foreign craft coming from the sky.

*A curious one*, she decided. She motioned for Thoth to follow her to the back of the cargo bay by the door.

"Let's go say hello."

. . .

Alan's toes curled in his flimsy shoes as soon as his feet hit the snow outside, but he trudged on toward the saucer. He saw a glowing mark on the hull and decided that must be the front of the craft. There was a metallic clang as the museum door behind him opened. He turned to see Louise holding it open.

"Alan, get back here!"

"No can do! You should come see this, you won't believe what symbol this is!" he said, tracing a marking on the underside of the saucer with his finger. He heard the door close then the sound of feet crunching through the snow.

Louse's feet took her forward as though they were arguing with her urge to stop, and they were winning. She grabbed Alan's sleeve. "This is not safe. We need to go back inside."

He took another step forward and raised his hands to frame the marking again. It was an eye with an angled line coming off the bottom. "Recognize that?"

She looked up, and her mouth fell open. "Impossible," is all she could manage. She stumbled forward and stood next to him, staring up at the symbol. "It's a hieroglyph. It's the Eye of Ra!"

"That's what I thought," he said. "I think we're safe. This thing, and whoever is inside it, has been here before."

"You can't be sure, Alan," she urged.

He nodded. "The ancient Egyptians knew something. The pyramids, Louise, the pyramids represent the asteroids. And the Egyptians learned about that from whoever is inside this flying saucer, I'm sure of it."

Her bewildered expression showed that she didn't disagree, or at least didn't have a good argument to the contrary, yet.

A hiss emanated from the craft, and the symbol blinked off when a crack appeared in the hull. Alan felt Louise tugging him backward again, and this time he complied. The crack in the ship grew to the size of a door, and a large ramp descended from its curved base. The snow, already melting, crunched as the black ramp touched down on the ground. Shadows moved about in the opening.

Something, or someone, was inside.

. . .

Kaia and Thoth exchanged glances, then took a deep breath and slid their helmet visors down. They ducked through the doorway and onto the ramp. Kaia looked down at the white powder that squelched under her foot but appeared to be stable. She looked up and saw two Kemites outside the building. Both were short, with wrinkled skin on their faces and gray-white hair on their heads. One had hair on the lower jaw.

She whispered, "A male and a female, I think."

"It appears so."

"Are you ready?" she asked.

Thoth nodded and pressed the power button on the babel speaker in his hand.

Alan's heart raced in his chest; he couldn't believe what he was seeing.

The imposing figure said in a female voice, "Hello, my name is Kaia."

Here was an eight-foot-tall person stepping out of an impossible craft, introducing itself, or rather, what appeared to be herself, in perfect English. Alan opened his mouth to reply, but found his mouth too dry to speak.

The shorter figure stepped onto the snow and said, "I am Thoth," in a deeper male voice.

Alan couldn't contain himself. He blurted out, "Where are you from?"

Louise grabbed his arm and whispered, "Start with hello."

Alan corrected himself. "Hello! Where are you from?"

The two figures looked at one another and the male bowed to the taller female, who seemed to be in charge, he decided.

She bowed respectfully and said, "We are from here, like you. We are from Nu."

"Nu?" Alan said, angling himself toward Louise. He'd heard her use that word before.

She whispered out of the corner of her mouth, "Nu is the ancient Egyptian word for the primordial Earth."

Alan angled his head up to the aliens, or, not aliens, he now suspected. "You are from Earth?"


"You are from Nu?" Kaia heard the male say after he conferred with the female.

She turned to Thoth. "They used an unfamiliar word to describe our planet, er-th?"

He pointed down at his hood. "Our babels don't have that word, so it translated it back to Nu for us, but I think they call this planet, our planet, or I guess their planet now, *Earth*."

The male Kemite seemed more comfortable talking to her, so she bent over to get on his level. "Yes, we are from Earth, like you. We call ourselves Jacana. What are you called?"

He answered right away. "We are humans."

Her babel translated it to "Kemites", but one glance at Thoth, and he made sure the system learned the new word. "Humans," she said. "We once knew you as Kemites, but 'humans' sounds nicer."

The female human leaned in to say something else to the male. Kaia thought she heard a strange new word again, something like *ee-jip-shun*.

Thoth turned to her. "You should tell them we are here to teach them, not hurt them."

"Good idea," she said and turned to the humans. "We come in peace. We would like to work with you."

The male pointed to himself. "Work with us?"

She nodded. "Yes, this planet is in trouble. We know its troubles well because we made the same mistakes you are making."

The humans looked at one another, then back to her with bright eyes. They knew what she was talking about, she assumed.

The male seemed enthusiastic by the lilt in his voice. "We would like to work with you!" He bowed, picking up the customary Jacana greeting, Kaia assumed. "My name is Alan."

The female let go of the male and stood up straight. "And my name is Louise."

Kaia bowed. "It is very nice to meet you, Alan and Louise."

Alan pointed to his ear then to the box in Thoth's hand. "That box in your hand is translating for us, yes?"

Kaia handed the device back to Thoth.

"We call it a babel," she explained.

Louise grabbed his arm again. "The story of the Tower of Babel!"

"From the Bible?" asked Alan.

She nodded. "And many other religious books. After the great flood, the humans united in a land called Shinar and built a great tower to reach the heavens. God did not like this and made them speak different languages, then spread them around the Earth."

"But how can you understand us?" he asked Kaia.

"We have smaller versions in our ears," Kaia explained.

Thoth looked at Kaia, and she gave him an approving nod. He handed her the translating box, put both hands on the sides of his helmet, and lifted it off.

Alan and Louise froze when a feather tumbled from the helmet and a bright blue plume rose on the short one's head.

*Impossible,* he thought. *Impossible.* The short figure had large gleaming eyes, two slits for a nose, and its mouth protruded from its face to a point.

The crowd behind the glass in the atrium shrieked so loud that Alan could hear it from outside.

"Do I look familiar?" asked Thoth.

Alan felt like he was having an out-of-body experience. He could see himself floating up, looking down on the scene, but also felt himself living through every ounce of the excitement. At this point, the frontal lobe of his brain felt empty. That very special part, the part where humans evolved the ability to reason, plan, and make rational decisions, was offline. He'd never lived so in-the-moment and never felt so alive.

He heard Louise swallow her nerves to answer the question. "Yes, you are familiar. You came here thousands of years ago, didn't you?"

Thoth, the bird man, nodded.

She had another question. "And you tried to tell the ancient Egyptians, the Kemites, your story?"

Thoth nodded again.

Kaia sighed. "Thoth visited them, but I did not. The ancient Egyptians did not understand our message."

Louise shook her head. "No, they did not. They worshipped you, Thoth. Your image is everywhere. There is another image, as well."

Kaia's shoulders sank. "Horus?"

Louise nodded. "A second bird-god. The ancient Egyptians revered birds."

Thoth sighed. "Now, you know why."

Alan was about to speak when sirens rang out. On the highway, he saw a huge mass of blinking lights making their way to the museum.

"We're lucky Egypt doesn't have snowplows, or they'd be here already," he said. He turned to Kaia and Thoth. "You two should go. They will not understand as Louise and I do."

Kaia and Thoth exchanged a glance, then Alan heard the door open again. He turned to see Daxia running outside, phone held high.

She ran up to him, panting. "Are you able to talk to them?" she asked, looking up at Thoth.

"Yes," Alan said. "They have some kind of translation technology."

Daxia wiped a cold sweat from her forehead and held her phone up to Alan. "Remember South Dakota?"

He nodded.

"It's them," she said, pushing her phone farther into his face.

It was a photo of a fossilized skeleton. Then he saw it, too—the same backward-bent knees, beak-like mouths, and feathers. Feathers everywhere. "Is this what Seagraves found?"

"Yes, I thought it was one fossil, but there are actually three, two different species. There is a baby and an adult T. rex, along with an eight-foot feathered one, kind of like a theropod. They all died together, I think."

"When?" Alan asked. "When did this happen?"

She swiped over to a wide-angle photo. "Look at this one," Daxia said, handing her phone to him.

He took it and saw the unmistakable gray band of the K-Pg layer right above the skeletons. "Sixty-six million years, right before the impacts," he looked at Kaia and Thoth with new eyes. "Show them," he said. "You have to show them, Daxia." He handed the phone back.

She took a few cautious steps up to the creatures. "My name is Daxia," she said, and held her phone up for them to see.

Kaia saw a skeleton on the screen. It looked Jacana.

Thoth stood closer to her to look as well. He held his breath for a moment then asked, "Daxia, where did you find this?"

Kaia felt her heart wrench as if it already knew the answer.

Daxia brought the phone down and dragged her finger across the screen.

It was a map, Kaia saw. And that device, it was like a glyphpad and a viewscreen combined into one.

Daxia spread her fingers on the device and zoomed in on the location. "Here," she said, pointing to the west central part of the state. "It's one of you, isn't it? This area would have been a wetland sixty-six million years ago, on what we call the Western Interior Seaway."

Kaia leaned in for a closer look. "Show me the skeleton again, please."

Daxia lowered the phone, swiped again, then held it back up.

Kaia felt tears well up in her eyes when she noticed the small bundle of bones between the skeleton's arms. *How*, she asked herself, *how is this possible?* She reached for the phone screen. "Mother," she said, trying not to lose control of herself. She backed away from the phone and steadied herself against the shuttle. "Thoth, it's her," she said, holding her eyes shut.

Thoth bowed to the three humans. "Daxia, Alan, Louise, you must take us to this place called South Dakota."

Alan looked at the many flashing lights entering the parking lot then at Daxia and Louise. "We won't get another chance," he said. "And who knows what they'll do to us?"

Daxia shuddered. "They'll quarantine us, at a minimum."

Louise rubbed her shoulders. "I don't know…"

Alan wrapped his arms around her. "This is the answer, Louise. The answer to everything we've been working toward." He let go and gestured to Kaia. "She can explain everything on the way to South Dakota. Right?"

Kaia took a deep breath to collect herself.

She would be able to say goodbye.

"I can explain, yes. We are here to help, Louise. It won't take long to get there. The shuttle is fast."

Louise grimaced and held her eyes shut. She opened them and said, "Let's go before I change my mind."

"Thank you," Kaia said, and motioned them all into the shuttle. They walked up the ramp, but Kaia lingered. She rested her hand against the shuttle and took in the view beyond the museum.

The smaller pyramids of Khafre and Menkaure flanked the Great Pyramid of Khufu, which shone pure white, snow-covered under the midday sun.

"I wish you could be here too," she whispered. "Thank you, Apep."

# CHAPTER 17
# REMNANTS

Louise did her best to settle into the shuttle's cargo bay seat between Alan and Daxia, but she couldn't stop staring at the Jacana named Thoth seated across from them. She'd known her husband for decades, and they'd done some crazy things, but looking at the strange creature was far and away the craziest. Though, she admitted to herself, she felt the same feeling of connection and safety that he must be feeling to make such a nonsensical decision. There was no way she would have gone along with him otherwise.

Alan was looking to the front where Kaia and another Jacana drew hieroglyphs on giant touchpads to prepare for takeoff.

Louise watched Daxia's eyes dancing between the skeleton on her phone and Thoth.

*Paleontologists don't get to see living versions of many species they study,* she realized and let herself share some of the excitement Daxia must be feeling.

Alan broke the silence, as usual, with a question. "So, that skeleton in the ground is one of your people, right?"

Kaia and the other one up front in the cockpit exchanged a glance. "Yes," she said.

Daxia glanced up from her phone. "And, they're sixty-six million years old?"

Louise noticed Kaia squirm a bit in her seat.

Professor Thoth nodded. "They are. In a way, I suppose, that is how old the three of us are as well."

Daxia asked, "How is that possible? No species lives that long."

Alan jumped in, "And where have you been hiding for tens of millions of years? Some kind of stasis?"

Thoth laughed. "No, we have no such technology. But we do have the lightdrive."

"Lightdrive?" Alan asked.

Thoth nodded. "It enables acceleration to near the speed of light without the inertial effects associated with such rapid acceleration. Your species may not know this yet, but the faster you travel, the slower time moves for the ship while it keeps passing on at normal speed for everything outside the ship."

Alan rubbed his chin. "We three aren't physicists but are familiar with the concept, it's all over our time travel movies. How long have you had to travel to be alive for sixty-six million years?"

Thoth looked forward to the cockpit. "Kaia, how long has it been?"

"About eleven days," she said.

"Eleven days!" Alan exclaimed. He turned to Louise. "Can you believe that? Wait until Dr. Howe in astrophysics gets a load of this!"

Louise could not believe it but had watched enough documentaries to understand the concept. "That kind of speed is still science fiction for humans."

"Well, for us, that science is not fiction." Thoth clasped his hands in his laps. "So all three of you are scientists, too?"

"How could you tell?" Louise asked.

He waved toward Daxia, "She studies bones," then to Alan, "he studies asteroid impacts, and you," he said, looking into Louise's eyes, "are studying us."

Louise had not considered others might notice she was studying their behavior instead of interacting with them on equal terms. "Sorry," she said. "You must understand how unusual this is for us."

Thoth nodded. "And for us. We three are scientists, too. I study both people and technical systems, which we've learned aren't as different as we once thought."

He nodded to the front of the ship. "The one next to Kaia studies rocks, like Alan," then to Kaia, "and she studies animals, the same animals Daxia is studying in fossilized form."

Alan chuckled. "Better for six scientists to make first contact with one another than a bunch of politicians, if you ask me. Or, even worse, our militaries!"

Thoth smiled. "We come in peace."

Kaia waved for them to come up front. "You should see this."

Louise followed Alan and Daxia, with Thoth joining behind her as they looked at the front viewscreen. A mass of white clouds swirled over open water on the hazy blue horizon.

Louise sighed. "The remnants of the hypercane."

Kaia sighed as well. "Your hypercanes have already begun. That is not good."

Alan shook his head. "No, it is not good at all. That is the first one. It killed over twenty thousand people and washed away entire cities."

"If your history repeats ours, it is just the first of many," Kaia warned.

Louise added, "We called it Hypercane Levi, short for leviathan." She caught a flash of recognition on Kaia's face.

Kaia leaned over. "Leviathan? What does that word mean to you?"

Louise remembered the translation might not work for odd words. "A leviathan is a mythical sea monster."

Kaia and her copilot exchanged a glance. "We also had a creature called a leviathan. It was real, though. It had a long body, four flippers, and a mouth full of sharp teeth."

Daxia gasped. "That sounds like a mosasaur. They've been dead since the Cretaceous. They looked like a cross between a whale and a crocodile."

There was a bit of static from the babel speaker, then it repeated the last word as, "Sobek."

The word puzzled Louise. It didn't make any sense. She asked Thoth, "Did you and Horus tell the Egyptians about the mosasaur, or leviathan, or crocodiles?"

Thoth studied the shuttle's ceiling. "I do not recall that being part of Horus's story, but it might have been in the book."

"You gave them a book?" Louise asked.

He nodded. "It was irresponsible, I know. It had a lot of information in it. About our world, our history, our science."

"Remarkable," Louise said, feeling lightheaded. "The Book of Thoth. It is real!"

Thoth leaned forward. "It's still around, you still have it?"

She shrugged. "Some conspiracy theorists think the government is hiding it. But most legitimate anthropologists think it is a myth, because the Book of Thoth we know of is a book of the dead and has instructions for resurrection." Then it hit her. "And, I suppose," she looked at the three Jacana, "it does."

A rush of static came from the cockpit. "Kaia, this is Captain Ra. I see you've left the Kemite city."

Kaia held down a button on the console. "We have, and three Kemites, or humans, came with us. They have made a discovery," she paused, and Louise picked up a quiver in Kaia's voice, "in a place called South Dakota, near the narrow sea."

There was a moment of silence from this Captain Ra.

*The ancient Egyptian sun god,* Louise knew.

Then he replied, "Understood. Please stay safe, Kaia." The static clicked off.

Louise leaned between the front seats. "You have another ship in orbit?"

"Yes," Kaia said, "called the *Meridian.*"

"Meridian," Louise repeated, wracking her brain for the word's origin. "Greek, that word is Greek. It means center, central, or sometimes refers to the beginning or zero point of something."

Kaia looked at her. "The *Meridian* was central to our plan. We started everything from onboard."

Alan leaned between the seats, too. "And what plan was that? The impacts? Why did you do that?"

"Alan," Louise said, pulling him back. "Perhaps we should listen to their story before jumping to conclusions." She took a seat back in the cargo bay and patted the one next to her. Alan sat down next to her and Daxia. "Kaia, please tell us what happened and what you said you are here to prevent."

Kaia looked to her copilot.

"The autopilot and I will keep us on course," he said and nodded that it was okay for her to turn around.

She reached under the seat and pulled a lever. Her chair swiveled around to face the cargo bay.

Louise saw a childlike wonder fill Alan and Daxia's eyes. It was story time, she knew.

Kaia rested her hands in her lap. "Sixty-six million cycles, or years, ago was the height of our civilization. We had cities all over the world. But our success came with a price, and the price we paid was high. We insisted on constant economic growth and consumption that led to a ravaging of the natural world. And, it turned out, nature is what kept Nu, Earth, habitable for our people."

She pointed to the suit covering her body. "The climate got so bad, we had to wear these to go outside because. As the world died, so did we, because our resources, important resources like food, dried up. Our planet could no longer sustain the population, and a third great war broke out over the dwindling resources. This was all a generation before I or any of us were born."

Louise nodded along. "There have been two wars like that on Earth so far." Images of the growing resistance to environmentalist change flashed through her mind. "But I worry one is looming if our current growth continues."

Kaia sighed. "I assure you it will happen if you do nothing. Our civilizations are not so different."

Daxia raised her hand. "There are paleontologists digging on every continent, but we've never found a trace of anything like you until South Dakota, or of your civilization. That seems impossible. What happened to them?"

Kaia looked to Thoth, and he explained, "Our people burn our dead and have done so since our first ancestors evolved. There may still be some buried in landslides or sunken vessels on the ocean floor, but for the most part, you would not find them because they are ashes."

"And the cities? It seems impossible that no structures have been found," said Daxia.

Kaia explained, "We have a technology—tiny machines called nanomechs—that can work at the atomic level. Our great war left many of the cities uninhabitable and so few of us alive to inhabit them. The effects of climate change, including hypercanes and the rising sea, left the rest too dangerous to remain viable. We moved everyone to a single city called Puna and set the nanomechs to work everywhere else. All traces of our time on this planet have been deconstructed atom-by-atom and returned to the soil."

Louise nudged Alan. "Poon-ah is how *Pune* is pronounced," she looked at Kaia. "That city name still exists in a country called India." Her brain was trying to piece everything together as Kaia continued.

"But even Puna was not viable for long. The whole world was dying, and we had to leave. So, our global Council devised a plan to use nanomechs to drill deep below the city after they evacuated everyone to cityships in space. That was the exodus phase." Another word came out unchanged, surprising Kaia. She repeated it, "Exodus." *Remarkable.*

"Exodus..." Louise stammered in response, "a mass departure. That word still exists, unchanged!"

Alan's eyes grew as wide as saucers. "Forget the word... your people created a flood basalt lava eruption with the drilling!"

Kaia nodded. "The largest Nu had ever experienced. We tried to bring it back in balance, but a Jacana named Captain Set sabotaged the plan, and it failed. We almost turned Earth into a lifeless ice world with the volume of volcanic gases we released into the atmosphere."

Louise's mind flashed back to the view from Matheran. The striped hills were made of the world's largest lava flow. "Our city, Pune, must be in the same location as your city of Puna. Sixty-six-million-year-old lava flows cover the region around Pune." Louise shook her head. "How is that possible? The same place, the same name?"

Alan raised his arms and yelled, "I told you! Someone knows about all this! We've known it for thousands of years!"

"I'm not sure how," Kaia said. Louise saw that Kaia also realized there was something deeper behind her story by the way she hesitated, but that she couldn't place it either, yet.

Alan shook his head. "But Pune is nowhere near a mantle plume. You'd have to drill so deep to reach the lava, and even then, it wouldn't flow like that."

The copilot turned for a moment. "Our planet's land moves, as I'm sure you know. When we drilled, a mantle plume was present, but now the land has moved far to the north and collided with another continent."

"Yes, of course," Alan realized. "Réunion Island! That is where India was, where Pune was, during your time. The mantle plume is still active after all those millennia. Our own Climate Council is investigating plans to drill into it and do just as you described."

Kaia looked to him. "That is not wise," she turned to the copilot. "Right, Enki?"

He nodded. "Too difficult to control with your level of technology. Even we were not sure we could do it without killing everything. Plus, the model is too difficult," Enki said.

*Enki*, that name stuck in Louise's mind. It had been too long since someone put her linguist skills to the test, but she pushed it into her subconscious to keep mulling it over.

Daxia leaned forward, like an eager kid on the edge of their seat. "What did you do when the eruption failed?"

Kaia smiled. "I think you three have figured that out already. The lava flow was not the only part of our plan. We were also to have one hundred small asteroid impacts—"

Alan jumped in, "To clear the volcanic sulphates from the atmosphere and stir up dust!"

Kaia nodded. "But that would no longer work, since the flood basalt, as you called it, failed. We needed a lot more dust all at once, and so we used nanomechs to combine the small asteroids into four much larger ones. But Captain Set returned with his cityship and destroyed one of them."

"Four!" Alan held up four fingers. "Like the four horsemen of the apocalypse!"

*The Book of Revelation*, Louise realized. But she filed it away too, because she also caught the name Set, another ancient Egyptian god, and noticed Kaia's voice growing tense. *There's something more there.*

"What happened, Kaia?" she asked, trying not to prod beyond her comfort zone.

Kaia shut her eyes for a moment and took a deep breath. "The refugees from one of our cityships and three of our very brave crew members gave their lives. The three remaining crystals needed to impact faster than they could pull them and still escape."

It clicked in Louise's mind. "Those three asteroids saved the Earth, and you left at light speed only to return and find the ancient Egyptians. You decided to intervene and told them this story with the hopes they would not repeat your mistakes. But..." she trailed off.

"The ancient Egyptians were too primitive," Thoth finished her thought. "I was there, with Horus. They thought we were gods."

Louise turned to Daxia when she heard a sniffle and saw tears in her eyes.

Kaia took a deep breath. "We lost two great pilots to the impacts, and the original captain of the *Meridian*, Apep."

Daxia wiped her brief tears away. "I'm so sorry for your loss," she said. "They did save the world, though."

Louise nodded. "We wouldn't exist without their sacrifices, and I imagine our society would not be the same had you not tried to tell the ancient Egyptians."

"Well," Kaia said, "not everyone wanted to let the Egyptians live at all. Head Councilor Hegira wanted to eradicate your species. She was sure you'd end up destroying life on Earth again. But I wouldn't let her. She was the one who convinced everyone on Nu that we needed to leave, to journey through the stars on cityships to other worlds."

Louise couldn't believe it. "Hegira?"

Kaia nodded.

"That means journey or migration. One of our world's largest religions, Islam, uses the name to describe their prophet's journey from Mecca to Medina in the mid-600s AD."

Louise noticed Kaia's eyebrows scrunch up.

"*Mecca* and *Medina*?" Kaia asked.

Louise nodded.

"Those were the names of two cityships."

"Thoth and Horus must have left quite a story behind," she said, looking across the cargo bay at Thoth, but she didn't see a guilty look on his face. He looked puzzled.

"That's strange," Thoth said. "The book I left was written before the exodus, and Horus did not tell the Egyptians those names, either."

Alan clapped his hands. "There is so much more to this story! And to think my research on impacts matches what you needed to do, and what we may need to do in the future. Unbelievable!"

Louise pressed on, wanting to hear more about the story itself and how it became so widespread. "Other than Captain Set, do you know if anyone else returned?"

Kaia shook her head. "That isn't likely. We gave no timeframe for when our plan would heal Nu. It would be too risky for any other cityships to return."

"How do you know they didn't figure it out?" Alan asked.

"I suppose we don't, but we also left behind ten specific rules on each ship. I do not believe they would have returned if they followed those ten rules."

Louise couldn't help it and chuckled. "Ten? Ten commandments?"

Kaia tilted her head. "Yes, though they're more like principles."

Alan crossed his arms and narrowed his eyes. "What were the first two?"

Louise wasn't sure where he was going with this but looked to Kaia.

Kaia looked to Thoth, embarrassed. "Thoth? I do not remember them."

He looked at Alan. "The first is 'Maintain a population under five hundred million in perpetual balance with nature' and the second is 'Guide reproduction wisely, improving fitness and diversity.'"

Alan slapped his knee. "I don't believe it!"

Louise put her hand on his shoulder. "What? Those are not the first two in Judaism or Christianity. They can't be the same."

"Not our religions, I mean the dang Extraterrestrialists! The same words are carved on nineteen-foot pieces of granite on a hill in Elbert County, Georgia. In eight languages, no less!" He thought for a moment and said, "I guess you all aren't extraterrestrial, though. All those ancient alien people are wrong, too. Either way, not only did some of them somehow know about your influence on ancient civilizations, but the cooky ones who think there are 'aliens' visiting us may be right, too."

Louise's brain could not believe such things. "There has to be another explanation."

"No, I'm telling you, Louise, someone alive today knows all about the Jacana! Remember? They put the words 'For our Future' on an octahedron made from iridium as an award for receiving funding to research iridium asteroid impacts as one way to engineer the climate!"

Louise stared at Thoth, still unable to believe it. "Did you leave the ten rules with the Egyptians?"

He shook his head. "No, we considered it, but thought the Kemites, Egyptians, were too primitive." He looked at Kaia with a very concerned expression.

Louise's subconscious roared through the confusion with an answer to the question she gave it earlier. *Enki.* "Enki's name is one of the oldest known gods. He was, or perhaps is, the Sumerian god of knowledge and wisdom."

Enki tilted his head as if considering that connection. "I never went to the surface, though."

Thoth nodded along, "And I don't recall Councilor Horus saying his name."

Kaia grinned. "I don't know how these Sumerians knew it, but Enki is the smartest Jacana I've ever known."

Enki glanced over his shoulder. "We are nearing the location Daxia provided at the place called South Dakota."

Louise was still trying to put the pieces together. "Alan, do you remember the name of the pyramid in Mexico? Where you discovered the true size of the Chicxulub crater?"

He shook his head.

She turned to Daxia, hoping her younger mind would remember.

Daxia nodded. "Dr. Pearce thought it was Pyramid of the Magician, but you said that was a poor translation and that a better one was Pyramid of the Prophet."

"Yes!" Louise exclaimed. She let the waves of information that had been eons in the making sink in. "I'd say that was quite prophetic, wouldn't you?"

"Alan," she began, "you have to be correct. Somehow, people alive today know this story and have known it since before the time of the Egyptians. There are pyramids all over Earth."

Alan laughed and put his hand on her shoulder. "Now *you* sound like one of those people even the Extraterrestrialists would call fringe! Secret societies with ancient wisdom."

He waggled his eyebrows. "Maybe the Freemasons? Or the Illuminati!" He made a triangle with his index fingers and thumbs. "Both groups use the pyramid shape on their insignia. And don't forget about this," he leaned over, pulled his wallet out of his pocket, and removed a one-dollar bill. "Look here!" he pointed to the Great Seal of the United States, "a pyramid with the Eye of Providence over the top of it."

Louise read the Latin phrase surrounding the pyramid. "*Annuit Coeptis, Novus Ordo Seclorum.* Translated, it says 'God has cleared the way for a new order of the ages.'"

She knew it sounded preposterous, but now she had to admit it was all possible. The Jacana reset Earth, and humans evolved in their wake.

Someone had to keep this knowledge alive for the world to progress as fast as it did, while also hiding the true origins, lest a total collapse of society follow. For the first time, she feared what was to come of this contact with the Jacana.

Enki announced. "We're here."

# CHAPTER 18
# REUNION

Kaia kept her eyes on the viewscreen showing the front camera's view. Her hands danced over the controls as the terrain changed from flat to rolling hills. The shuttle flew over a shallow valley lined with trees and a stream winding down the center. Her mouth turned dry in an instant. The morning sky's orange glow faded to black as rain streaked across the window. She felt her heart clench and looked down at the glyphpad. Someone else was controlling the shuttle. The roar of the rain was loud, so loud. Fear gripped her body, and she froze. A hand rested on her shoulder.

"Kaia?"

She turned, wide-eyed, and saw a concerned expression on Enki's face.

"Kaia, are you okay?"

She looked down at her hands and felt as though they were moving over the glyphpad on their own. He returned her focus to the viewscreen. The sun peeked over the horizon. Not a drop of rain in sight.

She gulped, "I've been here before."

"Yes," Enki said, looking over the green hills, "many cycles ago, Kaia."

"It looks so different now."

"The narrow sea is gone, and the coastal wetlands with it, yes, but millions of cycles of geological uplift and erosion have brought our history, your history, nearer to the surface."

Kaia noticed a white two-story dwelling near the destination and steered toward it. The blocky structure looked nothing like the smooth surface of Jacana buildings, but it reminded her of the facility, nonetheless. She noticed a silver box with wheels near the edge of a cliff some distance behind the house, and her mind jumped to the memory of the last time she was on Nu.

She raised her hand and pointed. "Enki, from this distance, that reminds me of seeing your shuttle on the plateau just before the eruption."

He followed her finger. "Yes, but the view from this plateau is much less grand without Puna's skyline."

"I disagree," Kaia said, settling into a gentle smile at the sight of so much green.

Daxia got up and stood between the seats. "That's where we're going. You can land next to the truck."

"Truck?" Kaia hadn't heard that word before.

"The silver vehicle," Daxia explained, gesturing to the viewscreen.

"Ah," Kaia said and steered the shuttle toward it as they descended.

Kaia set the shuttle down a few yards from the edge of the plateau, just as she had done some sixty-six million cycles ago before the eruption. "Thoth, can you get the door?"

"Of course," he said and headed to the back of the shuttle.

Kaia got up and stepped down into the cargo bay then turned back to the cockpit. "Enki, why don't you join us outside this time?"

He swiveled the chair around. "Is it safe?"

She nodded. "We were able to breathe."

Alan chimed in, "And we're far from anyone who might try to take you, or us, into custody. Nothing out here but sunshine!"

Enki rubbed his hand along the edge of the glyphpad. "Okay, I'll go with you."

"Good," Kaia said, turning back to the cargo bay.

Thoth had already stepped down the ramp, with Alan and Daxia behind him, but Louise hung back.

"Kaia, Enki," she said, bowing. "I want to apologize in advance for any skepticism you sense from me about your story. It is just so hard for me to believe, even with all the linguistic evidence. Please do not take it personally."

Kaia bowed in return. "I understand. We Jacana also lean toward questioning everything."

"I must say, though," Enki added, "skeptical questioning must come from scientific motivations over political ones. I hope you have positive intentions, Louise."

A slight smile spread over Kaia's face. "Well said, Enki."

Enki faced Louise and raised his eyebrows. "All the linguistic evidence in the world pales in comparison to what you are about to see."

As soon as Enki said it, Kaia felt her body tense and her mouth seize up at the realization. The sudden look of concern on Louise's face showed she noticed Kaia's reaction, too.

Alan waved his hand in the doorway. "Come on out, you three. Get some fresh air!"

Kaia stepped out into the sunlight. The sky glowed a warm orange as Earth turned toward sol. No Jacana from her time had ever seen such a sunrise. It energized her. The humans had not ruined the world yet, she realized.

Kaia inhaled. "It smells so, so..."

"Alive," Enki said.

"Yes, alive," Kaia agreed.

The dewy grass reflected the morning light and dispersed it through the air. Her gaze swept over the expansive prairie extending to the horizon in every direction.

An unfamiliar sensation washed over her. Her body felt relaxed, her nostrils opened, and she couldn't help but take several deep breaths as the sweet scent filled her lungs. She closed her eyes and reveled in the feeling. *Fresh air*, those were the words Alan used, and they fit.

"Daxia!" a man yelled. "I'm coming!"

Kaia jerked her head to the side and opened her eyes to see someone charging at them with a large, sharp tool raised in his hand.

Alan stepped in front of her, waving his arms. "Stop!"

Daxia shot forward, running to the man. "They're friends!" she yelled. "Seagraves, they're friends!" She caught up to him, and he stopped in his tracks.

The man lowered his weapon. "Friends?" He looked back at the creatures. "So, tall... Nothing like... They're birds," he said, shaking.

She shook her head. "They have feathers, but they are not quite birds. You know what they are, yes?"

"The flying saucer... aliens, but no, they're... from here? They have to be from here because..."

Daxia nodded. "Yes, Seagraves. They had a civilization here. They polluted Earth, tried to clean it up, and left. They succeeded, and that led to us. We evolved in the climate they created."

"They created..." he stammered.

Kaia saw the disbelief in his eyes. She yelled to reassure him, "We come in peace!"

Then the man's expression changed. His eyes widened, and his jaw fell open. He pointed with his free hand and blinked hard. "It's, it's..."

Daxia waved Kaia forward. "Yes, Seagraves, it's... them."

Kaia weaved around Alan and took a tentative step toward the man. "You've seen our kind before?"

Seagraves nodded. He clenched his eyes shut for a moment and opened them again. "In sixty-six-million-year-old stone."

"How many?" she said, taking a few more steps.

He stumbled backward. Daxia grabbed his arm and patted his head. "It's okay, Seagraves." She let go and pointed down the path. "Kaia, there is one of your people in the rock face over the ridge."

Seagraves shook his head. "No, there are two."

Daxia cocked her head. "You found another one?"

He nodded, keeping his eyes on Kaia, and held up the pickaxe. "I've been excavating the second one all week."

Kaia felt Enki's hand on her shoulder. He was almost whispering when he said, "It has to be them."

She gulped. Her eyes followed the path over the ridge. "Seagraves, my name is Kaia." She gestured to her side then behind her. "This is Enki, and that is Thoth."

"N-nice to meet you…" Seagraves stammered.

She walked toward him and bowed. "Please, show us what you found."


Kaia kept an eye on the man named Seagraves as they followed him along a narrow path hugging the cliff face. The valley floor stretched out twenty feet below.

Daxia tapped on the rock wall next to them. "Be careful, everyone. The wall is prone to rockslides."

"Got it," Alan said, taking Enki and Thoth's hands next after they helped Louise over a boulder blocking the trail.

Kaia stopped in front of a blue tarpaulin on the wall and turned to Seagraves. "Behind here?" she asked.

Seagraves nodded. "Yes, there."

Kaia pulled the tarpaulin down, revealing the *Tyrannosaurus rex* skull.

Thoth jumped back. "I've never been so close to one's head before!"

Kaia then said to Daxia, "And you wouldn't want to be here if it were still alive. We called this creature a phara."

Louise stepped forward. "Phara?"

Kaia nodded. "It was king of the forest."

"Well," Daxia said, "we call it a *Tyrannosaurus rex* or T. rex for short."

"Of course, 'king' is 'rex' in Latin," Louise said. "The Romans based Latin on Greek, and Greek is derived from a combination of ancient Egyptian and Sumerian with a few more languages thrown in. But the connection is obvious because the Egyptians called their rulers pharaohs. Phara is right in the title of their rulers."

Thoth sighed. "That was Horus, too. He told them about pharas, in a sense. Their king at the time, Djoser, seemed very impressed."

Kaia shot him a look then softened her eyes before turning to Seagraves. "Where are the other skeletons?"

"Over here. There are two of you, and one baby T. rex," he said.

She reached up and pulled the tarp the rest of the way down.

This time, everyone gasped.

Kaia took a step toward the dark bones surrounded by light-colored rock. She puffed and blew the dust away from her mother's hands. She reached out and touched the small bundle of young phara bones between her mother's arms, then her mother's head, and on to her father, who was holding them all.

"They're both... here," she managed, then fell to her knees.

Enki knelt beside her as she tried to speak through the tears.

Her throat constricted, and she tried to speak. "They rescued the baby, and then they died alone." She pounded the ground. "Councilor Hegira, it was all Hegira. She wanted my parents to be martyrs, for me to be a martyr."

Enki was doing his best, she knew, when he said, "No, Kaia, they were not alone. We were all there, with them. We all know their story. We all know your story."

Alan cleared his throat. "I am sorry, Kaia. These were your parents?"

Kaia couldn't take her eyes off the skeletons, so Enki explained it to him. "Yes, this is her mother and father."

Alan leaned in for a closer look at the two figures. "I do not mean to be insensitive, but how do you know it is them?"

Enki continued, "The Jacana government established refuges for endangered wildlife. This area was a phara, or T. rex, breeding ground. Kaia's parents were leading experts on the species. They were—" he paused.

"Thank you, Enki," Kaia said, rising to her feet. "I'll explain." She wiped her eyes. "The Council stationed us alone at this wildlife refuge, but a tidal surge from a storm, like Hypercane Levi, washed it away. I escaped in a shuttle remote piloted by, I believe, Horus. He and Hegira were not councilors, yet. She was the Director of Relocations, and he was her lieutenant."

Louise stepped up to the rock face and lowered her eyes. "You said she made them martyrs?" She held her hand over her heart. "How awful."

Enki nodded. "There is a recording of the events that every Jacana child sees in school. The Council used it to gain support for their plans."

Daxia looked up at Enki. "A recording?"

Kaia gave him an approving nod. "Go ahead."

He pulled a round box from his pocket and set it on the ground. He then drew a symbol on his forearm glyphpad. An image appeared, projected in the air above the box. Alan, Louise, and Daxia stood still, entranced by the technology as much as by the image.

Kaia observed their reactions as they watched her father's gloved hands pass a very large, speckled brown egg to her mother. A tiny arm popped out after a crack spread across the top and her mother pulled away bits of dead grass.

Daxia whispered, "That's a dinosaur egg…"

The camera panned up, darting back and forth across the horizon.

"He hears something," Alan observed.

Lightning flashed long enough for them to see trees shaking, then falling, in the distance.

Kaia watched the fear spread across Louise's face as the storm surge snapped trees in half and carried their sharp trunks forward like battering rams.

The two Jacana set off through the muck only to arrive at the flooded stream. Kaia's father turned as the wall of water burst through the trees into the clearing.

The video switched to her mother's view as she watched the shuttle rising over the facility. Then the video transitioned to an aerial view from the shuttle itself. The storm surge raced across the nesting ground.

Another transition showed a young female Jacana, beating on the glass of the shuttle's window as it rose above the coming surge. A screen next to her showed her parents' faces, filled with tears. She was in tears, too, still hitting the window and swiping incoherent streaks over the glyphpad. The girl looked down and pounded the emergency stop. The shuttle kept on rising.

Her father's soft voice said, "Kaia, you can save the world from us."

The camera switched back to the shuttle's exterior view as the surge hit the dead mother T. Rex, pushed her body into Kaia's parents, then faded to darkness.

Five hieroglyphics appeared.

Louise reached out to touch them. "This first one is a symbol of divinity, and this one means Earth."

Enki nodded. "It reads: 'Kaia, you can save the world from us.'"

Kaia stood up, wiping the tears from her eyes. "My father's last words."

All three humans huddled together.

Louise looked up at her. "How could Councilor Hegira do that to them? To you?"

Kaia took a deep breath. "They had a mission. They had to save the world." She looked at Alan. "We still need to save the world."

Daxia wiped the tears from her eyes and took Kaia's hand. "I'm so sorry. We dig up these bones and think about how they got there, but never assumed they were something more than animals. Because no paleontologist has seen a video of fossils being created. We've never seen the terror of dying. Fossilized bones are not specimens."

She looked to the wall where the final terrifying moments of two Jacana lives were frozen in time. "We need to respect them for what they are, remains."

Kaia stepped away from the wall, looking back to her parents. "Their devotion inspired me. It led me to care for the animals."

Thoth stepped up next to her. "It inspired a whole generation, Kaia."

Kaia reached up with her right arm and rubbed her hand along her father's skull. "We did it." She started to cry soft tears. "Nu is alive. More alive than you could have imagined."

She turned to Alan and Louise. "And a new species has risen. They have made mistakes. Mistakes like ours. But, I think, a new understanding is emerging. One that will ensure Nu's, Earth's children never threaten it again."

Daxia and Alan smiled at her and Enki as they all turned away from the wall. The light of sunrise was pouring over the valley floor. Louise stepped forward and rubbed Kaia's back. "Kaia, what were their names?"

"Rhea and Ory, short for Oranus."

Louise held her eyes shut for a moment, then opened them and softened her voice to say, "My dear, the story of your parents lived longer than your time on this planet. They are the names of Greek gods. One of our greatest civilizations knew their names, Kaia."

Kaia struggled to comprehend what it all meant. How was it all possible? She mustered a simple, "I would like to hear more about that sometime, Louise."

Alan cleared his throat. "There is only one problem with all of this. While you might have saved Nu from your civilization, we now must save it from ours. Earth is still in danger." He began to pace back and forth, rubbing his beard.

He paused and looked around at the group. "But we have everything we need right here. Biology, geology, anthropology, history, and heck, we even have an oil man!" he exclaimed, nodding to Seagraves. "And now, we have more facts than anyone can deny. We can control the future—" he waved toward Kaia, Enki, and Thoth, "with your help."

Thoth drew a hieroglyph on his forearm, and an image of the book he had left behind appeared in the air. "Is your society ready for the knowledge this time?"

"There's only one way to find out!" Alan said. "Let's have a look at what's inside."

Thoth swiped on the glyphpad, and the holographic book opened. Alan stepped forward first to get a better look, then Daxia and Seagraves joined him.

Enki leaned in and cocked his head. "Does the scientific evidence not speak for itself?"

Alan shook his head. "I've been trying to convince skeptics all my life, and let's just say we still have a lot of convincing to do."

Kaia looked at him sorrowfully. "Our people could not handle the truth of what we were doing to the world, either."

Alan looked up for a moment. "We'll see that humans can handle it this time. Right, Louise?"

Louise kept her distance from the book but said, "The Climate Council will grow more powerful, yes."

Kaia twitched inside at the thought of another council taking on plans to save the world. She turned away from the hologram and left them to it.

She walked a short distance back up the path, then sat down on the ledge and removed her gloves. The cool, damp grass felt like nothing she'd ever experienced. One more small thing on the growing list of things to like about this new, vibrant world she helped create. She surveyed the sweeping valley below, broken only by a lazy river meandering between the hills on each side.

"May I join you?" Louise said, eyeing a spot next to her.

"Of course."

Louise's knees popped as she lowered herself down to the ground and scooted to join Kaia at the edge of the path. She took a deep breath, and Kaia did the same.

*So many smells,* Kaia thought. There was a strange noise from the sky, and she looked up to see a group of winged creatures flying overhead. They began their descent over the ridge, swept over the grass, and landed on the river.

Kaia had never seen such a species. She had seen wings, and creatures in the water, but never both in a single animal.

Louise nodded toward them. "We call those geese. They're a type of bird," she explained.

"Bird?"

Louise chuckled. "In a way, they're the legacy of your species on Earth. A species related to yours must have survived the impacts and evolved alongside mammals, until," she nodded to the creatures again, "birds."

"A nathus, that's what we called the relative. They became birds," Kaia said, astonished.

Louise leaned closer. "The Jacana relatives may not dominate the world as you once did, but birds are everywhere in our mythology. *You were always with us.*" She shielded her eyes from the rising sun and watched as the geese paddled around the river. "We always revered them, but I never understood why, until today."

Kaia heard Alan yelling, and they turned to see what was happening, but everyone quieted down and huddled around the holographic book again. "Louise, do you believe saving Nu, Earth, is possible? Alan says you know the most about human behavior."

"If I'm being honest, Kaia... I don't know." Louise's eyes sank to the ground. "Your story taught me that humans have more control than we realize. Too many of us like to think the climate of Earth does what it does, that there is no way we could influence it, that it is beyond our control, but now I understand. We can warm the Earth up, or we can cool it down. We can destroy life or create it. That is the power of the gods. *We* are the gods, and *we* are in control."

Kaia nodded once, and said, "We are in control, yes, but we don't always know where that control leads because we don't understand how everything works together. Our simulations only helped us to a certain point."

"Interesting you say that, Kaia. Some Earth scientists believe in a theory of interconnectedness. They believe we can't just look at geology, or climatology, or even just look at life to understand the Earth's systems. It's all interconnected in a self-regulating way, almost like the entire planet is one massive animal."

"That is not far from the truth," Kaia said. "We couldn't get our simulation to work well until I included biological data in it. Everything is connected, yes, but that cannot tell you what to do about climate change. It is much more difficult than having enough data."

"I suppose you're right. Humans are always looking for the silver bullet to our problems," Louise said.

"Silver bullet?"

Louise chuckled. "It is from folklore about a terrifying mythical beast called a werewolf. The only way to kill them was by shooting them with a silver bullet."

"Ah," Kaia said.

"These days we use it as shorthand for a simple solution to a very complex problem."

Kaia looked out over the valley. "If humans are like the Jacana, there will be no silver bullet. While this theory of interconnectedness is true in some respects, I do not think it can help you understand intelligent life, because it couldn't help us. We could never simulate Jacana behavior well. Nothing worked until we left, removing ourselves from the equation. And then, when we returned... well, you see what happened."

"I've never thought about it that way," Louise said. "You're right. The interconnectedness hypothesis does not account for culture. Culture determines values, values determine behavior, and certain behaviors can have catastrophic consequences for the planet." She pondered it for a moment. "A culture-climate connection... Yes, that's where we should start with our plan. There are almost 9 billion humans and thousands of cultures, though. It won't be easy."

Kaia sighed. "We were not able to figure it out in time. Too many Jacana liked simplicity, and interconnected systems on a planetary scale are difficult to understand. In the end, billions died before our Council formed a tenuous agreement with those who resisted it out of desperation."

"Humans are the same," Louise explained. "We like things in what we call black-and-white, clear delineations between what is good and what is bad, what is right and what is wrong."

"The answers are never that clear," Kaia lamented.

"I agree. That's why I study people," Louise said. "I'm fascinated by us. We have a powerful intellect that can reason through ambiguity, but we default to the extremes, especially in our political structures. We have the right and we have the left, and too few in between."

Kaia's eyes fell over the lush valley. She thought back to a conversation with Enki about how valleys and canyons formed.

A river cut deeper and deeper, he explained, creating two sides out of one piece of land. Over time, the water eroded the sediments, widening the gap and altering the landscape forever. The ground that fell in, though, became part of something special. The current carried it away and deposited it where the river met the sea. This new, fertile land could only be created by leaving its old world behind.

Kaia connected the thoughts, and said, "If we are to create a new way of thinking, we need to move beyond the two sides," she said.

Louise looked over the valley, too. "Yes, we need to bring people together."

Kaia's eyes followed the river at the center of the valley as it flowed toward the rising sun. "The best way to do that is by charting a path in-between, like a river. We need to flow at the center of the division, forgoing those who imagine a utopian future as well as those who want to hold on to the past. Progress, not idealism or tradition, is the way forward."

"I believe so, too," Louise said. "That will take compromise, but it is in short supply these days."

"Why?"

Louise sighed. "Because our institutions, especially our governments and media, use the most powerful force on Earth: fear. Fear of one another, fear of losing our lives, fear of persecution, are all wielded to keep us divided in their pursuit of another powerful force."

Kaia thought about it for a moment, remembering what drove the Jacana apart and corrupted their best, like Councilor Horus. "Money?" she guessed.

Louise nodded. "Money." She brushed bits of dirt from her pants. "It isn't bad in itself, it is a tool. How we use that tool depends on culture. But one thing is for sure. Your return is going to change everything. This might be what it takes to snap us out of our shortsightedness and see the bigger picture."

"Councilor Hegira tried to get us to see the bigger picture, too, but it wasn't possible, and now I believe it isn't the best way, either."

"Why do you say that?" Louise asked.

"The Council tried and realized it is impossible to change enough people's minds through education because other interests, like money, competed with their message. When that failed, the Council turned to other powerful emotions, like anger, and shame, and even took forceful and sometimes violent actions against those who resisted the regulations."

"Anger, shame, and force do not convince humans well, either. Where are the Councilors now?" Louise asked.

"Locked up in their quarters on the *Meridian*, where they belong. They used my story, my tragedy, to accomplish their goals. They were noble goals, but," she remembered Apep's words, "a smart person once told me: 'You can do the right thing the wrong way.' The Councilors are a perfect example of that sentiment."

"Well," Louise said, "we have to do it the right way this time. There will be no more martyrs. No more forced change. People need to understand that Earth is special and worth protecting."

"It is indeed special," Kaia acknowledged. "We studied the stars and never found another place as lush, or as fragile, as our home." She looked up at the sky. "We sent out colonists on cityships but have not heard from them. I hope we are not the last."

Louise puffed her cheeks and exhaled. "I can say with absolute certainty that you are not the last."

Kaia turned to her, brows furrowed. "How do you know that?"

"Your name, Kaia."

"My… name?"

Louise nodded and turned around. "Many languages have an alphabet made of letters. But, before letters, we started representing speech sounds with pictures of objects or animals whose names comprised those sounds, like your glyphs. Over time, those glyphs were simplified and became our modern letters." She put her finger in the dirt and drew the letter K. "We call this specific letter *K*. Like in 'Kaia' or kid."

Kaia got a better look at the letter. "So, my name starts with this letter in your language?"

"Yes, but like all things, our language and letters change. They evolve. This letter originated from the ancient Egyptian hieroglyph for an open, welcoming hand, which was often used to depict sharing knowledge or sharing love. The Egyptians pronounced hand as 'deret,' so, that is how they would have read the hieroglyph out loud. The Jewish people, another group who lived in ancient Egypt, pronounced hand as 'carat' and evolved the hieroglyph to resemble the 'k' shape, so the shape came to represent a hard 'C' sound."

Kaia nodded along. "Our languages evolved and mixed many times over tens of thousands of cycles as well."

"I am sure we have much more in common," Louise said. "After Egypt, the Western Hemisphere had two more great civilizations. The Greeks and the Romans. The Greeks came first and continued the Jewish language tradition of the K symbol being a sharp sound, like the word 'carat.' Later, the Romans also used the shape of K but pronounced it as 'gee' or 'guh,' creating an opportunity for misunderstanding. They caught on to how confusing this was and created this new shape."

Louise drew a second K to the right of the first one, but she didn't add the long vertical line and left only the sideways V.

Kaia sensed Louise was leading her to an unfathomable answer to the original question.

*Did other Jacana survive?*

"Now the Romans had two shapes, but this new one still confused people because it looked too much like K, so they added another line." She dragged her finger over the bottom half of the sideways V. "Over time, the V shape turned more into a C with a line through it." She drew another shape to the right. "The letter G, to follow the gee or guh pronunciation."

Kaia looked at the three letter shapes. "You said this had something to do with my name?"

Louise nodded and folded her hands in her lap. "You are an ancient goddess, Kaia, one of our oldest. Thoth said Horus didn't tell the ancient Egyptians your name, it doesn't exist in their language, but someone shared it with another civilization. They must have, because we know your name to this day, and some even still worship you."

She looked into Kaia's eyes. "Your name, to us, is Gaia."

"Gaia?"

Louise grinned. "We have known a version of your story for thousands of years. You are the goddess of the Earth. That interconnectedness theory? Some people call it the Gaia hypothesis."

Kaia felt electricity course through her veins. *Humans know me.* "How is that possible?"

"I don't know, but I can't deny the connection. Modern pagans, another type of religion still on Earth, have continued the Greek tradition of calling you Gaia, the ancestral Mother Earth."

"Mother... Earth?" Kaia couldn't believe it.

Louise reached over and patted Kaia's shoulder. "Yes."

Kaia watched a group of thin quadrupedal creatures gathered at the edge of the river for a drink. She took a deep breath. "We can't let this planet's life die."

"No, we can't." Louise smiled at the gentle creatures. "We call those deer."

A large one with horns on its head stood tall and seemed to look straight at Kaia, flicking its ears. This world was so alive. She scooted closer to Louise and turned to smile.

Louise was already smiling. "Wait until we tell the world that Gaia, Mother Earth, has arrived and is staying true to her sixty-six-million-year-old intentions to protect the planet," she joked. "No culture will remain the same."

Kaia took another deep breath. "It feels good to know there may be a place for the Jacana, for me, in the future."

"Yes," Louise agreed. "You may be relics of the past, but you will usher in the dawn of a new age."

*The Dawn Project is not finished,* Kaia thought as she looked back to the geese paddling on the river, then to the grass waving in the gentle morning breeze and up to the brilliant blue sky dotted with pristine white clouds. Her heart swelled.

*It may never be finished.*

She pulled her shoulders back and filled her lungs with the sweet air.

"We can save the world, from us."

# EPILOGUE

"Do we have an update on the Giza situation?" General Walker said as he returned to the control room from the hot Nevada desert outside.

"Not yet, sir, but we're monitoring it," Major Velasquez replied. "The craft abducted three humans then disappeared."

The general kicked an empty chair. "How could we lose it?" He stomped toward the far side of the room and got into the elevator.

It descended at an ear-popping pace, which irritated him more. The elevator chimed, and the doors opened into a cavernous underground hangar. A Jacana shuttle sat in the center, encased in scaffolding with cords running in every direction into rack after rack of computational hardware.

Ruth, the Chief Scientist of Project Blue Book, was standing under the black ship they repaired after it crash landed on a ranch outside Roswell, New Mexico decades earlier. Though, because of the time dilation tests, Ruth didn't look a day over forty years old.

General Walker stormed past the ship and felt the warmth still radiating off it from the last time dilation test flight. "Have you seen what happened today?" he asked, surprising her.

She looked up from her tablet. "Did someone see our last flight and report a UFO again? We left in 1972 and were going so fast I don't think anyone could have seen us. Or did another crazy post online about what they think we're doing down here?" She laughed a little but stopped when she realized he was serious.

"A little ship, just like that one," he said, pointing up at the battered black shuttle, "landed in Giza at the United Nations Climate Council summit, abducted three people, and flew off!"

Her eyebrows flew to the top of her forehead. "What?!"

He rolled his eyes. "Just look at the news. We need to ask Big Bird One what is going on here. Now!" the general demanded.

She began scrolling through news stories on her tablet. There was a blurry photo of the encounter from Giza. "Yes, sir, right away. He has a name, you know," she said as a tall figure approached.

"You can ask me yourself, General Walker," an unmistakable voice boomed from behind him.

The eight-foot-tall feathered reptilian man was hobbling toward them. He rested each hand on two men's shoulders to steady himself. The men, tall and stocky by human standards, were tiny compared to the figure.

"Give him that tablet!" the general barked to Ruth.

She handed it over to him, almost dropping it on the concrete floor.

The man they called Big Bird One took a look at it and began to laugh. A laugh deeper than any human could muster.

"Fools. I tried to tell you I am not an extraterrestrial. I am from Earth. You know, here, same as you," he insisted. "It looks like my old enemies have arrived, just as I'd warned. I'd recognize them anywhere."

He grinned and pointed at the image. "This is Kaia, she is a biologist. She's a smart one, the smartest of this group. She studied what you pathetic life-forms call dinosaurs back when they were walking around breathing, blood pumping through them. And this is Enki. He was a geologist on the Dawn Project. He is the one who picked the spots where the crystals impacted. The one who killed the colonists I tried to save. This last one is a clown. He's a waste of space if you ask me," he said, pointing at Thoth.

Ruth peered over the top of her glasses. "I know you don't believe him, General, but I do. The other one tells us the same thing, when we don't have him sedated. And, if you want to learn anymore from either of them, I suggest we stop calling them Big Bird One and Two."

General Walker scoffed. "This changes nothing. It still doesn't prove anything he says is true. They're both named after evil Egyptian gods for God's sake!"

Big Bird One swiped through more photos. He handed the tablet back to Ruth and looked up at his black shuttlecraft. "I bet you'll find a larger ship orbiting Earth right now called the *Meridian*."

Ruth joined the alien-looking man as he marveled at his own shuttle. "When do you think they'll try to destroy the planet again?"

He smiled. She knew he liked that she always treated him with respect. "It is hard to say. I'm sure they're already working on a new plan, though. And you should hope that no other Jacana have returned to Earth in the sixty-six million cycles — sorry, years — since we first left Puna."

Ruth looked up at the ship. "I believe they have and that they are hiding."

He looked down at her, interested. "Why do you say that?"

She took a deep breath. "Well, we know your kind made contact in Egypt and sparked a powerful civilization, even a written language with those hieroglyphics and the rebus principle. The Egyptians weren't the only ones who built monuments to your stories. There are many examples of similar sparks, similar structures."

She had his full attention. "Go on..."

"The Mayan pyramids, Stonehenge in England, which looks like the rotating circular orbital lab plans you've drawn for us. The Nazca Lines in Peru even show what looks like a Jacana in a habsew. On top of that, there is a drawing of something that looks like a dinosaur in Angkor Wat in Cambodia. And don't forget Göbekli Tepe in Turkey. They're still uncovering odd sculptures and carvings that bear more than a passing resemblance to Jacana ships. All of this tells me it is unlikely that Egypt was the only point of contact between our people, Captain Set."

He nodded in agreement. "You may be right, Ruth. Many Jacana left for many worlds. I tried to tell you. Humans are not alone, or special, in the cosmos."

The blood drained from Ruth's face. "I'm not sure our society is strong enough to endure the truth."

# AFTERWORD

Thank you so much for reading Relics of Dawn, A Story Carved in Time. If you enjoyed the book, please consider leaving a review, and sharing it with your friends. Us indie authors depend on readers to help spread the word!

As you can imagine, it is impossible to write a book about climate change without a heavy nod to the many contributing factors. Both the political left and right over-simplify and exaggerate the data, solutions, and reality in general. It is happening, yes, but I don't believe more rules will help us. I have a lot of other opinions, most of them unpopular to those on either extreme. I am happy to discuss them via email in good faith if you're so inclined.

As for the story, it has a lot of science, and science fiction - some well-researched and some nothing more than wild notions. Much of the geology in this book is real, as well as bits of the human history. I encourage you to check out a few of the links from my research notes.

I began writing Relics of Dawn in 2012, but it really began in 1993 in my grandmother's sunroom. To my little-kid-self, her enclosed back porch was a magical place filled with National Geographic magazines and kooky ideas she shared from Art Bell's radio show, Coast to Coast AM, which aired long after my bedtime. I remember the 1977 cover with King Tutankhamun's gold funerary mask and images of pyramids from all over the world contained in the pages of others. Ancient civilizations built pyramids because it was the only way they knew to build tall, but it sure is fun to think about other explanations.

From there, the story picked up scientific details from decades of watching science documentaries with my dad and hiking with the rest of my family around the crinoid-laden 340-million-year-old fossil beds of rural west-central Indiana. The tone and sense of adventure and mystery come from the Clive Cussler novels my mom shared with my sister and me on the countless hours of road trips crisscrossing the spectacular visible geology of the western United States.

As I started thinking about having a family, the challenges of future generations became tangible. The climate is changing due to human activity, and we may need to turn to geoengineering, but we have so much to learn and need to be cautious. We've already engineered the climate for the worse, so our next actions need to make it better. Hopefully, we will change before we need to take actions as drastic as the ones in this story. We need to work together, For our Future.

I'd love to hear from you!
author@awdavidson.com

www.awdavidson.com

# AUTHOR'S NOTES

Multiple passionate scientists and researchers contributed to this work, from geology, anthropology, climatology, linguistics, and more. We all hope you enjoyed the ride. Please take a few minutes to learn more about the theories that informed this book with the links below. You may discover some truths are more unbelievable than this work of science fiction.

Here are some recommended Wikipedia pages to get you started:

- Silurian hypothesis – a thought experiment from Adam Frank and Gavin Schmidt, inspired by the Dr. Who TV series, on how we might know if there was an advanced civilization on Earth prior to our own.
- Climate engineering – aka geoengineering, purposely altering the Earth's climate through solar radiation reduction and/or greenhouse gas reduction.
- Georgia Guidestones – mysterious granite monuments erected in Georgia with ten rules for living in balance with nature.
- Shiva crater – an unconfirmed (as of 2020) impact location

around the time of the Cretaceous-Paleogene (K-Pg) impact event.

- Chicxulub crater – confirmed impact crater in Mexico from the K-Pg impact.
- Deccan Traps – one of the largest volcanic features on Earth.
- Rebus – linguistic principle of using pictograms to represent sounds.
- Proto-Human language – theory of a root language of all languages.
- Uxmal Ruins – an ancient Mayan city near the epicenter of the confirmed Chicxulub crater.

# A.W. DAVIDSON

A.W. DAVIDSON grew up on a farm and now, somehow, works in fast-paced technology by day while writing as slowly as possible by night. Writing is how he stays (arguably) sane. When not tech-ing or writing, he enjoys spending time with family in the great outdoors and is sad to see it disappearing.

I'd love to hear from you! author@awdavidson.com

Join my mailing list at: www.awdavidson.com

f facebook.com/authawdavidson

𝕏 twitter.com/awdavids

📷 instagram.com/aw.davidson

ⓐ amazon.com/author/awdavidson

g goodreads.com/awdavidson

BB bookbub.com/authors/a-w-davidson